Caden,

Keep your eyes

Peeled for your own Seagull

OBSIDIAN FEATHERS

N. Cáceres

Cover Design by ebooklaunch.com
Interior Illustrations by N. Cáceres and Rowan Merrick
Line Editing, Copy Editing, Proofreading, and Interior Formatting by
Samantha Pico, Miss Eloquent Edits

ISBN: 979-8-9876885-1-9 (Paperback)
ISBN: 979-8-9876885-0-2 (Hardcover)
ISBN: B0BH3RYPLB (Ebook)

Published by N. Cáceres
www.authorNCaceres.com

Dear Dad,
I'm not sorry about what I wrote, but you're not
allowed to read it until you're older.

The rest of you heathens?
Remember to hydrate between chapters.

In Smut We Trust,
N. Cáceres

AUTHOR'S NOTE

(Please note I have done my best to cover as much of the potentially triggering content in this book as possible but may have missed some. Please read carefully. If you believe I have not listed a trigger that is worth being added, please contact me at triggers@ authorncaceres.com with your concern and the information so that I can consider adding it.)

The enclosed story will feature the following sensitive subjects:

General Content Warnings: graphic depictions of cannibalism, mild discussion of self-harm, ritualized self-harm, murder, graphic language, panic attacks, child abuse, mentions of needle-based drug use, parental abuse, guns, murder, depictions of indigenous rites in a fictionalized universe, discussion of sexual assault (including coercion based rape), death of an adolescent, partial loss of mental autonomy, and discussion of suicide.

Social: colorism, ableism, fatphobia, racism, prejudice, discussion of historical genocide, body shaming, discussion of deportation, trivializing mental illness, self-destructive coping mechanisms, emotional self-harm, self-sabotage, and confrontation of an abuser.

Romance: dubious consent, breeding, masochism, graphic sex acts, choking, large objects, sexualized violence, intense language, graphic sex, masturbation, stalking, kidnapping, forced captivity, brat taming, somnophelia, praise kink, orgasm denial, domination/ submission, anal, spanking, knotting, cum worship, primal play, breath play, and D/S dynamics.

ADDITIONAL INFORMATION

This book takes place in a fictionalized world and references multiple real-world indigenous cultures. Many of the depictions of these cultures have been altered to fit within a fictionalized world and modified for use within such context. This is not to say that the content within is a wholly fictionalized depiction. Much time and effort was spent in researching to ensure that the roots of the cultural perceptions and positions were maintained.

There are surviving Nahua, Mexica, K'ekchi' Maya, and Poton Lenca indigenous people struggling to this day to receive recognition for their validity, connection to their heritage, and to maintain the sacredness of their traditions.

If you are curious about or intrigued by any of the concepts shown here, please take the time to learn about these amazing, rich, and vibrant cultures.

This book takes place in a region of El Salvador, where, for thousands of years, my tribe, the Poton Lenca, have flourished. Today, they are dying out. Their culture is disappearing, and as of today, there are only a mere 400 known words of their dialect. Their contribution to the vivid and lush world of Mesoamerica is almost completely lost to the world. If you are so moved by this story and the individuals listed here, please consider contributing to the **Museo Nacional de Antropología** or to the **Cave of Creation** (a historical cave site).

One of the age-old traditions of Mesoamerica is storytelling with an eye for the love of the people. This is my love letter to my people and a love letter for my homeland.

Imapil ten El Salvador.

LEXICON

K'ekchi' Maya • one of multiple Mayan dialects native to the horn of the Yucatan Peninsula

    Ah Kin • a member of the clergy, used as a rank title and occupational designation

Nahuatl • an indigenous language of the Azteca people or the Nahua people native to Central Mexico

    centecpanhuia • literally translates to "to plunder a woman," a euphemism for a rapist

    Cihuapilli • noble lady, a rank title

    cihuapiltzintle • my beloved lady

    cihuatl • wife

    Cihuatlatoani • female monarch, a rank tile

    Cuacualti • beautiful, in reference to a woman

    cualcihuatl • beautiful wife

    nonamic • my wife

    monamic • my husband

    nayeli • princess, a term of endearment, not a rank

    nonayeli • my princess (when a male is speaking to a female)

        Note: The addition of mo (female speaker) and no (male speaker) indicates a possessive, "monamic" my husband or "nonamic" my wife, where "namic" means spouse.

    noyzotzon • my heart, a term of endearment from a male to a female

    tecutli • a ruler, informal rank title

    teocuitlateotl • golden goddess

    teocuitlayocatl • golden beast

    teopixqui • a priest

    Tlacualiztli • a traditional greeting for dignitaries or important events, literally translates to "eating of the earth"

    Tlahtoani • a king or male ruler, a rank tile

    tlamacazto • a young priest or a priest in training

totocan · an exile, one who has been banished. Alternative: A member of an extended family, tribe or clan of cadejos, whether they are themselves a cadejo.

totoco · to be sent into exile. Alternative: An extended family, tribe or clan of cadejos

Poton Lenca · an endangered indigenous language of the Poton Lenca or Taulepa people of South East El Salvador

Elentios ala nam · Blood of the Gods, a sacrifice

Ik'an Lepa · Fire Jaguar, the name of an extended family or totoco

janaw · crocodile

Lets'a Wehle · Honey of the Moon or Honey Moon, the name of an extended family or totoco

sija · daughter

Ulkin Sila · Flower Dancers, the name of an extended family or totoco

wewe · child

PROLOGUE

Sticky hands, sweaty foreheads glistening in the late afternoon sun of mid-July, and that special cologne of rubber shavings mixed with the scents of San Francisco, coloring the air in a cloud of pixie dust. Cars rushing past the playground in Balboa Park were almost loud enough to drown out the sound of exuberant childhood joy. Almost. Nothing could truly drown out the magical sound of kids playing games only they knew the rules to. Especially with the sugar rushes, courtesy of the ice cream truck now sauntering victoriously down the street. Angie fussed with the barrettes holding back the raucous dark curls from her face. The humidity had not been kind to the special care her mother showed to them before she'd hustled out the door to catch a bus to the Embarcadero, but she wanted it to be perfect. Her skin felt like it was buzzing with the excitement her little 10-year-old body could barely contain.

Sal had told her to meet him by the big dogwood tree near the edge of the park, where he and his friend César would meet her right as the sun set, and that he had a surprise for her. Sal was her neighbor Javier's strange cousin, who was visiting for the week, whom she had just met the day before.

She loved surprises. She secretly hoped that, after her very meticulous recitation of all of the virtues of clear quartz, he would surprise her with one. After all, it was by far the most superior of the quartz family, especially when compared to the weird cheap ham-slice-looking rose quartz. Angie was sure to inform Sal of how weird it was that rose quartz reminded her of a sandwich her tío Raul once made her with that gross ham from the corner store. How, when she tried to eat it, it was so salty she had to spit it all over him. She told him she couldn't look at that stone without remembering the way her mouth felt. Just thinking of that repulsive-looking processed meat stone made her skin crawl.

Angie decided rose quartz should be banned from the face of the earth and that, when she ran for president—because she was most assuredly going to be the first female President of the United States on her off time as a geologist—she would pledge to eradicate it and its floppy deli equivalent.

"Hey!" Sal shouted over a car horn as he loped up with César in tow. Both boys were gangly and awkward in ways only an 11-year-old and 12-year-old respectively could be, all elbows, knees, and oversized feet slapping sun-baked concrete. A wide grin split his sun-warmed face, which reminded her of the tiger's eye chips tucked away in her desk drawer. His voice curled around the simple word in a way that made her smile just as brightly. He stumbled a half step and grinned sheepishly over the shaggy black locks that fell over his face. César rolled his eyes and helped his friend make it up the small slope of the grass, as if he'd forgotten how to drive his scrawny legs.

"Hey, Sal! What's up? What did you want to show me?" Angie blurted out in a rush as she bounced on her toes.

"Oh." He chuckled nervously, the toe of his beat-up sneakers pushing a rock across the grass as he fished something out of his pocket. "Well, since I'm leaving in two days, I just . . . pero . . ."

His thick accent swallowed up the rest of the words, and he looked up to the older César to take the lead.

César, once again, rolled his eyes and pushed Sal, speaking to him in that language they had told her was what everyone in their hometown spoke that she had never heard before. It wasn't like the Spanish or Mandarin she was used to hearing on the streets of the Mission Terrace area. She was proud of knowing a few phrases in Spanish, which was how she had met Sal and César when Javi refused to introduce them.

Sal fell into the grass, his knobby knees grinding into the green spikes through his jeans. "Xochitl Angelica Esparza, marry me?"

He released his clenched fist, revealing a rainbow-filled, rounded tumble of clear quartz the size of her thumb that glittered in the golden light of the first rays of sunset.

She giggled, a bright tinkling that danced around the trio on enchanted notes. "I can't marry you, Sal! You don't even know my name! I told you it's Zocheetel. Plus, no one calls me that. It's Angie."

Sal frowned. They'd argued about this at great length the day prior over a patriotic-colored popsicle she called a Bomb Pop. He assured her it was absolutely not Zocheetel and that it was a hideous name. She'd punched him in the kidney with a quivering bottom lip but brightened when he assured her the proper way of saying it was Shocheet and that it was a name for his favorite flower, which wasn't half as pretty as her. He wisely chose not to remind her of this argument, lest he start his matrimonial life on the wrong foot.

She interrupted his brooding over how to navigate the resurgence of an argument she had obviously forgotten about by adding, "Plus, we don't even have a priest! We can't get married without a priest!"

His brows shot up, his mouth curving into a grin. Did that mean she would say yes if there were a priest?

In a rush, he motioned to César. "César is going to be a priest. So, it'll be like practice for him. That counts, I'm sure. Right?"

Her small deep amber hand shot up to her chin and gripped it as she thought. Did it count? She was pretty sure, after exactly three seconds of consideration, that it did, in fact, count.

She shrugged her acquiescence before her eyes widened like saucers. "But there's no ring! We can't have a wedding without a ring! Or a bouquet! I'm already in a dress, but it's not white. I don't think that matters, though. My tía Cecelia got married in her mama's blue dress, and my dress is blue, so that should count, I think. It counted for her, so I think it does."

As she prattled on about the very important list of things that were absolutely required for a wedding—that they absolutely couldn't have a wedding without—César collected daisies from the riotous bush not far from their perch. Sal carved holes into stems of clover buds to make a chainring. By the time she completed her very exhaustive list that included flower petals, an audience, and a dog—because she once saw a TV show where a dog carried the rings down the aisle—the two boys had completed what they deemed the reasonable tasks on her list. Three daisies and four stabbed clover buds later, Angie, once again, shrugged and nodded.

Sal pushed up from the grass and took her hands as César positioned himself with his back to the setting sun, frowning into the words Angie couldn't understand.

Four sentences in, she frowned again and groaned, "You're doing it wrong, César! I have no clue what you are saying."

César rolled his narrow shoulder in a half shrug and softly and slowly—as if he were thinking too hard on how to craft the English words—said, "It's all I know."

"I guess it counts." Angie sighed.

"It counts," Sal said.

He'd learned the day before that anything that mattered had to count, according to Angie. Though, he thought it was a weird way of saying things. She had dutifully explained that, if it counts, it counts and settled it at that. He also learned their foot race didn't count because she wasn't ready, so they had to do it again four times until she was actually ready. It was only valid when she was ready and she won.

She shrugged, and César continued on. Somewhere into the monologue, which Angie could only guess meant basically the same thing, she rocked on her toes. When César looked to Sal expectantly, he nodded and grunted a response, then Sal lifted his brows expectantly to her.

Again, she shrugged. "Me too."

Sal grinned bright and wide, and Angie had the strange thought that he looked almost like a grinning wolf when he did that. César mumbled something else, and Sal leaned in to kiss her. She laughed and pushed him away as the sun fully set and the streetlights came on. She darted away with her treasure tucked neatly in her pocket. "Sorry! Gotta go! Streetlights are on, and Mama will wonder where I am! Bye, Sal!"

Sal and César watched her run across the grass, down the street, and out of sight. Something unspoken passed between the two boys, but they knew it was not the last time they would see the sparkling chestnut-and-gold eyes of the girl with a Nahuatl name and not a clue what it or any of what she had just agreed to actually meant . . . or that it counted.

CHAPTER ONE

Deep breaths. That was the only way I would get through this.

My mother, seemingly disappointed by my silence, frowned at me over her coffee. Four times now, she'd mentioned the fact that I hadn't purchased anything, but I'd stopped making excuses long ago. I tried explaining the fiscal irresponsibility of purchasing a blazer for nearly $700 when I could purchase the same item for a fraction of the price. I also tried explaining that my sensible, sturdy leather messenger bag suited me just fine. Ultimately, what she wanted was an opportunity to voice her disappointment with my body. She wanted to goad me into admitting the only reason I hadn't purchased something was that it wasn't in my size, not because the prices were ridiculous.

It was an old argument. My mother was a wispy woman, narrow and bird-like. From her stick-like fingers to her pinched beak-like face, with dark eyes I hadn't looked into in years. Her pale uniform of cream, ivory, white, or soft blush pink and her cameo did not help with the appearance. I was everything she'd found completely unacceptable.

My hips were shapely and wide. My stomach rounded slightly, even with the dramatic nip at my natural waistline. My legs were strong and thick, with generous thighs and calves. My feet, not dainty but sturdy and sculpted for traveling. My chest was full and heavy, the envy of many women, the object of lust for many men.

I was the culmination of healthy, hearty women dating back to antiquity who survived the ages, not solely by the strength of their minds but by the strength of their bodies.

I cherished the health and vitality of the body my ancestresses had gifted me. Was it the current standard of beauty? No, but it was mine, and despite all of their attempts to turn me against it, my body was one of the few things in my life I truly delighted in. It was mine. It carried me from day to day and, for the most part, never failed me. And, for that, I was eternally grateful. Not everyone in this world had the luxury of saying that. My refusal to hate my plush, curvy, full figure was a never-ending font of disappointment for my mother, and she lamented that I did not "favor the aristocratic" at every opportunity she could. I'd long ago given up trying to convince her that's not how that—or any of this, really—worked.

We were shown to our reserved seat at The Rotunda café, at the top of the luxury store that overlooked Union Square. The reservation for our monthly luncheon was years old, and my mother never missed it, even if I hated these visits. My mother, true to form in all things, immediately ordered us the seasonal salad, two glasses of water and, for herself, finger sandwiches and a cafécito. Some habits died hard. She hadn't missed the opportunity to skim her dark-brown gaze over my simple boat-necked navy dress and matching cardigan, always searching for the next flaw to henpeck.

"I see we have decided to forego the sunblock recently."

Her mild tone could have been about anything, the weather, the price of broccoli, or a quiet admonition of the slight tan from my time walking the Japanese Gardens over the past weekend. I'd run out of sunscreen right as I got to my arms, and it was either roast in a long-sleeved shirt or hope that the ever-present Bay Area fog offered some sort of protection. The change was imperceptible, so little that even my foundation still matched but enough to draw her disapproval.

I sat quietly, nearly statue-still. I could feel my skin thrash under the appraisal. It was best not to show it. My mother hated when I fidgeted, and the Adderall I had been taking since childhood killed that urge, at least on a physical level. The agony of the constrained physical urge to fidget was a never-ending source of torment. I could still feel the urge in my very cells. It was a living thing, squirming and crawling under my skin, forever searching for an exit from the medicated fleshy prison that kept it from tapping my toe on the ground or my fingernail on the linen-covered tabletop. It slithered outside of my view, right under my flesh, writhing and searching.

"Robert has invited Shayne and you to his fundraising dinner," she said in that well-crafted tone that my siblings and I had learned to decipher since the cradle.

This specific sentence, of course, meant I was expected to attend in my most coiffed state, on Shayne's arm. I was expected to represent my politician brother, who dropped the O at the end of his name in high school. I was to represent him to perfection and impress his city hall friends with every last molecule of my existence. I was expected to ensure he received exactly what he needed for the upcoming campaign and influence both the attendees and my partner to lock in their votes. She had spent years crafting me to be the perfect conduit for the ambitions of those around me, and she missed no opportunity to test her training. This simple sentence was a command, divine directive, and an existential imperative.

After lifting my ice water to my lips, I took a sip as she watched my movements, always searching for a single arm hair that might have accidentally been missed to mar the excellence she demanded.

I wish I could say that my mother, Anita—who renamed herself Annette for some reason—was always like this. It probably would have made it easier. No, she changed when she married Edwin Yarbrow, banking millionaire and San Francisco elite socialite, when I was eleven.

From the moment she started dating him, things changed in our household. Roberto, Elida, and I all were pulled from public school and immediately placed in Catholic school. Things progressed from there in little ways. We had stopped speaking Spanish, and I was placed on medication to stop me from "acting like a wild child." We moved out of my grandparents' house and never spoke to them again, despite Elida's and my wailing to keep in touch. Any trace of our heritage, our roots, was scrubbed away. And my world narrowed to school, homework, and whatever activities my mother deemed acceptable for "a lady of standing."

I remember distinctly thinking she'd fallen into a Jane Austen novel and hadn't figured out that she was living in the '90s.

When the silence dragged on, she sniffed almost imperceptibly, finally finding that unpolished corner she had been seeking. "Mrs. Ellington phoned me yesterday to announce the happy news."

Dear God, it's me, Angie. I know we haven't spoken much since high school, but if you could please make a guest appearance and perhaps priority express my soul to purgatory, that would be great. Appreciate it, Big Guy. I'll bake you some cookies or something. Anything is preferable to what's going to happen next.

These were the words I was hoping that she would accidentally forget in her other designer handbag. I lifted my brows in question. Maybe, just maybe, if I said nothing, I could just disappear off of the face of the planet.

She carried on, wielding simple language, like perfectly aimed, razor-sharp flechettes. "I was more than happy to accept her happy congratulations on my daughter's acceptance of her son's proposal."

I secretly wondered if it would be too much of a fuss if I launched myself over the stone railing to the marble floor three floors down. Sure, it would inconvenience the cleaning crew and possibly the piano player in the splash zone, but it would save me the inevitability of my life careening out of what little control I did have. I was sure they'd forgive me if they knew the suffocating weight of the glare she'd flung at me across the starched linen.

My mother's stare was a tangible slow coil of a python around my throat, squeezing with sadistic glee as I clawed and squirmed to disentangle myself from its clutches. Every scale of the creature was a single grain of sand in a beachside grave—never enough to kill you outright, but the slow accumulation would choke you nonetheless.

"He sent a text," I murmured to my empty plate and ice water.

"Excuse me? Speak up, Angelica. You know how much I hate when you mumble. A lady does not mumble."

Deep breaths. *One.* Deep breaths. *Two.* Filling my lungs, I centered myself as the panic and anxiety raced through my veins, scoring and scraping. The image of a disembodied wolfish grin and amber dripping sunsets filled my mind. The scent of rain-soaked, rich earth mixed with bright green foliage permeated my senses. It was a coping mechanism for my anxiety that I'd picked up in my early teens. I had no clue where it came from, but one day, mid-panic attack over an A- in calculus, it swept in. And, ever since, it had been what I gripped close to my being to still the cacophony of disjointed sensations crashing into me. It saved me from having to add to my mother's ever-changing cocktail of prescriptions she managed me with.

"Shayne sent me a text three days ago asking me if I would marry him," I stated in the flattest, calmest tone I could manage.

I had hoped to keep this between Shayne and me. We had been dating for four years, and it was one of many lifestyle concessions I made to please my mother and meet her expectations.

"And did you accept?"

My chestnut gaze snapped up to her. "What? *Mother, he sent me a text message.*"

She angled a scimitar-shaped brow up at my tone. The command was unspoken but crystal clear.

"No, Mother. I had not accepted."

The defeat in my voice was as familiar as my heartbeat.

Shayne Ellington was my mother's choice. I was barely twenty-eight, and the introduction all but engraved our relationship's permanence. He was an influential software guru based out of Atherton, whose legacy of money dated back to the California railroads. His father all but whispered ideas into Bill Gates's ear. They had an obscene amount of connections and money. It was too bad that all the money in the world couldn't buy a drop of personality or emotional intelligence. Despite having the finances to buy a small country, Shayne had never even bought me a single two-dollar teddy bear because "material things are just that, babes. Materials. We are so much more than that on a cosmic level, yanno?"

Her pale olive hand extended over the table, demanding my phone. I sighed, knowing exactly what came next—because, of course, it did. It was the plan, after all. I was to marry Shayne Ellington, have at least two babies, a boy and a girl—any other order would be unacceptable—and disappear into the sprawling suburbs of Atherton. I'd quit my accounting job, of course—not that that would be a big loss because I hated it anyway—and dedicate myself to philanthropy and bolstering my brother *Robert's* career. He was on the fast track to the White House, after all . . . if you believed my mother's tall tales, that is. Elida escaped the crushing expectation machine at eighteen, disappearing into the arms of some Japanese cartoonist, never to be seen or heard from again. *Lucky bitch.*

Lighting up my phone's screen with lightning-fast fingers, she tapped out the staccato of my death warrant. An incongruously cheerful ding came a few seconds later. She made a soft, pleased noise and handed the phone back.

"He will have his girl send over the prenup and the ring in the morning." I was saved from embarrassing myself in a wailing fit by the arrival of our gourmet seasonal salads.

Fuck. My. Life.

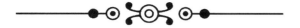

I adjusted the ten tons of the hideous canary diamond perched on my finger. It might as well have been a sizzling iron collar around my neck. Every time I looked at it, my anxiety cackled wickedly, kicking my heart rate up, causing a cold clammy tingle to spread from between my shoulder blades to wrap my body in a stranglehold. It was like walking upstairs at midnight in a power outage, thinking there was one more stair at the top when there wasn't or not knowing if you'd closed your front door, being six hours away with no cell service. In a nutshell, agony.

"Angie, did you hear me?" Colin, my boss, asked in a huff.

"What? Huh? Sorry, Mr. Spiker. I drifted off there for a second."

He chuckled patronizingly, brushing at the mustache that reminded me of the one attached to Groucho glasses. He leaned against his desk to stare down at me. "It's okay. My sister was the same way when she got engaged. Always staring at it, like the diamond would disappear. You ladies are so obsessed with shiny rocks."

Something inside of me screamed like it was on fire. I hated jewelry. I hated everything about it. I hadn't owned any since I'd moved out of my parent's house and refused to wear a single stud earring, let alone a necklace. The perverseness of the gaudy ring on my small hand made my stomach roil, and I hated Colin right then even more than I did on any general day.

Pulling on the poised mask I had learned to craft around me from all of my mother's loving lessons, I smiled the cold, condescending smile of a woman petting a man's ego. "I'm glad you understand, Mr. Spiker."

Appeased, he repeated himself. "The El Salvador client. Jake's having some issues with the local finance guy there. Says he can't understand a thing that the guy is saying, and the numbers are all over the place. We need this account, Angie. With the rumblings about this new president of theirs shaking things up, if we secure it now, when he inevitably shits the bed, we will make a killing on the referrals and conversions. So, I'm thinking . . . you haven't been on vacation since we hired you. What do you say? We fly you out there and see if you can translate for Jake?"

I blinked. This finance bro was not saying what I thought he was saying, right? Not only was he insinuating that I burn my vacation days but that I play second fiddle to Jake Lassiter of all people. Because what? He thought I was a translator? I wanted to snatch that stupid fishing trophy perched on the corner of his desk and shove it through his eye. I wouldn't, though. The firm I worked for was the chief donating partner to my brother's campaign, and my stepfather was on the board, a point sweet Pàpa always insisted on bringing up whenever I thought of switching careers. They knew I wanted out from under their thumbs, and whenever I wriggled in my tight bindings, they would tighten them further.

"If that's what needs to be done, Mr. Spiker. Of course."

"Ah, that's my girl!" He laughed and clapped. "I knew you spoke Spanish. Jake said he was sure you didn't. But with a last name like Esparza? You'd have to, right? Great! I'll have Mandy set your flight up. And, Angie?"

Retreating before committing career homicide—or just regular homicide—I placed one hand on his office door. "Yes, Mr. Spiker?"

"No wandering off and getting lost in the jungle, okay?"

I bristled under the cloak of my skirt suit, nonexistent hackles raised, a snarled growl scratching at my glossed lips. I sincerely hoped that, one day, I would wake up and some angel would have tattooed "insufferable" on Colin's forehead to warn the rest of humanity. I politely chuckled.

"Oh, and congrats, Mrs. Ellington!" he called out.

Mrs. Ellington.

The name hung in my mind like the solid presence of an executioner, following me to my apartment, haunting me with its final proclamation to the certainty of my destiny. Home. Or a reasonable facsimile. Not the safe harbor in the storm but a shanty against the roaring winds of the world's fury.

The prenup papers that had been delivered promptly at 7:05 a.m.—Shayne's assistant knew I woke up at 7 a.m. on the dot every day—were still tossed on the kitchen counter. I hadn't had the strength that morning to sign them. There was something too final about it. I lifted the cheap pen Shayne had sent over with the papers so many times I could probably identify it in a bin of its cheap brethren. Regardless of my hand's comfort and familiarity with it, I couldn't force my shaking hand to comply and sign.

Even the sight of the innocuous sheets of bone stopped me in my tracks. I stared, and it seemed even a single whispered breath would launch them off of the counter to attack me if it were too loud. Shaking from head to toe, barely holding it all together, I slid that vulgar ring from my finger and shoved it back into the navy-blue velvet trifold ring box.

When my finger was released from its platinum noose, I stumbled past the soulless designs of my stark apartment through my bedroom and into my sanctum. The silent condemnation of that horrid name dissipated as I stepped into the tight confines of the space. The only place in my entire world that was mine, my sanctuary hidden away from the rest of the world. This tiny little speck of space, my bedroom's bathroom, was the only place that was truly mine. Everywhere else, other people traipsed through, hanging their expectations, judgment, and disappointment like paintings on the walls of my life. Here, I could close the door, and in thirty-six square feet, I could truly *live*, exist as myself. Though, who the hell she was, I barely even knew at thirty-two years old.

Where my life was cast in navy-blues, taupe, white, cream, and gray in every possible aspect, here, in this bathroom, I could release myself. It was bedecked in rich mosaic tiles of golds, oranges, yellows, and spikes of vivid pink. I had decorated it in every color and design I was not otherwise allowed to express outside of its confines.

I collapsed against the dark wood door and sobbed. It was all too much, but in this small space, I could let it all go for a few minutes. I could let it all crumble in on me and crush me under its weight. I could let the broken, sundered pieces of myself mourn the loss of freedom, even if it had been an illusion for the last twenty years. I sobbed into the bright orange-yellow terry cloth robe hanging on the back of the door and screamed into its fabric arms. I wept for the lost dreams I wasn't allowed to have. I wept for the hopes I wasn't allowed to explore. I broke apart into the thousand pieces I wasn't allowed to be outside of this space.

Dark streaks of mascara coated my cheeks and chin and stained the top of my white blouse when I finally had the strength to pull myself off of the floor. What a mess. What a fitting and perfectly apt mess. My hair, tamed by the searing heat of a flat iron, lay stick-straight like a shroud of dark chocolate around my shoulders. My top was ruined. As I reached up to smear the streaking black rivers, I noticed the distinct red outline of that horrid ring on my finger. Of course it was still there. Even having taken it off at every opportunity I could, that damned thing still clung to my skin, burning the inevitability of ownership into my very essence.

"Fuck," I whispered to the beaten girl in the mirror.

How had I let my life spiral so out of control? I barely recognized the woman in the mirror. Oh, I knew it was my face. I knew every line and scar intimately. There, right next to my left eyebrow, was a tiny nick from when my mother decided cheerleading was for me and insisted that I learn "how to fly." I had been violently scared of being picked up, preferring to keep my feet solidly planted on the ground, but when the coach flipped me up over his head to the ear-piercing sounds of my mortal terror, she merely scoffed and sniffed her disapproval. My clumsiness and lack of coordination didn't live up to the standards she had set for me. Perhaps another mother would have encouraged me to keep trying—it had been only my second time to cheer practice—but not Annette.

Though smeared and smudged from the sobbing, the traces of the classic cat-eye eyeliner I had toiled an entire summer to perfect—per my mother's demands—clung on. Oh, yes, that was me for sure, the culmination of every single grain of sand that had added up into the shifting dunes of who I was. I envied those people who, at my age, knew themselves so solidly that they never questioned what tomorrow would bring. My tomorrows were full of only one certainty, that my choices were not my own.

And now I was on my way to some foreign country to act as a translator for a man I had no interest in helping. Could I even still speak Spanish? They say you never really forget a language, but it had been years since I spoke it. Years since I was anything more than the pale shadow of Annette and Edwin, years since I was Xochitl Angelica Esparza and not Angie Yarbrow. I had lost every connection to my true self; piece by tiny piece had been extracted and reforged to fit into my mother and stepfather's perfect pawn.

Knowing I was dwelling on things I couldn't change, I sighed. Knowing that the lost pieces of me would never come back. I would never be Xochitl again. I would be Angie forevermore, and not even Angie Esparza, *Angie Ellington*.

The only thing I was looking forward to with this trip was the two weeks and thousands of miles between Shayne and me. It would give me time to mourn the loss of the last piece of my inner self, time to accept it. Over the years, I had let little pieces of myself slide through my fingers with barely a twinge of feeling, but this engagement was killing me. It felt so wrong. It felt like I was being pulled through blackberry bushes, naked. Every inch of my skin prickled with the absolute *wrongness* of it. I felt hollow yet filled with futile rage, like a creature in a dark warehouse trapped under layers of crates and locked behind solid steel bars.

As if thinking about him summoned him into existence, my phone went off in my pocket.

S. Ellington: *Hey babes. Did you get the papers?*

He knew I had received the papers. His secretary must have told him she hand-delivered the two items. No matter how incompetent someone was, there was no way someone would be incompetent enough to drop an extravagant diamond ring and legal documents at a front desk or in front of an apartment door.

S. Ellington: *Dad wants the papers signed by tomorrow. L said she dropped them off to you this morning.*

Again, I didn't respond.

S. Ellington: *Mom's set up an engagement party for fri. She'll run the announcement on thurs. And she's got the venue reserved for Aug 2nd. Annette ordered your dress this morning. She said to tell you to pick it up two weeks from tues and that she got it in a 12. Not sure what that means but okay. Gotta go babes. See you fri.*

I rolled my eyes. He would not go away.

Angie: I've got a work trip.

S. Ellington: *k*

"K?" That's it? Insufferable. I wasn't sure what made me angrier, his mother's efficient audacity or the slap in the face. A twelve? My mother was keenly aware I was a size eighteen.

Angie: I'm leaving tomorrow.

S. Ellington: *k*

Angie: I don't know when I will be back.

S. Ellington: *k*

I wanted to strangle him. Why did I even bother?

Angie: I'll be without cell service the entire time.

S. Ellington: *that sucks babes!*

I typed out some sort of gibberish message just to get a human response but quickly erased it. Shayne wasn't human, and, ultimately, I didn't care. Hell, I was sure he didn't care. No part of our relationship ever seemed passionate or loving. He had always been pleasant enough if one squinted hard, but I was nothing more than a thing to him. A checkbox, nothing more, and he treated me neither with revulsion nor with wrath . . . just apathy.

A normal girl would call her best friend, perhaps have a pizza night in, and sob into each other's shoulders. I wasn't a normal girl, though. Not in the fun I'm-not-like-other-girls way but in a depressing one. I didn't have a best friend, not really. I had friends hand-picked by my family to further Robert's career. Influential women of standing and connections who could be moved and positioned to help his next campaign. It didn't matter that Robert was barely qualified to run for an office or that his chances were slim at best.

My brother, at his heart, was a wonderful person, but he was as much of a pawn as I was, propped up on the altar of expectation as much as me. Only, instead of the sacrificial lamb, he was the petrified effigy of success, terrified of dropping a hand from his crossbeam lest he find himself demoted to my servitude.

I confronted my reflection again. As I watched her rounded shoulders slump and hunch with the weight of others' ambition, anger seeped into my edges. I thrust my burdened, sloped shoulders back and flipped my unnaturally tamed hair over them, rebellion sparkling in my chestnut-and-gold eyes.

Fuck this. Fuck my mother. Fuck my stepfather. Fuck my brother. Fuck San Francisco. Fuck every last thing about this sham of a life. Fuck all of their expectations and their demands.

I was going to El Salvador, and when I got back, I would be done with it all. If I ever came back.

Don't get lost in the jungle? *Ha.* That's exactly what I would do. I was going to disappear into the jungle and never be seen again.

Something crackled to life deep in my soul, and it felt *right*. It felt absolutely and stunningly right, like smelling the crisp scent after a torrential downpour when the skies finally cleared. Even the girl in the mirror seemed to shift, and I could see her clearer. I saw less of her flaws. I saw around the manufactured image to the root of my essence. Oh, the veneer was still there, of course, but now, it felt and looked like a costume out of place and just as foreign as it should have been all along. I felt like a wild thing shoved and whipped into docility. The cream blouse hanging off of my shoulders, too loose in the bust, looked like it belonged to someone else. I recognized her, though. I recognized the wild glint in her eye when the light caught the golden flecks in the rich chocolate depths.

The feral, wolfish grin curling my lips seemed all too at home on my face.

Fuck this. That was my new mantra.

CHAPTER TWO

My 3 a.m. alarm clock jarred me out of the stupor I had drunk myself into. I sat up bolt-straight in my bed. Big mistake. The bottle of red wine I'd chugged while listening to Halestorm at full volume and packing my bag seemed to cackle its malicious betrayal in my pounding head. My eye sockets felt five sizes too small, and my stomach felt like I had guzzled lava. What was I thinking? I rarely drank anything aside from water and the occasional cola when no one was looking. What made me think it would be a great idea to change that by pounding back the bottle I only kept on hand on the off chance my mother stopped by?

My life flooded back like a tidal wave. The crushing weight of it threatened to pull me back under the warm cocoon of silence that was my comforter. Maybe I could hide from all the inconvenient truths I still had to face. Maybe I could sink into my bed and disappear forever, and it would all be okay when I finally surfaced.

My snoozed alarm shattered that half-baked idea with a reminder that my flight would leave in two hours. Two hours to figure out my entire life? Or perhaps just to avoid thinking altogether. Panic shot through me as I burst from the bed. A laundry list of items I needed to do to get out of the house crashed into each other like bumper cars. Taking deep breaths, I tried to fish through the wreckage of their various parts and pieces to find the first step.

Shoving my Adderall, vitamins, and birth control down my throat was step one. I hated those pills so much. They made me feel like a sloshing bottle of water on a thrashing boat. Sure, the water was all contained from splashing all over the nice clean carpets, but that did nothing for the swirling eddies raging within the confines of its container.

Thirty minutes later, I was pouring my pounding head and the rebelling body into the pre-scheduled car service that buzzed up to head to the airport. Deep breaths. *One*. Deep breaths. *Two*. The barely contained shaking, the living thing crawling under my skin, was an unseen manifestation of my nerves. The driver put my bag in the trunk before we began navigating through the dark streets of the city I hoped to never see again.

I shouldn't have, but I glanced at my phone to verify I had my itinerary. I knew it was there. My nerves had me checking the blasted thing every few seconds.

> **A. Yarbrow:** *Mrs. Ellington told me you hadn't signed the papers we drew up, yet. I'll be by while you are gone to sign them for you and drop them off at Shayne's office. Don't embarrass your father in El Salvador.*

I sighed heavily. Of course. "Don't embarrass your stepfather, Angelica." Not "Have a good trip." Not "Be safe." Not "Call me when you get there." Not a single word for me. Just more demands and more expectations.

> **A. Yarbrow:** *You owe us this. Especially after all Edwin, and I have done for you.*

Which did I owe her? Marrying a man I didn't like, let alone love? Or locking in a client for them when it wasn't even part of my job duties? Either. Both.

It always came back to this. How much they had done for me. I didn't respond. What was there to say? I knew what I had to do. I knew exactly what they expected. Was it bad that I focused on that part and not the threat that, whether or not I wanted to, those papers were getting signed? My mother had gotten power of attorney over me, "just in case" when I turned eighteen. I was too young at the time to understand what I was giving her but old enough to predict it was another tool for her to control me further. She had used it at every opportunity.

When I didn't want to go to the university of her choice, she enrolled me anyway, using the power of attorney as leverage. When I didn't want to rent the apartment I was speeding away from, in the building her friend owned, she signed the lease under my name. No choice was ever my own. Everything served my mother and her ambitions for Robert.

I had once dug my heels in on something small—a simple thing, really—just a cellphone plan. I needed to claw some scrap of power back. She had calmly, quietly—as we were in a public place—explained to me how easy it was for her and Edwin to have the power of attorney upgraded to a full conservatorship. I had never heard the word before. She explained to me how simple it would be for her friends to forge psychiatric history logs for her to get one and the extent of power she would truly have over me. I never bothered calling her bluff again. Not in person. Only in ways I could hide, like the tile in my bathroom or the lingerie I had custom made once a quarter.

"Rough morning?"

The voice of my driver called me away from the depressing reality of my life, dragging my eyes away from the stark reminders slithering by the windows. I looked out of the corner of my eye, my head not leaving the cool kiss of the glass. I caught the side of his face and the reflection of his eyes in the rearview mirror, but it seemed so familiar. I squinted, trying to place the face, which made him laugh, a laugh I remembered.

"Javier?" I asked incredulously. "Javier Hernández?"

He laughed again, the sound a comforting hand petting the jagged and bristling edges of my psyche. It stroked that pain-soaked spot in my soul like the feeling of coming home in the dead of winter to a warm apartment that smelled of freshly baked bread.

"Hey, Xochi."

The nickname, a shortened version of Xochitl, should have pulled those bristling edges back up. After she'd married my stepfather, my mother had called me Xochi a few times, always to cajole me into peacefully doing as she bid. It had never worked. Ever since then, the nickname from anyone's mouth felt like they were waging a personal war against my defenses. But on Javier's tongue, the name felt easy, like pulling on an old comfy shirt.

"No one's called me that in a long time."

His smile pushed through a filter of barely contained dejection. "Well, then, Angelica, it is."

He'd said it with that soft accent he had, even as children. Ann-hell-ika. I'd always liked the way it sounded. The way it curled around my head like the stroke of a treasured pet I had not seen in years. I never had a pet, but I imagined the way my body eased into the seat was the same way a cat purring in my lap would make me feel.

"Just Angie," I murmured, and his smile deflated to a half smirk. "What are the chances? I haven't seen you since we moved out of Outer Mission."

Polite. Had to be polite. I hadn't seen the man since we were kids. We had been close but weren't allowed to stay in touch when my family moved away. Just like everyone else, before Edwin Yarbrow, Javier had been shoved out of my life without even a goodbye. I was a ghost to them. One day, I was at school, laughing on the playground, and the following Monday, I never showed up. It was so sudden even *I* didn't know when I had crawled into the car that morning to head to school. My mother hadn't even bothered to give the three of us any warning. When I was a child, it seemed odd. Now, as an adult, having learned the slithering ways of my mother's mind, I realized it was disgustingly normal.

He smiled again, this time a genuine and bright smile.

"Yeah. I hear you are up to big things these days. About to grab that happily ever after."

Did everyone in the entire universe know that I was marrying Shayne? I wasn't even wearing that awful anchor. I'd left it in the box on top of the prenup papers. I didn't know exactly why I hadn't grabbed it, but when I stepped out into the hallway, the decision sparkled in my blood like gold flecks in a river bed drawing in the light and scattering it across mirrored surfaces.

"I guess so." I huffed out in a fake laugh. "How's Juanita? Last I heard, she was about to retire from the school?"

I hadn't heard anything about anyone from the old neighborhood, but a bit of quick math said it was plausible.

Javi's mother was one of my favorite teachers before I was pulled from public school. I remember distinctly being so upset I wouldn't be able to see her again. Mrs. Hernández was immortalized in my childhood mind as the mother I wished I could have had, the mother I wished my mother would have been. She always smelled of carrot cake and had the brightest smile, a trait I could see Javi had inherited from her. She was warm, kind, and caring, never being shy about affection or tender words.

"She's great, actually, Xo—Angie. She and Pops moved up to Merced not too long ago. She's got a garden now. She keeps sending me tomatoes and squash. No clue what I'm going to do with them, but the missus loves it."

I grinned, remembering the lessons we had on Botany. It was impractical, living in a city where each square foot of real estate was jealously hoarded and more valuable than gold, but I loved those classes more than anything. The rich scent of potting soil and freshly watered plants had been a balm to my soul even then.

"Sounds like the dream. Congrats, by the way."

"Thanks."

We pulled up to the international gate, and Javi helped me with my bag. He was much taller than I would have expected. He stayed fit, though. I could tell by the way the white button-up shirt clung to his well-muscled shoulders. I should have felt a larger twinge of irritation with myself. Not only was I checking out a married man, but I was engaged, and all I felt was mild guilt for having ogled a married man. Even though that was the first I had heard of Javi's wife or even thought of him in the last fifteen years, I wanted to believe that he was very happily married. Blissfully, happily married, even.

I tried to wave him off, but he shrugged me away, saying it was the least he could do for someone like me. When I shot him a quizzical look, he grinned. Someone like me? What did that even mean? Was I so isolated and different from my childhood friend that he felt I was somehow Other? That thought pulled the familiar frown to my face, but I let it go. There would be no point in fighting him on this, no use in pushing him to explain. The odds of me seeing Javi again were slim, and it would be impolite of me to leave him with a poor impression of me to report back to the chismosas of the old neighborhood.

He walked me to the counter, clearing the way with his larger body. After ensuring I had my ticket, he grinned at me and snatched my mere five-foot-three frame up against his way-above-six-foot body.

I shrieked and fought him off but not before he whispered "Congrats, Xochitl" in my ear.

As he put me down, I frowned and said to his retreating back, "Thanks. I'll tell Shayne you send your regards."

He spun on his heel, walking backward. "Who's Shayne?"

I sputtered. What? My lashes blinked wildly, and somewhere between blink seven and eight, Javi was gone. I stared, dumbstruck by what had happened and how weird it was to see Javi again. I stood there, gawking at the exchange. Who the hell did he think I was marrying? Or, if it wasn't my engagement he was congratulating me on, what was he talking about with all that nonsense about grabbing happily ever after?

I was blocking traffic in the airport atrium, drawing glares and a few grumbled choice words before my phone blared, snapping me out of it.

"Hello?"

"Mrs. Ellington?"

I gritted my teeth. "Not yet."

"What?"

"Nothing. This is Angie Esparza."

The woman paused on the other end. "Uh . . . sorry, ma'am, I have this number down as the contact number for Angie Ellington, who I'm supposed to pick up for a drop off at the airport."

She must have taken my stupefied pause as I stared at the empty space Javi had just occupied as an excuse to go on.

"Anyway, ma'am, I'm outside. I tried to buzz you, but you didn—"

As the gears in my head whirred in double time, they finally engaged with the parts that mattered in the moment.

"Yeah . . . yeah. Sorry about that. I am so sorry, miss. I called an Uber. I totally forgot that the company would have sent a service."

A grumble settled in the silence. "It's okay, ma'am. Have a safe flight. I'll let the dispatcher know not to bill for the service."

"Wait! No. Don't do that. You came all the way out. Go ahead and bill the firm for your time . . . Heck, I am pretty sure you hit traffic, too. As a matter of fact, you almost didn't even make it. But you were such an excellent driver that you called ahead to get me checked in to make sure I didn't miss my flight. And you carried my bag all the way in. And, uhm, I promised you a hundred-dollar tip, too." I could almost hear the woman on the other end mentally stammering, trying to catch up to the revisionist history I was blurting out. "At least that's how I remember it."

A nearly microscopic pause spun the gears on the other side of the phone.

"That's exactly how I remember it, too, ma'am." I could hear the grin in her voice as she caught up. "You have a safe flight, ma'am. And have fun on your trip, too."

"Thanks," I mumbled while disconnecting.

This one time, when I was maybe fifteen or sixteen, I went to an arcade and played pinball. I remember the slapping of the flippers so clearly. I felt like that little silver ball right now. Bouncing and ricocheting off of the walls in a dizzying, unstoppable path toward whatever the next thing I slammed into sent me after, with no clear destination or map.

CHAPTER THREE

The entire six-hour flight to El Salvador, I fidgeted, twitching and picking at my fingers the whole hour-long drive from the airport to my hotel in La Libertad. Through the check-in process and all the way to my cabana, I twitched, my mind pacing. Even with my Adderall caging the most ferocious of my squirming nerves, it was still too weak to shackle its mighty strength. My fingers, naked except for the imagined indent of that awful ring, tapped on any surface in front of me.

Who's Shayne? kept echoing in my head. I replayed the entire interaction with Javier and the driver. What did he mean 'who's Shayne?' What did he mean 'someone like me?' And how had he known to pick me up? Or where I lived? Or even that I was taking a trip?

It was driving me up a wall. Nothing made sense. It was the sensation of an itch right between your shoulder blades, persistent, nagging, but out of reach.

It *was*, however, a great distraction from hyper-focusing on the absolute mess that my life was. I hadn't thought of the engagement or my mother the entire time I was mulling over the strange morning. Instead, I fixated on every single word and gesture until I could probably have painted it from memory. And, still, none of it made a lick of sense.

Pacing my cabana, I only occasionally cast my gaze out the wall of glass facing the coastal paradise that serenaded me from forty feet away. My mind would occasionally register my upstairs neighbor shifting, reminding me of how different it was in La Libertad. In San Francisco, there was a crush of humanity. Everywhere you went writhed with life, and, here, there was breathing room with so few people. My foot caught on a green stem as I shuffled across the tiles for the seventeenth time, and I crouched to fish it from under the bed. It was a single white rose.

My brow shot up. *Shayne.* I hated roses, but Shayne insisted on always sending me white roses every Friday, like clockwork. It struck me as both desperate and weird that, every Friday, at exactly 3 p.m., I would have two dozen white roses delivered to my desk. At first, it was sweet. After the fifth delivery, I worked up the nerve to tell him I didn't like roses, especially not white ones. I loved marigolds and peonies.

He chuckled, face still buried in his phone, and said, "Okay, babes."

The next Friday, I was looking forward to the delivery, and when the white roses were delivered anyway, I sighed. Just like everyone else in my life, Shayne didn't care about what I liked and never made any excuses about it. It was then that I realized that the roses weren't for me but a visible claim on my space and person, a way for Shayne to flex his ownership and show what a great partner he was. My coworkers' *oohs* and *awwuhs* had solidified it.

It was a Wednesday, and I was not at work to show off. Why was there a white rose in my room? Hunting around the room, I found two more petals and a leaf, but the usual two dozen roses were nowhere to be found. After a full circuit of the suite, every surface inspected and trash bin searched, I discovered one more petal under a pillow. I didn't find another full rose. And I didn't know where the one I held had come from.

I left the crushing weight of my life in San Francisco only a few hours ago, and for that mere eight hours, the incessant scratching of my anxiety had stilled to a whispered tapping on the edges of my psyche. Then the single rose and a handful of petals had the beast rearing up to claw at my throat. I was in a foreign land, where I barely spoke the language, thousands of miles away from anyone I knew, not counting Jake Lassiter—the man was as useful as chopsticks when you have a bowl of soup—and a simple flower had cold sweats prickling at my temple.

Get it together, Angie. It's just a flower.

Maybe the hotel left them as a nice check-in service and the bellman knocked it to the floor when he put my bag on the bed. Yeah, that sounded perfectly reasonable and not strange at all. That was it. There wasn't some creepy kidnapping cartel guy sneaking into cabanas, leaving white roses as warnings to his future victims, like some weirdo comic book villain.

One. Deep breath. *Two.* Deep breath. That old, familiar wolfish grin and natural scent filled my awareness, bringing with it the comfort it always had. But a new scent joined the mental image, and I couldn't quite place it. It reminded me of the warmth of spiced rum sliding down my throat, quelling the rising panic and the worst of the intrusive thoughts.

I needed air. I needed space.

Kicking off my tennis shoes, I flipped open my suitcase and winced. Fishing through it, I found one navy-blue pump, its mate somewhere in my catastrophe of a bedroom in San Francisco. I found the belt to my favorite bathrobe but not the matching robe. Chaos reigned supreme in the contents of the bag, and I couldn't be bothered to deal with it. Seeing the jumble of clashing colors, shapes, and textures reminded me of a shattered gumball machine. Mental note: never pack for an international business trip during a mental breakdown. I hoped there was a store with my size somewhere close by, or this would be one very interesting trip.

On the bright side, I did manage to get both a left and right flip-flop into my suitcase. Too bad they were different cuts, styles, and colors. Well, that settled it. I was going walking on the beach. No shoes required, right?

Pushing open the sliding glass door, I turned, then locked it behind me. I dragged in another deep breath, trying to calm my frayed edges as I pressed my palm to the glass. The scent of the pool between me and the ocean mingled with the bright scent of tropical flowers. I rested my head on the cool glass before me. It helped, but I let the rhythmic pounding of the waves pull me.

Smiling softly, I ran my hand over the sunny blossom heads of marigolds lining the pathway down to the sandy beach. Their scent wrapped me in a warm, welcoming hug, and paired with the sounds of the ocean, I calmed more. The sand crunched between my toes, the small, water-rounded stones pebbling the beach adding a distinct ring. I walked to the edge of the waves and meandered the trek down the beach. The cold kiss of the water pulled my anxiety and panic away, lick by lick.

I'd never been out of the country. Before my family lived in the lap of luxury, growing up, my mother was a single mother of three kids. She was the daughter of Mexican immigrants barely scraping by, wavering between outright destitution and tolerable poverty. Depending on the week, she'd rely on the strength of the community more than whatever meager wages a day's backbreaking work would earn her. We lived with her parents in a small house that barely contained all six of us. We were happy—or so I thought. The turn started when my father was deported back to Nicaragua shortly after Elida was born, and we never saw him again.

I'd occasionally hear my mother crying in the bathroom or the garage, whispering a prayer for him through her tears. But, after it was clear he was never coming back, he disappeared. He was cut out of family photos. Pictures of him and my mom miraculously vanished, as if they never existed. I'd found his favorite mug, a navy-blue monstrosity Robert had made in summer camp, shattered in the trash. When I missed him most, I would crawl into the closet where all his clothes hung and wrap myself in his scent.

Eventually, those, too, disappeared without comment. Any time we brought him up, we were scolded severely or beaten, though that was rarer than the verbal lashings. On one such night, as I huddled in the corner of the room I shared with Robert, baby Elida, and my mother, my abuela came to hold me.

"Ay, mija, I know it is scary and confusing," she whispered into my mane of curls, stroking her gnarled hands over the ringlets. "Your mamá is very sad, and when creatures are sad, their tears blind their eyes. Her tears will dry up, and she will be able to see again. Be patient with her, mi corazón."

I don't think my mother's tears ever dried up. If they had, they poisoned her so completely that the woman that came out of that sorrow was not the same as the one that went in. Abuela had told me stories of women in the old country who would cry so hard, and for so long, they would die from heartbreak and come back as horrible monsters. The terror of my childhood was La Llorona, and I could almost see the resemblances between the original story and what my mother had become. I remembered the day she began donning her pale uniform and the bone-deep terror that ran through me whenever I saw her in white.

The first time that realization hit my young mind, I began to believe in monsters and my abuela's old stories. I hadn't slept well for almost two years after that. I saw the weeping lady in every mirror, every window, but the most terrifying was when I began to recognize her in my mother's cold gaze.

The cameo she wore was a constant reminder of the day I saw her. I was cleaning our room when I knocked over her jewelry box. When I picked it up, the carpet snagged the cameo's chain, and the dainty links snapped. I expected rage, anger, or a scolding, but the look in my mother's eyes had turned cold, like she expected it and was just waiting to mete out the brutal punishment I would receive. I swore there was even a ghastly smirk on her face as she smacked me.

My head was far away, bobbing on a sea of memories in a state of post anxiety afterglow, when I felt the warmth of a solid wall collide with my body. I felt myself falling, waiting for the sand and sea to rush up and cradle me close, but the salty arms of the ocean never found me.

"Easy there, nayeli," a thick-accented voice purred.

I had never heard a more comforting and enthralling sound. It was the sensation of freshly shaved legs crawling into clean sheets just out of the dryer on a cold winter's night. It reached down into my very center and wrapped it in a warm blanket.

My lashes fluttered wildly, and I stared into the face of the wall of a man I'd walked into. His skin was rich, like the dark heart of an ancient forest, his eyes the loamy earth that lined that wood, his cheekbones high and prominent, his nose elegant and hawk-like. Lips that curved into a gentle smile were deep oak-brown and plump. A sparkle of mischief in his eyes drew me into the luxury of their depths. His powerful shoulders were clad in an ash-gray button-down shirt open at the V of his collar, revealing the golden links of a Figaro chain dipping below it.

He held me perhaps for a little too long, and perhaps I let him. The rightness of the embrace extended that deep, comforting ease settling into my psyche. While I was busy making excuses for myself about letting a stranger hold me, his scent enveloped me. It was familiar in a way I couldn't place but had me fighting the urge to nuzzle into his neck and grip his shirt. I could feel the muscles of his arms tensing, not struggling with my weight, but seemingly struggling with the exact distance to hold me. His fingers would clench, drawing me an inch closer, then relax to ease me back, as if he, too, felt the magnetic pull tethering us and tightening with each passing second.

A lazy smile curled at the edge of his lips before he straightened to his full height and towered over me by at least a foot or more. He set me down gently on the sand, like I was made of spun sugar and ephemera that would break apart and scatter in the tropical breeze should he handle me carelessly.

"Uhm. Thanks," I mumbled awkwardly. "I, uh . . . didn't see you there."

That smile never left his lips, and I wanted to trip again to fall back into his arms. The lack of their warmth seemed like a crime, and my body leaned toward him without my consent, longing to be closer to him.

"It was my mistake, nayeli. I was watching the waves come in and looking for sea glass."

The way his clever tongue curled and rolled around the English words spoke of long, hot nights in the tropical climate and years of switching between Spanish and English. It was an accent rich with spices and history. I wanted him to read a phone book to me to hear the words dance in his soft, deep velvet voice.

"Sea glass?" I asked stupidly.

He chuckled, kneeling next to me on one knee, plucking a pale green stone from near my foot. The action brought my gaze down his length to the muscled thighs hidden behind a pair of sensible charcoal slacks cuffed at the knees, baring his toned shins, ankles, and feet. I understood now why ankles were such a big deal back in the day. How could a man have such attractive ankles and feet?

I shook myself before a cartoonish gulp could make its way down my throat. From the way his black brow ticked at the edge, the corner of his lips following suit, and his nostrils flared almost imperceptibly, I was pretty sure he knew exactly where my scattered thoughts were headed. He, thankfully, said nothing about it and offered me the thumb-sized chunk of weather-beaten glass.

A memory of a sunset-drenched park from my childhood splashed across my mind's eye, too far and blurred by age to remember clearly. Like with all memories, the harder I tried to focus on it, the more it slipped from my fingers like soap in slick, wet fingers.

"Sea glass," he whispered, as if saying it too loud could shatter the moment and cast us back into the bleakness of reality where magic didn't draw two strangers into a single throbbing moment of light.

When had my heart started racing? It barreled down my internal track toward the man before me, offering up a rounded hunk of glass like it was the greatest treasure he had ever possessed. Every strike pounded out a drumbeat in my ears, and the world around us narrowed down to this and only this. To this man, this tiny section of ocean-kissed beach. To this weathered piece of glass and to my trembling hand as I plucked it from his fingers.

His smile grew tender and doting as he tracked the minty tumble, my fingers drawing it up to my eye. Examining it, I saw the tiny crack that ran through the center but didn't terminate at the edges, oddly reminding me of myself. *I, too, have a crack running through the center of my being, little glass piece,* I wanted to whisper to it.

"Thank you," I breathed.

He rose, purposefully blocking out the mid-afternoon sun, so I didn't have to squint. It was a kind and strangely thoughtful gesture. He was so close I could feel the heat of him radiating into my skin. If I were to have moved a fraction of an inch, I would be pressed to that toned chest again. I needed to lean a hair closer to the body that beckoned my own.

I looked up, both of us taking in the other. I noticed that, at the corners of his temples, a suggestion of salt mixed with the peppery black of his hair. The length of which was swept into a braid that plunged behind his shoulders. Nicks and cuts peppered his tanned skin, from his hands to his face and throat, had long since healed over, just barely visible. His ears were pierced, the plug in each lobe the circumference of my pinky. The stone was almost like jade but had a richness to the green that I hadn't seen before and a pattern that reminded me of turquoise.

A seagull called overhead, drawing my attention away from dark eyes that sucked me in and held me in a vise grip. A flash of white and gray marred the perfect azure sky for a moment before I felt something collide with my shoulder. Horror washed through me as the shoulder of my baby-blue cotton dress grew damp with a fat splatter of white.

I was mortified. In every movie, every book, and every imagining of the perfect moment on a sunlit beach with a handsome man, none of those women were subjected to such a hideous affront to their dignity. Especially not in front of the man of her dreams.

His laughter, deep drums pounding out a primal beat, washed over me. I whipped my gaze back at him.

"What's so funny?" I exclaimed.

"Your face! Mira, es buena suerte." He moved closer into my space, plucking the limp strand of my humidity-ravaged hair out of the mess.

"It's what?" Hysteria crept into my voice. "How can a bird shitting on me be good luck?"

He grinned, settling large hands with blunt fingertips below the peaks of my shoulders, wisely out of the splash zone. "It is good luck. I don't know why. It just is."

I could feel the vibration of his voice in my chest. The last spike of anxiety eased, scattering like leaves in the wind. I felt . . . relaxed. Truly *relaxed*, fully and completely, for the first time in as long as I could remember. I wanted to bask in this feeling of ease, bask in the looseness of every muscle and thought. Even my jaw had unclenched, and I was sure those muscles were permanently locked from all the tension.

"Come. The café over there will have some napkins. Maybe, if some of your luck rubs off on me, you will share a drink with me?"

The hope in his voice was intoxicating, so tantalizing I demurred from the obvious next course of action: smear the bird poop on him. That'd be a sure way for my luck to rub off on him.

I followed him down the beach to a small building with a grill out in the sand, three tables under its palm-thatched roof, and a small bar separating a home kitchen-style stove top range and refrigerator. On the counter of the bar were two large terra-cotta tanks that glistened with condensation.

My rescuer pulled a chair out for me. "Por favor, siéntate, estrella hermosa."

I blushed under the compliment and complied. He tucked the chair in under me and went to collect the promised water and napkins. A brief conversation between him and the weathered old man behind the bar was too fast for me to catch, and he made his way back to the table with that pleased grin on his face again.

He leaned over me, dabbed the napkin in the water, and swabbed the mess on my shoulder. A distant hissing voice in my head mumbled something about how I probably shouldn't let this incredibly handsome stranger be so familiar with touching me. The way the warmth of his hand melted into my skin made my eyes roll back, scattering any thoughts of proprietary. The way his other palm rested possessively on my other shoulder made my soul purr with delight. My breathing picked up, the shallow rhythm pulling through my nose to feed my suddenly starving lungs.

Warmth traveled down my body, swirled around my chest, and peaked my nipples against my satiny bra. It traipsed across the rise and fall of my chest to tumble down the tightening nip of my generous stomach and teased the lines of my wide hips to pool seductively in my center. My core flexed and clenched as if to beckon him closer . . . and lower.

The hand on my shoulder flexed, gripping the meat of my upper arm. My eyes flickered open in question. A strange, pained look twisting his face faded away when he realized that I had moved.

"Lo siento." He cleared his throat and passed the napkin to me, embarrassment blooming in my cheeks. Those wonderful hands flexed against my skin again but didn't grip as I wanted them to. All too quickly, their warmth faded from my skin as he found his seat across from me.

"Está bien," I mumbled back to him, wishing he would scoot closer. Stiffening my back as I dabbed at the last bit of the avian humiliation, I let my eyes wander his frame from behind lowered lashes. "So, do you often loiter on beaches hunting for sea glass?"

He grinned over the milky substance that was brought in glasses to our table. "Not often. Though, if I'm sure to run into more beautiful American women on the beach, I'll be a resident by sundown."

I grimaced. "Is it that obvious?"

"Your accent . . . it could use some work. Not terrible, though. I've heard worse."

My brain just now registered the compliment enough to blush. I stared at the drink in front of me.

"It's horchata. Drink, nayeli. It's good. It's a favorite here in El Salvador."

I had heard of the drink before. My friends in high school were fond of it. I couldn't remember ever having it myself, though. He seemed overly pleased with himself for introducing me to the drink, so I didn't disabuse him of the notion.

He kept calling me that, nayeli, but it was a word I hadn't heard before. A word that, as I searched my very rusty Spanish lexicon, didn't seem to have a place. Maybe it was a local term of endearment or slang I just didn't know yet.

I followed his lead and tipped the glass up. The cool, milky drink was refreshing against the heat of the day. Flavors of rice, milk, and cinnamon mingled on my tongue. "It's wonderful!"

"I'm glad you like it," he drawled over his glass. "To answer your question, no. Not often. I own the hotel up the beach some, and I've been in business meetings all day. I needed some time to decompress."

My eyes skipped down the beach to the hotel the opposite way from my own. "Ah, I see. It's a beautiful hotel."

"Would you be uncomfortable if I told you it and no other thing in creation is more beautiful than you?"

I blinked again at him. A deep breath was pulled in. Years of the lack of compliments made me exceptionally grateful for them. I always felt I was beautiful, but my family had taken every opportunity to convince me otherwise.

"Thank you."

We talked for hours. The conversation was easy and flirty. I found my smile came just as easily as the discussion. By the time the older gentleman had packed up, the sun had set, and the moon came up over the waves.

"I should really get back. I have an early day tomorrow."

I hated to leave. His presence was a comfort I didn't know I needed, the balm and soft space my aching soul had been crying out for, never knowing what it yearned for. A small part of me was ashamed of that. Despite the fact we had never been happy together, I was technically engaged to another man, and I was sure this beautiful man would find it offensive I let him flirt with me all day if he knew.

"Let me walk you back. La Libertad is not as dangerous as it once was and not as dangerous as San Salvador at night, but you can never be too careful."

I nodded, and we bid the café owner a good night. The stroll along the moonlit beach would have been romantic in any setting but standing next to this tall, dark, and handsome stranger was something out of a fairy tale. It was a moment I never thought would be mine. I always thought I would wither away doing what my family had bid me, doing what was best for those I loved. Yet, there I was, strolling barefoot on the black sands of a tropical paradise with a man whose name I didn't even know.

"You know, I don't think I caught your name," I said into the conversation's natural lull as we reached the stairs to the hotel's entrance.

A slow, wolfish grin that tugged at my heart—and, frankly, my pussy, too—flashed over his face. "It's Itziquetzal. But my friends call me Sal."

Itziquetzal, what a beautiful name for such a dangerously handsome man. His mother knew what she was doing when she named him. Something about it, though, itched at the back of my brain, like a dog scratching at the back door.

"I'm Angie."

"Are you now?"

I tilted my head. "Well, I figured since we were on a familiar-name basis, Sal, that was enough. But, if you must know, no, it's Xochitl Angelica, actually."

"Sho-cheet," he corrected, and that itch became a clawing.

I frowned but let it pass. It had been a long time since I used my first name and this perfect stranger correcting my pronunciation of it wasn't something I felt like arguing about. It was best to avoid simple arguments, I had found. Some things didn't need to be bickered about, and this was one of them.

"Good night, Sal. It was lovely meeting you. Thank you for introducing me to horchata."

I pulled the mask of placidity back across myself. Something about the spark in his eye when he corrected me had me feeling like he wanted to argue. I learned from my mother how best to avoid that look in someone's eye. A polite, pleasant tone and a soft voice usually took the wind right out of a verbal combatant's sails.

Disappointment, a look I was so familiar with, flashed across his teasing features before he could pull it back. *Ah.* I'd seen it, though, and it was a look I knew far too well to not understand. He had expectations of me, just like everyone else.

I turned to walk up the stairs that would bring me into the pool area and lead me back to my solitary cabana. My fingers idly caressed the tops of the marigolds as I passed them, deep and angry orange in the moonlight.

"Xochitl," he said in a voice almost edging with command.

I stopped, inhaled, and turned. "Yes, Itziquetzal?"

It was his turn to frown at my formality. "Will you meet me for dinner tomorrow? I fear I might have . . . soiled your opinion of me. Allow me to make it up to you?"

What was the point? Why should it matter to him if he had "soiled my opinion?" But a girl has to eat, and unless I wanted to eat room service in my cabana like a sad sack, someone would have to show me around. And it sure as hell would not be Jake goddamned Lassiter.

Jake had, once upon a time, imagined a world in which I would be attracted to him. He was fifteen years my senior, and while handsome enough in the way most corporate men kept up their appearances, he had the personality of dirty dishwater. I let him take me out on one date. He had made *me* choose the location, the time, and the day. He'd made me carry the entire conversation, as well as order, even though the tapas menu was in English and Spanish. It was "so sexy" that I was a Latina who could speak Spanish. When I told him I hadn't spoken it since I was a little girl, he pressed, and I'd relented.

When I declined a second date, Jake tried every dirty, underhanded corporate sabotage tactic he could think of to tank my career. He would invite me to nonexistent meetings and write emails that insinuated heavily that my numbers were off. He'd alter billing cycles to ensure they fell on an odd day, throwing off the invoicing process, making me stay late to correct it. Jake, unfortunately, never got the memo that I had absolutely nothing to lose with my accountant's position, and an act of God himself couldn't fire me unless it benefited the Yarbrows.

"I would love to, but unfortunately, I only packed for business meetings."

The excuse was lame but not untrue. I could probably make one of my boring sheath dresses work for dinner, but he *had* soiled my opinion of him.

"You'll find that, when faced with a beautiful woman, she could be dressed in rags, and most Salvadoran men would still do their best to woo her." The frown he was given spurred him on. "Allow me to take you to the dress shop, then? And if, by some miracle, you find one to your liking, perhaps then you will let me take you to dinner?"

I did need to find a clothing store. And I knew I wouldn't find it on my own. Flashes of horrific shopping sprees with my mother, where I found a frumpy potato sack stashed in the back on the clearance rack, the only thing in my size in the entire store, flashed across my mind. I had no interest in the humiliation of that experience playing out in front of this god of a man.

"How about this: you tell me where the store is, I will go on my own and if—and that's a big *if*—I find something I like, I will meet you somewhere for dinner."

Hope sparkled in his eyes.

"That is a deal I am willing to take." He gave me the name of the boutique and instructions to give to the concierge, who would order me a taxi. "I will leave the name of the restaurant and time with the clerk at the boutique. Should you find a dress, that is."

A half smirk was his reward and nothing more, but he seemed grateful.

"Sleep well, Xochitl. I look forward to seeing you in the moonlight again."

Thankfully, he didn't attempt to kiss me or hug me. He stayed a respectful two feet away, though his hand wrapped around the metal railing flexed with the strain of the unheeded desire.

"Good night, Sal. I might see you tomorrow."

And, with that, I retreated to the safety of my cabana.

CHAPTER FOUR

My hand trembled with my pounding heart as I closed and locked the sliding glass door to my room. It shook as I pulled the wall-length heavy curtain across the glass. Only when I was positive that there was no way Sal could see or hear me did I finally exhale.

As soon as the grounding breath left my lungs, my entire body moved. Hands shaking out like they were on fire as I hunched over and stamped my feet, screaming silently in the international excited girl-freak-out flail. What the actual fuck? What the actual *oh-my-god* fuck just happened? Was I dreaming? Did I just meet a tall, dark, and handsome stranger on a tropical beach, who was charming and seemed very into me? I wished I had someone to call to freak out with.

Instead of reaching for a cell phone, I flopped myself on the queen-sized bed and grinned up to the ceiling. My upstairs neighbor was pacing while I snuggled into the crisp cotton linens around me. I stilled for a few seconds, but my skin was too tingly, too excited and alive to stay in one place.

Jumping from the bed, I stripped off the puffy-sleeved, peasant-style baby-blue dress and tossed it in the corner under the vent. I paced like a caged tiger, the air from the fan above the bed, ubiquitous in this climate, cooling the skin not covered by my matching white satin bra and panties. My fingers occasionally grazed my hot skin, making me gasp with need at the contact.

Closing my eyes, I let my mind wander back to Sal's face, imagining his teasing grin and the feel of his calloused fingertips. I imagined the warmth of those blunted fingers were my hands running up my generous thighs, across my slightly rounded belly, up my large, satin-covered breast to play at my throat.

You're soaking wet for me, he purred in my ear in that beautiful, accented voice in my imagination. *Show me.*

Allowing my mind to dictate the scene, I saw him sitting in his slightly crumpled business attire in the chair across from the bed tucked in at the desk, intensity burning in his stygian gaze. I bent to face my ass to it, giving him a show as I slowly slid the panties from my dripping pussy. I stepped out of them and tossed them to the pile near the vent.

Sal leaned back in the chair, sucking his bottom lip between his teeth, then ran a thumb over it as his hungry eyes traveled up my plush form. I shivered under the gaze of the illusionary man.

Bra, too, came the starved voice, dripping with command.

My fingers danced along my stomach, teasing the straining flesh before circling behind me and unhooking each of the four clasps with practiced fingers. It, too, joined the growing pile under the ceiling vent. I swayed to the moody music playing in my mind, letting my hands roam, tease my pebbled nipples, then curl around my hair. I loved the idea of Sal sitting there, watching me, nude and glistening with the need for him to touch me.

I fell back onto the cloudy comfort of the bed and let my knees fall open, never losing contact with the imaginary man who was the voyeur to my evening delights. I was so wet from the whole day of being inches from mauling him I could feel my juices sliding down my ass onto the bed. I licked my lips and dragged my nails down my hyper-aware breasts to play at my nipples, rolling them gently at first, then increasing the pressure until it was teetering on that sumptuous precipice between pleasure and pain. I squirmed on the bed, my heartbeat throbbing in my aching depths.

A moan slipped through my lips, and I crossed the threshold between pain and pleasure by letting just the edge of my nail dig into the stiffened flesh before pinching and rolling it. The upstairs neighbor slid a chair across the floor, and I folded it into my fantasy, seeing Sal pull his chair up to the foot of the bed to be closer.

More, he demanded.

Giving him more, I pulled, rolled, and dug the nail in until the throb drove me insane, and I was panting with desire.

I imagined a groan from the apparition haunting my thoughts. He leaned forward, elbows digging into his knees, that heated stare fixed on me as if I were the only thing that would ever matter to him. I blossomed under that imaginary gaze, legs spreading wide to let him feast, the fingers of one hand teasing me as it slid down the slope of my stomach to play in the trimmed hair at the top of my flushed, throbbing flesh. They were as ghostly in their touch as his presence was in my room. A mere suggestion of touch, there one second, then gone before I could lean into it. The heat of the fingertips was the only thing left in their wake to suggest they had been there.

Again, I moaned, this time thick with rapture and desire. I wished I could feel his hot breath on my skin. Wished I could hear that spiced accent rolling through the words playing in my mind. Wished I could fill my aching with his and we could slake our thirst in each other's bodies.

When my fingers grazed the wanton, swollen bud, I gasped, trembling, so close to the edge. Sal's ghost moaned at the foot of my bed. My fingers played in the slick, drenched folds, teasing me more, occasionally flicking my fingertips over my nub. Each flick elicited a gasped moan from my lips and a pained groan from Sal.

Harder, he murmured into the hush of the room, the only sound the soaked slip of my fingers and my whimpering.

Positioning my fingers on that sensitive, quivering button, I stroked it, thinking of him watching me and refusing to touch me while I pleasured myself for him. I was already on edge, the day with Sal playing out in my mind, my fingers on my clit while the others brutalized my nipples. My hips rose and fell with my stroking, that feverish heat coiling furiously in my center, as if I had not come in years.

Panting, wild with need, and my hollow pussy gripping at thin air as I yearned for nothing more than a cock filling me, I rode the edge as long as I could until I thrust pruned fingers into my aching flesh and pinched my clit with my other hand.

I came so hard I couldn't even make a sound. Light flashed behind my eyelids, the sharp sensation rushing through my blood swallowing me. I crumpled, moaning and panting like I had run a marathon as shuddering aftershocks rippled on the waves of my heartbeat centered squarely in my cunt.

A door slammed upstairs, and I groaned into the fading sensation.

Had I masturbated to the thought of a man I had met . . . when I was engaged to someone else? Sure, that someone else was absolute trash of a human being and probably wouldn't have cared if I fucked Sal instead of just gotten off to thoughts of him, but that didn't change who I was.

Shivering, I got up from the bed to shower. It would help clear my mind and help me sleep. In the morning, I could feel bad. No one else would ever know.

CHAPTER FIVE

Itziquetzal

I t had been twenty years. Every year of my life since she had refused my kiss and run down that street into the fading light was spent carefully planning her return to my arms. In the early years, I would lay awake in my bed, staring at my ceiling, and see her gold-flecked gaze. When the memory of her smile and her beautiful curls faded, her laughter haunted me. Even that faded with time until all that was left was the hole where she should have been. It tore at me like shards of glass lining my shoes, dogging every step.

Sometimes, the call to go to my mate was too strong. My blood would boil with rage, and I would find a means to cross the many borders between us. In those stolen snapshots of her life, my cousin helped me find her. Even as children, Javi had known what she meant to me and what she would mean to my totoco. I made him swear a blood oath before his totoco leader to never let her come to harm, never allow her to stray so far that she was lost to me completely. He was instrumental in allowing me to see her in those times, when my cadejo would not let me go another day without dulling the ache that had cut us both.

That was all I had, though, for so many years. Standing outside of her life, catching stolen glimpses of the woman who would be my mate and was already my wife by totoco law. Seeing her, snapshots in time, was enough. But as she grew, I grew with her. I feared the time when it would no longer be enough to see her across a crowded mall with her mother or brother once every four or five years. I knew, eventually, the spirit within me would not be content with the simple ceremony and the vacuum her absence left.

César, though just a tlamacazto, a priest in training at the time, was already ordained by the teotl, and the exchange of vows witnessed by my patron teotl, Huitzilopochtli, and blessed by his golden rays as is the tradition of my totoco, had bound us, according to totoco law. The mating ceremony would have to come later. I had always known that. Only when I rose to tecuhtli could I take my mate. Our traditions, while not the traditions of the area we now called our territory, were still deeply rooted. No warrior could take a mate without my father's approval, and the heir apparent could not take one at all while he still lived. I had two choices to take her, live to be strong enough to challenge him or leave my totoco forever.

The latter was not an option.

Though my family was Mixtec from Mexico, we traveled as a band of warriors called by the Council to help the local totoco stand against the atrocities happening to their human tribal counterpart, the Lencas. Though I was too young to remember. Our totoco fought with them when the rising tides of human violence threatened their already-diminished foothold and population. So, many of my uncles and aunts died alongside them. When the totoco's leader, Antu Silan Ulap's—named for her ancestress, who fought valiantly against the Spaniards—mate died, my father was the only cadejo willing to step into his shadow. She took him as her companion, passing the totoco to him when she followed her beloved mate into the afterlife. This place, this totoco, was all I had known from childhood.

When my father sent César, the rest of the children, and me from our totoco to stay with Javier and his totoco in San Francisco, fearing another rise of violence to rival the massacre of El Mozote, it felt like he cut me in half. One half stayed in El Salvador, longing to fight beside my father, the other half caring for the scared and lost children of our totoco in a strange land with people who barely spoke our language.

Some children did not even speak Spanish, let alone English. Only the older children, like César, two others, and myself spoke English well enough to navigate the city and its human denizens. Those of us who could wore bracelets to stave off shadows leaking into an accidental trade and prevented any mistakes of passion riding our wild spirits too hard. They prevented the micro exchanges of mouth, eyes, hands, and ears that were part of our common body language at home. Those of us who could not trade shadows were not even taught how to cross the realms and merge as one with our spirits until we returned to totoco territory. It was too dangerous.

When I met her on that playground, I understood why I was always going to go north, why it had always been my fate to shepherd the young into that bizarre country. I was not split in half when leaving home. I was split in half at birth, the other half finding its way into her. All my goodness, all my purity, and light had gone into that innocent young girl. I knew it when I saw her. At the time, I did not recognize her as I would later in life. My soul recognized her, the spirit I had been partnered with solidifying the union of our kind recognized her, and that was all I needed to know.

Now she was here, in my country, staying in my hotel. I finally had a chance, after twenty years, to speak with her. Her voice had changed, but it still had that softness I remembered, clutching that song that had been haunting my dreams for years.

Something had changed about her, though. The last time I saw her was almost two years ago in a museum. I wanted to talk to her then. She looked so worn thin, and at first, I thought she was alone. If she were alone, I could speak with her, remind her of who I was. But as our eyes met through the glass of an exhibit, a man came to stand at her side, and there was no spark of recognition as I hoped there would be. It wasn't her brother—I would have known Roberto from a hundred feet away. This was a man I had never seen with her before. He pulled her against him, kissed her forehead, laced his fingers with hers, and pulled her away from the dusty dress she had been looking at in the case.

Rage filled me, and the only reason I had not traded shadows and mauled the smirking toad was the lack of joy in her eyes when she looked at him. No smile adorned her lips when she followed him toward another couple. Nor did she speak to him or the others. She was a silent shadow standing next to him, seemingly wishing to be anywhere else. I watched her for an hour and a half until the four of them left. She had not spoken a single word the entire length of my spying, and the man she was with seemed all the happier for it.

When I sent Javier to escort her to the airport, I needed to lay the foundations to reintroduce myself to her. He said she remembered him. Why, then, were her eyes devoid of familiarity when I positioned myself to have her run into me on the beach? We spent the entire afternoon talking, and she had not remembered me for who I was to her. My beast had snarled and gnashed his teeth, pacing in my mind at the perceived slight by his mate. Her not recalling his scent or the comfort of his body infuriated him. I struggled to keep him from handling her too roughly. He wanted to mark her as his there on the beach for all to see. He wanted to dominate her, press her into the black sand, sink his claws into her tender flesh, and force her at the tip of his thrusting cock to remember us.

There was a moment, though, when she ran her fingers over the marigolds I had placed on the walkways I told her my name, and I thought she would remember me. The spark faded so quickly. At that moment, something changed in her. Something that neither myself nor my beast liked. It was a coldness, an iciness that did not belong to our sun goddess. She was warmth and sunlight and summer in the flesh, not meant to be cold and placating. She was born to burn and scorch and be the softness to my razor's edge.

And there I was, pacing above her, breathing in her intoxicating scent, listening to her pant in solitude. If I did not know for certain that there was no man in that room with her, I'd have suspected that simpering little shit, Shayne, flew in. I made sure that a totocan was stationed at the airport to ensure that, should that blonde-haired buffoon choose to step onto my people's land, he would be quickly dealt with. He would not get to my nayeli again. He did not deserve to be in her presence, let alone see her. I would rip out his eyes and feast on his screams before he saw her again. It was bad enough he insinuated himself into my plans for her with those damned flowers.

When his secretary called to have two dozen white roses delivered to her room for her arrival, I was in the market, ordering the supplies the totoco needed for their monthly supplement. Graciela, our front desk clerk, had no idea who Xochitl was to me and delivered them to her bed, as requested. When ensuring her room was perfect, I saw those damned flowers, and that old rage welled up. I had torn them into pieces. How dare he mark her in my territory as his possession. She was mine. She had always been mine. And she would be mine again.

It took every last bit of my effort not to reveal my presence above her when I heard her whimpering and moaning what sounded like my name. After pacing, I pulled out a chair and sat, staring at my empty bed, imagining her sprawled naked atop it and writhing for my eyes. It was too much to bear. I leaned my head against the wall where the vents connected my room to hers and listened. I could hear the wet, slick sounds, smell her arousal, and hear her begging. Knowing she was below me, I wanted nothing more than to sink my cock deep into the drooling satiny flesh I could practically hear begging for me.

The thought of her tan skin covered in my cream and her begging me for more nearly undid me. I fumbled with my cock, wrestling it into my hand and stroking as I heard her stroke. Mirroring the movements I could not see, I tried to keep up with her. Her scent was calling to my beast, making him whine for her under my skin.

He did not want to spill our seed outside of her body anymore. He did not want to bed another woman other than his mate. He wanted his mate, and he kept me from falling with her over that precipice of pleasure when she finally came, murmuring my name as clear as could be.

I could not take it after that. I needed to be out of temptation. Years of planning could not go to rot now that I had her so close to me. I could not allow myself to break down her door and kiss her with twenty years of pent-up passion. If I wanted my mate, that golden princess who danced into existence and stole my heart and soul, I had to continue being patient and convince her she still loved me.

After hearing her start the shower, I slammed the suite door behind me and stripped from my clothes to stalk the beaches. The hotel's walls were far too thin to contain my cadejo and me. We needed to hunt the streets of La Libertad and feast on the fear, the only way to distract the beast that we both were. To stuff his gullet with the shrieks and terror sweats we could find lurking in back alleys and preying on others. A true predator would walk among them and vent his need.

CHAPTER SIX

I woke up to my ringing phone. Groggily, I slapped at it a few times before I could finally wrestle it into my hand.

"Hello?"

"Good morning. It's 7 a.m. This is your wake-up call."

"I . . . uh, thank you."

"You're welcome. Have a wonderful day." The woman on the other side of the line hung up.

I had not scheduled a wake-up call. I'd intended to but forgot, what with meeting Sal and then . . . *ugh.*

Sliding from the bed, I did my best not to see the evidence of my cupidity under the vent and aimed for the open suitcase on the desk. Fishing through it, I found a flowy navy floor-length skirt and a cream satin blouse I could pair with the only blazer I had brought with me. I had forgotten to pack my flat iron, though. That would have to be changed quickly. At least I had the mind to toss in both shoes of my favorite pair of loafer pumps.

I popped my Adderall, vitamins, and birth control in my mouth, then got into the shower. Afterward, I tossed my hair into a French braid and grabbed my messenger bag with my laptop in it. I was armed for my day, rescuing some perfectly competent individual from the ridiculousness that was Jake. We were to meet in the hotel's conference room, and I made short work of getting there.

When I approached the closed conference room doors, I could already hear the mayhem I was about to enter. Jake, in classic Jake fashion, was berating the man over some perceived slight. The man was quickly explaining in Spanish that Jake was being rude and offensive. Not that Jake would have cared, even if he understood him.

"Good morning, gentlemen," I said, pushing into the room with a bright smile.

The two stopped dead in their tracks to stare at me openly. The client reminded me of Sal. He had the same coloring, the same proud features, but his hair was cut short in a more western style, and his ears only held one much smaller jadeite plug.

"Good morning, Señora. Please, perhaps your beauty can calm this baboso."

The simply stated compliment was polite and fell from his tongue with an uninhibited casualness that spoke of truth. He pulled out a chair for me near the two laptops that were set up, and motioned offhandedly for me to sit.

Pulling my laptop from the bag, I eyeballed the numbers the two argued over. It seemed straightforward. Why did I have to take a plane ride down here just to look over these?

Idly setting my laptop up, I spoke in Spanish to the man, taking a chance to match his casual comfort with me. "Please excuse my ignorance, sir. Can you explain to me, slowly please, my Spanish is not the best, why the buffoon here needed me to come down to help him?"

He grinned and sat at the head of the table, dismissing Jake, who was not ignorant to being cut out of the conversation. He'd asked for a translator, right?

"This man is absolutely bone-stupid, miss. I hope you do not like him too much. If I thought my boss would not be displeased, I'd throw him out a window," he grumbled.

I tried my best to suppress my smirk. He wasn't wrong. Not even a little bit. "You'll have no arguments from me. Please, show me what he couldn't understand?"

His smile was warm and gave me a distinct feeling of being at home in his presence.

"Of course, señora. I am Antonio Roque, Chief Financial Officer. And you are?" He lofted his bushy dark brows.

"I'm so sorry, so rude of me. Angie Espar—"

"Ellington," Jake said, earning a scathing glare from me that, if I were lucky, would have melted his flesh from his bones.

I was not that lucky, and he sniffed his indignation.

Antonio didn't seem to catch the correction or chose to ignore it and trudged onward. "This jackass seems to think that, despite the evidence in front of his face, my numbers can't be correct. There are few things I have more pride in, señora, than I have in the veracity of my work."

He slid his laptop to face me, and I skimmed the numbers as I spoke. "And what makes him think they are falsified? These seem like perfectly reasonable figures, given the scale of your companies and the industry you are in."

"He seems to think that all of us sell drugs and that's the only reason or way that we could be so profitable."

Antonio could barely hold back the rage flashing in his burnt amber eyes. It wasn't misplaced anger, either. If I were in his shoes, I probably would have broken Jake's nose a few times over for suggesting that.

How the hell had Jake not already blown this deal? It was incredibly difficult for an investment firm to build trust with a foreign business when they sent someone who bought into ancient stereotypes and couldn't read the damned spreadsheets in front of him. It was almost doomed.

Antonio and I worked on the numbers, and sometime around lunch, Jake disappeared, secure that he was no longer needed and would get all the credit nonetheless. Good, he was more of a deadweight than helpful, since Antonio practically bristled any time he even got near us. Something about that casual brush-off evolved the cordialness into a companionable rapport.

"Is he your boss, señora?" he asked over our lunch brought in by the staff, having switched to English as soon as Jake left.

I was more than happy for the reprieve, as I was sure my rudimentary and weak Spanish would eventually fail me in translating his words.

"Thankfully, not at all."

"Your, eh . . . novio?"

Choking on the fruit salad, I almost spit my mango back into it. "Jake? Absolutely not. Antonio, I thought we liked each other. Would you really wish me to be attached to that boar of a man?"

He laughed. "Truthfully, señora, I'd rather imagine you unencumbered, but I fear that I am far too late to meet such an enchanting creature."

I grinned at him. "You flatterer, you." Sighing, I put down my spoon and took a sip of water. "If you must know, I'm engaged."

"Are you now?" The familiarity in his teasing tone seemed far too pointed, but he covered it swiftly. "I see no ring. What man lets his amor run around without his ring proudly perched on her finger?"

"A man who picks out a hideous ring," I teased back, trying to avoid further discussion of Shayne.

The shame of my late-night activities was still slinking along the edges of my mind, crouching and waiting to strike at a moment's notice.

Antonio was kind enough to laugh heartily with his full body before barking out, "My condolences, señora."

We worked companionably for the rest of the day. If all went well for the rest of the week, I could be home far sooner than I'd like. I'd have to convince Antonio to perhaps fudge the ease of our work a little, somehow. There was no way I would be ready to go back to San Francisco in a week.

Pulling up my email to send over the document I had prepared for the contract lawyer, I flinched when I saw an email waiting for me from my mother and two from Shayne's assistant. I didn't bother opening them. Not today. I wanted to breathe my own air for a little longer.

"Troubles, Xochi?"

He had switched to calling me by the nickname after we had had a raucous conversation about my full name. He proclaimed it a shame I let myself be called by Angie instead of Xochitl.

"Nothing that can't be solved by ignoring it." I grinned at him.

"Then, leave it for another day. I will take you to my favorite bar, and we will talk more about how wonderful I am."

Clicking the laptop shut, I chuckled. "I wish I could, Antonio, but, unfortunately, I got drunk and packed nonsense and need to go shopping."

"Any excuse for a woman to shop." He laughed.

"You're awful!" I giggled with him. "Thank you, though, perhaps tomorrow?"

"I will hold my breath until then, señora." He winked and slid from the conference room as I followed him.

After a quick stop at the front desk to request a taxi, I dashed to my room to drop off my laptop and collect my wallet. One fifteen-minute wait later, and I was on my way to the boutique Sal had recommended. The receptionist assured me it was her favorite shop and that I would love it. Despite her shorter height and curvaceous figure, I still held very little hope.

The drive was short and slow, but I enjoyed seeing the beautiful sparsely populated streets of La Libertad. When we pulled up to the shop, the driver waved off payment, saying it had been taken care of. I frowned but didn't press further. I did not like the idea of someone having paid for this little jaunt.

Two hours later, I was shocked to find that Sal was not wrong. The shop not only carried my size in almost everything that I wanted, but a tailor on site stood by to alter any items to my size. The clothing style was a little different from what I would have normally worn but was comfortable and favored flowing skirts and tops, with expertly worked embroidery of abstract designs, flowers, and birds. They also carried a few dresses and a few pieces of more American-style garments, but I kept those to a minimum. The pieces I chose were practical but stunningly well made and could be swapped around to build multiple outfits.

It felt good to pick items that spoke to me instead of items that would not inspire a sniff or eyebrow from my mother. And I was smiling brightly by the time the clerk rang me up. I handed over my credit card, and she waved me off.

"No, señora, it's already paid for. Señor Almendárez left clear instructions. You were to pick whatever it was you liked, however much you liked, and I was to charge his account."

"Oh, this is ridiculous. I expect he took care of the cab, too? And who the hell is Señor Almendárez?"

This was out of hand. A stranger taking care of the cab was one thing, but my bill was easily over five hundred American dollars. A perfect stranger should not have paid for that.

"Ah . . . uhm. Señor Itziquetzal Almendárez? He assured us that you would know him?" The sweet woman wrung her hands in distress.

Sal. Sal paid for it all. A war raged inside of me. Half of me wanted to rebel against being taken care of by this presumptuous, sexy stranger, and the other half purred with delight. Chewing my lip, I watched as the two parties battled it out in my mind. I couldn't accept this . . . could I? What would he expect from me in return? What was the harm? He was merely courting me.

Courting me.

Shame washed over me, but I didn't want to inconvenience the clerk, so I accepted. I'd meet up with him that night for dinner, pay him back, explain that I probably shouldn't see him again and that I was engaged . . . to a man who gave zero fucks about me. Maybe I'd leave that part out.

"Ah . . . one more thing, señora. He wanted me to give this card to you if you found the items to your liking. And there was another item. You'll find it in your bag." Smiling, she slid a thick sealed black envelope into one of my three large shopping bags and wished me a good evening.

CHAPTER SEVEN

The cab ride back to the hotel was a silent affair as I tapped the thick envelope against my navy clad thigh, my mind a swirling mess of thoughts. By the time I got back into my room, my fingers itched to tear open the letter.

Xochitl,

Thank you for spending time with me tonight. Your laugh made my heart warm in a way I have not experienced in a long time. It has been only three hours since you left my side, and I am already miserable without the sound of your voice. I'm glad that you found the shop to your liking. I've picked out something I would like you to wear to dinner tonight, please. Meet me at the below address at 8 pm.

I will be waiting.

Yours,

Itziquetzal

I blinked several times before tears came to my eyes. Never had anyone sent me a note like that before, the emotion bald and unapologetic. With shaking hands, I dug into the bags to find a package at the bottom wrapped in soft orange tissue paper with a green ribbon and a marigold stuck in the knot. I took the flower from the ribbon and placed it in my braid. Unwrapping the dress with shaking fingers, I pulled it from the bag.

It was stunning. A creamy white cotton dress with smocking at the bust, a tiered skirt, and softly puffed sleeves that would drape off my shoulders. Intricately embroidered black feathers that glittered in the light with beadwork adorned the hem to weigh it down enough to keep the airy fabric from kicking up in the tropical breezes. Small clear beads caught the light, interspersing the feathers' border and casting a slight rainbow effect. As I held it to the light, a small palm-sized box tumbled out onto the bed.

Setting the dress down reverently, I picked up the box. Inside was a pair of obsidian earrings that matched the dress, beautiful inky feathers dripping from delicate silver chains. Two barrettes, with the same obsidian feathers set on silver filigree, lay nestled in the box with another marigold.

My hand began to tremble, and tears tumbled down my cheeks. I had never been given a gift so beautiful nor so intimate. The items radiated the foreign feeling of adoration. Who was this man that I'd stumbled into, who gave so freely without thought? No, not without thought. The dress, earrings, and barrettes were not without thought. He picked this specifically for me. My heart soared.

Specifically for me.

It was not a gift given out of obligation or selected without thought to what I would like. No, these items were selected with care and consideration for me, and it was overwhelming.

I let my hair out of my braid and ran hotel gel through it. I would need to acquire better gel in the morning. After misting it with water, I slid the barrettes in to keep my long curls from swallowing my face. I dressed and struggled to put on the earrings. It had been a while since I wore any, and my holes were almost closed.

As I looked at the girl in the mirror, my breath caught. The white sleeves clung off my shoulders, and the feathers danced at my collarbones, flashing in my chocolate locks. I wore little makeup, eyeliner, mascara, and a simple tinted lip gloss, but I looked like a different woman than the one who last examined herself. I looked . . . like a goddess.

After fishing a pair of flats out of my chaos bag, I slid them on, then the phone by the bedside rang again. It was the front desk advising that a cab was waiting outside and asking whether I'd like to have them sent away. I was being given a choice, and some part of me wondered if Sal had any inclination as to what he was doing to me. How could he, though?

The cab took me to an open-air café at the fringe of the town's center. Sal was pacing in front of the restaurant in a pair of black jeans and a black button-up shirt. His hair was, once again, pulled back in a braid, and as he paced, I saw the worry etched into his features.

Our eyes met as I emerged, relief smoothing the doubt from his expression and awe replacing it. His smile said, *You came*, but it was my name he breathed. My heart twisted painfully with a heady kaleidoscope of emotions: fear, hope, longing, shame, and exhilaration.

I had never heard my name whispered with such reverence and yearning. His hand reached out for mine. I smiled, sliding fingers into his palm. All the shame, doubt, and anxiety melted away, leaving behind an easy silence. I inhaled his scent: rich earth, spices, and rum undercut by the scent of wild things. He mimicked my inhale, scenting me, too. We both smiled stupidly at each other.

"You look . . ." He cast a hungry gaze down my body. "Wow. I . . ."

I laughed, a strange tinkling lightness that was foreign to me, making the sound melodic even to my ears. "Thank you. This dress is . . . it's the most beautiful thing I've ever seen."

"It doesn't hold a candle to you, Xochitl." His voice was soft and tender around the edges, like drinking rum and floating in a hot tub, warm inside and out. "Come, let's eat before I make bad decisions."

We ate dinner in an empty restaurant by the glow of low lights, with the conversation floating at the surface. I wouldn't let it get deeper than that. I kept falling into the glint of his eyes. I had made a promise to another man. I needed to be sure not to forget that.

The promise was made by your mother, a voice whispered in my ear, blooming to remind me that Shayne was never my choice, and I had lain with him because of someone else's ambition. If I let that little voice guide me, I would regret it, but I wanted to stray so badly. The more it whispered the more I leaned closer to Sal. I found my hand drifting toward his on the table and saw his finger twitch with the urge to grip mine.

"Do you dance?" he purred over the rim of his raised glass of water.

"Hmm?" I asked dreamily, wishing I was made of glass so his lips would press against me.

"Dancing? Do you dance?"

His smirk was back, a wolfish thing that made me squirm in my chair.

"Oh. Uhm, not really. Too much hip."

He made a tsking sound in his teeth that reminded me of the way he said my name, and pushed from his chair. "Come."

I didn't particularly care for the demanding color to that word, but it wasn't worth mentioning and ruining the beautiful evening. I slid my hand into his waiting hand and let our fingers intertwine naturally. When our hands fell to our side, he squeezed mine just slightly, causing me to smile.

He led me out of the restaurant and into the town square strung with lights and bustling with couples. A band was setting up on the grass. "Just follow my lead. Your body will know what to do."

I doubted that sincerely. I had never been able to pick up the dancing lessons my mother had insisted on. The complicated steps and timing eluded me, and I felt like a drunk flamingo prancing about and squawking, just short of laying an egg in embarrassment. But when Sal rolled up his sleeves, stepping into my personal space, I completely forgot about any previous disagreements with dancing.

Dancing was now my favorite thing in the world. I intended to never leave this small courtyard of fairytales and dreams.

He searched my face—for what, I didn't know—but it made my heart skip several beats, my breathing a shallow pant. There was an intensity, an all-consuming hunger in his gaze that made my blood boil and my skin writhe to touch and be touched by him. I didn't hear the music, but I didn't care. I was hyperfocused on him, his breath mingling with mine, his body pressing against me through the thinness of my dress, the feel of his hands hot on my hips. His eyes locked with mine, and I had the faintest impression of a dangerous carnality in them, one I longed to chase and tease further to the surface.

We swayed, his hips leading mine, as our eyes devoured each other, my hands pressed to his chest, feeling the rise and fall of his breath and the strong, even hammering of his heart. Electricity crackled between us, burning the air and scorching the presence of others from my awareness. Once again, it was just him and me, alone in the universe. My heart squeezed painfully with the vibrant swell of emotion I shouldn't have been feeling for him.

"The moon is jealous of your beauty, Xochitl."

His voice caressed my ear as he leaned in to nuzzle my curls. My heart exploded and dripped through my body to create a puddle in my core, where it thudded to match the rhythm of his. Leaning my head against his chest, I tried to catch my breath. I breathed in his scent. It curled around my essence and wove into an intoxicating trance I needed to shake off.

Tears pricked at my eyes, burning around the edges and strangling my throat. I needed to tell him. No one as wonderful as him deserved to be wasting his romancing on someone like me.

I tilted my head up and caught his gaze. His hand left my hip to hold my cheek, his thumb stroking my heated flesh.

"I need to tell you something, Sal," I started. His brow ticked up, and I forged onward before I lost my nerve. "Y—You need to know something. I'm . . . I'm engaged."

He smiled slowly, his hand never leaving my cheek. "I saw no ring on your finger."

"It's a long story."

That smile didn't leave his mouth, but he said nothing for a long time and simply swayed with me and stroked my cheek. Unable to stand the silence, I choked out, "I'm sorry."

"Is he worthy of you?" he asked.

"Wh—What?"

"Is he worthy of you?" he repeated, his tone soft and conspiratorial.

I might have forgotten everyone around us, but it seemed he had not and that he was keeping this moment for only us.

"I . . . I don't . . . What?"

"It's a simple question, Xochitl. Is he worthy of you?" He leaned down and pressed his forehead to mine, the sensation causing my eyes to flutter shut with indulgence. His next breath was a caress against my lips. "I would do anything to be worthy of you."

My heart hammered in my panties, my breath ragged. I wanted this man so badly I could hear every cell in my body screaming to be touched by him. I couldn't, though, not while I was engaged to Shayne. Sal deserved so much better than to be a vacation fling on the eve of me being married to someone else . . . someone who was not worthy of me.

Shayne never made my heart race. Shayne never made my pussy drool with need like it was right then. Shayne had never done any number of the tiny things Sal had done in the short time I had known him, and since he had pointed it out, I could practically hear the reaper of that chapter in my life swinging its scythe with finality.

I knew what I had to do. Not just because it was all too clear to me now that I wanted Sal in a way I couldn't comprehend but because I was worth more. I owed it to myself to reach for more.

I clung to him, his hand petting my curls, not making the mistake of running his fingers through them. After a few moments, he rested his head on mine, his chin pressing into my scalp but avoiding the two silver-and-obsidian barrettes. He crushed me to his chest, comforting me as I did my best not to crumble into him. It felt like he was pressing those errant pieces of me back into place. They would need glue to stick, but his strength alone could hold them in place a little longer.

"Would you like me to take you back to the hotel?"

His voice was soft velvet caressing over my raw edges.

Did I want him to? No. Did I need him to? Probably, yes. I nodded into his shirt.

He hummed, the sound vibrating through me, then he squeezed me one last time. "Come."

He led me from the courtyard to a small alley, where a black truck was parked under a streetlight. He opened the door for me and rounded the vehicle to get in. The drive to the hotel was quiet. He sat as a silent, fixed point as I tried to quell the racing thoughts and feelings before they eluded my control.

He parked and opened my door, taking my hand to lead me out of the parking lot.

"You don't ne—"

"I do," he said simply.

He led me down the hallways to my room. When I cocked an eyebrow at him, he smiled sheepishly. "I said I owned a hotel. You assumed it was another. I own this one."

I blinked wildly at him, and he chuckled. "I'm actually staying upstairs. Should you need to talk or anything."

I wondered if he knew what I had done the night before. Oh god, was I loud about it? Anxiety stabbed through the welling whirlpool of emotions and choked back my words.

"Good night, Xochitl. If you want to, I'll be having dinner by the pool tomorrow. I would still like you to join me." He kissed the top of my head, and before I could answer him, tell him he deserved better than me, and not to wait for me to show up because I wouldn't be taking up any more of his time, he was already retreating down the hallway toward the stairs at the other end.

I stood there, watching his back until he paused at the stairwell to look back at me, the longing in his smile as deep as the longing in my heart. Then he was gone.

I felt sick. Nausea swirled in my guts, fueled by the discordant emotions waging war throughout my body and mind. I shut the door behind me, then went straight for my cellphone and laptop. I had no clue if I truly didn't have any cell service, but I was about to find out.

I opened my text thread with Shayne. No new texts had come through, so I began typing.

> **Angie**: *Shayne, I'm sorry, but I can't do this anymore. Neither of us actually wants to be married to each other. I know you aren't happy. Neither am I. I left the ring and the papers in my apartment. Robert has a key. I'm sorry. It's over. I can't marry you.*

I sent the text, then opened my laptop. I sent Shayne an email with basically the same message. I knew the Wi-Fi worked but wasn't sure about the cell service.

The ding that came through five minutes later as I was taking off the earrings Sal gave me scared me so badly I let out a little squeak of surprise.

> **S. Ellington**: *You don't mean that.*

> **S. Ellington**: *Let's talk about this when you get home.*

> **Angie**: *I'm sorry Shayne.*

> **S. Ellington**: *It's cool babes. We all have doubts.*

> **Angie**: *No Shayne. I meant what I said.*

> **S. Ellington**: *That's not how this works.*

> **Angie**: *What?*

S. Ellington: *You don't get to break it off.*

Angie: *Uhm, I'm not marrying you, Shayne.*

S. Ellington: *We'll talk about this when you get home. I'll have Edwin reschedule your flight for tomorrow. I'll pick you up from the airport.*

Angie: *I. Am. Not. Marrying. You. Shayne.*

Fifteen minutes later, there was still no response from him. The tightness in my chest released like a bubble popping, splattering all over the landscape of my mind. It was done and over. I would never have to see Shayne again, and I would never have to wear that awful ring again. I was free of him. I flopped onto the bed and stared up to the ceiling, salty tears streaking down my temples and into my hair as I stared at the ceiling between Sal and me. I could almost feel his strong arms around me, holding me tight, his deep voice rumbling over me, telling me it was going to be okay.

I fell asleep dressed, tears still rolling down my cheeks, staring up at the ceiling between us.

CHAPTER EIGHT

I awoke a few hours later to the sound of my cell phone ringing, as well as the phone near the bedside. When it would switch over to voicemail, both phones stopped ringing for a few seconds, then started again. I groaned, my throat hoarse from the clenching stress of my anxiety. When I finally swiped my cell phone, I could see that it was my mother calling. Eyes snapping to the bedside phone, I assumed that was her as well.

Fear spiked through me. What had I done? What was she going to do to me for this? An oily, slick, crawling sensation oozed through my blood, flashes of needles and dead skin bursting in the back of my mind as dread gripped me. Taking a deep, shaking breath, I sent the current call to voicemail and shut off my phone. The nightstand phone kept ringing, and I could almost hear the shrill hushed screaming of my mother in its tone.

I yanked the cord from the wall, cutting off the sound sharply.

Gathering a pillow into my arms, I crushed it against my chest, rocking back and forth at the head of the bed. Terror over what my mother and stepfather were going to do about my decision poured through my blood, drowning me in panic. My heart was racing so fast I was starting to get light headed. Unfocused, I gazed blindly into the liminal space between me and the wall, seeing the erosion of the little freedoms I'd earned over the years.

I could see them gathering my apartment keys, slamming the door closed, and shoving me into the bedroom on the third floor of their Seacliff district mansion. No light, no bed, nothing but windowless walls. I could see myself being forced down the aisle in whatever hideous dress my mother picked out and into Shayne's waiting arms. I could see her taking my birth control pills from me when she decided it was time I gave Shayne a child and the cycle of control repeating. And if I dared to fight back or squirm away like Elida had when she was a teen, I would be slipped quietly into a mental health facility until I finally acquiesced.

Snuffling came from the sliding glass door, the scent of rotting meat finding my nostrils. I whipped my attention to it. I had forgotten to pull the curtains across the wall of glass. It was dark out, almost pitch-black, except for the slight outline of the shadows cast by the moonlit plants. Something moved, a dark inky smear darting across the line of glass.

I froze. Spikes of fear turned into great glaciers of dread that slid through my veins and clogged them. Another snuffle sounded from the junction between the sliding glass door and the frame. Had I locked it? I was certain I had, hadn't I? A small whimper— barely even a sound, really—slipped from my lips. The moment the squeak fell into the chilled silence, the smudge moved and solidified into the shape of a giant dog the size of a small horse. Twin torrid orbs slid to stare directly at me. The glow from their red embers cast an eerie halo around the beast's head, pooling on the floor beyond the glass like spilled blood. A vivid red tongue slipped from between jagged teeth and licked the glass between us in a clarion, morbid promise.

The creature pawed at the door, shaking it as I cowered and calculated the thickness of glass and how many milliseconds I had left to live. All that was between me and the nightmare outside was sheet glass, perhaps twenty paces of bare floor, an arm's length of bed, and a thin hotel pillow. My body quaked as the claws scored the glass, and the feral grin became more and more a menacing promise.

I couldn't move. My mind screamed at me to do something, dart out the door, and run down the hallway to the brightly lit reception area, to the safety of the people who were surely there. Or even to take the stairs three at a time and run to Sal to protect me. To do anything, even just scream for help. I could do nothing but stare as claws scraped the door, degrading its stability more and more.

Scratch, scratch, scratch.

I was going to die. I knew it in my bones. And I could do nothing about it.

The shattering inwards of the glass was the only sound I heard. I could not hear my heart thrashing to escape my body's fate. I could not hear my ragged, panicked panting. I could not hear the nightmare's slow approach over the glass shards. The only sound that rang through my reality was the echoing decimation of that too-ephemeral barrier.

Until there was another sound. A yelping whimper. At first, I thought it was mine but then it registered in my tremulous connection to my mind that another larger inky creature had joined us in the room. Its massive jaws had clamped the other dog's head, wrestling it away from my bed. Thick rivers of blood ran through smoky black fur. Yelping snarls came from the smaller creature as it fought to free itself from the lurid black fangs of the other. Onyx eyes in the massive head of the large monster connected with mine as it dragged the other creature out into the pool area.

The spell broken, I screamed at a pitch I was sure my estranged sister, an ocean away, could hear. I kept screaming as the creatures battled on the deck of the pool, hunks of flesh ripped from the shoulder and face of the smaller dog as they fought. I screamed as I heard the shouts at my door and the pounding fists on it. I screamed as I watched the two creatures disappear over the small hill that led down to the beach. I screamed as the night clerk finally beat down the door to my cabana, my eyes frozen and unable to be ripped from the place where the two horrific black nebulas had disappeared. I screamed as the clerk pulled a gun and swept the room. I screamed as two security guards joined the other man yelling at me to calm down in Spanish.

I didn't know when I stopped screaming. It was sometime after two police officers with assault rifles, Jake and a woman I had never seen before, a haggard Antonio, and several terrified guests crowded my room with light. It was sometime before I passed out, unable to take the weight of the monster-filled waking world any longer.

CHAPTER NINE

Male voices arguing in Spanish woke me, ripping me from the blissful black blanket of nothingness. I didn't want to wake up. My entire body was limp and exhausted, like I had run for hours and cried for days. I was bone-tired from the tips of my hair to the deepest parts of my soul. Lifting my lashes was a herculean effort, but focusing my eyes in the dim afternoon light filtering in from the window was even more of an exertion. Eventually, I managed to coax my wrung-out body to sit up from the confines of a massive nest-like bed.

I had no idea where I was. From the lack of squawking seabirds and incessant lapping ocean waves, I knew I was not in my cabana. And that was it.

The bedroom walls were painted cinder blocks in some places and mudded adobe in others. It was an especially masculine room, with dark woods and dark colors splashed around on the bedding and furniture. It contained all the usual items you would expect in a bedroom: a massive bed, a pair of dressers along one wall, the outline of what I assumed was a stand-up mirror under a black sheet, the top of a trunk at the foot of the bed, and two nightstands. The usual. There was no television, though, and the ceiling fan had no lights attached to it. The oddest piece in the room was the floor-to-ceiling pillar of rough obsidian that had been cleaned of dirt but, aside from that, had not been touched. Its edges jagged, scalpel-sharp, and inconsistent in its glassy polish.

The scent coming from the sheets finally penetrated the thick fog. Sal. Sal's scent clung deep to the bedding and room. He came for me. It made sense in a small part of my mind. Whatever had happened last night, I knew that he was in the room above me, and it struck me as odd that the one face I wanted to see crowding in to try and see why a banshee had taken up residence in my room wasn't there. A small pleased hum rumbled in my chest as I snuggled into the comfort and strength of the scent. The scent of rich earth, rain-drenched woods, rum and cinnamon, mixed with what I assumed was the faint scent of a campfire, calmed me and enveloped me in warmth and serenity.

The voices raised again, then drifted off. I was having trouble identifying the words, and though I didn't want to, something poked me in the brain, insisting I concentrate. Frowning, I pulled myself from the confines of the black bedding. I was not in the beautiful white dress I had fallen asleep in but an oversized men's T-shirt, a shirt I didn't recognize, but a content smile played on my lips because it hung on me like a tent. It was not a fit I was used to when wearing men's shirts. I was, however, absolutely bare under the shirt. One problem at a time. I had no clue where I nor my clothing was.

I stripped the bed of a cozy-looking woven blanket and wrapped the handcrafted riot of dark grays and faded shades of black around myself as I went after the voices. One of them vaguely sounded like Sal, and while the other seemed distantly familiar, I couldn't place it. The first door I opened was a bathroom, which tugged a frown at my lips. I did not like this disoriented feeling. The second door opened to a long hallway I'd never seen before.

I followed it to where it opened to a living room. Sal was pacing, wearing nothing but a pair of black jeans slung low on the chiseled rock of a drool-worthy adonis belt. His long hair was unbound. Gorgeous, deep tan skin wrapped around muscles that I had felt but only guessed at. Now, here I was, able to feast my eyes on his body as agitation forced his bare feet back and forth over a woven rug on the adobe-tiled floor. As I watched him prowl and talk to another man in a similar state of undress, I noticed freshly healing claw marks on his stomach and arms, and one caught the strong edge of his jaw in its journey to slice at his shoulder. Bruises bloomed dark under his skin in some places. He looked like he went ten rounds with a panther.

". . . had I not been there, she'd be dead," he raged at the other man, his voice barely more than a fiendish growl.

The other man was still, calm, and reverie radiated off of him. He was tall, almost as tall as Sal, though much leaner. His frame was wiry but well muscled. He looked as though he was built for speed rather than the raw power of Sal's bulky muscled form, which was built for violence. Unlike Sal, whose body was decorated in a constellation of brutality, the only adornment to the other man was a set of what looked like glyphs riding the cobbles of his ribs. His tousled mop of dark teak curls bobbed as he rolled his shoulder in a shrug to deflect Sal's rage.

Neither of them seemed to notice me tucked into the corner of the doorjamb, spying on them.

"And, yet she is not."

His voice was warm milk after a nightmare: soothing, easy, and softly masculine.

Sal snarled. "She is my *mate*. He had no right to try to feed on her!"

"You wish to go to war over a cadejo attempting to feed in neutral territory on a woman that is not totocan, wears no charms of protection, and has no ties to any tribe?" His tone was flat. None of what he said made any sense to me, and I blamed my rusty Spanish for the poor translation as he went on. "Yes, his feeding is distasteful, but, brother, we both know that is lunacy. The Council will never let you go to war over him feeding on her in neutral territory. No matter how vile it is. Why do you rage?"

Sal growled again, then scrubbed his hand over his face and seemed to relent, defeat bowing his shoulders and deflating his body. "She's . . . César, she's so . . . so different. You should see her. She's nothing like she was. She barely laughs. She barely smiles.

She doesn't even fight back. It's like she's hiding from me. Me! Her damned mate."

"It's been over twenty years, brother. People change."

"No, César. Not that much. She's doing it on purpose. I know it. She's nothing like I expected."

I could almost hear the other man rolling his eyes.

My heart shattered so loud in my ears it was surprising that neither of the men responded to it. *Nothing like I expected.* Those words ricocheted within me, breaking me, stabbing deep into my being, crushing the last bits of control I was holding on to by my fingernails. *Nothing like I expected.* More expectations. Always expectations. Everyone had them of me. Everyone wanted something from me. Everyone made demands of me. Everyone wanted something from me. Even Sal.

A pointed sniff and a soft snarl snapped me from the internal collapse and electrified me into motion.

"Xochitl."

Sal's voice breathed behind me as I ran down the hallway, escaping in blind fear and pain. I had no clue how to get out of this place. I knew nothing about the layout of this . . . wherever I was, but I knew that room, and I knew there was a window. If I had to, I would go out that window and find my way back to somewhere more familiar. Somewhere I could escape. Somewhere safe. I had no idea where that was, but I knew it was not here, in this hallway with those words flaying my soul.

His feet pounded behind me as I slammed the bedroom door in his face. With no time to get to the window, I went for the bathroom. I flew past its door jamb right as Sal breached the other door after me. I slammed it and locked it, slid down the door, and tucked my frame into a ball. Tears fell from my eyes, silent sobs racking my body.

"Xochitl," Sal's voice demanded from the other side of the door. "Xochitl, open this goddamned door."

I thought Sal would be different from Shayne and my mother. I thought, for once, I found someone who wanted me as I was, could adore me for who I was and not for who they thought I could be to them.

"Open. The. Fucking. Door," he snarled at me, fist pounding on the wood separating us, rattling it down to its hinges.

Plaster holding the door in place cracked, and chips of it fell to the tiled floor.

"Go away," I whispered, my voice dripping with the torn edges of the small scrap of hope he had ripped away from me.

A dark laugh wriggled through the door as he stopped pounding. His voice was deeper, dangerous. "Oh, Xochitl, that's not how this works. You don't get to shut me out . . . not anymore."

The door groaned, straining under his force, bowing out toward me, the grain straining under the power. I scrambled away from it, tucking myself into the corner next to a bathtub. Moments later, the door came away from its hinges, and the thing that stood in the doorway made the creatures in my room last night look like a sweet, summer-lit dream.

A massive form ducked beneath the door frame and stood to its full height, the points of its jackal ears bending down as they pressed into the ceiling. Shadows gathered around its huge, muscled body, rolling off of it like plumes of inky smoke. The black fur along its body bristled as it tracked me, finding me cowering next to the tub, my bare legs kicking along the slick tile as my T-shirt covered bottom tried to skid away from it. Intelligent black eyes rolled back into its head with delight as it took a deep breath. Its lip curled over a wolfish snout that lolled open, revealing sharp, pearly, midnight dagger teeth. Its broad chest heaved, and long talon-tipped claws flexed into fists, restraining itself.

"Oh, my sweet flower. You are begging me to lap at you until you scream my name."

The creature groaned in a voice reminiscent of Sal's, as if it had been run through a nightmare filter. Or through the maw of a lupine horror rejected from a horror movie for being too graphic.

I shuddered, my body betraying me by making my pussy clench with a need that had no logical explanation. The beast before me grinned as he smelled my dampening folds, and he advanced on me. His claw-tipped, paw-like feet took slow steps as he hunkered down so as not to brush the ceiling. Intent eyes locked on mine.

"Were I a better man, I would woo you, as you deserve. But I am not. And I am ravenous for you." He growled, lips pulling back across the sharp teeth.

My back hit the door to what I assumed was a closet, and I slid into a corner, trying to get as far away from him as possible.

He grinned, wrapping an enormous clawed hand around my ankle, forcing my legs open wide for him. Letting the sharp talons prick my tender skin. The other claw caressed the inside of my thigh in a whisper of a threat. *Move an inch without my permission, and I will rip your femoral artery from your body*, it said without words.

My heart raced for a different reason. Lust poured through my veins. I wanted to be terrified of this creature—even repulsed, at the bare minimum—but he smelled like Sal, he sounded like Sal, and torn heart or not, my pussy longed to have him sinking deep inside of me. The fur on his paws stroking my thighs, pushing them wider for his view, was soft and silky where I expected it to be coarse and prickly. It tickled in a way that made me want to moan for more.

"Fuck. I have waited so long to have you spread out in front of me. You smell like a dream." He took a deep breath in through his wolfish nostrils, and I shuddered with need, a small whimper slipping past my parted lips answered by the beast who was Sal-but-not-Sal's groan.

The clawed talon on my leg moved and brushed the shirt past my wide hips and over my rounded tummy. A long pink tongue snaked out to lick his lips as his gaze traced the line of my stomach down my hip to the tops of my pillowy thighs, leaving a slight red mark.

A roughened, dagger-tipped finger slid between the swollen petals of my pussy, and I gasped, my hips shifting to give him more access without me bidding them to do so.

"You're so wet for me, nayeli. Even like this." His voice was husky, barely above a groan. "I've dreamed of how you'd cream for me, but I never thought this form would leave you so soaked and ready for me."

A wicked grin sparkled in his lust-glazed eyes. His finger never stopped stroking my engorged clit, never venturing lower, sending tremors of pleasure to dance along my skin and sparks to gather in my field of vision. An ache bloomed deep within my flooded cunt as my hips rolled into every rub of the leathery, calloused pad of his fingers.

"Tell me what you want, nayeli," he growled above me. He released his claw from my ankle, tracing a searing line up under his shirt and over my waist, my legs still spread.

I was silent, though, lost in the sensation of his fingers finally on my body. It felt like I had been aching for him for years, decades.

"Tell me," he demanded again, having found one of my nipples, rolling it between razor-tipped fingers. I whined in response, my hips chasing his fingers. He was teasing me like he knew the exact spots that called to him and only grazed them to keep me balanced on the razor's edge of pleasure and frustration. "As much as I love my scent all over you, I need to see your body. I've waited so long to see you, dreamed of you dripping wet and begging for me so many times. My hand gripping my cock could never compare to this."

The sound of ripping and the breeze of his breath on my bare skin made my lashes flutter as I watched him peel shredded fabric away from me. We both groaned, me because his fingers dipped to finally play at the tight opening of my clenching, aching, needy slit and him from the sight of my curvy bare form fully on display before his monstrousness.

"My gods. Do you have any idea how beautiful you are, teocuitlateotl?" He leaned over me, his long snout nuzzling into my hair, snuffling and nipping my ear.

A yearning, groaning whine escaped his wolfish lips, and my hands slid up arms the size of my thighs to curl into the black smoke-covered fur. The moment my fingers touched his skin, he moved. Snarling and growling into my ear as he scooped me off the bathroom floor and stalked toward his bed.

"I will wait no longer. I have waited too long. You are *mine*."

My back hit the bed, and my body flopped against it before I was dragged back to the edge of the bed by my ankles. My thighs were spread. That long pink tongue slid up my leg, rough, thick, and strong. A shared shiver passed between us. My fingers found a tuft of silken fur at the top of his lupine head and gripped it as my hips lifted to offer my nectar to him like a gift. A rumbling chuckle passed through sharp teeth and puffed over the sensitive meat of my thigh.

"Yes, my mate, you have longed for me, too, haven't you? Mmm, I can smell your need. So strong. I could smell that scent for the rest of my life and be a happy creature. I wonder, my golden mate, do you taste as good as you smell?"

What came over me to respond to his lewd words that crawled into my skin and took up residence in my pussy, I didn't know, but my lips were moving before I even thought the words. "Why don't you find out, Big Bad Wolf?"

His claws dug into the flesh of my thighs, piercing my skin as he answered with a deep roar of lascivious approval and desire, pulling my thighs wider to accommodate the girth of his head. His tongue snaked out to taste me, and my eyes flew open as I gasped, gripping his wrist and hair. The heat of his tongue and the rasping sensation gliding across my sensitive skin made every cell in my body writhe with pleasure. My heart became a rabbit fluttering around a cage, kicking at the walls. My hips pressed into that clever mouth, and I began to pant out, longing, begging. His tongue dragged against me again, pulsing and curling around my clit before plunging into the flexing sheath of my pussy to lick and suckle at my entrance.

"Mine," he moaned against me, nipping at the petal of my soaked lips. "Mine," he said again every time he licked, lapped, and nipped. "Tell me who you belong to, teocuitlateotl."

The pain of those daggers slicing into my thighs pricked into my awareness but only dully compared to the pleasure leaking through my blood to swallow me whole. "Sal . . . please."

"Say my name, nonayeli."

His hard cock pressed against my ankle. I needed him to fuck me so badly that I felt like I couldn't breathe without him buried deep inside of me and pounding me into the mattress.

"Please, Sal . . . Please . . ."

He groaned and pulled away. My eyes slid shut in a wince at the loss of contact mingled with the pain from the bleeding cuts at the tops of my thighs. Before the wince could fade, he pressed his body to mine again. This time, I felt the soft velvet skin of the man who whispered such sweet things to me on a dance floor. His unbound hair pooled around my chest as his hand pushed back my bed-rumpled curls.

His lips were on mine before I could blink at the sensation shift. I imagined kissing Sal since the moment I met him. My imagination and reality were nothing alike. In my imagination, it was fireworks exploding over a tropical volcano and a kaleidoscope of butterflies exploding across the landscape of my body. In reality, it was that and so much more.

In reality, my heart squeezed, and my legs pulled him into me. My arms circled him in a movement far too natural and felt all too right, like the gears of a mechanical puzzle clicking and locking into place. His lips moved on mine in an elegant dance, his tongue pressing into my gasping mouth, as if it were always meant to be there. My stomach clenched, my whole body kissed him, and if I were being realistic, a piece of my soul crawled up to intertwine with my tongue to kiss him, too. To call it the best kiss of my life would diminish it. It was the only kiss that ever counted.

His hands were in my hair, sliding up the nape of my neck to tangle gripping fingers at the back of my head. The sensation pulled a primal moan of pleasure from my lips, drawing me away from his. He echoed my groan when my hips rose to press my achingly bare, empty pussy against his hardened length. The warmth of his body surrounded me and flowed through me, mirrored by my own craving flowing into him. He pressed his forehead to mine as he panted into me. Grinding on my slick folds, he slithered against my painfully swollen clit, teasing us both.

He pulled back my head so that my eyes flew open to meet his. The cunning in his feral grin made me shiver. His eyes searched mine for a second before he plunged himself into me, his eyes locking onto mine, holding me captive in his gaze. Sal was not as massive as I imagined his length would be, but the girth of his cock was a solid presence that split me wide for him. Wedging into me, he rocked his hips from side to side, stretching me like no other had before. He was enough to hit the back of my walls without trying but not long enough to hurt. The girth, though, left a burning ache where it stretched my soaked depths around him. Stars danced behind my quickly closing lids as we both stilled to enjoy the sensation of that first stroke, our first connection. I felt his heartbeat pounding next to mine. Felt his breath drawing alongside mine. I felt his hand cup my cheek, his thumb gently caressing my face.

That moment of tenderness was over far too soon, though. A few seconds of rapture, and he was plunging into me again. He started slowly, rocking against me as I clung to him, with an exploring stroke meant to test my limits, as if asking me if I would stop him. I would absolutely not. I was riding so close to the razor's edge of orgasm that, with even just a little breath, I would scream, coming all over his cock.

"Look at me when I fuck you, nayeli." Dropping his hand from my cheek, he trailed to my nipple and tortured me as he fed my hungry depths his thick length. "I want you to watch me fuck my mate for the first time. Share this with me."

A slow devil's grin spread across his features as my eyes fluttered open.

"I want to watch you explode for me, nayeli. I can't promise I will ever be this sweet to you again. I have spent so long dreaming about fucking you within an inch of your life."

I clenched around his cock as he pushed especially deep, pressing into a sweet spot deep and to the back of me. The clench made him smirk. "My mate likes it when I tell her how much I have wanted and dreamed of her?"

Groaning, I clawed at his arms as he jerked my head to the side and leaned over to whisper into my ear, "I have dreamed of feeding you my cock. Dreamed of the sound of you coming for me, my name on your lips. Dreamed of you swollen, with my get and on all fours begging for me to fuck you deep and hard. You are mine, nayeli. And I've dreamed of hearing you say it."

He picked up his pace, slamming into me mercilessly with every word. Pounding into that spot with laser focus, like he had a visual bead on its exact location. His precision was that of a man on a mission. And I felt his brutality with every inch of my being, my body flooding with pleasure from the follicles of my hair to the tips of my toes. He was keeping me on the edge, though, keeping me just a hair's width away from shattering into a billion sparkling shards. It was a wonder I could breathe at all from the want. I needed to come. I needed to bathe his cock in the pressure and the flood building behind the thinly stretched walls he viciously assaulted with meticulous accuracy.

"Tell me you are mine, nayeli . . . and I'll let you come for me," he purred.

My mouth wouldn't work. All I wanted to do was come. I had no clue how I was holding out. How he was keeping me from spilling over the edges of my dam and drowning the world in my ecstasy. I had no clue how he was keeping me from going over that edge and taking all of humanity with me. I felt like I would come apart if he didn't let me fall into its swirling eddies. My clit had become so sensitive to the barest touch of his hips against mine that it shot fireworks through my brain, and a ballista slammed into my heart. My pussy ached from clenching. Every single hair on my body held its breath for the precise moment he would let me go and release his spell.

"Please, Sal . . . I . . . I need . . ."

The refusal to tell him I belonged to him was clear. Not even my lust-crazed, orgasm-blinded brain would let me lie to him. I wanted the man, but I barely knew him.

"Good. You will not come until you tell me you are mine. Until you give me what I need . . . all of it."

Cold metal was slipped around my wrists and clamped shut before my arms were hoisted above my head, stretching me out under him and across the bed. Confusion exploded across my face as I whipped my gaze from my handcuffed wrists tethered to the headboard to his cheshire grin. His body slid from mine, leaving a hollow emptiness. I had felt desolation before. I had felt abandoned before. This was different. This was a bone-deep ache and longing I couldn't have even fathomed existed before this moment.

"Since you are so good with your fingers . . ." He grinned at his cleverness.

As recognition of my situation clanged in my lust-fogged mind, I scowled. His words reverberated through my mind. *Until you give me what I need . . . all of it.* Of course. *Of course,* how could I have been so stupid? I knew he wanted something from me. I knew that his expectations had not been met. And I knew, viscerally, what unmet expectations meant. I had been taught that lesson repeatedly throughout my life. I hoped he would be different. I hoped he would treat me differently.

When would I learn? When would I learn I was just another vehicle for everyone else? A beast of burden meant to shuttle folks from one place to another in their life, uncaring of my needs or wants. And he was no different.

The glare I gave him said all this and more. Told him clearly what I thought of him and his expectations. He would hear not a single word from me again. And he would certainly not hear any arguments from me. He was just like the others, and I knew how to deal with people like that. I knew how to suffer the weight and shifting landscape of the expectations of others. I knew how to weather the shifting sandstorms of not living up to those expectations and how to navigate the dunes of demands.

Even if the whiplash of his lightning-fast switches from sweet to primal to demanding to domineering and back to sweet kept me from being able to predict who the next breath would bring.

Sal was not prepared for the war he started. His consternation and the scowl he returned, his gorgeous cock slick with my juices, and his hair unbound as he crossed his arms across his muscular chest told me he was stumped at my reaction. He subconsciously widened his stance as if readying for a fight. Good. There was one thing my mother had taught me all those years that she had not realized, a lesson wedged into the margins of her twisted textbook: how to give without losing a single millimeter of ground.

Game on, Sal. Hope you brought your big boy panties. You're going to need them, fucker.

CHAPTER TEN

He loomed over me. His eyes, obsidian in the shade of the bedroom, searched mine for an answer to a question he didn't ask. It was as if he was staring down a jigsaw puzzle that had no picture on the top, just blank white space where the image should be. I gave him not a single inch. I schooled my face into empty placidity. No fight, no stubbornness, just pure nothingness. At least as much as I could with the raging maelstrom of fury roiling within me. I wanted to claw at his face, bite at his throat, and tear out the flesh hiding the pulsing throb of his heart. I wanted to rend him for his betrayals and ravage his body for inspiring such a heady lust in me. Instead, I stared at him.

A slow, teasing, wicked grin pulled at those soft lips, swollen from our passionate kisses. His gaze traveled down my plush, naked form stretched out in his massive bed. His pink tongue flicked out to lick at his lips, and I wondered if, in his transformation, my taste would linger.

"My mate wishes to play hard to get?" he crooned, like I was playing some game with him. I wanted to rail against him and tell him what I wanted: his cock, sure, but also his blood as payment for his perfidy. "She longs for my cock inside her but wants to make me work for it? Hmm? Is that it nayeli?"

His fingers traced obscure patterns into my bare skin as he whispered his seductive words, trying to wrap them around me and tug me from the security of my internal hiding place. "Perhaps you just want to see how much I have desired you? Hmm? Let me show you, cihuatl."

He rose from sitting on the bed with me, his eyes and fingers never ceasing their roaming. He reached for the impossibly thick length that, moments ago, pounded into me and made me forget my name. He stroked it slowly, matching that same carnal rhythm, a rhythm I would carry in my soul to my grave.

"Shall I tell you how I stood over the vent in my room and listened to you play with that delicious pussy of yours that night?" He stroked harder, tugging and pistoning his hips into his hand, while the other tweaked and pinched at my nipples, trying so hard to get a reaction out of me.

The pleasure from the way he rolled my nipples swam through my blood like a drug. "Give in," it whispered. "Give him what we both want," it hummed as he tugged his cock and my nipple in the same rhythm.

Biting the inside of my cheek with my back teeth, I fought the overwhelming urge to speak, to tell him what he wanted to hear, to let my traitorous body give in to the tantalizing beat and the bewitching voice purring in my head. Not yet. This war had just started, and I would not be losing the oldest game in my repertoire. I had studied too hard for this test to fail in the first round.

"Should I tell you how I took this cock in my hand and listened to you moan and beg and stroked with every sound I could hear from you?"

Having not received the response he wanted from my nipples, he slithered his hand down my stomach, his blunted fingertips caressing the swell of silky soft skin he found there as if entranced. He lingered there a few moments, his hand spread wide over its expanse before he moved lower to the drenched cleft of my sex. As he teased the pearl of pleasure coiled taut, shards of crystalline pleasure lacerated the walls of my resolve. When my eyes pressed shut, trying to force the moans of delight back down my throat, he went on. "I was moaning your name into the wall, cualcihuatl. I imagined you writhing on my bed, just like this, moaning for my touch. Begging me for release. Begging for me to touch you like this."

His breathing became ragged, and I found I was holding my breath more than I was drawing in vital air, trying not to react on the outside and not to let him know sumptuous, aching pain had been gathering in my core, begging him to let me fall over the edge again. My fingers, held captive by cuffed wrists, biting hungrily into my palms, longed to sink their sharp little nails into his flesh.

"I wanted to break down your door and fuck you as you deserved, Xochitl. I wanted you at the end of my cock and dripping with my cum so bad. You weren't ready for me then, though. Even though you called my name as you came. You weren't ready. You needed to know how deep my love for you is."

My eyes snapped open, and I glared at him. *Love?* He just met me! How the hell could he love me? Oh no . . . had I traveled to a foreign country and fallen into a Lifetime movie? Was this guy obsessed with me? Go figure—the first time in my life someone shows me a little romancing, and it's a crazy guy with a penchant for giving life-altering dick and tying random chicks up. Just my luck. Someone find that seagull and shoot it immediately.

He pinched my clit. "Tell me you are mine, Xochitl."

He was right on the edge of coming. I could see it in the way his face contorted and could see the strain in his pumping arm. It was the slight edge of desperation and sadness flavoring his words that was confusing. Remaining silent, I bit down on the inside of my cheek again, the taste of blood blooming on my tongue. I huffed out a single sound, and he shuddered, splashing the thick ropes of his pleasure all over my stomach as he strained over me, his eyes locking onto mine as if the mere sight of me was all he needed. A distant sound in the back of my head sounded like the soft, whined whimper of a creature mourning the loss of the opportunity to lap at that heated fluid as it pooled in my belly button.

He took several deep breaths to steady himself. "Fuck."

As if I had offended him, he snatched a pair of jeans off the floor and stalked out. I heard him snarling a barking order in another language to someone and the livid slam of a door somewhere far deeper in the building.

Once I was sure he was gone, I exhaled the breath that felt as though I was holding it for months. I pulled at the handcuffs, tugging at them to test their strength. There was no give at all. The metal dug into my tender skin as I yanked, and I cursed under my breath. In the utter stillness of the heavy room, I took stock of my situation. My fingers were getting chilly, a precursor to circulation issues. My thighs were burning, and I didn't want to look down to see how bad off they were. The fire that licked at them could either mean I was about to bleed out in a crazy man's bed, or I'd need a lot of bandages. I felt the claws sinking into the meat of my thighs, but it was so dull at the time. Now the throbbing pain was telling me it might be a lot worse than I thought. My pussy was aching and burning, too, and I was starting to suspect that it wasn't just from the fact that I had been edged within an inch of selling my soul.

Fuck.

Death to all seagulls. As soon as I figured out how to get free of Creepy Guy, I was going to buy a shotgun and go after every single one of those feathered fuckers.

A long period passed in utter silence as I seethed in my anger before a soft tapping came from the bedroom door. It paused and tapped again.

"Cihuatlatoani, if you can hear me, I'm coming in." The voice of the man I had found Sal talking to—César, I think was his name—came from the other side of the door before he pushed it open slowly. His shaggy head poked into the room, his eyes locking with mine before darting back to the floor immediately. "I'm sorry, Itziquetzal said you might need seeing to. I'll try not to look where I don't have to."

He advanced into the room, shutting the door behind him. His eyes remained on the floor as he came to the side of the bed where I was trapped.

Medical attention? My eyes finally dared to look down at the sticky mess of my stomach and beyond to the pooling ruby streams slipping down the ravine between my thigh and puffy, ravaged lips.

"Fuck, my thighs are bleeding pretty badly. Shit. Shit. Shit." I could feel blood beginning to pool and soak the bedding beneath me. For now, I decided that, if I didn't look, it wouldn't be that bad. Right? If I just didn't acknowledge my slashed thighs, they wouldn't be that bad. Right? The pain was a sharp searing in my periphery, but it seemed dull.

He smiled softly. That same sense I had of him when he was talking to Sal, of calm serenity, washed over me, and I wanted to curl into the comfort it offered. I couldn't move, though. Not only was my thigh bleeding from the claw marks, but Sal's icy cum had caked on my stomach, and I had no desire to smear it everywhere and have it crusting up my skin.

"I'm César, by the way, if you don't remember," he said in that soft, steady manner of his.

"Remember?" I asked as he unpacked bandages and a few other items.

A brow kicked up, and he met my gaze. Rich hazel and moss-green eyes searched mine, never straying below my nose line. I could tell he was trying to see if there was any deception in my face. Sal had told him I was hiding things, so he had a reason to doubt me. I let him see what he could, letting the fake emotions wash away from my visage. It felt the most open I had been in so long. It felt raw and brittle, like the fresh scab on a deep, oozing wound. I didn't like it.

"You really don't remember?" he asked, tilting his head. No accusation accompanied his tone but almost a sad wonderment, like it seemed tragically obscene I didn't remember him. "Who I am? Who Itziquetzal is?"

I shook my head. "I have no clue what you are talking about, César. Are you sure you've got the right girl? Would be a shame if your crazy friend kidnapped the wrong American. You won't get any ransom, by the way. If that's your end goal. No one's going to pay to get me back."

He was not nearly as guarded as Sal, his emotions rippling across his face like rings in a pond. First remorse, then confusion, then amusement, and, finally, a shocking sadness that pulled at his otherwise sincere face in strange ways. His face rebelled against the foreign emotion and sought to push it from his dark features as quickly as possible as he exhaled and pulled a pillow—the closest thing at hand—over my body to hide my nakedness.

"I will have him tell you the story of who we are to you, Xochi. That is not my story alone to tell. He should have told you by now." He cleaned the blood on my thighs, pulling a deep wince from me. "I can tell you who I am, though. My name is César Osario. You and I met when we were very young. I believe you might have been ten? It's been a very long time. Sorry. I am the totoco's healer and teopixqui . . . a priest or religious person. That's why he sent me in to see to you."

He motioned to the bloodied cloths and set them aside. "This may sting a little, by the way. Just breathe through it."

I shouldn't have, but I looked down past the pillow to my thighs. Just a few inches above my knee were four lacerations that bubbled and oozed sparkling crimson blood against my fawn skin. They were clean, with no ragged edges or tears, but angry. The other thigh sported a matching set. I tried to move my legs and was greeted with an instant and vicious reprisal for my audacity as the torn flesh cried out.

He held up his arms, and before my eyes, they shivered, the skin rippling and churning on the bones that it encased. Patches of dark black fur similar to Sal's sprouted from his arms like smoke from a snuffed candle. The skin turned dark as Sal's had, but unlike Sal's, the skin was mottled, ashy, and pallid. Where Sal's forearms were strong, rippling with muscle and power, César's were thin, emaciated, nearly transparent in the gauntness of his flesh. The claws that tipped his lengthening hands were ragged and chipped, the knuckles gnarled and grotesque. Where Sal's beast was all potency and might, César's seemed to be the opposite, deathly and diseased.

I gasped, my feet trying to kick myself away from him as I scrambled against the sheets to tuck myself up against the headboard. My thighs, ravaged as they were, cooperated but at the cost of pain so keen it stole the breath from my lungs and iced over the edges of my vision. "What the actual fuck?!"

He sighed as the blood from my claw marks began weeping again. "Calm, Xochi. I'm not going to hurt you. I know Itziquetzal is not exactly the best example of our kind, but I promise I won't hurt you. Calm. It's okay. Just breathe."

"No! What the actual fuck! What the actual fuck are you? And him? What the fuck is going on here?"

My mind was reeling. It was like the shock of everything from my mother's machinations crashing in on me but so much worse. It was the cataclysmic crush of signing away my adult rights, but at least then, I knew how that would play out. Here, it was all topsy turvy, like walking into a funhouse blindfolded, only to have it ripped clear while you were on the tilting bridge. This was something else. The creatures in my room, brawling and snarling at each other, were horrific. Then there was that thing that Sal had turned into. Now this. Whatever the actual fucking fuck *this* was.

César, placid and unruffled as ever, sighed again. Muttering something about the hard way, he reached over, grabbed one of my ankles, and yanked me with great effort down the bed toward him. He growled, the first sign of any reaction to my kicking at him. The hand he used to protect his face from my thrashing foot slammed down on the slashed wound on my thigh.

I screamed then, for real. My throat felt like I was gargling shards of glass as I screamed as loudly as I thought was humanly possible.

Milliseconds later, I learned that was not the loudest a human could scream. Lava flowed into my bloodstream and liquefied my bones. It raced a path through my body, scorching every nerve as it went on its chaotic pathway toward the source of my scream. Fire radiated from the wounds that César clutched roughly. Once the agony reached my throat, it was too sharp to scream through it, and my scream turned silent, as if my body had forgotten how to produce the sounds.

Had it been hours of torment? Or merely seconds? I couldn't tell, but when it eventually ended, César's face was close to mine as he pushed back my curls with a caring, tender hand. "Shhhh, Xochi, it's okay. It's okay."

A roaring rattled the windows before that familiar beast broke the bedroom door down and stalked toward César. It barked out a growled order to César in a language I didn't recognize but figured was their mother tongue. César rolled his eyes and turned to the creature, his nightmarish hands lifting in the air. His compassionate tone softened more, his head tilting to the side as he stepped toward the creature, speaking his language back to him. The monster growled again, the sound a low, dangerous warning as César advanced on him.

The shadows gathered around the monster I knew to be Sal as, to my shock, golden light glimmered from César's hands. He was speaking, never stopping his very one-sided dialogue as the monster's gaze darted between me and César. Blood oozed down one thigh, and the beast tracked its course for a moment too long. Quick as a spider catching a fly, César's hands were on the creature as he crept toward me, and he held on tightly, groaning with the effort. The creature howled in rage and tried to shake him off, but César wouldn't let go, that golden halo seeping in and cutting through the shadows that gathered around the other beast.

Slowly, so agonizingly slowly, the shadows pooling at his knees rose up to engulf the two. The beast shivered and evaporated as the tendrils of shadows dissipated, all ten feet or more of him swallowed by the hungry shadows. When he was left standing naked before César, he panted and nodded to a question César had asked him. Angry coffee eyes held me in their depths before he nodded again and padded out of the room, not looking back at us.

César exhaled, exhaustion riding the sound. "I'm getting too old for this fucking shit."

He turned back. "Now. Xochi, I need you to promise me that you aren't going to scream again. If Itzatecuani hears you, I won't be able to hold him back. And as much as I'd like to say that Sal cares deeply for you, his beast has different primal imperatives. Now . . . can I trust you not to scream while I heal your wounds? Because, as much as I like you, Xochi, you're going to get me killed if you do that again. Got it? Calm. Bite the pillow if you have to."

My head was still swimming in the cloudy waters of hysteria, but I kept whispering, "What the fuck. What the fuck."

Shoving the pillow at me, he rolled his eyes. "I'm going to count to three, and so help me, if you scream, I'm letting him at you. Got it? Good."

He counted to three, and when the fire licked through me again, it was less painful. A small snarling grunt echoed in my mind. Or had I made the sound aloud? I couldn't tell. All I knew was that the second wave of white-hot violence rampaging through my body was almost tolerable. Almost.

When he was finally done with my thigh, he shifted me so I wasn't so contorted. Blood dribbled from between my legs where the claws of the beast cut little nicks into my tender folds. I hadn't even noticed until right then, swallowing the scream threatening to claw its way past my resolve. All that came out was a yelp.

"Absolutely not. No. Not going to happen." He backed away from me until he found a chair near the bed. "That's going to have to heal up the old-fashioned way, Xochi. With the mood he's in—if I go out there smelling of your scent like that?—he'll rip my head off. I'm sorry but absolutely not. I am rather fond of breathing at the moment, and I need to survive at least another year."

"What?"

"Nothing. Nothing. It's just not happening."

"Wh—I mean, what the actual *fuck* are you?"

He scrubbed a hand down his face and leaned forward, his elbows braced against his knees. He looked bedraggled, like he had gone twenty rounds with a gorilla and lost. "Remember, you promised not to scream. Okay?"

I nodded weakly. I couldn't do much, handcuffed to a bed and stark naked, blood leisurely weeping from my pussy.

He sighed again. "First, I know you are already thinking it. No, we aren't werewolves. Everyone thinks that. We aren't. Werewolves are native to Europe and more animal than we are. We've been here much longer than the fucking Spaniards' taint."

He spit or at least made a motion like he was spitting. From the lack of wet splat against the tiles, I imagined he had the sense not to spit in his boss's bedroom. He leaned back as he went on.

"Nor are we shifters, not by their standards, at least. We are what they call now cadejo. Ghost dogs. Though we aren't ghosts nor dogs. Ghost implies that our spirits were once human, mostly. They never were and never will be. Our connection to them is as close to humanity as they will ever get. We are a symbiosis, a conduit between the divine and the flesh."

Watching him, I focused extremely hard on each and every syllable of every word. I was sure they would make sense eventually. My mind had been rebelling against the images of what, up until I left San Francisco, would have been grounds for a padded room and heavy drugs.

"Our ancestors came from all around Central America, but the legends say we were born to the Olmecs first. The stories say that a woman fell in love with one of their gods. Their love was forbidden, of course, and the rest of the teotl cast him out, cursing them both. They walked the earth between worlds, cursed to neither be truly mortal nor truly divine, nor to pass into the other world. They were alone in the world, stuck between realms, able to see everything that went on around them but unable to interact with the land of the living nor the land of the divine. Eventually, as things usually happen, they had children. Seven of them. Three boys and four girls. These children could pass through the barrier of the in-between world their parents were cursed to reside in and interact with the land of the living but were barred from the land of the divine, being mortals themselves."

My eyes were bolted to his lips, that soft, easy way his voice stroked over the words with the seasoning of an accent reaching into my body, forcing my lungs to draw slow, measured breaths. It convinced my blood to whisper *truth* into my brain. I shifted on the bed, leaning in, nearly hypnotized by the story he was weaving effortlessly. My shifting drew a wry smile to his lips as he forged onward.

"These seven children were not like the mortals of the world, though. Their father being a teotl, they held a connection to the spirit world and could call to themselves the power of these spirits. They could manifest their power and might in various ways. One of those ways was by taking in the spirit of their godly father, a teotl of beasts. When the teotl saw that their curse had gone awry, they waged war on their children and killed all but three of them. Those surviving three are our ancestors. They were scattered across the land. The only way the teotl could rid themselves of the three strongest children was to separate them.

"But where they had truly made the mistake was not killing all of them. As the knowledge our ancient ancestor had, how to bond themselves to a spirit of the other realm was passed down. Crafted. Perfected. Refined and honed until the spirits that came forward from the field of bones were no longer just merely beasts that had passed but entities that could rival those same spirits that had cursed their progenitor and called themselves teotl. Some spirits chose again and again to come across the river between worlds and bond itself to a cadejo. Some came once and never again. Each brought a blessing of its own, unique to the realm they come from, giving part of that power to its mortal host." He paused and lifted his arms, returning them to their mundane, familiar human shape. "My ability to heal is one of those blessings."

He smirked down to his arms as if acknowledging the humbling of such a mighty blessing. Sure, his healer's touch was just as painful, if not more than the wound itself, but it had knit my flesh together with not even a single mark left behind. People back home would easily call that magic and not merely a blessing.

"It costs us, though. We must feed our spirits what they need to thrive, just as we must eat." He took a deep breath as if the worst was yet to come. "Cadejos, like myself and Sal, we feed our spirits fear, sorrow, anguish, terror, and all that goes along with it."

My mouth had gone dry, parched and dusty as I whispered, "How . . . How do you feed them?"

Images of that beast I had let between my thighs ripping chunks of flesh off of my body, gorging itself on my fear, ran rampant in my mind's eye.

"That . . . is much too complicated to explain to someone who will not experience it." He replied in a tone as soft as a baby's sigh, trying to comfort me and give me back some semblance of courage. He watched me, his eyes darting between mine, before it seemed he decided that the slight shivering of my thighs was no longer from fright but from the chill before he finished. "And, so, we are here. And have been here since before memory."

His slim shoulders rolled in a shrug. "That is the short of it, at least. I am no storyteller. I'm sure one of the others would be able to tell it more elegantly. We can transform our bodies into a dog-like form. The two creatures that were in your room at the hotel, both of them were cadejos. One is known to us and shouldn't be an issue again. The other was Sal, protecting you. And then you saw . . . well, you saw Itzatecuani."

I took deep breaths. This was insane. Absolutely bonkers. Yet, somewhere inside of me, I recognized it as truth. I had seen and touched, at least, the proof. "So, you're . . . magic?"

He huffed out a surprised laugh. "Not really. Not like you see in movies, no. More that we are connected to our ancestors and the power they tapped into. As you saw with Sal, he is physically strong. He feeds his other side—we call him Itzatecuani out of respect for his position—for his strength. And, as you saw in my arms, I feed mine for other purposes. I channel all of my power into my connection to the spirit realm. It leaches my other form of physical strength, but allows me a connection with our totoco's teotl and the powers and spirits that protect us. Healing takes a good bit of energy from me, but it can be done. So, no less magic and more connected to our teotl in a way most mortals have lost."

He nodded to my thighs. "And it leaves no scars. Which is why Itziquetzal sent me in to see to you. He didn't want you scarred from his, um . . . failed mating."

"Failed . . . mating?"

I sounded out the words as if he were insane. He was, but who was I to tell him that he was bonkers when I had seen the evidence of at least some of his claims myself? I was pretty sure it wasn't a great idea to piss off the crazy guy in the room when you were naked and chained to a bed.

An adorable blush dusted his cheeks. He waved an awkward hand at my bare form on the bed. "You didn't permit him to mark you, to seal the mating with you, so he could not. And he didn't want you to bleed out or scar from his . . . eh . . . failure, if you will."

He was still blushing, shifting awkwardly.

"So, he's—what, your king?"

A barked laugh came to his lips. "Please, Xochi, not so loud. If he hears you call him a king, he will be insufferable for the rest of his days. No, no, sweet Cihuatlatoani, he is not our king. He is our leader, our tecuhtli. I said we aren't werewolves. And our totoco is structured . . . a bit different than others."

"And you are . . . what? His second? Uh . . . prince?"

My mind was a whirlpool of thoughts, Charybdis squatting in the center, slashing her tail, about to taunt me further.

The cool serenity was back around him. "Something like that. Our rank within the totoco is pretty similar. Where he leads the totoco in their mortal lives, cares for them, and ensures that they have everything they need to be healthy and happy, I lead them in their spiritual life. I tend to their spirits and their bodies. I nurture the connection between us and our divinity and the spiritual world. When I cannot heal them by touch, I heal them with simple modern medicine."

"So . . . a doctor?"

"Of a sort. I have a small clinic here at the compound and occasionally do rounds down in La Libertad when I can. But, mostly, I spend my time as a gate messenger between our patron teotl and the totoco."

He rose and rooted around in the chest I had seen at the foot of the bed like he owned the place. He found a thin blanket and covered me.

"Any chance you can get me out of these?" I asked hopefully.

"Not even a little. If I take you out of them, he'll just find some other way to punish you for whatever it was that you did."

I snorted a decidedly unladylike sound, but Annette was too far away to bother me over it now. "Punish me? He's kind of a piece of shit, isn't he?"

A sharp brow, a cold, dangerous flash of his eyes, and curling of his lip slipped past his easy demeanor. "Itziquetzal is many things, a brute, an oaf, and, certainly, an idiot at times but a piece of shit? No. Do not insult him like that again in my presence."

I'd tested the lines of loyalty and lost. Thoroughly chastised, I winced and slunk down in my lean against the headboard.

"Sorry," I whispered as he glared at me.

The ease came back, and he nodded his acceptance of my apology.

His boss was a piece of shit. I wasn't going to tell him that again, but we both knew it was true.

He turned and made his exit since I was patched up. Calm leached into my emotionally exhausted bones. Then a small scratchy voice itched a hiss at the back of my mind.

"César?"

He turned, smiling softly at me. "Yes, Cihuatlatoani?"

"I had some medications with me at the hotel. I don't know how long I've been here, but I'm supposed to take them daily."

He frowned consternation, and a bit of trepidation curled around his face. "Are you sick, Cihuatlatoani?"

"What does that mean? And no . . . but yes. I have ADHD. It helps me focus, and the rest are vitamins, to keep me from getting sick."

"It's your title. Well . . . might be. I like to assume the teotl only whisper lies when they are bored. They have deemed it so." He shrugged and smirked again. "I think I saw some medications in your bags. I'll have them brought in for you to take. I'd like to draw blood, if you don't mind. I felt a strangeness when I was healing you. I thought it was just unfamiliarity with your essence, but I'd like to run some tests. If you don't mind, that is. Perhaps I can find a natural compound to replace the chemicals in your medication for when you run out."

I nodded. I'd had enough blood drawn in my life to fill an Olympic swimming pool. My mother was always shuttling me to and from new doctors, speaking in hushed tones about what might be wrong with me. I'd lost track of how many times she'd squeezed my veins dry. "Sure. I guess."

He nodded and padded toward the hallway, leaving me alone to stew in my thoughts. "For when you run out."

So . . . I was a prisoner. Great.

Fuck seagulls.

CHAPTER ELEVEN

Waiting in the quiet of the room, I lay on the bed, shifting occasionally to ease the tension in my wrists. My skin crawled at the unnatural stillness. My entire body ached to move, to fidget, as it was forced to stay still on the bed. At least I was warm. The chill from the ceiling fan blowing on my skin, paired with the living thing in my skin raging to move, would have been too much.

While I fought the urge to thrash, my mind worked through everything I'd learned and seen. I was in survival mode. I had to survive these absurd people . . . and my inconvenient attraction to their leader. I needed to make it out, but the one thing I knew for sure—from my conversation with César—was that Sal was not going to just let me go, no matter what I said or how hard I begged him. I would have to free myself.

Plans flitted through my mind, each as diaphanous and immaterial as the next. I wished I could sit still and focus on a step-by-step plan, but it was too overwhelming. So, I decided on the first step that I'd figure out the rest as it came. And my first step in my war against my cadejo captor was to lull him into a sense of security that I was his. I would treat him like I treated my mother. I'd go along, get along, and placate him without digging myself deeper if I could. He, unlike Annette, had a certain knack for pulling out reactions I didn't want to feel or give him. I'd have to ballet dance over that minefield with care. And when the opportunity arose, I'd run.

That small voice was getting louder and louder since I'd touched down in this country. It grew from an inaudible hoarse croak from ten thousand miles away to the sound of someone whispering in the next apartment. It hummed in my ear that, if he got his hands on me, I'd crumble. It was true, but I wished it wasn't. My body craved him from the moment I set eyes on him on that beach.

I met you when you were maybe ten. César's voice tumbled around in the whirlpool of my mind. I tried to focus on memories that might help me piece him into my chronology when a woman with glowing terra-cotta skin and a bright white smile came in.

"The priest said you needed your pills?" she asked me in Spanish.

She had a glass of water in one hand, the other grasping my tidy square daily medication kit.

"Thank you . . . uhm . . . I'm Ang—Xochitl," I replied as she set down my pills. "Do you speak English? My Spanish is not that great."

She shook her head and dumped Friday's medication into her hand. Friday? It was Friday already? She sniffed the pills and scrunched her face in disgust. "No, sorry. Only Spanish and Nahuatl. These pills, they smell . . . spoiled."

I smirked and opened my mouth when she tipped them up. After I swallowed them with the water, I smirked at her. "They taste it, too. Thank you."

"I'm Julia," she said as she fluffed my pillow, noticing the cuffs around my wrists, then conspiratorially winked. "You're very flexible, Cihuatlatoani."

Her hands moved quickly. One second, both hands were cuffed, and the next, I was free. She snapped the cuffs closed again. With another wink, she slid the key under the mattress near my foot. "Just in case he gets ideas again."

I rubbed the ache in my wrists and thanked her, resisting the urge to eye the key's placement skeptically. She must have really thought I was a contortionist if she thought monkey toes would help future me in getting that key. "Won't you get in trouble? For freeing me?"

She made a tsking sound in her throat, reminding me of the way Sal had said my name. "And what will he do? Hmm? Spank me? Ha. Not likely. Not while you are here, Cihuatlatoani. He wouldn't dare touch another woman. Itzatecuani wouldn't let him. No, I think not, Cihuatlatoani, as long as you are here we are safe from his grumpiness." She sat on the bed with me.

I liked Julia. She was sassy, and I'd always wanted a sassy friend.

"Thank you, Julia. It's very kind of you to do," I gulped down.

She tsked again. "Think nothing of it, Cihuatlatoani. Now, let's get you dressed, hmm? We cannot have Itziquetzal thinking that he can hide his mate in his room away from his people. That's not how any of this works. And he should know you aren't going to stand for that, too."

I cocked a brow at her. "Uh . . . I'm not his mate . . . whatever that means. I'm just his prisoner."

She barked a laugh. "Nonsense. He marked you, no?"

I shook my head, and she frowned.

"Ah . . . that explains his mood, then. His failure is not your fault, Cihuatlatoani. You make him earn that mark. Hmm? You are our Cihuatlatoani now. Don't let him forget that."

I laughed, a little drizzle of hysteria flavoring the edges of the sound. "I don't even know what that means!"

"He . . . He didn't tell you?" She devolved into a flurry of Spanish cuss words I couldn't follow, but I was certain that it was condemning. She huffed, punching her hip as she leaned into it. "It means queen. Well, close enough. It means you are equal to him in the ranking of the totoco. You are not below him, not a nothing. You are not a prisoner. You are our princess, the mate to our tecuhtli. So . . . do you plan on letting him treat you like that? Hmm?"

What. The. Hell. From accountant to princess—yeah, fuck seagulls. I was not emotionally or mentally prepared for this.

After Julia dressed me in a top and skirt from my bags, she clucked, letting an approving eye sweep over me as she grinned. "I'll have someone unpack your bags and replace that door, Cihuatlatoani. Now, let's go introduce you to the totoco. He should have done that yesterday when he brought you here, but as we both know, men are stupid."

I decided that Julia was the best thing in El Salvador, and I'd punch a moose for her. Okay. Maybe a stuffed moose, but still.

"They won't care that I'm not like you? I'm not a cadejo?" I fretted as she walked me down that hallway of horrors and into the living room.

I memorized the pathways as we wound out of the living room to another hallway lined with bright windows. I could see marigolds interspersed with a voluminous white flower that reminded me of hyacinths or lilies of the valley dancing in a slow breeze beyond the panes. They were beautiful.

"No. It won't matter. But are you sure you aren't? How do you know? The priest said you just learned of us today. You never know. And if you are not already spirit touched, the priest can perform the ritual to call the spirits near. Perhaps one will choose you." She shrugged and smiled, tracing my gaze to the flowers. "He tried growing peonies for you a few years back. It's too hot here for them."

My eyebrow shot up. How had Sal known I liked marigolds or even peonies? One could guess easily from my name about the marigolds, but the peonies? How would he have known a few years ago? César's voice ghosted through my mind again. That was going to be a conversation I'd have to approach carefully. I didn't want to let my heart get too far into his clutches. The man who I met on the beach and the man or *thing* that had brought me to the edge of paradise, only to leave me cuffed and covered in his cum, were not the same. I needed to guard myself against his changeable nature.

We stepped out into a bustling courtyard that was the totoco compound. It was larger than I thought. At least fifty people milled around what reminded me of a medieval castle in its scale.

The compound was just that, a square with three two-story-tall buildings flanking three walls of the courtyard, and smaller single-story buildings made up the fourth with a large metal gate between them. Each building had an alleyway that led somewhere I couldn't see. No cars occupied the courtyard, but I could see them parked outside the gate's metal bars.

Within the courtyard, all manner of industry was underway. Women sat at looms, some men at candle pots, children running with chickens and goats. A kitchen of sorts was tucked under the roof of an open-air patio. It was a thriving, living village tucked within the walls protecting it from the incursion of prying eyes.

Julia walked me around, introducing me to people whose names I struggled to remember but did my best. It was an overwhelming amount of people, though I suspected they were secretly the creatures I had watched Sal and César turn into. They were all welcoming and warm. I had imagined that they would be put off by a foreign woman in their midsts, but they all seemed happy to have me in a way I had not experienced before. It was . . . touching.

CHAPTER TWELVE

Hours later, after night had fallen, I hadn't seen Sal at all. I'd shared a meal with César, Julia, and a few others. I was left to my own devices. I wandered the compound, memorizing its layout and any exit points without being too obvious. Eyes didn't follow me as I suspected they would, as I, a stranger, wandered what I learned from Julia was the home of most of the totoco. I also learned that the clan of them, some family, some extended family, some not related at all, called themselves a totoco. Some lived down the mountain, in the tiny town of Chinameca that the compound overlooked. Others resided in small one-room houses that dotted the jungle, whose canopy I could see peaking above the walls.

I found two exit points aside from the main gate. One behind the large building that Sal had rooms in, and one behind the kitchen that led out to flat farmland that the totoco used to supplement their hunting and livestock. Julia had been a wonderful guide, unsuspecting of my true motives, and told me that the other gate led out into the jungle and up into the caldera of a slumbering volcano. When the time was right, that would be my best exit point. She'd said that, at night, it was incredibly dangerous but offered to take me on a tour of the volcano's vista point another day, where I could see San Miguel in the distance.

Watching the stars from the front gate, I felt a warm body press against me and a hand slide along the nip of my waist to spread across the cotton-clad front of my belly. My muscles tensed for a single second before they relaxed into the warmth of Sal behind me.

He pressed his chin to my scalp as we watched the stars. "They are beautiful, no?"

He was right. The lack of light pollution made the stars brighter than I had ever seen. I wanted to lean back into his body and take from him the heat and security that his presence offered. I needed to keep my wits about me, though. I needed to not fall into this man the way that little voice insisted I should.

I hummed a noncommittal sound, and he stilled.

"Are you ignoring me now, Xochitl?" His tone wasn't the apologetic tone I expected of a man who'd edged me, jerked off on me, then abandoned me, leaving me shackled to his bed. I didn't reply. He stiffened. "I told you, Xochitl. You don't get to shut me out anymore."

He spun me in his arms and glared down at me, searching my eyes for that reaction he so wanted. I gave him nothing but the same placid mask I'd worn on the beach. He could steal me away and hide me in the mountains, but he didn't get to win the war. This was a game he was a novice at, not me. He could make my body and soul ache to be touched, loved, and caressed by him, but he couldn't make my mind bend to his will. My heart and body might have been weak, but my mind had been tested in the hellfire forge of a villain far outside of his league, and I would not break.

He growled, low and soft, as if he didn't notice it. "Speak, woman."

I narrowed my eyes at him but said nothing.

"Dammit, Xochitl, speak." He gripped my jaw and squeezed as if he could force my tongue to give him what he wanted. "Why won't you talk? Why won't you fight with me? Tell me off. Anything is better than this . . . this ice. You are not ice. You are not cold. So, speak, dammit!"

My resolve to freeze him out cracked slightly at the corner.

"And how would you know what I am? How would you know who and how I am?" I spat at him, pushing him away from me. He barely budged.

His glare was pointed and dangerous. "You really don't remember, do you?"

"César said the exact same damned thing. Remember what? Who the hell are you people?"

He sighed and ran a hand through his unbound hair. "We met when we were younger. You were everything I ever wanted in a mate. You were fire and sun. You were rainbows and gold. You really don't remember? Balboa Park?"

I huffed and crossed my arms. No . . . I didn't remember. Or did I? The image of a sun-drenched park, heat, and sticky hands filled my mind's eye. It was still so blurry at the edges, but I felt . . . warmth. Not just from the summer heat beating down on the grass but from something else I couldn't place.

He paced, watching me with a predator's gaze. "I gave you a crystal. Do you remember? A thumb-sized clear rock with rainbows in it. You met César, too. My cousin, Javier, introduced us."

Javi. How was Javi caught up in this? I narrowed my eyes further as a foot race came to memory, but it was like trying to grasp sand in gloved hands, sliding from my mental fingers before I could get a full grip on it.

He growled and grabbed my shoulders, shaking me. "How can you not remember? César married us! At sunset. How can you not remember that?"

I slapped at his hands, my tone forced but even. "You're insane! Is that what this is about? Some sham of a ceremony in a park at sunset? We were *kids*! Please, for the love of god, tell me you did not kidnap me because some ten-year-old version of me agreed to marry some kid at a park that she barely knew! That's insane!"

Victory splashed against his starlit face as he ate up the space he had paced between us and pressed my body between his and the gate, the night-kissed bars licking frost through the thin barrier of my cotton top and skirt. The scent of rain-soaked dark earth, rich green plants, cinnamon, rum, and sun-warmed skin crashed into my mind as he held my chin again and flashed that wolfish grin. That earthy scent. My eyes slid shut, and I saw the amber rays of a beautiful sunset behind my lids.

I shuddered in his grip. All this time. All these years, when anxiety scraped and clawed at me the hardest, in my darkest moments, I had clung to that mental image and scent to calm my nerves. And there, in that moment, this infuriating brute of a man pressing his knee to my dampening core was the source of it. How? How could I remember it so clearly but not remember him at all? And why had it calmed me so many times when I was at my lowest and about to shatter?

I needed air. I needed space. The emotions and sensations swirling around me were too confusing. Nothing made sense. I dragged in a ragged breath and pushed him away—or tried to. He was a massive unmovable object, crushing me against the gate's metal bars, unwilling to let me squirm away from him, unheeding to my thrashing.

"No, Xochitl, we were kids, but we knew each other. My cadejo recognized you as his mate even then. He knew who you were. We know who you are now." He pressed me still against the bars, his knee working my throbbing core that begged for me to succumb to his temptation. The occasional pinprick of fire licking from the nicks and cuts only added to the cocktail of seduction. When he finally spoke, his voice was a whisper edged in steel. "You will give her back to us. We won't accept you keeping her from us."

"You're sick. You're fetishizing a *child*! Get off of me!" I hissed at him.

"No child. The woman you are is our mate. We merely found you when you were a child." He growled, vibrating my bones.

I wanted to melt into the sound, into the rightness pouring through me. I wanted to give in to the way something inside me clamored to be closer to him. I wanted to curl up in his arms and take from him the solace I knew I would find. I wanted to give in to the swirling emotions that were so new yet felt like a well-worn favorite hoodie.

"What do you even know about me? Hmm? That was twenty years ago! You know nothing about me!" I snapped back, nearly a snarl as I tried to find some means of getting away, so I could just breathe.

"Everything I have ever done has been for you, Xochitl. You loved crystals. I bought three mines. You loved the sea. Javi said he would often track you to a beach and could smell the fear and anxiety drop off of you. So, I bought a hotel on the ocean. And you loved marigolds, so I planted them wherever I could." He stroked my cheek, his forehead pressing into mine. His breath was warm and sweet on my lips. "When I could support the totoco, I honored my father's wish for me to take the totoco from him and made myself worthy of claiming you."

I was hyperventilating. Gasping for breath that wouldn't fill my lungs, gulping down air to force the heat of my denial hotter. His other hand came to my chest to lay his splayed hand across my sternum. It was strange, but it was like he pressed my tattered edges back into place. Shadows grew around his hand, like the smoke I had seen before. It licked and kissed at my skin, melting into it.

"You're mine. You will be mine on the day I pass into the next world. You will be mine when you join me there. I will never let you go again. You will give me back my golden princess, eventually. Now, breathe."

I drew in a single breath, ragged and brutally stinging. I needed to calm myself, but how was I going to do that when the very source of my crumbling edges was connected to the one thing that I found in my life that had ever calmed the raging storm within me when it got the worst? Instead of the vision that kept me from the edge, even when I considered ending it all, I pictured the sensation of cool glass pressing against my flushed skin. I imagined its firm, icy grip drawing away my anxiety and fusing my shattering pieces with the ice slithering through it.

"Why me?" I whispered when the ice fused enough of my edges to allow my voice to work again.

He tilted my head up to meet his gaze, ferocity and tenderness warring in the swirling depths of his eyes. "How could it be anyone but you?"

He kissed me, fire licking over my lips and saturating my pulse with the heady sensation of satisfaction oozing from his pores. The kiss was chaste compared to our last. That one was all scorching heat and ferocious need. This one spoke of his hopes and dreams that I could not afford to share with him. I could let him indulge at least until I found a way out and back to some other life. I couldn't go back to the life I had led, a prison with a different set of bars, but I could not stay, either. Not with him. Not with them.

"Let's go to bed, nonayeli, but no tempting me." His tongue flicked a searing lash across my kiss-swollen lips. "César has told me I was . . . a little too rough on you."

He had the good sense to look at least somewhat abashed at the damage that had kept me standing most of the day to prevent the stinging from getting too bad.

"You'll get used to my touch, though. Both of our touch. Soon," he purred down at me, sweeping me into his arms bridal-style, then took me to bed.

CHAPTER THIRTEEN

I slept naked beside my captor all night, or at least laid next to him until I was too exhausted from the out-of-control roller coaster of emotional turmoil that had become my life, and finally succumbed to sleep. To my surprise, he didn't lock any doors, handcuff me to the bed, or do any other brutish thing that would have kept me by his side. Instead, after we showered and cleaned up for bed, he quietly tucked me into his warm body and laid an arm over me, gripping one of my generous breasts in his hand and kissing my shoulder. He whispered something in his mother tongue, then fell asleep without fuss.

Replaying the events of the last few days in my mind, I shored up the walls of my reality. I planned. Tracing the lines of the fractures, I found them still sharp enough to cut my mental fingers. I knew where the new boundaries of my life were, and I needed to reign it in and remember he was just another face in the game. Another challenge to my self-preservation. I'd survived thirty years of Annette. I could survive a few days of Itziquetzal and his merry band of weirdos.

In the morning, I woke alone with a pang of yearning and loss in my stomach. A soft whimpering huff echoed in my ears when I had finally cleared the sleep fog from my mind. It was soft gossamer on a breeze, though, a memory of a whimpered sound I had heard before but couldn't pinpoint. I tried to chase it, a strange sense of comfort trailing behind it like the tail of a comet in my mind. It receded into the void that swallowed dreams faster than I could grasp it, and it was gone.

Dressing, I found the tray of pills Julia left on the nightstand closest to what I assumed was now my side of the bed and took my Adderall, vitamins, and birth control. Then I wandered the halls to the courtyard, where I found Julia preparing breakfast with two other women, stirring a batch of eggs in a large terra-cotta pot, while one made dark rich beans and the other grilled plantains. Taking an offered cup of coffee, I smiled. I would miss Julia when I finally left. She was the only sweetness in this entire ordeal.

"Itziquetzal went hunting with the others early this morning, Cihuatlatoani. He should be back soon," Julia explained as she stirred the eggs.

The other woman chittered in that musical language that made my nerves stand up and vibrate pleasantly. Julia listened and then turned to me. "She wants to know if you will tame him or let him tame you."

I cocked a brow and sipped my coffee. "Having met *him*, I'm surprised that you speak so . . . casually of him. He doesn't seem like he forgives easily."

Julia translated and chuckled with the other woman.

"He is not the worst of them. Yes, he will snap and snarl like them all, but Itzatecuani has always been very reasonable compared to all except César. You will find that the men are stupid. They need a guiding light. You will see." She shrugged. "He is fair, though. The rules here are simple. We know what we must do and what we must not do. And we know the consequences when we do what we should not do. His father was much the same. It has always been the way of our totoco. Others? Not so much."

"What happened to his father? And his mother?" I asked, curious when I shouldn't have been.

Julia cocked an eyebrow at me and put a hand on her hip. "When he decided it was time to claim you, he killed him. His mother? She died before they came here. I do not know what happened to her."

I sputtered and choked on my coffee. "He killed him?"

She watched me skeptically for a moment as if judging my rather reasonable reaction—wholly unreasonable—and then went on. "Of course. It is the way. Itzatecuani was the son of the Tlahtoani. To claim a mate or take tecuhtli of the totoco, he needed to defeat his father in combat. When it was time, they stripped, traded shadows with their cadejos, and fought to the death. That was seven months ago."

I gawped at her, my mouth slack, eyes locked on her. "There is so much in that statement that was—no, is, absolute gibberish."

Julia crossed her arms over her bosom and leaned back on one foot as she glared at me. I'd offended her, of course I had. I felt like a stool with one broken leg, tottering to and fro, trying to find balance.

"What is a Tah-twani? Why did he have to kill his father? And what is trading shadows?"

The women helping Julia with breakfast tittered their laughter and replied in the language they spoke that reminded me of the flap of luminous feathered wings among the canopy of the jungle. Julia smirked at them but never relented. "Tlahtoani. Tl. Tl." She over annunciated the subtle tap of her tongue along the front of the roof of her mouth in a hard T sound cupped in her cheeks, and I tried to mimic her. The attempt returned the determined but friendly cut of my only companion's face. "You will get there. Keep trying. It is hard for English speakers; your language is so . . . dull. No flavor. As for why, it is the way of things. A Tlahtoani must feed the cycle of spirits so that their heir may stand among the demanding howl of the dead lands, unchallenged and mighty. As for trading shadows . . . it is an old term. From before the Triple Alliance was even dreamed of by Huitzilopochtli, from before the Lenca grew roots and their great feathered ancestor rose from their nest. It translates poorly. The original word our ancestors used was xonotáni. It means to release your spirit, the control of your born flesh, and to fall back into the spirit realm while your partnered spirit comes forward, breeches the boundary that has held them in their realm, reshapes your skin to suit their desire, and take its place on this plane. Most chose the easier path of reshaping the flesh to honor the god whose brood we came from. It takes more precious energy for them to shape it in other ways, but it can be done if they wish."

She shrugged casually, as if she hadn't just described the inner workings of a magic so old that the mother language for it had gone to dust on the tongue of the world.

"And seven months ago? That was when it was his time."

The simple answer she offered for the timing made the deep secrets she had revealed all the more stark in comparison.

Seven months ago. The mines. The conglomerate. That was about when the firm started courting the conglomerate. Before then, I had never heard of the business that the Yarbrows were sure would solidify their foothold in the Latin market to milk it for all it was worth as it went through waves of destabilization. Had he really, with his own father's blood on his hands, set into motion what I thought he had done?

A shiver crept up my spine. It was a move worthy of my mother's cold, calculated manipulations. It also made that little part of me deep down that longed for him this morning purr with delight.

After breakfast, Julia and I took up pulling weeds from the crop of corn growing in a field while chatting personably about our lives. I found, as I struggled through the conversation, she would naturally slide in to offer me a word I perhaps didn't know, and it became easier and easier to find the right words to guide me through Spanish. I guess the adage about never forgetting a language was true.

After dinner, a venison shank from the morning's kill, César drew the blood he had requested of me. He frowned deeply at the old scars of previous blood draws.

"It's not that," I said, rolling my eyes at the perceived implication of something illicit.

"Not what, Cihuatlatoani?" he said, puzzling over the five vials he had pulled.

"I was never into drugs." I shrugged and pressed the cotton ball closer. "I was just sick a lot as a kid. The doctors took a lot of blood pretty regularly."

"Oh? How regularly? And what did you have, Cihuatlatoani?" His manner, like always, was soft and implacable.

"A bag or two every week for about two years. It started clearing up after a few treatments and vitamin supplements. My mother never told me what it was, but I guess it worked, since I never got sick again."

He frowned again, closing up the baggie encasing my blood. "Was it serious?"

"Not really sure, honestly. I just remember feeling like I swallowed magma. My entire body was on fire, and my skin felt like it was made of glass. Like, at any moment, I would shatter if anyone touched me too hard. And I was always hungry, but any time I ate, I threw up. Then there was the exhaustion I felt—like even growing hair was too much energy."

Concern washed over his face. "That sounds pretty serious, Cihuatlatoani. And you said there were treatments and vitamin supplements? And that's all that it took to cure it? It never returned?"

Sipping the cool coconut water that I'd helped gather with Julia for dinner, I nodded. "Yep. I occasionally still get the stomach trouble, but aside from that, no other symptoms ever came back."

"And the pills you take?"

"Adderall, for attention-deficit hyperactivity disorder. Then there's birth control. That's pretty obvious. And then just vitamins to supplement my diet like most people."

The furrow of his brow deepened as I spoke, now deep enough for me to plant irises in. "Hmm. That seems like a lot of blood for that. I'll see what I can see in these. I might need to run additional tests. One of which might be fairly invasive."

I cocked my head. "César, once a year I climb up onto a table and let a total stranger stir my guts like chow mein. You wouldn't even heal my pussy cuts. I can't imagine you'd possibly be more invasive than that."

He snorted his amusement. "Some things are more invasive than that, Cihuatlatoani. It involves me examining your spirit. It can be . . . disturbing for some. And, as he is your mate, I will also need to get Itziquetzal's permission or the teotl will not allow it."

I snorted in an unladylike manner. "He's not my mate."

"Oh, but he is."

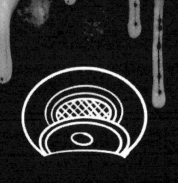

CHAPTER FOURTEEN

Itziquetzal

The sun was kissing the night goodbye, my fingers wandering the paths of my beloved's defiant curls. It was not an easy night for her, nor for me. Her thrashing whimpers woke me with a start deep into the night, the blunt spikes of her nails digging into my bare chest in her sleep. She'd curled into me as soon as she fell asleep, our bodies two flesh-sheathed magnets drawn to each other. The fear rolling off of her twitching body made my stomach roll with disgust, the press of a primal need to protect her scraped layers of humanity from me. When a quick sniff of the air yielded no disturbances, I let my eyes adjust to her tightly hunkered body. She winced, whispering terror-filled gibberish into my skin, lighting it aflame with the burning twist of wrongness as she nearly climbed atop me.

It took me well-spent hours to keep her from waking by pressing her body to me tightly, forcing the nightmare from her mind as I whispered to her in Nahuatl. "Ni mitz tlazohtla ta ma miqui in tonaltzin." *I will love you until the sun dies*, I told her.

She may freeze me out, glare at me with glaciers in her eyes in the day, but in the night, and—most importantly—in those moments, she knew who she belonged to.

When whatever creatures lurking in her mind had finally loosened their claws, she slumped, loose and liquid against me, finding her way onto my shoulder. Her face slackened with blissful peace, and I felt myself drawn down into it with her, sleep reclaiming me after knowing she was safe. As I woke to the wink of the still living sun, her cheek flattened against my chest, and I hummed with delight.

When I scooted up, she hadn't roused, and I spent far too long with her head in my lap, stroking those curls, letting their silken length pool and slip through my fingers. I had thought that the deep aching in my body was just to sate myself on her flesh, but moments like this ground the blade of it to a nub, reminding me she was so much more to me. These moments gripped me with cruel talons and ripped away any doubts I had about my path. She would need a firm hand, a callous hand to guide her back to me, but it would be worth it. The soft, content sighs into my skin would make the hatred that boiled just under the surface worth it in the end.

It had taken every last drop of my willpower to inch out from under her. The mornings started with the rising of the sun for most. For me, it started even before then. The moment my toes touched my bedroom floor's tiles, I longed to slink back into the inviting heat of her body, to smell that sweet mix of marigold, rain, and almonds from its source nestled right between her breasts.

I dressed quickly, my eyes often finding their way back to the fall of her tresses cascading over the sheets in ringlets of mocha. My beast was trying to talk me into crawling back into our little den with his mate and lavishing her with attention. He was even harder to resist when I didn't want to be more than a foot from her ever again. Gritting my teeth, I forced myself back into the hallway, past the small living area, and out into the courtyard. I had to see to the harvest numbers, check on the progress of the yield, go to the office, and cut paychecks for totocan at some point that day.

Counting up the food stores, I made a note of what would need to be refilled, regrown, harvested, or brought in to feed the totoco, its children, and any additional visitors that might wander in took about an hour. After that, it was time to swing through each of the small workshops that faced the open courtyard. Any of the various crafts the totoco employed, from leather-working to weaving to candle-making to pottery to the tending of herbs and spices, could require any number of different tools and materials to be refilled. My father had trained me to know each of them well enough to leave the craftsman to their devices and unobtrusively check to see that they were well supplied before they returned to their trade. He had believed that the job of the tecuhtli was to steward, not to lord over his people, and by extension, this was also how I cared for the totoco.

After tallying the restocking, the sun's golden rays breached the horizon, and the totoco would wake soon.

I went to the grills and lit them from the ever-burning fire kept in a special pot created anew each year, nodding to the night watch, Elian. I dropped a large, metal percolator-style coffee pot into the waking coals and filled it with water. Totocan would start flooding out of their rooms and from the surrounding small satellite huts that dotted the road up from the small town of Chinameca at the base of the volcano. This was one of my favorite things to do for the totoco. Wake them with the scent of the coffee roasted from the fields around our volcano.

I grinned at my cousin as she stumbled into the courtyard from her shared rooms. "Good morning, Julia."

"Go fuck yourself," she snapped before eyeing the pot. She was up earlier than usual . . . or I had lazed about in bed with Xochitl longer than I intended. "You're late. Dibs on the first."

Julia wasn't my blood cousin. She was the daughter of Antu's sister. And while we would never truly be blood-related, she had been just three years my junior by the time we had migrated here. We grew up together and were as close as they came. I'd call her my sister, except that would make that summer when she was seventeen exceptionally awkward. More awkward than it had been.

When the coffee was done, I snatched a clay mug from the cabinet a few feet away. As demanded, Julia got the first cup. She took it with grateful hands and didn't even bother to wait for it to cool off. Julia had never been a morning person, and I doubted that would ever change. The pain of the burn made her snap and bite at the air trying to cool it.

Between snorted laughter, I blew on my coffee, watching her carefully. I knew the deal. Four sips. That was the exact amount of coffee that was required not to end up at the business end of whatever Julia could find to hit me with should I talk too much. Sip two came with much the same, biting and snarling at the agony, but she was still determined to down the piping hot ambrosia. I took my first sip, my own having cooled. Sip three. Her shoulders uncurled from around the mug, and she rolled her neck to the sound of popping and a groan. Sip four had her eyes open to a normal aperture, her mouth uncurling from the angry-zombie scowl.

All safe.

"So," I opened.

A lame salvo, but I anticipated the fight that was coming.

She cocked a brow at me. "So help me, Itzatecuani. If you ask me to do something despicable to that girl, I am going to castrate you *and* make you do it yourself."

I feigned offense. It was a fair accusation. She knew exactly how calculating I had been in acquiring my mate again. I had hunted down any method by which to bring her to me and stopped at nothing. Including challenging the sitting head of the Council, who objected to my claim that the ceremony was valid, then doubly objected to my refusal to let country borders dictate whether I could have her. César and I would never let it slip she was human.

"Nothing too unsavory. Just a simple recon mission." She sipped again, letting me hang myself, most likely. "Something is . . . different about her. She—"

"Do you mean aside from the fact that she's not ten fucking years old and in pigtails still?"

I scowled at her. "Don't interrupt me. And yes, aside from having grown up. Something is different. She feels different. Not just in body. Shut up. I know, and I never thought of her like that at that age. Fuck, Julia. I mean it. I don't know what it is, but something is completely different. If Javier hadn't kept an eye on her all these years, I would swear she isn't the same person."

She sipped again, emptying it, then shook the cup at me in a silent demand for more. Julia was many things, but a well-mannered lady before noon was not one of those things. I filled her cup, then set another out to cool.

She took it gratefully, mumbling a "thanks," which was the closest thing to manners one could expect before cup two. "And you want me to do what about it?"

"See if you can find anything out. See if you can figure out anything. Even just something small. Something I can work with. She would never tell me, at least not right now, that is. Maybe in a few months, but now? When she doesn't trust me, remember me or know who I am to her? Never. She's too guarded. She wasn't this guarded before." I frowned into the last bit of my coffee.

It bugged me all night and chased me in my dreams, where she was an ever-present figure. The distance I felt was something more than the distance of time. It was something deeper than that, but I could not pin it down nor wrestle it out from her grasp so I could examine it in the light.

Pensive, Julia sipped. "I can try. She is just as guarded with me. Well . . . maybe a little less, seeing as I didn't handcuff her to a fucking bed the first day she was here."

She glared at me over the cup. "Don't think I have forgotten that shit. That was fucked, even for you. Do it again, and you'll be guzzling rue with your dinner."

I snorted and handed her the mug I had let cool beside me. "It's about time for her to have woken up. Let me know."

"You know your whole stalker thing probably isn't helping. Knowing when she wakes up is a little weird, even for us." She chugged the last bit of her coffee and chucked the cup at my head. Wild beasts were how we bred them, and I maybe was a bit too lenient on that particular cadejo. She took the cup from me and flipped me off as she sauntered in to wake my mate.

CHAPTER FIFTEEN
Itziquetzal

I paced, checking my watch, itching to be near her again. It had been a little under twenty minutes since I sent Julia in. "Fuck it," I grumbled before making my way into our rooms.

I could hear her chatting with Julia in the bathroom. A deep breath filled my lungs as I reached out to the spirit that coursed through my soul. I gathered the shadows my kind was known for and wrapped my bare feet in them, letting the icy sensation pump through my heart and blood. My footfalls were swallowed by the deafening of the inky smoke around me as I stalked my prey. My beast paced with delight between the shards of spirit energy, grinning at our game.

I made it to the cracked door jamb of the bathroom without being heard by Julia, who was teaching my glorious goddess of a mate how to braid her hair in the traditional style. The ribbon often worn around her wrist was woven into one half of Xochitl's head, and she instructed her to do the other side.

I watched, a silent observer to their grooming lesson, just out of Julia's periphery and out of the angle of the mirror they were sitting at. The sun streamed through the bathroom window, painting Xochitl in gilded beams that lovingly stroked her cheek, and I was struck again at how beautiful she had grown up to be. Her dark brows were delicately drawn down in concentration as she parted her earthen hair into three parts, then placed the end of the ribbon on top of the middle section. Slowly and methodically, she plaited the silk tresses I loved to curl around my finger, keeping the ribbon flat on the section. When she completed the braid, she executed the two knots that held the ends.

"Good, Cihuatlatoani. Now, wrap the ends of the braids around the back of your head, cross them in the back and then bring them up to the band at the top. Don't put it too low in the back, or it will bother you all day. When you get to the front, I want you to find the band and tie a tight knot to secure them. One or two should be fine. Then tuck the tails of the ribbon under the band and the braids. Bring them to the front and then tie a pretty bow." Xochitl tied the bow in the front. "Good. Now, simply tuck the ends of the braids under themselves, and you're done."

Julia beamed down at Xochitl, and she gazed up at my cousin in a way that made my gut churn with jealousy.

"Perfect."

"She is, isn't she?" I said, cutting into their conversation.

Both women turned to face me, pushing up to stand, as if caught with their hands in a cookie jar. Julia glowered at me. I'm sure she expected me. Xochitl flashed a quick quirk of her lips into a smirk that was gone as fast as a flash, then replaced it with a scowl and then the imperious cold mask that she liked to use in my presence.

"How long have you been standing there?"

Her voice was flat, my beast writhing under my skin at its emotionless void.

I rolled my shoulder in a casual shrug, my simple white T-shirt straining against my muscular form. "Long enough. You look beautiful, nayeli."

Julia rolled her eyes and excused herself, passing through the bathroom and trying to exit.

I stopped her at the door and switched to Nahuatl. "Did you find anything out?"

She smiled with feigned pleasure. A smile I knew far too well. She was trying to lead Xochitl into a misunderstanding about the nature of our conversation. Julia was as smart as a whip and just as brutal. Her cunning was one of the many things I adored about my cousin.

"It's been less than an hour, you impatient swine. But, if you must know, yes. She blooms under praise. Specifically, when she is given a task and earns that praise. It's like she's never received a single compliment. Now, if you don't get out of my way so I can get another cup of coffee, I'm going to gut you like a fish and use your parts to shovel goat shit."

"There should be at least two cups left for you by now, I wager. Get out of here you snapping dog. Oh, and tell Nopaltzin I'm assigning him an apprentice." I smiled after her retreating form, then zeroed in on Xochitl.

Her plush, curvy form, built for sinking fingers into the flesh while she screamed my name, was hidden from my eyes by the thin cotton nightgown I'd set out for her that morning. The sight of her wrapped in clothing I'd provided for her had a primal effect on me. My cadejo and I purred internally with the ability to provide for her, keep her comfortable . . . even if seeing her hidden from my hungry gaze made me want to shred her clothing and make her beg me for release again.

Memories of being in this bathroom with her and shredding her shirt made me grind my teeth against the urge to wrap my hand around her throat and have her kneeling before me. I swept my gaze up and down her body, imagining running my tongue along her heated skin and tasting her sweat again. She shivered as I prowled toward her, set on getting my fingers on her silken flesh.

She rocked back on one foot, her eyes meeting mine. "What does that mean?"

A slight tremble clipped her voice, one I would have missed if it weren't for my hyperawareness of the littlest things about her in this tiny space.

"What does what mean?"

My beast inched into my voice, husking and deepening it with our shared lust for her.

"Nayeli. You've been calling me that since we first met."

She turned to the mirror, trying to act normal, as if I couldn't smell the sweet, slightly salty scent of her pussy weeping in invitation. She fidgeted with the bow atop her crown of braids. A hint of a tremble to the dexterous fingers drew my predator's eye.

I sniffed, scenting the air. The bloom of her arousal was sorted through in search of the mouthwatering aroma of fear, but I found none. That was already an improvement from the last time we had shared this tiled space. My cadejo snorted his disapproval. He liked the taste of his mate mixed with the flavor of fear.

"Not since I met you. I called you teocuitlateotl when we first met. But that was a very long time ago, wasn't it? And you've already taunted us enough with being unable to remember." I sucked my teeth in disapproval, finding them elongated just enough to be noticeable in my mouth. I crept behind her, within arm's reach of my prey. "But, to answer your question, it means princess in Nahuatl."

I caught her gaze in the mirror. I could almost see the slightest shimmer in her chestnut gaze. A hint, a little fairy glitter marking out the path ahead. "Which you have always been. You have always been my golden princess."

My hand snaked out, unable to keep myself from feeling the heat of her against me any longer. Blood raged and howled with the acute need just to feel her against me again, to feel the solid weight of her body pressed against my own. I flexed my fingers against the rise of her hip and slid against the thin fabric possessively, pulling her toward me. "And you will be again."

Menace dripped in my voice, the power of the spirits emboldening my cadejo, who lurked at the edges of my psyche. Ever since I had first held her again on that beach, the barrier between my world and his had become thinner than a wish. His needs became mine, and mine, his. It took more of an effort not to give in to the whispering temptation of him when we were so close to her. We both had been starved of her for far too long. I should have collected her sooner.

I pulled her back flush against my chest. Her heat melted into my skin as I lowered my face to the crook of her neck. My nose nudged at the tender flesh where, one day, when she agreed to it, I might carve my mark upon her.

"I don't know who you think I was before, Sal, but I'm not her anymore. I doubt I will ever be her again. You should get used to the idea of disappointment if that's all you wanted me for . . . to be here and fulfill that weird obsessive image you have in your head."

I snarled a warning into her ear. In the world of black cadejos, who fed on the fear of others, it was a tempting sound. It was a sound to lure the fear from the pores of our partners so we could lick it from their flesh like an intoxicant.

The sparkling chill of the spirit power manifesting shimmered through the base of my spine and, like a gusting blizzard, rippled through my flesh to slice shallow paper cuts at my nail beds, lengthening my fingers into claws. I let those sharp black talons prick into her hip, just enough to let the slight amount of pain trickle into her mind.

"You will be. Or you will regret it."

That rumbling growl was all beast-powered. He let the claws sink into her flesh deeper than I had intended. He sensed her growing desire just as I did.

So, my little mate enjoyed the games we played just as much as we did. My beast chuffed with delight and nipped at her ear lobe with his sharpened teeth. She squirmed just slightly in my arms, and I let my lips travel down the hammering of her heart in her throat to that junction again.

Games would be played. I was a master at these games, and leaving her on the precipice, begging for me, had become my new favorite drug.

"Get dressed. We have things to do today, nayeli. And as much as I'd like to sink into your flesh and explore all the ways I could remind you of who you are, I do not have time today." I whispered into her ear, dark and dangerous, watching the hairs on her arms rise and her toes curl. "I'll be in the courtyard with the others. Come find me when you are dressed."

I placed a chaste kiss on the place where my mark would one day live, then stepped away, heading for the door. I could smell the heavy perfume of her wanton need in the air. I licked my lips, hoping to catch the ghost of her taste.

"You don't get to boss me around like that, fucker."

My cadejo perked up. The sound in her voice, the sound of golden bracelets tinkling against each other, was the sound of our mate. I turned on my heel, hopeful I would finally see her again after all this time, but if she had been there, she had already retreated behind the glacial walls of the woman before me.

"Fucker? Yes . . . Indeed, I am. And I will show you . . . soon. And, yes, I do get to boss you around. I am tecuhtli here. You are on my lands. In my home. In my territory. And you are my wife. I could throw you against the gate and fuck you until you bleated my name for the teotl, and no one would stop me." Microscopic flecks of gold winked in her eyes as I stepped closer and leaned down until I was nose-to-nose with her, hunting those sparks like the predator I was. "Or I could drag you out by your hair into the courtyard and claw ribbons of your skin off of your body, and no one would stop me. Do not test me, nayeli. I love you, and you are my mate, but never forget who and what I am."

She glared up at me. A tempestuous hurricane mated with a violent earthquake rampaging across the oak and chestnut planes of her eyes. Those microscopic specks became full-fledged flashes of glitter, and my beast and I held in our venator's grin. She was in there. We just had to keep pushing and pulling until we could free her.

"Now, get dressed." I flicked her nose with the end of my claw and sauntered out of the bathroom, leaving her there roiling in her anger.

I loved the flash of defiance in her eyes. It called to me like a siren perched atop razor-sharp reefs. It burned through me and thickened my cock. I adjusted the heft of it in my black jeans and chuckled silently. That flash of gold felt like it had been attached to my balls.

I grinned into the burning bright sunlight bathing the courtyard in fire. Two of my hunters were getting breakfast from the cooks, with Julia tending to them. Ixchel reclined against one of the tables, blood weeping from a nasty slash on her muscular calf. I lofted my brows at her in question as I passed and took a crockery plate from Julia's extended hand.

"Caymen. Big fucker." My brows nearly lept off of my face, and she went on. "Tracked a boar into the swamps of the river a few miles from here. Didn't see it hunting the boar, too, when I took it down. It snapped and only managed to get my leg. Cheeno pulled me free before it could spin, but I nearly lost my leg."

I looked over to the tall cadejo, who was kissing his mate's cheek as he handed Cheeno a plate. Maneuvering behind him, he prepped to brush out his hair to braid it.

My gaze darted back to Ixchel. "I'll expect you to honor him and his mate."

She tilted her head to the side in a sign of obedience and nodded. "Of course, Itzatecuani. I wouldn't dream of it being otherwise. Without him, I'd be legless *and* mateless. Not a fate I want."

Grunting my approval, I nodded.

Cheeno and Rafael came to our totoco only recently, from being exiled from a totoco in Honduras. While it was not entirely unusual for males to mate with each other, few totocos accepted this mating, instead holding to the Invader's assumption of the sanctity of male-to-female unions. It was a foreign concept to most of our ancestors, and, often, the spirits favored these matings with additional gifts. My totoco embraced them the moment they petitioned us to allow them sanctuary.

César finally appeared, medical bag in hand, and unwound the shirt Ixchel had wrapped around her leg. I nodded to him, shoveling the food Julia had offered into my mouth, unconcerned. Ixchel was in safe hands. She could heal the human way, or she could petition César to speak to the spirits on her behalf. Knowing Ixchel as I did, she would choose the human way. No hunter would miss the chance to add a scar to their ever-growing tapestry of accomplishments emblazoned upon their flesh. So, it came as no surprise when she whispered a request to enter the temple and dedicate her suffering and blood to the teotl. César would take that as an honor and would guide her, as he had always done, in finding an appropriate sacrifice of honor to Cheeno and Rafael.

I turned my attention away from them, safe in the knowledge that my second had Ixchel and her needs well in hand. As I tore a bite from a strip of spiced meat, my eye caught on the loping gait of Antonio as he approached.

Fuck.

My eyes darted between Ixchel, who was still wrapped in conversation with César and Antonio, who didn't seem to notice that the blood-stained rag he was frowning at belonged to his ex-girlfriend. The last time the two had been in the same place, I had to break them up from killing each other. Antonio had committed the ultimate sin, one I had just threatened my mate with, violence upon a woman in the totoco. She had every right to kick his teeth down his throat, just not at the totoco compound and, certainly, not without a single totocan to witness it but me.

She could have called the rite of contrition to order. She would have the right to take his life for the sin of striking her in anger. She knew, though, that, while it would be her choice—had she brought the priests and the rest of the totoco to the fight grounds in the heart of the slumbering giant of our home—he would have been forced to settle his debt to her, and that would have meant his death. The only other option for him would have been to walk away in shame with whatever wounds she deemed acceptable, and he would have been exiled from the totoco. Antonio was a financial pillar of the totoco, and that choice, while no one would have held it against her, would have impacted the entire compound.

I had always treasured Ixchel for her dedication to the stability of the totoco over her desire for retribution and justice. That didn't mean Antonio had gotten off clean from his crime, though. I made sure that he had an appointment with the rest of the hunters to ensure that mistake would never be repeated. An appointment that still pained him on cold days and had kept him under César's care for close to two months.

There were few things that this totoco did not tolerate between couples. Striking your partner was tantamount to signing a death warrant. I had put several cadejos to death, returning their spirit to the realm beyond for harming one of our own before, and would not hesitate to do it again. While the world around us, from the border of the United States to the tip of South America, waged a hidden war on the women of their communities, turning a blind eye to the femicide, rape, and abuse they'd face daily, we did not. The cadejos of that same area had all sworn an oath never to allow it on their totoco grounds.

The women of our kind, while just as common as normal human women, were cherished as the warriors they were. Only they could bring new life into the world. They not only held the map and keys to the gates of life, but they also held the same for the path to the afterlife. Only a female priest could properly perform the intercession prayers, sacrifices, and rituals befitting a cadejo. Only their hands could guide our human spirits and the spirit of the cadejo nestled within it to their appropriate places in the beyond.

César had always been a spot of contention for the mystic women for being one of the few males called to their path. He was called as a child to walk the worlds between, and it had been reflected in the appearance of his traded form ever since. His cadejo form, as well as his half-traded monstrous form, had sacrificed its physical prowess to turn its strength toward its connection with the world of our ancestors and the spirits that resided there. He had to prove himself before the Council of the Smoking Sun, a yearly convening of totoco leaders throughout our continent and their spiritual advisors, numerous times when he was younger. No one wanted to believe a male could be properly devoted enough to the cause of the teotl, offering his might to their hunger. Their doubts had turned to dust and ash by now.

Tension rippled through the air of the courtyard as the other members of the totoco watched Antonio stride toward me, and, by extension, within clawing distance of Ixchel—should she notice him. He seemed focused on me as I scrubbed at the unshaved bristle at my square jawline. Thankfully, the two of them seemed not to notice each other, and by the time he made it to me, I knew that he had other things on his mind.

I angled my body to block his view from Ixchel and the kneeling César. "Piyalli, Antonio."

He scowled at me. "We have a problem."

It was not Antonio's usual way to be so abrupt with me in earshot of the rest of the totoco. He preferred to pretend that he hadn't broken my nose once or twice when I was lost to the rage or drunk on the fear, lost to the clutches of Itzatecuani.

"What problem could we possibly have?"

"That useless baboso she came with? Jake? He's starting to ask questions about where she is," he grumbled. "I've told him she got food poisoning and has been in her room, but it's been a few days now, and he's not accepting that anymore."

I took the strip of spiced meat from my plate, folded it around a bite of beans, and popped it into my mouth, sucking the juices from my fingers. "And? You know my answer. I don't care who is looking for her. Kill them if they get too nosey."

With a long-suffering sigh, he rolled his eyes at me. "You can't just go around killing everyone who annoys you, Itzatecuani."

I lofted my brows at him from over the plate I was holding up to my chin as I stood, eating. "Can I not? Says who? The police? The totoco? The Council? Who says exactly?"

He threw his hands in the air and barked, "I don't know, Itzatecuani! You just don't do that!"

I shrugged at him, scooping up the last of my beans with a spear of plantain. As far as I was concerned, this was a nonissue. "It's simple, Antonio. If he comes here, I will kill him. To the rest of the world, he will simply leave the country. He will be seen at the airport by our totocan, boarding a flight to Ecuador with that prostitute he picked up. The tickets will show that they both got on the plane. She will find a nice cozy house somewhere in Komat's territory, where she will be cared for when he eventually breaks her heart to run off with someone else. It's that easy. I don't see why you are upset. Xochitl is mine now, and she will never leave me again. They relinquished their claim to her the moment she got into Javi's car."

He sighed and shoved a hand through his short black hair. His eyes cast to the sky as he mumbled a prayer. If he were looking for the teotl to save him, he was looking in the wrong place. It didn't matter who was looking for Xochitl. She was my mate. I had her, finally, and I wasn't letting anyone come between us ever again.

"Your fucking schemes will be the death of me."

I smirked. "If you think I'm letting you off that easy, you're very wrong, brother."

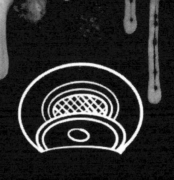

CHAPTER SIXTEEN

ITZIQUETZAL

I t was late afternoon when I spotted the plume of dust rising up the road that led to our compound. My gaze darted around the open courtyard from the hood of the flatbed truck I was working on with Phelix. Xochitl was nowhere in sight. Good. She would be with the potter, Nopaltzin, who had taken her on as his apprentice that morning. Whatever was coming would be away from her until I deemed it safe.

As the black Cadillac, now covered in a coat of red dirt, rumbled up to me, I gripped the thin veil between our world and the spiritual realm. I felt the icy fingers of spirit power caress the nape of my neck before soaking into my essence. I kept the exchange on the razor's edge, waiting for whatever danger there was to announce itself.

The driver climbed out of the front seat, then opened the passenger door as I grabbed a rag to clean my hands. The man climbing out of the vehicle wasn't who I was expecting. I anticipated another cartel enforcer to try and strong-arm me again. Instead, a man nearly half a foot shorter than me, his skin a split tomato red from too much sun in a tight-fitting business suit, climbed out and sniffed his disapproval.

"You. Do you live here?" he asked in the worst accented Spanish I had ever heard.

It was so bad, even the driver winced.

"This is mine," I replied in English back to him. "Can I help you?"

"Oh, good. You speak English. That will make this much easier."

I rolled my eyes. Who came to a Latin American country and didn't at least attempt to learn some of the languages and instead assumed everyone should speak English?

"What do you want, gabacho?" I asked, tossing the rag onto the open engine.

I held up a hand to Phelix when he made a move to come around the other side of the flatbed to stand with me. I didn't need him. Whoever the noodle-armed white boy was, even without my cadejo, I could easily punch his ticket to the deadlands.

"Have you seen this woman?" he asked, shoving a picture of Xochitl into my face. "She's an associate of mine, and I was told she was seen up here."

I frowned down at the picture of her in her drab navy-and-cream business suit standing next to Roberto and Shayne. The latter had his arm draped possessively over her shoulder. "And if I have?"

"If you *have*, then you need to go tell her to come out. It's time she went home."

He was annoyed with me . . . good.

"And you are?"

"Jake. Jake Lassiter."

Ah. Of course. The hot steaming pile of garbage Antonio kept complaining about.

"Well, Jake Lassiter, I have seen the lady. And she is perfectly happy where she is. So. Either get off my fucking volcano, or I'll feed you to the crocs."

He chuckled the dark derisive laugh of someone who had gotten confused and thought he was in control. "Nah, I don't think so, pal. Her dad is my boss, and that's not how this works. So, be a good boy and run along. Go get her."

Cocking a brow at him, I folded my powerfully muscled arms over my chest. "I said the lady is happy where she is. I will tell you only once more. Get off my volcano."

Jake made the mistake of reaching back, a sudden movement that perked my beast up to the scent of prey. The ripe tang of terror bloomed redolent on the mid-afternoon air like split peaches basking in the sun from where they had fallen from the tree—sticky, sickly sweet, and musky. Jake might not have shown it on the outside, but he was scared, afraid of something. Either me, the smartest choice at hand, or something else.

Phelix sniffed behind me, smelling it as well.

"Look, how much do you want? I know you people out here all speak cold, hard cash. Just give me the girl, and I'll give you . . ." He flipped through a fistful of money. "A thousand?"

I didn't move, didn't speak. A thousand fucking dollars. Was that Xochitl's worth to these people?

Seeing my lack of movement, he threw the cash at me.

Phelix snorted. "Big mistake. Big."

The snap of my wrist was faster than Jake could react to. My massive hand circled his throat and drew his body toward me as I let Itzatecuani bleed into my voice. "Xochitl is mine."

"Wh—Who?!" he choked out, his red-backed fingers coming up to claw futilely at my iron grip.

Smiling down at him, I let him see the fangs that studded my jaws with deadly purpose. "You've made a grave error coming here, gabacho."

Terror pulsed through him, stiffening his muscles and bulging his eyes. I could hear Phelix trading shadows behind me.

"Oh, fuck this!" screamed the driver, who jumped into the Cadillac and floored a full-speed, backward descent of the mountain.

I smirked as the realization that he was right and properly fucked dawned in Jake's eyes. I licked my fangs, then turned to the towering beast Phelix traded into. "Eat well, my friend. When you are done, kill him. Feed him to the crocodiles or the sharks. I don't care which one. Just make sure he's not found."

I turned my attention back to the struggling man held by the throat. "You should have never come, Jake Lassiter."

Jake found his tongue then and screamed at the top of his lungs. I shrugged and tossed him like a rag doll to Phelix. Seconds later, a pale inky shadow surrounded Jake's mouth, silencing his still screaming head.

I walked away to find my mate. As long as she never knew Jake had come for her, all would be well. I couldn't afford for her to know.

CHAPTER SEVENTEEN

I woke to the sensation of a large, warm hand snaking under the coverlet and slithering up my thigh. If I moved or breathed too hard, would he stop? Keeping my breathing the same—or trying to—I held still. The callouses and the rough palm of his hand made me want to shiver. If I stayed here, in this shimmering in-between time, where neither of us was at war, and it was just two hungry bodies in the sheets, could I savor this without guilt?

The hand unfurled across my lower belly, pressing softly into its supple flesh. His chest pressed against my back, and the thick stiffness of his cock wedged itself between my ample ass cheeks. His breath dusted across the expanse of my naked shoulder, silken raven tresses whispering across my bare neck. I wanted to lean into him, to reach up and capture his head in my palm so he couldn't pull away.

Feather-soft kisses rained against my skin, kicking my lazy heartbeat into alertness. Goosebumps rose against my arms and legs as he pulled me back snugly against him.

"Nayeli. Beautiful mate. How I have longed for you to be here with me. How I have dreamed of touching you in the mornings like this. How I have dreamed of tasting your skin. Amo nica in atle tehuatl . . ."

He murmured first in Spanish, then trailed into soft words in that gorgeous language I had learned was Nahuatl, a language spoken by so many indigenous peoples across Central America. Julia promised she would teach me some, but lessons hadn't started, and I had no idea what he was saying. At least not in the way of understanding the words. I knew deep in my soul he was murmuring words of passion.

I shifted, unable to hold still, with his hand roaming the rounded flesh of my belly. My slight shift brought a hint of friction to the length seated between my cheeks, and he groaned.

"Are you awake, my beautiful golden girl?" he murmured in English in my ear.

I purred a low hum.

My response emboldened his stroking hand that now traveled up my belly to cup one of my large breasts. Nimble fingers gripped the dusky brown peak of my hardening nipple and squeezed gently. I groaned at the sensation and stretched languidly against him.

Kisses rained down on my neck and throat. The sound of my heartbeat thrummed in my ears in an intoxicating bass.

His scent filled my senses, warm and bare of perfumes. Just the scent of his skin and the spices that his special musk inspired in my periphery.

His fingers rolled my nipple, and spikes of delicious pleasure throbbed lazily into my blood. This was a slow seduction, so different from the intensity I associated with him. He made me feel like I was on fire on an average day, but in that moment, I felt like I *was* the fire, merrily chewing at the logs of delight he fed me from kiss to rolling fingers. My hips moved without me telling them to, responding to the slow, dulcet temptation his solid body posed.

He sighed into the delicate shell of my ear and drew heavy breaths. Neither of us was in a rush to frantically come together like we had done that first time. We were just as content to lay in the warm cavern of the blankets for however long it took us to drown in each other, with the early summer air dancing through the open window to skirt across our exposed skin.

Sliding a hand under my body to drag fingertips along the length of my side, he elicited a gasped moan. I had never known how soft, sensual touches to my sides could make my pussy weep with longing.

Burying his nose into the nape of my neck, he drew in deep breaths as my languorous hips drew him across their velvety flesh, teasing him just as his fingers playing across my hip and nipples teased me.

"Beloved," he whispered in a pleading whimper.

"Sal," I responded in kind.

Heavy breaths disturbed the drape of my curls he buried his face in.

"I can smell how much you need me. Tell me what you want."

His demanding tone would have otherwise put me off, but my brain gripped onto the other thing he said.

"You can smell me?"

He chuckled darkly. "I can. You smell like need and want. You smell like a meal I could gobble up for the rest of eternity, and if you don't let me feast on you soon, I'm likely to go mad."

I groaned in embarrassment, and he chuckled.

The hand that had been playing at my tits finger-walked down my belly and began caressing the short cropped thatch of hair between my closed thighs. The threat of more made my pulse rise, and I rocked back into him in a silent request.

"You smell like a promise I've been waiting my whole life to fulfill." Slipping his finger between the puffy petals of my pussy, he dipped into the dampening nectar dripping from it. Teasing nudges to my clit drew gasps from me as I returned the favor with more rocking along his length. "I could drink you for breakfast, lunch, and dinner. I smell you dampening for my touch, and it drives me crazy with need, nayeli. I want to bury my face in you every time I see you, but when I can smell your need calling for me, it takes every drop of my willpower not to throw you over my shoulder, find a quiet place to sit you on, and just eat your pussy until you scream yourself hoarse."

"Neanderthal." I snickered up to him as he played with the throbbing pearl of wantonness at my apex.

I wanted to be wittier. I wanted to tell him all the same things or even dare him to do so next time, but a little snake dripped poison in my ear to be careful of this man.

Another finger joined the other and slid lower and lower in his enervated enticement. I groaned a needy sound that dripped from my lips and forced my hips to meet his fingers.

"Please," I begged softly, grinding my pussy into his teasing fingers.

A growl snapped from his lips. One moment, I was on my side with Sal pressed against me, and the next, I was flat on my back with him kneeling between my legs.

"Again. Say it again," he commanded.

I fluttered my lashes at him.

He grinned wickedly, teasing my opening, just enough to give me a taste of what was to come. Just enough to tease my hungry slit with the promise of more to sate her hunger. The other hand snaked up around my throat and nudged against it. Alarm slithered through me like molasses on a cold day, dribbling into my blood with difficulty.

I wanted to bravely dare him to choke me, to carry out the bodily violence he had threatened before, but I felt no real danger in his touch. Instead, his tightening grip drew out a thorn of lust.

He grinned down at me and pressed harder. "Say it again, nayeli."

"Please," I whimpered, need and excitement coloring the words into a kaleidoscope of emotions.

The feral grin I was so familiar with took up residence on his face again, and he notched his cock at the teased, drooling flower he had been toying with.

I moaned and shifted my hips to welcome him deeper, only for his grip on my throat to tighten.

"Greedy princess. You beg so pretty. It's music to my ears."

He slowly stroked his cock into my clenching depths, just the head. Just enough to keep the tease up for both of us. The way his girth stretched me shot sparks of pain wrapped in intoxicating ecstasy to smash against my grip on reality.

"You will have only what I give you." He stroked in a bit deeper as he talked.

My hands reached out to hold on to his hips, trying to pull him closer. I needed him to be buried so deep I could taste his cock. I needed him, the sensation tightening in my core, drowning my better senses.

He swatted at my hands, then looped them into his grip. "Only what I give you. And nothing more."

"Please, Sal. You left me wanting the other day. Please, I need to come so bad," I whimpered up to him.

Grinning down at me, he loosened his grip on my throat just enough for me to feel a little more comfortable, but his hand didn't wander too far. "I did. And now, here you are, squirming and begging for my cock. Begging me to fill you up and plant my get." His eyes traveled down my body to where we were joined, his hips leisurely drawing his length in and out of my grip. His mouth dipped, searing heat circling my nipple as his tongue rolled and sucked greedily at that bundle of nerves. Teeth pressed into it, as he assaulted the other with his nimble fingers, washing my senses in a twin spark of pleasure. The icy chill of his mouth abandoning me was quickly replaced by the heat puddling in my depths as his molten whisper came to my ear. "Beg me. Beg me to let you come for me. Beg me to fuck you deep and hard. Tell me how much your needy cunt wants to milk my cum from my cock until I fill you to the brim. Beg me, sweet flower, to plant my get in your womb, and I'll let you come for me."

I snorted. "Pregnant? With your child? I doubt it."

His wild eyes flashed up to me, anger sparking behind the cool pools of darkness. "Is that so?"

"Yup."

"We shall see." That grin curled up again, erasing the existence of the anger that had, just a moment ago, sparked in them. "We shall see."

He finally thrust himself all the way in, splitting me wide around him and burying himself deep inside of me. We both groaned with the sensation, the relief of finally fitting together the way we were supposed to.

Sal made love to me, slow and gentle, a passionate edge to every moment until we fell over the edge together, and he drowned my pussy with his hot, spurting cum.

I expected him to roll off of me immediately, but he stayed buried, staring down at me, stroking my cheek with his thumb.

"We will be going into town today, nayeli." He pet my mussed curls. "I want you to wear the barrettes I gave you. And the dress."

I cocked a brow at him. "Weird request but okay. It won't get dirty?"

"Oh, it will get very dirty. Especially because you will be walking around with my cum inside you all day. Smelling of our rutting."

I sputtered. "What?"

He grinned and snatched a roll of medical tape César had left on my nightstand. His cock, still stiff and ready for the next round, slid from my aching pussy. I tried to roll away, but his strong arms caught me before I could wriggle out from under him.

"Oh, no, nayeli. You will learn. Your smart mouth has consequences here."

"Let me go, you big oaf!"

"Never." I heard the stretch of the tape, then felt him pressing my lips together, the cold kiss of the tape sealing them. "Keep squirming, princess, and I'll fill your ass, too. I haven't tasted that delight just yet, and I do encourage you to keep it up. I hadn't planned on reveling in that just yet, but you could certainly convince me."

I bit my lip, holding so still a statue would be jealous of my form.

Sal burst into a roaring laugh as he flipped me with ease, my face pressed into the pillow. "Awwuh, nayeli, you would deny me?"

he said, his finger stroking my taped-shut pussy, gathering what small bit of our mingled juices he could find on the tip of his finger. He traced a lazy line up to my stiffly puckered hole that tried to hide from his attention. The tip swirled teasingly against the little hole, and I felt his head lean down closer to my flesh. I could feel his hot breath on the skin of my full ass cheek. "Mmm, I wonder if it's cheating to tickle you just a little here . . ."

Dropping his teasing finger, he danced it along the crease where my ass met my thigh.

I bit harder on my lip. Still. Stone still.

"Reach back, nayeli. Spread your ass wide for me," he purred, heating my skin. I didn't move, just in case this game was higher stakes than I thought. He barked a laugh again. "So . . . she can be taught to follow orders."

"I'm not a fucking dog, Sal. You'd think you, of all people, would know that," I hissed acerbically.

A crack of his hand on my ass sparked knives at my boundary walls, thinning them to a moan that gathered on my kiss-swollen lips.

His hand, hot from the stinging slap, stroked over the burn. "Spread."

I obeyed this time, not wanting a matching handprint on the other cheek. Leaning all the way forward so that my face was nearly buried in the pillow, I gripped each generous soft cheek, and pulled them apart from each other.

A murmuring of approval was my reward, and it felt like my throat seized and twitched with the knot that grew in my stomach, both from being so exposed and the sound of exultation in that simple hum.

His fingers began their exploration of my flesh again. My grip dug into the skin, desperate to yield to his whims and to the urge to thwart him.

"I wish I could explain to you how good you smell, cualcihuatl. You smell like heaven." He leaned down, his long hair brushing the backs of my thighs and fingers as he nuzzled the tape binding his gift within me, then the slope up to my ass. "A man could fall into your depths and drown happily."

The squeak of surprise cut off my wanton, hot moaning as the molten-hot tip of his tongue laved my ass in languid circles, then nudged at the tight band of my entrance. I relaxed into the slow, taunting strokes of his attention. I gulped deep and hard when I felt his searching fingers join his tongue by pressing the point of his knuckle into me.

Even with Shayne, I had never done this. I was nervous, intrigued, and most unsettlingly, I was enticed by the discordant emotions as my heart pumped them through my heated blood.

Sal's thick club of a cock nestled against my calf as he worked me to a cliff I had never explored before.

"From now on, noyzotzon, you are not to come without my permission," he murmured against my asshole, still working it with the tip of his knuckle, pressing, circling, thrusting millimeters at a time. "Do you agree?"

He could have asked me to fight a moose, single-handedly pull the moon from the sky, or go skinny-dipping on my period with a hundred great whites, and I probably would have asked him if I got to at least wear a hair tie to my execution. Anything he wanted, just as long as he gave me more of the sweet torture he had been drawing out with such wicked precision.

Pressing his knuckle farther, he breached the barrier. His other hand reached down and around to press against the flushed lips of my sealed pussy to tease my clit with a dull stroke when I longed for harder and more. "Say it, cihuapiltzintle."

"I don't get to come without your permission," I gasped out, unable to hold my whimper from seeping into my voice.

"Good girl."

Had two words ever sounded so inviting? I felt numb. I felt like I was on fire. I felt like, if it were possible, I would puddle up on the floor happily and ooze into the cracks.

My fingers were slipping as I ran joyfully up that cliff, blind to what was on the other side. Desperate to hold on and not to have him take away those priceless two words that made my very soul sing with an aria I had never heard, I dug my fingernails into my skin.

Sal hummed his approval. "Very good girl. Obeying at all costs. Now, if you remain a good girl all day, I will let you pick what method you earn my cum tonight. Hmm?"

Sharks, then? Sounds fun. Let's go swimming.

"Mmhmm," I purred out, unsure of what else to say.

When his fingers pulled away, and I was left bereft, cold, and unfinished, I cried out at the injustice. A playful smack came to the other ass cheek, one I knew from the slight bite, but no sting, wouldn't leave a mark like the other, which was still burning hot.

"Now, get up and get dressed."

CHAPTER EIGHTEEN

I did not expect our day out to be half as difficult as it had turned out to be. I had pulled my curls back into the barrettes, making do with extra conditioner from the shower to tame them. I put on the dress Sal had requested and a pair of flats that materialized from the chest at the foot of the bed. When I attempted to slip into a pair of panties, Sal, with a devilish grin, snatched them from my hand with a wink and slid them into his pocket.

Walking around in the tepid heat, with only medical tape as a barrier between me and a determined gust of wind, kept me on the edge of nervousness. Anxiety curled into a pulsing thrum of excitement, which was tempered by the heady knowledge that, at any moment, Sal's handprint would be on full display.

It wasn't until the end of the first hour, walking around the little rural town of Chinameca while Sal met with various townspeople, that the chafing of my thighs rubbing together cut that intoxicating thrill of the disparate emotions in half. Soon, the edge lost its novelty, and the stinging shuffle of flesh against flesh grounded me to reality.

I watched Sal talk to the mayor of the small town in English—thankfully—about the tourism to the volcano that was starting to encroach on the totoco's territory.

They were chatting amiably, in the way two serious businessmen—who were unwilling to budge from their respectful positions without serious concessions—did when I spotted it. A sleek black Cadillac prowled the street, the same type of Cadillac I had seen in La Libertad that catered to the few who could afford it as a taxi between towns.

My eyes snapped toward Sal, who was deeply engrossed with his back turned to me.

My heart pounded a battle drum in my chest, adrenaline ricocheting through my blood. I kept my eyes glued to the carved obsidian feather that dripped from the tie at the base of Sal's head by a silver chain. When I saw him first loop it into his hair, a smile of recognition passed my lips. It was the mate to the two in my hair currently.

I took a hesitant step backward, a spooked deer staring down the back of a predator's head. Sal did not react. I took another step back, eyes slicing between the sleek panther of a Cadillac as it prowled and the wolf in man's clothing in front of me. I was sure that, at any moment, Sal would catch my movement and whirl on me to snatch me back to his side. I made twenty backward paces before I hit the corner of the street. Ten steps to the left, and I would be out of sight.

A breeze danced around my ankles as if to shout, "Take the steps! Take the steps! Fly!"

Eyes never leaving that glistening black feather, I took one step to the left. Another. My heart screamed in its cage that, if I didn't do something soon, the entire country would hear its staccato rage. I took steps three, four, five, six all on my tiptoes, like a cheesy cartoon robber. Nothing. He didn't notice. He just nodded to the elderly man half his height. Could I really make it?

Two more steps between me and the car. The sting of my chafed thighs was drowned out by the narrowing of my field of vision, which focused on nothing but the back of Sal's head, until it finally disappeared behind the stucco wall of the building.

I was off as soon as I lost sight of that carved feather. My heart and lungs clanged with the fury of a thousand church bells as my feet brutalized the pavement with frantic footfalls. My skirt billowed in the breeze, giving everyone behind me a free peep show, but I didn't care. As if the heavens opened up and poured down golden luck, the Cadillac pulled down the street I was plunging toward.

I was going to make it! I was absolutely going to make it. I just had to keep running, and I would make it to that glossy black angel and be in La Libertad by the end of the afternoon! Just ten more paces!

I raised my arm to hail it, caught the eye of the driver, and he nodded to me. The knight in ebony armor was right there.

When my hand closed around the sun-warmed handle, I nearly cried with relief. After sliding into the back of the car, I closed the door behind me, daring to look down the street I had just run down. No sign of Sal.

Okay, so maybe I won't kill every last seagull on the planet. Maybe just one.

"Can you please take me to La Libertad, sir?" I asked, forcing my heaving lungs to gulp down a breath so I didn't sound like I was fighting for my life.

"Anywhere specific, señora?" he asked, catching my eye in the rearview mirror.

Think, Angie. Think, you stupid beast. Think!

"I think the hotel is called Encanta something?"

Wild guess. It's a tropical paradise. There had to be at least one enchanted something hotel, right?

"Acantilados, señora?"

"Yes! Acantilados, please. Sorry about that."

He shrugged dismissively and pulled out into traffic.

I wanted to scream. I wanted to laugh so loud that I'd sound like a maniac. I made it. I was free. I was going to make it back to La Libertad, and from there, I could contact Jake and get the hell out of this gods forsaken country. That's what I wanted, right?

I relaxed back against the seat and took three deep gulping breaths, trying to calm my heart that was still doing its best impression of a speaker at a dance club.

We turned down the main street and headed out toward what I assumed was the main highway out of the town, and the driver slammed on the brakes, forcing me forward.

Half a hitched breath later, the door to the opposite side of the car opened, and Sal slid into the back with me.

"Ah, there you are, mi cielo." His voice was even, so level I could hang shelves on it, but the eyes that locked on mine were blazing with fury. "Thank you for getting a car service. So thoughtful, my wife is."

The driver screwed his face up in confusion. "Señor?"

"Up to the rancho at the top of the volcano, por favor," Sal said with the fakest grin I'd ever seen, and that was a pretty high bar to set.

The driver frowned back and turned fully. "The lady said she needed to go to La Libertad."

Sal shrugged, nonchalance dripping from him. "She was mistaken. Our trip to La Libertad isn't until tomorrow, mi amor." He cast his gaze directly to the driver. "She gets confused easily since the accident."

"Ah. I see. Not an issue, señor."

Fuck. Fuck. Fuck. Fuck.

The car ride back to the compound was pregnant with silent rage rolling off of Sal and agonized nerves from me. He held my hand, and while I expected him to crush it with the amount of anger pouring from him, he never did. He simply curled his fingers around mine and held them still against his.

As we drew closer to the compound, dread pooled thick like tar in my belly and made my forehead sweat. Sal turned to me and drew in a deep breath but said nothing until he shut the door to the Cadillac and it was turning around to depart.

"Why are you scared?" he said to the tail lights illuminated by the cloud of red dust in its wake.

"W-What?" It was not what I expected him to say. I expected to see Itzatecuani ripping through his skin and heading to do the same to me.

"I asked why you are dripping with fear and puddling it in my driveway."

His voice was cold. So frigid I could get frostbite.

"I . . . because . . . I . . . What?" I stammered, finally daring to look at him.

He stared into the dust, his hands in his pockets, the muscle at his jaw tap dancing. He was silent, though. He wanted an answer.

"Because I ran?"

He finally turned, his rage-filled gaze leveling on me. I stumbled backward, a new wave of panic danced with the horror already floating ethereally in my mind. "You did. Unsuccessfully, I might add. Are you scared because you were caught? Or scared because of something else?"

"I . . . because you're going to punish me again?"

The corner of his lips twitched in a suppressed smile, but the rest of his face was still, frozen over by the tone in his voice. "Yes . . . I will."

He tilted his head, his gaze making an indulgent pass over my body. "The tape?"

My lashes fluttered wildly, and I choked out, "What?"

"The tape. Is it still in place? Or were you naughty enough to take it off?" He advanced, and I retreated. He stalked me, slow steps guiding me until he had me penned in. The gate was at my back, with the road in front of me and nowhere to run to. "Did you?"

I shook my head in denial. I hadn't even thought of disturbing the tape a single time all day.

"Words, Xochitl. You will use your damned words."

"N-No."

"Show me."

"What?!"

"I said"—his words were soft but made of iron slamming shackles around me—"show me."

"But . . ."

He lifted a brow, and a shiver of delight mixed with terror ran through me.

With a shaking hand, I reached for the hem of the pretty white dress that was quickly becoming a flag for so many memories.

"Stop."

I jerked to a halt. My heart, the poor bedraggled organ, was pounding in my ears again.

"Not like that. Turn around."

I wanted to hesitate. I wanted to tell him to go fuck himself, but I also wanted to see how far this would go. I wanted to feel that same rush of passion and pleasure mixed with the exhilaration of fear. After turning around, my eyes darted the courtyard beyond the bars of the gate. The evening feast was being prepared, and people teamed in the open space, preparing for the communal meal.

"Sal!" I hissed in a whisper. "They will see!"

"And?"

I whipped a baleful glare over my shoulder at him. He was unrepentant. A brow lofted at me. It told me to obey, and it told me to see what would happen if I didn't.

That exhausted creature that was now doing double time, pumping blood through my ears at a deafening volume, took up residence in my throat. I leaned forward at the waist, my forehead pressing into the bars as my hands hiked my skirt up in the back to show him.

Silence reigned emperor as the chariot of dusk approached the afternoon light. I didn't hear him approach but felt the flick of his wrist moving the skirt up further to rest around my hips.

"Hands on the bars."

My fingers wrapped around the sun-warmed bars, and I wished with all my might that they were the cold night-kissed bars that I had been pressed against last.

His hands slid over the naked bounty of my pale terra-cotta globes. I felt him kneeling between my legs, his hot breath fanning over my skin, making goosebumps freckle across my ass.

"Mmm, I see it's still in place." He ran his fingertip along the taped-shut seam, finding the swell of my clit, and pressed circles into it. I jerked, my legs suddenly losing all feeling as I longed to collapse into the sharp veering from one extreme to the other. He knew exactly how to twist and pull me to keep me on the edge of whiplash. "You have a choice now, Xochitl. Take whatever punishment I dole out for running away, or you can select your own punishment and hope it sates my beast."

His finger never ceased pressing pointed circles into my clit, the sensation muffled by the pillow of my lips.

"I . . ."

I couldn't think with him doing that. I understood at the back of my mind that I needed to be smart about my decision, but all I wanted was for him to keep that pace up.

He chuckled. "Make a choice."

"Punishment."

It was the only word I could think of saying.

"Very well." He moved his finger away from my clit, and I slumped against the bars, not daring to move.

A loud crack echoed through the courtyard as fire bloomed across my exposed cheek. A moan slipped through my lips, and my eyes slid shut. Once again, with the calloused palm of his hand heated by the strike, he pet over the fire. The sensation fought with the pain of the smack, and I drew a deep, shuddering breath.

"Eyes open, Xochitl."

Lust-glazed languor made complying ten times harder than I expected. I didn't want to see the totocan staring at me as I got my ass battered. I wanted to just stay in the bubble, with Sal and me being its only residents. The surprise of not a single pair of eyes turning our way only barely registered before the next strike.

By the eighth strike, I was panting with the heady cocktail of need and pain. It drowned out everything around me except for the scent of Sal, the feel of his hand always connected to my skin until the next strike. It bled away the reality that just twenty feet away were the gathered totocan, blissfully ignoring my humiliation at their gate.

When his hand stroked away the burn of the tenth strike, he pressed me into the bars with his body, just like he had the other night.

"Never run from me again, nayeli." He leaned down and kissed a blazing path up my throat. "Now, go inside and clean up for dinner. You may take off the tape. You will not wear panties for the rest of the week. Any that I find on you, I will tear off, and I won't replace them. You will find lotion in the medicine cabinet. You may use it on your thighs but not on your ass. Those marks, I want to lick tonight, when the totoco goes to sleep."

A nip was given to my ear, a flick of his hand covering my molten-hot skin, and a gentle pat was given to my rump as I dragged myself past the gate.

"Good girl."

When had my legs been replaced by Jell-O? I wasn't entirely sure, but I was oddly not opposed to it.

CHAPTER NINETEEN
ITZIQUETZAL

She was sitting on the bed when I came to find her for dinner, one leg draped over the mattress, the other kicking over the lip at the floor. Her hair was dripping into the towel wrapped around her shoulders, and she was wearing one of my old shirts. It pooled around her and made her curvaceous body look tiny and frail.

Mine, howled my beast as he pushed me toward her. He wanted to curl around her protectively, like a dragon on his horde. I wondered idly if she knew how affected we were by that pensive look pulling her goddess features into a sad mask.

I shut the door and leaned against it, my arms crossing over my chest. My hand still stung from the spanking I had to give her. She had gotten into a car with a stranger in a backwoods town, with no money and no identification. She had no idea of the fear that seized my heart when Raul pointed out that she wasn't standing behind me anymore. I'd been in battles. I'd fought for my life and the lives of those inhabiting the town. I'd dragged brothers in arms from landmines. I've dodged bullets in the killing fields of the cartels. I've fought with all manner of spirits and creatures of the flesh, and only when I turned and saw no trace of her had I truly understood the depths of primal fear my kind could pull from the souls of our human victims.

I thought I'd lost her again. Visions of her smile, her laughter, and the fierce flash in her eyes being extinguished for good by some hapless human's greed were sabers through my heart and soul. My beast had panicked, thrashing against my tenuous connection to the spirit realm, clawing at it to let him find his mate. It is rare, at my age, to lose control over the open conduit that we foster with our cadejos. In that moment, I almost lost my grip completely and let the flood open into me.

When I saw the driver's face, it took everything in me not to let the beast push through the barrier and paint the car's cabin with his rage. I knew that face, even if he hadn't known mine. She had crawled into a car, unaware of the magnitude of danger she was in, and had the audacity to be afraid of me and not the abomination behind the wheel.

Carefully combing through the soaked strands with her fingers, she added the conditioner I bought for her into the dripping tendrils. She hadn't noticed that I was watching her. I let the silence string out between us, content to enjoy this peaceful moment, when neither of us was warring against each other or moving chess pieces toward our own goals.

"Are we going to talk about it?" she asked, her voice razors slashing my soul.

So soft, weak, and broken, nothing like the sound I had come to know. Even in the coldest of moments, her voice held the burning edge of the fury of ice. But it had since turned too fragile, a papery wisp of a sound that hung on the weight of the air.

I lofted my brows. Pushing off the door, I strode to the bed and flopped onto it. She squeaked her protest when I gathered her in my arms and curled her into a ball on my lap. She struggled, trying to get away from me again.

"Still yourself," Itzatecuani barked through my mouth. He was on edge by the vast change in her attitude just as much as I was. I cleared my throat, clamping down further on my control of his access. "And speak."

She was shivering against me. I wanted to believe it was because of the fan and her wet hair, but I mentally squirmed under the idea that it might have been for other reasons. She was afraid of me when we got out of the car. The fear hung so heavy in the air that I was impressed by the restraint of my totoco to not come running at the bounty she offered them. Even I had a hard time not licking it from her skin and drawing it away from her. She was totoco now, though, and there were laws against that. Laws even I would never skirt the edge of.

She said nothing, just quaked in my arms and stared blindly at the band of muscle around her. She didn't draw from me the strength and security I wanted her to. As much as I pressed her to me, I could not feel the pieces of her jagged edges folding down into place again. Had I gone too far in my fury and fear?

Slowly, I turned her in my lap, letting her face the pillar of obsidian in the corner where I had pulled the materials for her mating gifts. I took up the conditioner from where she abandoned it and lathered my hands in it. I needed to tend to my mate. The cracks I had noticed when she came to me were starting to open again, and I needed to ensure they wouldn't form a deeper ravine between us. We could not afford the space and distance.

Methodically, I ran my fingers through her hair, finding tiny knots her curls formed as they dried and massaging the conditioner into them.

"You must know there are things you must be and do now. You are my wife, Xochitl." I softened my tone to a silken brush against her ear. "Nocualcihuatl."

"What does that mean?"

A chisel slammed into my heart at every syllable from her lips. She was so far away from me that I could feel her drifting on the breeze farther and farther into the darkness.

"It means my beautiful wife." I nuzzled her wet head and placed a gentle kiss on her crown. "It means that, as I am tecuhtli and César is my second, you, too, have a place here. You are their Cihuatlatoani. The feminine equal to me. Like me, you are to be bound to the totoco. You must nurture them and care for them as I do. I have shouldered the weight of your duties for too long. It is time that you took them from me."

"I don't want to be that."

A shard of my heart fell into a dark pit as she sliced at it unknowingly, with the battered fragility radiating from her.

"You do not have a choice. You are my wife. My mate. It is what is expected of you. And you will do this." I parted her hair into two sections, then braided one section poorly. "This is not up for debate. We were married in the eyes of the teotl. You will be their Cihuatlatoani, I, their Tlahtoani. You will come to see it for what it is: your destiny. It has always been your destiny. Since the moment you were born into this world."

She snorted, a little spice returning to her otherwise diaphanous voice. "So, that's it? I'm what? Fated to have been yours?"

Smiling softly, I finished off one of her braids and started on the other. It was a mess, not neat and tidy like she or Julia would have accomplished, but it pleased me to do this for her. I took that she allowed me to continue as a victory. "Some think so. Some think that when a cadejo finds its mate, it is because the teotl will it to be so. César thinks that it is because the spirits within us have their own lives in their realm and find their beloveds if they cross into this world, too. I don't know that I agree with either. No, Xochitl, it is not that fate or the teotl have made it to be so. It is that my cadejo sees you, truly and without blind spots, and he has chosen you. I have chosen you. You were everything I have ever wanted, Xochitl. And you will be again."

I buried my nose at the base of the column of her neck and closed my eyes as the perfume of her skin filled my senses. She smelled of marigolds, almonds, and a clean skin musk that drove me insane. "We will have many years ahead of us to settle into each other. You will return to me the teocuitlateotl inside of you, and she will birth me an entire litter of happy, fat babies who will flourish in the light of our love."

Again, she snorted. "Not likely."

Itzatecuani reared up and roared beneath my skin, flexing at the denial of his needs from his chosen mate. "And why is that?"

"You mean aside from the fact I am on birth control?" She turned to look at me, her eyes sparkless and detached. "Because I don't very much like you."

I grinned, the fangs filling my mouth from my beast riding me hard to get at her flashing in the dim light of our bedroom. A nip was given to the back of her neck, and I launched myself from the bed. She didn't need to like me for me to drag my golden goddess from under her skin. She would like me well enough by the time I finished my task.

I stalked to her nightstand and snatched the tiny case filled with the rattling pills.

"What are you doing?" Alarm flashed in her tone, and she sat up on the bed.

"One of those things is easily solved." I threw open the door to the bathroom and headed toward the toilet.

"Wait! Sal! Stop! I need those!"

"No, you don't. Not anymore. You took them to not harbor the get of that vile man you called a fiancé. I am not him. You do not need them anymore." I flicked the container open and reared back at the stench.

They smelled like death. I dumped the first compartment out into the pool of water.

"Sal. I need those! I need them for my ADHD!"

Turning to her, I glared up and down. "You will get over it."

"That's not how that works!" She clawed at my wrists as I flicked the last of the compartments into the toilet and barked a snarl back at her.

"You don't need them."

"Yes, I do! I can't focus without them!"

"Try harder," I snarled, pushing past her and out of the bedroom.

"You're such a dick! I hate you!"

Tears swam in her chestnut gaze as I turned to her.

"You'll get over it." I slammed the door behind me and headed out into the courtyard.

I needed space. The unstable shifting dunes of her temperament were grating at my willpower.

I paced, my bare feet eating up the length of the roof I'd long ago claimed as my retreat, when I felt the presence behind me. A snarl of warning rippled from my lips as I turned to take in the night-drenched figure of my cousin outlined by the spatter of stars.

"What do you want?" I barked out through razor-sharp teeth.

I felt more than saw César's cool gaze taking me in: half dressed, in nothing but a pair of dust smeared jeans hanging from my hips. He said nothing, just let me seethe as he watched me.

"Old habits," he finally said, crossing his toned arms over his chest.

"Fuck off, César. I'm not in the mood for your pompous bullshit tonight." I went back to pacing, shoving an agitated hand through my unbound hair.

"Ah. I see." He shifted behind me, going to the edge of the roof and sitting down, so his long legs dangled over the edge. He turned and waited expectantly. When I didn't move toward him, his golden blessing shimmered over him, lighting him up like a torch in the darkness. "Do I need to make you? Or are you done being a petulant twat?"

I narrowed my gaze on him. So, he wanted to push. The threat was tacit: obey my equal or he'd make me calm down and do it anyway. Whatever spirit had blessed him with the ability to draw the rage and fight out of his peers was a dick. I wished more times than I could count that I could kick its ass back into the spirit realm.

Growling, I stalked over to the edge, joining him as he stared out into the night sky. When I said nothing, he started.

"So, is it Xochi or yourself you're mad at tonight?"

The golden shimmer eased down, casting us back into the inky anonymity that would make this conversation half way tolerable.

"I don't need marriage counseling from a celibate priest," I snapped.

"Don't you, though? And who said I was celibate?" He smirked at me.

He had me there. Though I hadn't seen César with a partner, man or woman, in our entire lives, that meant nothing. My cousin was an enigma to the entire totoco, to me, only a little less. He moved in stealth, with a careful step, never rushing into anything or revealing what he did not want others to know.

"Yeah? And who was the last person you fucked? Your palm is smoother than a baby's ass," I spat.

He tilted his head and stared at me. I hated when he did that. It meant he knew what I was doing and wouldn't tolerate it. I wanted to be mad, though. I wanted to feel the indignation coursing through me and let it heat my blood. He wouldn't let me. This fucking annoying, calm man, who had been by my side through everything, wouldn't let me wallow in my own rage.

"Xochitl," I finally ground out.

"And what could she possibly have done in the time it took you to go from skipping on clouds, helping Ximena get her favorite flowers onto the table, and the time you went in to get her? Hmm?"

His voice was soft, even, no accusation or denunciation in the tone.

"She's refusing to give me children," I hissed, tossing a small stone from the roof out into the darkness.

I felt more than saw the cocking of his bushy brow at me. "You must be joking."

"Why the fuck would I joke about that, César?"

"Well, I'm hoping you're joking because, otherwise, you're the dumbest man I've ever met in my life."

"And what the fuck is that supposed to mean? She's my wife. She's supposed to give me children!"

"Keep your voice down, you fucking coconut," he hissed. "I mean that you can't possibly be stupid enough to think that broaching the subject of children so early is a good idea. Please tell me you're not that stupid, brother."

I scowled at him. "We've been married for over twenty years, César."

He rolled his eyes and pinched the bridge between his brows. "Gods give me strength to survive the overwhelming stupidity of my brother and not push him over this roof."

I snorted. "Good luck with that."

"Thank you. I'll need it." He drew in a deep breath. "Itziquetzal, you might have married when you were children, but it is beyond obvious that woman does not remember you nor hold those vows as sacred as you do. If you can't see that, you are a madman. You've done nothing to hold those vows up, either."

A growl of warning pushed past my lips. He was edging on dangerous territory, talking of my marriage that way.

But he forged on. "You've walked around here treating her like a toy. Worse than a toy. I've seen you treat your women rough in the past, and I assumed it was just a game you liked to play with them, but this is Xochitl. This is not one of those flings you buried yourself in trying to forget her for a few moments. You can't treat her like she is disposable."

He held up a hand when I opened my mouth, silencing me. "I'm not done yet. You'll hear me out, and I'll say no more on this topic. I know that you and Itzatecuani need certain things from your partners. I know you like certain games to be played. I'm not talking about that. Play your bedroom games all you want. From that display at the gates, she seems to like it just as much as you do. I'm not talking about that, though. I'm talking about how you are keeping her in the dark about her role here. You feed her snippets. Like, if you give her the entire truth, she will run screaming into the night. I'm talking about how she still doesn't fully know who she is to you. How she still doesn't fully know who she is to this totoco. I'm talking about all the things she doesn't know. Those things that are important—not just to you, but to the rest of us, too. I'm talking about this bullshit obstacle course you've set up for her to stumble through as you test her to figure out whatever it is you're trying to figure out. Drop the act, Itziquetzal. I know who you are. I know you better than any other cadejo in this totoco. You've been so lost in your schemes to get to her that you can't be real with her, and it's going to push her away more than it's going to bring her closer."

I glared at him but said nothing.

"You fuck her like she matters. I hear it through the damned walls when I'm here. But you don't show her that she matters. And, until you can figure out how to stop fucking around with her, you need to leave her be. If I have to, I will intervene. Don't make me, brother. I do not want to have to do that to you for her benefit."

"You wouldn't," I bit out.

He threatened to sever our vows, to cast her back into the world, and destroy the link between Itzatecuani and her spirit that he wound together when we were children. It was in his power to do. Rare as the ceremony was, it was something I had seen him perform before. A knot formed in my stomach, not of my beast's discomfort but my own. The idea of losing her again, of not hearing her breath in my bed or seeing her from across the courtyard going about her day, was a hot knife in the gut.

"If it brought peace to her spirit and was what she desired, I would. I would weep the entire time, but I would do it."

Turning my eyes away from him, I stared up at the stars and the heavy moon in the sky. We were silent for a long time, letting the cooling night kiss our skin. It was me who finally broke our vigil.

"I'm trying," I whispered to my life-long confidant. "There's something broken in her. I'm not trying to play games with her, César. But there is something there."

"And what are you doing to heal the breaks, brother?"

His calm voice wove into the silence around us, as if it were just as much a part of the landscape as the night creatures.

"I set her up an apprenticeship with Nopaltzin." I sighed and scrubbed my hand down my face. "I asked him to teach her his trade and to see if she would open up to him. I gave him leave to say whatever he needed to about me. She needs someone who is loyal to her, I think. Someone that she doesn't see as my agent. Like Julia. Someone to integrate her into the totoco and to be there for her when I cannot."

He snorted. "It helps that, of all the cadejos in the totoco, that old dog is still the best warrior in our ranks."

I smirked. "It helps, yes. I know that, while I'm busy with other things, no one will harm her."

He exhaled deeply, and I felt him rise from beside me, then his warm hand found my bare shoulder. "Take some time, brother. Write her a note and tell her you need to go to La Libertad. Take a few days to get your head on straight. And when you come back, be here for her. Be the mate to her she deserves. The mate that will make everything you've sacrificed and given, worth it."

He was halfway to the stairwell when I called him back.

"César."

He groaned and turned. "I knew it wouldn't be that easy. What is it?"

"Promise me, swear on all you hold dear that, if she asks to be severed, you will tell me before you perform the ritual."

He was quiet for far too long as anxiety twisted in my guts like a ball of barbed wire. "I will tell you, brother, but I will not deny her should she choose that."

"I couldn't ask you to deny your sacred duty, brother."

CHAPTER TWENTY

I wanted to talk. I felt raw and shattered completely for the first time since I came to this country. It wasn't like the feeling I had breaking down in my bathroom before my trip. It was worse—a foreign aching hollowness holding hands with an eerie, still quietness filling me and swallowing everything about me. I couldn't see around it, through it, or between it. It was a dark distance, like I was floating outside of my body, and it had chilled me to the bone.

Only when he pulled me into his lap and combed his fingers through my hair did I feel any semblance of ease leaking into the edges of the abyss, like veins of white light.

It had all gone off the rails so quickly. So fast I couldn't even track the zipping left to right of the winding path the zephyr conversation took. All I wanted was for him to hold me and tell me why he had been so angry. It was the first time I had ever seen him like that. I didn't want to wonder, didn't want to imagine a world in which it would ever matter to me, but something had shifted outside of the careful plan I made, and it all became a soggy paper bag in the rain, dissolving before my eyes. No matter how much I tried to claw the fleeing blocks of my resolve back into position, they kept escaping into the ephemera.

Then it shattered with the slamming of the bedroom door. His callousness to my medication had met not a scrap of resistance, as I had none left to offer. His cruelty, leaving me there all night in that cold black bed, sunk into my bones and rotted them from under my skin. I wanted to cry into the pillows, wanted to sob and scream the slivers of hurt all over the linens, but I had nothing to give. So, I lay there, staring at the spinning ceiling fan until I couldn't any longer.

We hadn't spoken since. It had been two days. Julia and I managed to excavate my prescription bottle from the hastily packed box someone shoved my already hastily packed items into. My birth control was lost somewhere between here and La Libertad. At least I had my Adderall and vitamins. Julia complained again about the stench of the pills, and I shrugged, saying something lame about Chinese herbs my mother had told me. César had been hesitant to replace the birth control, but one snarling snap of Julia's jaws, and he'd caved.

Sal had not come back to our room the entire time, and I had only seen him once. He'd stared at me from across the courtyard while I ate dinner with Nopaltzin, Julia, Phelix, and a few others.

César joined us initially but had excused himself when he noticed Sal watching me. I didn't like the charged air surrounding me, like everyone was walking on eggshells, waiting for something that only they knew was coming.

Here I was, two days later, awake earlier than normal, in a boiler suit-style of coveralls I found at the foot of the bed and a note to get dressed. I briefly entertained the idea that it was a gift or message from Sal, but when I examined the handwriting against the crisp, careful scrawl on the note from our first date, my heart fell when it wasn't a match.

Squinting, I looked up into the bright clean white rays of the early morning cresting over the lip of the volcano, stepping out into the courtyard with the scratchy suit's top tied around my nipped waist.

"Julia said you might do well with some time away," the gravelly voice of my tutor said from behind a pillar near the grills.

Nopaltzin had been a savior. He never let me spend a day inside wallowing in my self-pity. Instead, he had me up, out of bed, and working every day. Some of the tasks seemed disconnected from my lessons working the rich terra-cotta clay of the area, but he assured me that if I questioned him, I'd be spitting on the graves of his ancestors. That sounded melodramatic, but the older gentleman left little room for argument.

A bashful smile curled at the petals of my lips, and I nodded. "That'd be nice, actually."

"Well, come on, then. The daylight is burning, and you've got work to do." He hefted a large basket at me, and I instantly wrapped my arms around it as I stumbled back a little. He eyed me critically. "Need to get that arm strength up, chica. I've got just the thing for you."

I blinked up at him as he hefted a bundle of two shovels and a hunting rifle onto his shoulder and trudged toward one of the smaller trucks. He carelessly tossed the items into the bed and snatched the basket from me.

"Don't you think you should handle those with a little care?" I sputtered.

Shrugging, he seemed unbothered. "Why? The truck has enough holes as it is."

Were all the men just a little bit bonkers?

I crawled into the cab of the truck with him, and we were off.

An hour later, we pulled onto another dusty road that led to the river. Massive downed logs littered the banks on either side of the water and in the reeds.

I climbed out, and Nopaltzin reached across me, then slammed the door closed. "Stay here until I tell you to get out."

I stared at him as he jumped out of the truck, grabbed a shovel, and walked down to the bank. He barked something at the river and looked around. Displeased with the river's response, he clanged the shovel against the nearest log, and to my horror, a hiss exited the log, and a wide tooth-studded mouth shot back at him.

I gasped. Clamping my mouth with my hand, I muffled the scream as the enormous crocodile curled its tail and prepared to do battle with my tutor, who seemed unimpressed with the beast. The head came toward Nopaltzin, and he swatted it with the flat of the shovel, eliciting another clang. Logs revealing themselves to be crocodiles shifted on the bank and slid silently into the river's rush.

Nopaltzin barked at the creature again, haranguing with his shovel, and shoved its massive hindquarters toward the water. It hissed at him again, and he barked again. The last of the log-sized crocodiles slid into the water and disappeared, leaving the beast to square off with Nopaltzin. It maneuvered itself with each swipe of its powerful tail toward the water, never letting its eye leave the other predator on the bank. Slowly, it lowered itself into the black waters and edged out and away from the man standing alone on the bank.

He waited a good five minutes before he angled his body to keep an eye on the water and one on the truck. "All right. Come on out. Bring the other shovel and the rifle."

Fuck that. Absolutely not. I was not about to add *eaten by a crocodile* to my running tally of absolutely unreasonable situations.

"Get out here."

"Absolutely not. That is so not happening."

"I didn't realize that Itzatecuani had mated a coward."

I snorted and yelled back, "I'm not a coward! I just don't feel like being dinosaur chow."

He chuckled, the sound rich and full. "Tsst. The janaw just needed to be asked to let us use his home for a little while. Now, get out here. This clay isn't going to dig itself."

"They aren't coming back? Promise?"

He exaggerated an eye roll. "Not for a while, at least. Now hurry up."

I slid out of the truck and did as he asked, bringing the rifle and shovel with me. "So, if they aren't coming back, what's the gun for? And what does janaw mean?"

He took the gun and shoved his shovel into the bank's soft mud. "It's Lenca. Itzatecuani and his people might speak Nahuatl, but I'm from Antu's original totoco bloodline. One of the few of us left standing. I was raised speaking the language. It is the word we use for the spirits in the big beasts that line our rivers. And the rifle is in case your jabbering pisses off the rest of them. Dig here."

"So, it means crocodile?" I asked, lofting my brows, doing as he said.

"If you wish to say that." He scanned the water and the reeds around us.

The silent guardianship made me relax into my task, the simple *shink thud* into the mud. The slide of it along the metal was a soundtrack that calmed me, and he went on speaking as he had before in other lessons.

"When you pick mud, you will look for the janaw. They like the way it holds heat without drying their skin out. Their shit mixes with the mud and makes it black. But not all banks are the best. Look for one that has a big one, like the one that guarded the others. This one will be special. Perfect for ritual items. It has a guardian spirit that looks after the others. It will be the biggest. Find him and ask him to gather your mud. If he says no, then leave. If he says yes, let his wards back into the water unbothered, and he will keep them in the water while you gather. Don't be greedy. Take only what you need, nothing more." He looked over at me. "Stop digging. See that blackest layer there? With the white mixed in? Grab a handful. Feel it in your hand. Feel how it is silky and holds together? That is what we are looking for. Go get the bucket from the truck, three scoops. Nothing more. Take more and the janaw will come back hungry for payment. And since you are so convinced not to be dinosaur chow, I don't think you want that. Now, go."

I raced to the truck, grabbed the bucket, and ran back. By the time I got back, I could see the head of the large river monster watching us from thirty feet out into the river, two eyes bobbing above the rush of the river. I shivered. His gaze on me felt menacing and too aware for a reptile.

Setting to work, I counted out my scoops into the bucket, just in case janaw couldn't see well enough. It made Nopaltzin snicker into his scarred hand.

When I was done, with the bucket set aside, I filled the hole. He lofted his brows at me appreciatively and nodded. "Good. You're learning."

I patted the hole as flat as I could and swiped a few times to cover up that we had been there, earning me another approving nod. It made me smile inside my head. Nopaltzin was not as gruff as Sal but not as soft as César. He did not give out his approval easily nor without merit, and a warm bubble leaped in my throat whenever I earned a nod from him.

Before he could dismiss me, I was already halfway to the truck to stash the shovel and bucket. "Tsst. Not yet, girl. We have not paid the price yet."

"The what?" I looked over my shoulder at him, securing the top to the bucket in the back.

"Nothing comes free." He pointed his chin to the large set of eyes watching us from the water. "He expects payment for our collection and his patience. Come. Since you collected, you must pay the fee."

He unclipped a knife from his belt and handed it to me. I balked, holding the knife away from myself. Like, at any moment, it and the beast in the water would strike me dead. "What! You want me to, what . . . cut off something and feed it to him?"

He erupted into a roar, his head falling back as he rocked back on his heels and laughed. "No, foolish girl. Janaw does not ask for blood like the others. No, he favors secrets. It's why he's always grinning—because he knows what we do not. So"—he motioned again with his chin—"slice into the river bed and feed him a secret. Make it a good one. I don't want to be dinosaur chow, either."

I shuffled from foot to foot, uncomfortable and nervous. What would I tell a mammoth beast who would amuse him enough to keep grinning? I kneeled next to the water and cut a slash into the soft mud. He nodded again, urging me to get on with it, while he protected me from any impatient reptiles.

"Sal scares me," I whispered into the mud, then sat up straight.

Nopaltzin lofted his brow again with a tilt of his head for me to go on.

I sighed heavily and shifted. I didn't want to do this in front of him. I felt vulnerable and dangerously close to revealing way more than I had ever intended on revealing to anyone here. It was dinosaur chow or awkward future conversations. I had no way of knowing if Nopaltzin would use this against me, but it was better to just get it over with and discover the damage later. "He scares me because I want him all the time, but I don't belong here, and he'll never let me go. And I'm scared that, even if he does let me go, I'll only have my mother to go back to. I'm terrified of her. What she will do to me for being gone for so long. Scared of what she will make me do to get back on track. I'm scared that I don't want to go back. I'm scared to stay. And I'm scared if I don't go, of who I'll become. I'm scared all the time. I don't want to be scared anymore. And I'm scared that if I'm not scared anymore, what that will make me into. Who's left inside of me that isn't scared? I'm scared that I don't know how to not be scared anymore."

I looked up at him. A treasure trove of unreadable emotions swirled in his dark oak-colored eyes rimmed by heavy black lashes. He pursed his lips in thought for a while and then nodded. "Cover it up."

Already done, my friend, for years now.

I smooshed the thick mud into the cut, then stood up, handing the knife back to him.

He waved me away. "Keep it. You've earned it."

I smiled softly at him and mumbled my thanks. He nodded and walked to the truck. I took his cue and headed back as well. He sucked his teeth as I reached for the door handle. "Up on the roof. It's lunchtime."

I followed him up onto the truck's roof and winced at the crunch of it under our weight as he passed me a few of Pastora's pupusas. A small corked olla jar was placed between us, and one of the few pieces of plastic used by the totoco appeared. Two wooden straws were set next to the baggie full of juice, and he settled in next to me to watch the crocodiles return.

We sat quietly, tearing pieces off of the cheese-filled pita-like rounds, and folded them into tiny pincers to fish the curtido from the olla. All but the largest of them returned to their spots on the banks. To my untrained eye, it looked so organized, each crocodile returning to what looked like the same spot as before. The largest was the last to join them. He dragged his massive body directly over the place where I had buried my secret and settled into the mud.

I watched him settle in comfortably and sighed. "Is he satisfied?"

Nopaltzin snorted. "Fuck if I know."

"What?"

He shrugged and shoved a piece of food into his mouth, dusting off his hands. "It's just a crocodile, Xochitl."

I sputtered around my bite. "But you said . . . !"

He rolled his powerful shoulders again in a shrug. "You seemed like you had a lot on your mind. I knew if I asked you wouldn't tell me. So, I told you some story about crocodiles liking secrets to let you get it off your chest."

"You asshole."

He grinned at me. "Did it work?"

I sighed, the wind sucked out of my indignation. "Yeah."

"Then, it was worth it." He slid his straw into the juice and took a deep sip. "Do you want to talk about it?"

Nopaltzin looked maybe early or mid-forties at best, but, sometimes, the way he asked things made him sound like a doting grandfather—bristly and sharp occasionally but, for the most part, soft and caring. He seemed to know the exact thing to say and ask, no matter the situation. In this situation, he knew exactly how to get the crushing ache from my shoulders.

"Sal? No, not really." I pushed at the last piece of pupusa in my lap. "It's complicated."

He nodded and capped the jar that held the curtido. "And your mother?"

I exhaled a deep breath and leaned back, my palms finding the hot roof. My eyes shifted from the sunning reptiles to the bright clear blue sky. "That's even more complicated."

"Seems like everything is complicated with you. Must be exhausting. Ever thought about just . . . not?"

I gave him a scalding look. "That's very easy to say, isn't it? 'Just don't be complicated, Xochitl.' Sounds easy. If you have a map, let me know."

He smirked and rolled his shoulders in a shrug again. "I don't know your mother. From what I've heard from Julia and a little over the years from Itzatecuani, she's a piece of work. But I know Itzatecuani. He's hot-headed. He's stubborn. He's—"

"An insufferable prick?"

He barked out a laugh and let it trail off to a warm grin. "That, too. But the one thing that has driven him since he came back from America is you, Xochitl. Everything he has ever done is and has been for you. I'm not one to go poking about in other people's business. That's how you lose limbs, but I can tell you that that boy burns for you. So, toss a few logs on and let him feel what it's like to get burned by his fire. Or just stab him a few times until he gets the picture. Either one works better than what you've been doing."

Our eyes darted to the knife laying next to my knee, and we both snickered conspiratorially.

"Just don't tell him where you got the knife. I'd like to have all my fingers and toes when and if I ever meet my mate." He winked at me, and dawn broke within my heart and warmed the cold mountain range of my soul. "Now, get your lazy ass up. You've still got some ash to gather and goat shit to shovel before we can process this."

He slapped my thigh and jumped down with a grace that belied his age. I groaned and followed.

Gathering the volcanic ash was far more difficult than gathering the mud, and I had to do battle with more reptiles—this time, snakes. I decided that, as I was digging the hole to get to the ash, snakes were also on my extermination list, right behind seagulls. I hated seagulls far more that day under the burning sun than I hated snakes. Snakes just happened to be there. Seagulls had put me here with their damned poop luck.

By the time we got back to the compound, my body ached everywhere, and I felt like I was coated in a thick layer of crusty dried sweat, dirt, and dust. Even though I smelled like a dead goat, I felt clean from head to toe emotionally. Nopaltzin's methods were strange but effective, and I was ready to give Sal exactly what he suggested—the fire he didn't know burned inside of me. I hoped he had asbestos panties because I was tired of his bullshit in a way that felt like ice and lava swirling in my veins.

Waiting for him in our room all night, I sat up with a book on ceramics techniques Nopaltzin had handwritten over his years as the totoco potter.

The longer I waited for him to come loping through that door, the more ice joined the lava swirling inside of me. When I couldn't keep my eyes open any longer, I set the journal aside and turned off the light. I placed the knife next to the bed and made sure the sheath that Nopaltzin had given me was unclipped and at the ready, just in case Itzatecuani came through the door and not Sal.

CHAPTER TWENTY-ONE

It had been three goddamned days.

Three entire days since he deigned to speak to me. Two since I saw him staring at me from across the courtyard with those hungry eyes that made my skin tingle and my pussy clench with need. He hadn't come to me then, but here he was, sauntering up to me, like it had been just a few minutes since our fight.

I had almost forgotten how breathtaking he was when we met on the beach. His relaxed attire at the totoco compound had almost rewritten that fairy-tale meeting on black sands under the azure sky of a perfect tropical day. He had somehow accessed his wardrobe in the bedroom without me knowing, or he kept a separate room somewhere elsewhere in the totoco compound or down in the town.

Jealousy, hot and razor-sharp, sliced at my tender belly as I took in his powerful form wrapped in an exquisitely tailored charcoal gray suit, with a black silk vest and pocket square in the suit jacket that was folded over one arm. His sleeves were bunched and rolled up to his elbows, perfectly framing the length of dark skin that rippled with veins and muscle like driftwood. His black hair was pulled back into a single braid again, drawing it away from his strong features. The glint of the obsidian feather dripped from its silver chain wrapped around the end of the braid.

How fucking dare he look so absolutely lickable. I was offended by the gray-clad lust monster stalking me, to the roots of my hair.

A familiar sparkle in his dark oak eyes forced me to repress the shiver of delight that danced en pointe down my spine and settled in a shimmering golden pool in my core. When he licked his lips, his eyes taking in every swerve of my ample body, my knees rebelled and nearly gave out.

Of course he showed up looking like a GQ fever dream, while I was dressed in dirty coveralls folded down and tied off at my waist, along with a white tank top smeared with goat, pig, and chicken shit. I should have placed bets with Julia and Paloma that morning when they asked when I thought he'd show up again. I had finally gotten the clay Nopaltzin, and I gathered into a thin slurry that would be perfect to work and opted to clean out the animal pens that would need to be resodded soon. The physical labor kept my mind from wandering too much, keeping me focused on a single task I could do in chunks when it wandered to another task. It was a task that I could easily see progress in and one I could leave and come back to without any issue. It was also hard labor—and smelly. So, of course he'd show up right then instead of the day before, when I'd just been dusty and sweaty.

"Xochitl."

His deep cognac and spice voice rolled over the syllables of my name like his tongue was fucking them. Lecherous eyes drifted down my body again, setting micro fires under my skin with every flick of his long lashes.

The howling rage of the arctic swept in an unexpectedly swift blizzard of slicing fury. Did he think he could just abandon me and come sidling up three days later like nothing happened? Did he genuinely think I was so easily mollified and put aside when he got bored?

"What do you want, Itziquetzal?" I said as flatly as I could.

There was no getting around the torrential clawing of my anger, though, and it nipped at the edges of my tone balefully.

A dark brow twitched at me using his full name.

"Come have lunch with me," he demanded.

He had a way of keeping me on the edge of emotional whiplash that was commendable. Seconds ago, I had imagined climbing him like a lumberjack and begging him to fuck me. Now? I wanted to take a cheese grater to his face.

Nopaltzin's advice shuddered at the edges of my violent thoughts and begged for attention.

Someone get the ax. Time to split some logs.

"I'd rather eat with the goats."

I brushed him off and kept shoveling the pen, selecting the driest of the pellets into the bucket for the compost pile that would feed the crops that would, in turn, feed the totoco.

"It wasn't a request," he said, amusement slithering between each word.

High-handed as ever. I noted that, just like before, Sal had a tell when he approached the cusp of anger. His voice deepened and carved into his mouth with the same tones that his beast liked to use.

"Oh, I'm very aware it wasn't a request. And yet, my answer stays the same."

I didn't look at him. He didn't deserve the kindness of looking him in the eye as I worked.

"Come out of that pen and sit your fine ass down at the table, Xochitl," he barked, his voice now filled with the razor-sharp command I had first heard from his beast's muzzle.

I whipped my head up to meet him, his eyes flashing with obsidian menace. I met him spark-for-spark. He wouldn't be pushing me around anymore. Whatever he did to me paled in comparison to what I had survived, and I refused to live like a shrinking mouse for him any longer.

Burn, baby, burn.

"Oh, get fucked, Itzatecuani. And take Itziquetzal with you, too." I glared at him, fire roiling through my blood and licking at the air in the form of words.

I imagined myself as an annoyed dragon, claws and teeth ready for battle with the predator lurking in the skin of the god before me.

A wicked chuckle rolled from his lips, now stretched thin over a maw of sharp teeth. "Oh, I will . . . I absolutely will, nonayeli."

Sneering at him, I leaned against my shovel with feigned nonchalance, my other hand snaking to the knife in my pocket. "Oh? Is that so? Planning on kidnapping some other poor American girl? Do let me know when. I'll be more than happy to have my bags packed so she can wake up shackled to your bed, you fucking weirdo. Lord knows I'm not laying down and opening my legs for you ever again."

It was a low blow. Julia and I had talked about it the night before, when I was agonizing over whether he'd maybe found someone else. She'd told me his beast would never allow him to fuck another woman now that I was so close. He tried when we were apart a few times, years ago, and it had never worked out. Julia was vague about the details, but she had been clear that, of the women he courted, none of them lasted longer than a month or two. Itzatecuani had not allowed it.

He lunged for me. I darted backward, slicing at his arm with the concealed knife. I was by no means a trained combatant, but it took little effort to nick someone on the hand they were using to grab you. The roar of frustration that ripped through him as he teetered into the fence of the pen brought far too much satisfaction.

"Get out of the godsdamned shit and come eat with me. Or you will regret it, mate," snarled Itzatecuani from his thinned dark lips.

"Is the beast hungry? Fine. Let me make you a plate." I snatched up the shovel and dug into the pile of feces and urine that coated the animal pen two inches thick.

I loaded the shovel as full as I could physically lift and dumped it unceremoniously at the toe of his tanned leather dress shoes. "Eat up!"

Fury boiled through me as I tossed the shovel at him and stalked off toward the open gate to walk through the fields. I wanted to be away from him. Where, exactly? It didn't matter. I just needed space to cool down before I lost it. No matter where I was about to wander off to, it didn't matter because he darted in to block my path. A clawed hand reached for me, and I jumped back again.

"Touch me, and it will be the last thing you do," I warned, glaring at him with the same glint of feralness he had been feeding me.

"You think you can defeat me in combat, little cihuatl?" He tilted his head in amusement.

"Maybe, maybe not. But I'm quick enough to shove this knife into my throat before you can stop me. Now. Kindly fuck off." I diverted my path to the small gate on the opposite side of the courtyard that led out into the untamed jungle.

I unlatched it with ease and slammed it in his face. He didn't follow me, though. His steps stopped dead at the closed gate, then ground out an agitated pacing behind it.

I stomped my way down into the ravine full of trees, brush, and a wide, deep creek winding through it to sit on a large jutting rock and stare into the lazy trickle of water.

Righteous indignation pumped through me, shattering any hope of rational thought. I snatched a fallen stick from the leaf litter next to me and hacked at it with the knife. With each slice of the small steel blade, I imagined peeling the flesh from Sal's grabbing fingers.

I felt childish and stupid, but the hacking sliced off the edges of my rage until the knife nicked my finger and slid out of my hand down into the muddy water.

"Ugh! I hate this stupid jungle. I hate this stupid volcano." I petulantly pushed up from the rock and trudged after the knife. "I hate his stupid face. I mean, seriously! Who does this bullshit? First, he's all sweet and fairy-tale prince charming. Then, suddenly, he's a total asshole, ordering me around like he owns me!"

I shoved my hand into the cool water and fished out the knife, when a glint in the mud caught my eye. Curiosity licked away the last remnants of my tantrum, and I reached in after the shiny metal covered by the sediment. I noted that the creek's mud would do fine in a pinch for clay but wasn't nearly as silky as the janaw clay. Shaking my hand into the glittering water, I washed the small bit clean and poked around in the remaining clinging mud.

It was a ring. What was a ring doing out here?

I scrubbed the last of the mud from it and held it up to the dappled light filtering in from the canopy to examine it.

My blood froze in my veins.

Jake.

It was Jake Lassiter's class ring. He wore that stupid, gaudy gold ring everywhere he went, and I'd know it from a hundred feet away. He had a bad habit of twisting it and staring at me for long stretches at a time. It always made me think that he was secretly fantasizing about strangling me.

My body shook like I was standing in the tundra, suddenly naked and fully exposed to the capricious elements.

"What . . . the . . . fuck."

Why was Jake's ring here? Jake never took it off. Ever. How had it gotten into the creek behind the totoco compound?

Thunder rolled in my ears, drowning out the ambient bird calls and insect buzzing of the jungle, replacing it with the suffocating sound. I couldn't breathe. My lungs stuttered in my chest, clenching shut, unwilling to draw breaths as I stared at the nearly innocuous hunk of circular metal clenched in my fingers.

Had Jake been here? Did he know where I was? If Jake knew where I was, then my mother knew where I was.

Fear pulsed and throbbed through me, like a toxic sludge that coated my throat and squeezed it shut, whispering all the potential possibilities that could happen as I stood there like a stupid statue, paralyzed by my own terror.

Darting my gaze around, I searched the empty jungle canopy for signs of being watched by someone, anyone. There was no one.

I tried to hear past the deafening thunder of terror that blocked out everything, but the menagerie of spooked birds that had taken up residence inside the cage of my ribs.

I wanted to run. I screamed at my feet to run. I shouted into the sarcophagus that had become my body to just move. To find César. To find Julia or Nopaltzin. Hell, to even find Sal. Find any cadejo in the totoco house that would hide me from them.

I couldn't go back. I didn't want to go back. I'd do exactly as I threatened earlier—shove this shaking knife into my throat and bleed out into the creek—before I went back to living under her arctic glare and crushing control.

I drew gulping bites of air into my tattered lungs, but it wasn't enough. My mind screamed that I needed to get a hold of myself, that I was hyperventilating and needed to take a deep breath, but there was nothing I could do. Spidery claws slashed at my throat, and my mother's hollow black stare glared into me, finding me wanting.

Gripping the ring, I dug it into my palm and the knife in the other, but I still couldn't move my feet to flee, to go find somewhere to hide. I didn't need to hide, though. I just had to make it into the courtyard. I would be surrounded on all sides by great, hulking, predatory beasts that could shred anyone into ribbons. I needed to make it into the courtyard. Anyone lurking in the jungle to snatch me away, back to the prison of my old life, wouldn't be able to drag me from the depths of the courtyard.

Before my mind could fully register it, my feet were moving, and I was running as hard as I could for the open sanctum. It was so close but so far away. The forty-foot path stretched out in front of me for miles, distorting and contorting in a vortex into the abyss of my panic. I heard the leaves crunching under my punishing footfalls, the dull sound cranking the dial of my dread up to maximum volume. I scrambled up the rise and pushed through the gate. The incongruity between the relaxed air of the totoco mulling about, doing their designated chores and trades, collided with the tremors clawing into my muscles.

I just needed to make it somewhere quiet, somewhere away from the exits but close enough to the others that, should some horror leap from the shadows, they would see it. My frantic gaze slid across the familiar territory of the courtyard that could have easily fit the foundations of a McMansion from back home. The shadow of the massive totoco-shared home loomed like a guardian, casting its watchful gaze over the denizens as they busied themselves, unconcerned by my flight.

Passing totocan after totocan, I ignored the calling voices. My eyes were set on the picnic-style benches gathered around the grilling area, near the candle pots Paloma and her brother had been working. Nothing existed beyond the singular bench I had chosen as my refuge. When I finally found myself next to it, I sat down, movements forced into a false calm as I lowered myself to its solid wooden surface.

I stared, unseeing into the courtyard, hearing nothing but the shades of my mother's voice, feeling the slide of Shayne's hands on my arms as he steered me this way and that through our lives. I was vaguely aware of movement around me and distant voices somewhere in the courtyard. I stared blankly, trapped in the nightmarescape playing across my mind's eye. I felt the metal of the ring grinding into the softness of my palm, hot and molten, searing its taunting secrets into my flesh.

Somewhere. Somehow. Jake had been here. There was no other explanation for why he was here, aside from him attempting to collect me.

The edges of my vision blurred and smeared in sable inkblots, my eyes squeezing shut against its invasion. A rainbow of spots exploded behind them as I felt the presence of a body near me. Every hair on my body stood on edge for the executioner's ax that was to fall. I could feel it hovering over me with its stygian promise. Images of my mother's cold eyes hung in my mind's eyes, carving chunks off of me as I quaked and gripped the dreaded bit of metal harder. Perhaps, if I squeezed it hard enough, I could shove whatever ills had been let out of Pandora's box back inside, never having to face the possibility of being ferreted out by the demons of my past.

A hand, hot and final, fell to my canvas-covered knee. I felt it squeeze and was reminded of the early days with Shayne, when he showed affection like that in public. I felt more than heard the tiny thin whimper that snuck past my resolve to stay as quiet as possible.

Someone was calling my name, a male voice I didn't recognize. The sound twisted and contorted into a horror's groan and cackle.

Another hand came to my other knee. "Xochi . . . Xochi!"

The twisted, slithering voice called my name again, beckoning me to acknowledge it, so it could drag me off into the darkness, and deliver me to the harrowing creatures I left behind.

A body sat beside me, and I was pulled against its solid side. "Xochi. What's wrong?" The garbled voice coalesced into a less disharmonious sound, almost vaguely familiar. Who was it, though? "Xochi, shh. It's me. Shh. Tell me what's wrong."

Me? Me who? I tried to push away from the body, but it held me in an iron grip.

"Xochi, it's César. Xochi, tell me what's wrong. What happened?"

I elbowed him, his arms wrestling with my flailing form as I refused to open my eyes. I heard the words, but they didn't make sense. They couldn't penetrate the thick panic that gripped me stronger than the body holding me possibly could.

"Julia, call Sal. I don't know what's wrong. I've never seen her like this. Something is very wrong."

The tinkling of a woman's voice came from somewhere a few feet away from the hurricane of angry wings that had taken up residence in place of my heart and lungs.

"Just call him!" the man bellowed, his grip slipping on my arms before he corrected it and squeezed me so firmly that my already overtaxed lungs couldn't draw breath.

I felt his head come near my ear. His breath gusted against the shell of it as he whispered something I couldn't understand. I might not have understood the words, but I recognized, deep in the ocean of my panic, the characteristic tsst and cadence of the language I was struggling to learn. Nahuatl. The voice was speaking Nahuatl to me. No one back in San Francisco spoke it. I clung to it and dragged myself toward the surface, one drumming slam of a heartbeat after another.

"Xochi, are you in there?" he whispered again. He stroked the crown of braids. Soft shushing fell like the petals of hysteria on me. I eased down into the comfort and security it provided.

"Xochi, can you tell me what happened?"

His voice was so soft, like rabbits curling around each word, nuzzling my psyche with their soft fur.

I shivered against the comfort of his body. It was warm, and he was holding onto me like a broken doll. "It's . . . It's nothing. Just . . . just tell whomever not to call Sal."

He paused, considering my request. I loved that about César. He never acted rashly. He considered. He thought. He weighed the possibilities and what the person needed, not what he thought they needed. "Are you sure?"

I nodded, disentangling myself from him. As I started to calm, his presence a solid balm to my frayed nerves, I no longer needed the solid grounding his body provided. Nor the haunting slide of pale flesh against mine it brought to the surface of my mind.

"Julia. Tell Sal I have it in hand. Tell him not to come. Tell him I said so," he said over my head, then turned his attention back to me. His tender gaze pierced the last grip of panic and peeled its claws away from my throat. "You promise to tell me what happened?"

I nodded to him, and he turned his head again. "Tell him I said that's an order from his teopixqui."

I slumped against the table behind me like a wrung-out, wet towel.

César sat quietly with me for a long while as I peeled back the layers of fuliginous ooze that solidified over my vision. He waited for me. Never pushed, never asked. Just sat in the relative silence broken by the sounds of animals. The courtyard had been abandoned by everyone else, leaving me feeling exposed and vulnerable. He didn't fidget or stretch or make adjustments to his seat. He was merely content to be next to me as I clawed and scrambled at the disjointed particles of thought that zoomed through my mind, daring me to catch them.

"I . . . I found something," I whispered, when I could finally lay mental fingers on a single ribbon of thought, still clenching the ring in my vise of a fist.

He didn't ask what, just gave me the time and space to tell him what happened on my own. His patience made me want to cry into his arms.

"A . . . a ring. A ring that . . . that shouldn't be here."

As I swallowed against the tightness creeping up my throat, he reached out across the void between us and grounded me before I could float off into panic again by wrapping his fingers around mine.

I stared at the way my sepia skin looked against his deep ochre fingers. I was entranced by the tone against tone and oddly aware that my skin was once pale golden wheat rolling over the hills and valleys of my curvy body. But after so much time in the sun, it had matured into a golden moon over the cliffs of my plush form.

"Xochi?" He called my attention back to him, focusing my staring eyes back into the present. "Why shouldn't the ring have been here?"

"It was Jake's," I said with a hollow condemnation of myself.

I felt like a balloon abandoned by a careless child to float away into the sky, my ribbon trailing after me, begging for someone to grab hold and keep me from drifting into nothingness.

"Who is Jake?"

His words tugged at the string and pulled me a few feet lower.

"Jake Lassiter. He's . . . he's the associate I came down here to help." I gulped, forcing moisture into the desert that had taken over my mouth. "He . . . uhm . . ."

"Xochi." Curling his fingers around my jaw, he gently tugged my face to stare him in the eye. His soft philamot eyes, flecked with emerald, searched mine for an answer to the question he had not yet asked. When he wasn't satisfied, he frowned deeply. "Xochitl. Did this Jake Lassiter hurt you?"

The implications of his simple question were plain yet vague enough to give me room to escape them if the fears that swirled in his gimlet gaze were true.

"What? No. No, nothing like that." I scrubbed my hands along my arms, suddenly freezing cold. "No, Jake, and I went out on one date, but, no, he never touched me. Like that. Or any other way."

"What is it, then? Why did seeing Jake's ring scare you so much? The entire totoco is on edge, half of them stuffed to the gills just on the wake you left when you walked through the courtyard."

I blinked at him. Okay, those were definitely human words, but the way he put them together didn't make sense. They careened through the icy walls of my panic, punching holes in the barriers between me and linear thought. "Huh?"

The bewilderment in my voice made him chuckle. "No es serio. Go on. Tell me. Why did finding Jake's ring scare you so much?"

I frowned. He was avoiding my question. I wanted him to keep talking. The way his voice curled around me like a warm fur blanket, buffering me from the jagged shards of terror, helped. "No . . . tell me?"

He sighed softly and pushed his unoccupied hand through the mop of his shaggy curls. "I see Sal has done a bang-up job of explaining what's going on around you." He pinched his brows and grumbled in Nahuatl, then in Spanish. "Always leaving me to do his dirty work."

He pulled in a long-suffering sigh and exhaled it to the warm afternoon sky above us. "I know I told you a little about who and what we are. I expected your mate to tell you more, but it seems he's too preoccupied fucking or fighting with you. Typical." He rolled his eyes. "I told you about our beasts and how we feed them for different purposes. Cadejos are spiritual manifestations—the ghost, if you will—in the ghost dog."

His hazel gaze searched mine. Like a magnet pulling shards of iron shavings from deep within my soul, they sucked me into their comforting depths. Each sliver of panic-soaked metal they drew in left my lungs a little less burdened, my heart a little less vicious in its cacophonous pounding. He wrapped his arm around me and tucked me into his side, pressing me into the warmth of his body, like Sal was so keen on doing. It was different with César. Where Sal made me feel liquid and molten, César made me feel weightless, like I could slither past the holes his voice had punched into those slicing barriers and wriggle free of the suffocating press of my terror.

"As such," he pushed on, letting a comforting hand rub at my back, "they do not gain sustenance from food. It's not on their plane of existence. They must devour spiritual nutrients. There are two types of cadejos, the blacks, like Sal and I, and the whites. We don't have any white cadejos in the totoco anymore, but our progenitor, Antu, was a white cadejo. Each feeds differently, pulling out different energies from the prey . . . uh . . . humans. The blacks feed off of anger, pain, and fear. The whites feed on love, happiness, and hope."

I shuddered at the idea of a creature feeding off of the joy of another person, pulling it out of them, and leaving them with none. It reminded me of how my mother could sap every last drop of happiness and joy from me just by existing in my world.

He nodded. "I know. Each of them can inspire that in their prey, though. It's why so many of the locals will tell you of the ghost dogs stalking the darkness, leaving their children mute for weeks with fear. Sometimes, we inspire a bit too hard and make a meal a bit too large for our cadejos to consume down to balance." He shrugged with an apologetic half smirk pulling his lips awkwardly. "When you came through the courtyard, there was so much fear and pain radiating off of you that those closest to you are currently fallen down drunk on it, and the rest have fled back into the totoco house so as not to violate the laws on accident."

"Laws?"

He stared at me, incredulity wavering over his features. "He really hasn't told you anything, has he? I swear, when I see him, I'm kicking his ass for you, Xochi."

I snorted a laugh. It felt good to laugh as the claws eased away. The laugh slipped over my skin like an ice-cold drink slips down one's throat on a blisteringly hot summer day. "Thanks, César."

He grinned sheepishly at me. "Laws. Yeah. So, we are one totoco, yes? But we aren't the only ones. There are cadejo totocos from Canada down to Patagonia. Not a lot of them but enough that we have to keep a governing body. We call it the Council. The leaders, their mates, or their totoco spirit worker are the only representatives from each totoco."

Not really hearing much of his words, I nodded anyway. His voice was the solid ground in the floodwaters I needed to grip, so I let him keep talking.

"So, part of the Council's job is to enforce the laws we all agree to. One of those laws is that we are not to feed on people marked as totocan or potential totocan. It keeps us from draining each other dry and using our cadejos as war machines against each other, essentially wiping us off the map. Nothing stops us from waging regular war against each other, though. So, we can still occasionally get a few claws dirty." He winked at me. "But you are marked as totoco, and you are mated to the tecuhtli of the totoco. So, anyone caught feeding on you wouldn't just get beat to the ground. They'd be killed."

I choked on my own spit. "Killed?"

He nodded gravely. "But that's another bag of worms that I don't want to even imagine. So. Tell me about the ring."

I had almost forgotten the hunk of metal in my palm. Opening my palm, I saw the lurid red mark that it dug into my skin. "Jake's ring. He always wears it. I've never seen him without it. I found it in the creek out back."

He lofted his brows, asking quietly if he could take it. When I offered it, he plucked it from my palm with dexterous fingers. "And this ring, Jake's ring, had you so scared that you were disassociating with panic? Why?"

Disassociation. Is that what happened to me? I had felt like someone forced my consciousness out of my body, only a tenuous micro thread connecting the two halves of me. One was cast into the sea of nightmares, and the other had been left to bob and scuttle like a rudderless dinghy on a thrashing storm-churned sea of a different kind.

"I . . ." I snapped my mouth shut.

He cocked a brow again, turning the ring in his fingers. "You promised, Xochitl."

Gnawing on my lower lip, I began ravaging it, hoping the truth wouldn't pour out.

He frowned, pressing me for the first time since he laid a hand on my knee.

I sighed. He wasn't going to let this go. "Because, if his ring was here, that means he was here. And if he was here, that means that people from back home know where I am."

I hedged the facts, but it was close enough, peeling back the layers just enough for him to see the dewdrop of crystalline truth beading on the bloom of my life.

With a pensive look, he nodded, his eyes turning to the ring. "And you don't want to leave?"

"I don't want to go back there . . . ever again." His far too discerning gaze swept my face, searching for more information.

My heart pounded as I hoped against hope he did not push further. I wasn't ready to admit the truth he wanted from me, not even ready to face it myself.

"I see," he said, letting whatever questions he had been thinking through fall away. The shift in his body was almost imperceptible, but he softened, as if he had been on guard before. "Xochi, you need to know that you are totoco now. No matter what, no matter where you and Sal are with your relationship, no matter if you step up to your role of Cihuatlatoani or not, you will always be totoco. No one, not this Jake Lassiter guy, or anyone else, will ever take you from this place unless you wish to go. Even then, I doubt that Sal would let that happen quietly. You are safe here. You are safe with me. You are safe with Julia. You are safe with Nopaltzin."

He lofted his brows and stared directly into my eyes. "Sal is many things, Xochi. We've talked about this, but he would never allow harm to come to you. And I might not be the fighter he is, but I won't, either. And when Sal is not here, I am. When I am not, he is. No human will ever come into this compound and take you from us. Ever."

He tilted his head as I continued to chew on my lip, dots of blood speckling my tongue. "Do you believe me?"

Not really. He didn't know Annette like I did, didn't know the conniving manipulations she was capable of nor the harm she could bring upon them. The thought of her setting fire to this place twisted knots in my stomach. I hadn't seen her resort to violence since we were little, but I knew she was capable of it. The scars on Elida's back from a wire hanger when she was five were testament enough.

Despite my misgivings, I nodded anyway. The truth was a much more complicated mess than César deserved to have dumped at his feet. This burden was my own. And now that I had eased away from the cliff of chaos, the ring in César's hand told me I needed to leave soon. I couldn't stay here. If I wanted to stay living free, like I had come to enjoy, then I couldn't stay here. If I stayed here, Annette would come, and what would happen next could be easy or it could be hard. Either the cadejo would let me go with her, seeing me crumpled and defeated like a whipped dog, or she would harm them in some way to get me back into her perfect plan.

He leaned over and hugged me with one arm. "I won't tell Sal about this. I'll tell him you saw a snake and freaked out. Hmm?"

I smirked at him. "Thanks, César."

"Oh, no. Don't thank me. I just don't feel like dealing with him skulking about here, being an overbearing asshole while he prowls the perimeter like a juiced-up guard dog. And I don't feel like holding back Itzatecuani from slaughtering half the totoco in a jealous rage for them daring to accidentally be in the way when a fear buffet came barreling through the courtyard. So. Our secret."

He winked and tucked the ring into his pocket. "Now, Cihuatlatoani, I do believe you have a goat pen to finish mucking out. And I hear your tutor is a taskmaster when it comes to his kiln fires."

CHAPTER TWENTY-TWO

Itziquetzal

"**C**ome," I barked as I heard the knocking at the door to my office tucked into a small building we kept in the tiny town for business. My patience was thin after my argument with Xochitl earlier that afternoon, when I'd stopped by the compound to have lunch with her. I stayed away for three days, trying to get my shit together, and I couldn't stand it a second longer. I found her up to her elbows in goat shit, mucking out one of their pens, and she refused to have lunch with me. Once again, my godsdamned beast had reared up at the insult from his mate and vented his impotent rage at her. I'd have to apologize somehow when she was talking to me again.

As much as I hated to admit it, the fire creeping back into the corners of her walls turned me on. I fantasized about throwing logs on it to watch her incinerate everything around her. If she were crackling mad, at least the ice wouldn't crawl in further. It was in those times, when she was yelling—or like when she threw goat shit at me—I could just barely glance at the beautiful face of my mate again. I lived for those tiny glimpses. They gave me hope she wasn't gone, that Xochitl had not let her be killed over these many years.

My hand flexed as I remembered the way her eyes sparkled in the sunlight as she told me that, if I was hungry, she'd fix me a plate, then slopped a full shovel of goat piss and shit at my feet. Had I been sure she wasn't armed, I'd have pushed her into that muck and fucked her right then and there for the entire totoco to see.

Fuck. I adjusted the growing pressure in my slacks as Antonio closed my office door behind him and crumpled into the chair on the opposite side of my desk, causing me to quirk a brow. Antonio was many things. A slouch had never been one of them.

"Well?" I asked when he exhaled heavily and poured himself a glass of rum from my decanter.

"Well, I managed to cancel the contract with their firm. It took some talking, but their lawyer was happy enough with the breech of contract stipend I paid them to go away." He rolled the amber liquid in the glass, and I snorted.

Of course they were. If there was one thing I had learned about her teotl-cursed family, it was that they were money hungry in the worst way. Had I known sooner, I might have offered to pay them to let me have her. Though something told me the quick and easy way would have pissed my temperamental mate off even more than the kidnapping route.

"So, why do you look like you're about to shit in my chair?"

"Because that's not all I have to report."

"Well, then, get on with it, Antonio. I've got work to do aside from entertaining you all day." I growled at him.

Antonio was older than me by five or six years, we still weren't entirely sure. He had shown up on the caldera of the Chinameca volcano with a head injury seven years ago and had regained little of his memory since. The one thing he remembered, though, was how to be one hell of a numbers man. The man could calculate the square root of any number you spit at him in his head and carry large tallies of accounts to drop at a moment's notice. It had taken some time, but I trusted this cadejo with every last cent of my totoco's money and enterprises.

"They asked about her," he said quietly to the rum in his glass.

"And? Is that so strange? They are technically her family."

OBSIDIAN FEATHERS | 213

"Mmm. They are. But it's not necessarily that they asked about her . . . so much as the way they asked about her."

That caught my attention, and my gaze slid from the email I was reading to catch Antonio's. "What do you mean?"

He shrugged, considering the liquid before taking a gulp. "I can't say for certain. It wasn't the words they used, Itzatecuani. It was the way they said them. It was like they were asking about property instead of a person."

I frowned. "Who did you talk to? The mother? She's always been awful. Even from the small glimpses I had of her, she made me uneasy."

He shook his head. "The fiancé."

"Don't call him that. He is nothing to her," I snarled back at him.

"You sure about that? He seemed mighty intent on knowing about her whereabouts and movements."

"She is my wife, Antonio."

My beast snapped under my skin, prowling the perimeter, waiting for a moment he could sink his fangs into anyone that thought Xochitl belonged to anyone but us.

Antonio snorted. "I know, brother, but he doesn't. To him, she's to be *his* wife. And he was mollified by the scraps I gave him, but . . . I don't know, Itzatecuani. It felt different than a man asking about his fiancé. I can't say exactly what it was, it just . . . felt off. Something's there that we are missing."

I snorted and turned my attention back to my emails. "He's just annoyed she's not answering his calls."

Antonio wasn't convinced. I could tell by the way he shrugged and downed the rum.

"If you say so, tecuhtli," he dubiously replied, pushing up out of the chair, setting his glass on the edge of my desk, making his way out of my office.

What if I was wrong? What if, despite Xochitl not returning his affections, this man was in love with her? What if he never let her go? What if he was just like me?

"Antonio."

He paused, the door to my office ajar in his hand.

"If he calls back again, tell him if he comes for her, I'll rip his intestines out and fuck her raw on his still bleeding corpse."

Antonio barked a laugh. "Just like that, brother?"

I grinned menacingly. "Feel free to get more graphic if necessary. The point stays the same. If he comes for her, I will fuck my mate on his defeated body."

Antonio nodded with a wry smile and closed my door.

The fire of the bourbon sliding down my throat licked a hot path through the seething anger nursed by its amber depths. She had run from me again. Run from us. I wanted to go after her, but the beast had dug his claws in and forced me to stay my path. I had paced behind that gate for what seemed like hours, but she hadn't come back.

Abandoning her, especially when the fire and claws were out just where I liked them, had been the hardest thing I had done. I longed to feel her flesh against my own, to hear her sigh into my ear and curl my name into her mouth with the reverence she held while my arms were wrapped around her. It had been too long since I slept next to her, too many nights away from her, figuring out what I would do to get us back to where we needed to be. Too many nights spent staring up into the stars and begging the teotl and my spirits to show me how to get back the golden goddess shackled within her flesh.

He didn't knock, not my cousin. Oh, no, not in my most sacred of sanctums. Why would he? Not a damned care for my position, nor the rights afforded to the position of my title.

"We need to talk," he snapped, my office door slamming behind him.

My brow arched over the rim of my glass. This was out of character for my slithery cousin. He was not me. He was not one to barge through doors and demand an audience. He scowled at my amusement and crossed his arms, a habit he had recently picked up from me, and I didn't particularly care for the way it fit him.

"I'm worried about Xochi."

No opening salvo, no buffer, or easy slide into the subject. Who was this creature that had seeped into the careful skin of my cousin and taken hold of his spirits? Whomever he was, I liked him a lot more than I liked the creeping creature that formerly held his place.

My other brow lofted, joining its mate. "And what has she done to worry you now, cousin? Has she finally shown you the same thing that she has shown me? Do you believe me now that there is something wrong with her?"

"Stop talking about her like she is damaged goods," he hurled back at me, chasing the drunken edges from my vision as it narrowed on him.

Of course she wasn't damaged goods. Of course she wasn't anything to be tossed away and thrown out like garbage. She was just . . . complicated. A complication and a gordian knot I was itching to unravel as soon as I figured out what angle to attack it from.

"I'm not. You are. Now, spit it out, César. I have a date with a very pretty blonde that has been waiting thirty years for me to wrap my lips around her."

He glared at me, the fire of his cadejo finally ripping the surface as his brows drew down and flashes of deadly green played in his gaze. "You wouldn't dare."

"I'm talking about a fucking scotch, you jealous old hen. Fuck, man, do you really think Itzatecuani would let me even think about another woman, let alone actually touch one? I've never seen someone break their own bones from the inside out, but I think he'd figure out how to do it if I tried."

Mollified by the threat of internal bleeding, my cousin forged on. "Good. You led me to believe that maybe things weren't great with

Xochi, maybe she had some baggage, but I think you undersold it, brother. There's more to it, isn't there?"

The razor-slip slide of alarm slid through my spirit and severed the strength of the sludge around my brain. I didn't want to betray Xochi's confidence. What little she had actually given me was like nuggets of gold to be hoarded and stored for a rainy day, when she'd push me away again. I scowled at him. Not letting thoughts and memories of the times she had cried in the night, all the violence I had witnessed her wince away from in her sleep, or the haunted look in her eye when I moved a certain way, things I didn't think she realized she did, creep into my features.

"Tell me, brother," he commanded.

I hated when he used the ritual voice the priests mastered for ceremony. It crawled along my skin and seeped into my pores, nudging at the primal side of my brain that longed for a time when the nights were dark and the days were long, without the press of civilization.

I grunted, set down the glass of bourbon, and steepled my hands in front of me. This was a calculation, a risk that might not work out well for me, but if there was one person I could trust, aside from my troubled little flower, it was my cousin. "She has nightmares."

"What kind of nightmares?" He scowled as deep as I did.

"The kind that is remarkable enough to make me mention it."

I was hedging, and it was obvious.

"How often?"

"Nightly. Every single night, at least as far as I am aware. I've watched her through the windows while I've been away from her . . ."

I swallowed my tongue, unwilling to admit that a sneaking voice had skittered into my brain and that maybe I was the reason for those nightmares. When I saw her writhing in the sheets, fighting whatever demons she battled each night, a small breath of relief had gusted out of me. At least I knew it wasn't my skin pressed against her in the night that brought them to her.

"And you didn't think to tell me before? They could be spiritual in nature. I told you when I examined her, there was something off with her spirit. Something that I sensed that I have not encountered before. I have been meaning to examine her but just haven't seen a reason to step between the two of you trying to work out your . . . issues."

I grunted. "Issues."

A derisive snort. Yes. Issues. That was what we had, nothing more. Just issues. How neat and tidy was that? Just package up all the claws and the spitting rage and the carving of each other's skin into such a tidy little civilized package as "issues." If only they were as neat and tidy.

"I didn't think to tell you, César, because, despite the fact that you see spirits crawling across every little vine and spider in this world, some people just have nightmares. And that's a normal thing. You'd think a creature who can seed them in the waking minds of humans would know that, sometimes, it's just a fucking nightmare."

My beast awoke, realizing his mate was being discussed with another male. He was not normally a jealous creature, but when it came to Xochi, he saw any unmated male as a threat to his territory. Until he was satisfied with either his seed planted in her womb or a mate mark dug into her flesh, he would keep snarling under my skin and pushing me toward that inevitability.

"I don't know how to help her, César. The only time I see her at real true ease around me, when she feels like she is truly living in her skin, is when she is at my feet, kneeling to my whims." I frowned, disliking that I was revealing this to my assumably celibate cousin, who did not understand the things I needed to submit my partners to.

He certainly did not understand the way the golden meteors streaked across the sky of her eyes when she came for me with her ass on fire and my cock buried deep inside of her.

He drew in a deep breath and exhaled, staring straight at me. "Any other time, I would never advise this. Any other person. Any other cadejo. Any other situation. But I saw the way she melted into you at the gate—"

"That was not for your eyes, César. You would do well to forget that ever happened," I snarled, my beast controlling my teeth to snap the words.

"Then, next time, keep it in your fucking quarters, Itzatecuani," he said to my left eye, which I assumed, from the spike of discomfort, my beast decided to take as his own.

Snorting, I picked up my bourbon, washing down the push of my beast, who wished to crawl through my skin and flay my cousin alive for having the audacity to acknowledge the show we had put on for the totoco in full view, knowing that some might not have had the good sense to turn away.

Onward, he pushed, unhindered by the fear for his safety that any other sane person would have been subjected to under the gaze of the predator that stalked my born flesh. "I don't understand it. I don't understand how any of that works between you two, but if it works, and you have seen it help her . . . push harder. I'm scared we are going to lose her. She's drowning."

"What do you know, César?" I narrowed my gaze on him and pushed forward from my chair, leaning over the desk separating us.

He was smart enough to step back, the low dark rumble of his cadejo's growl of warning trembling in his chest. "That's between her and I. The purview of a teopixqui and his charge."

"Fuck that. You are not going to barge into my office, tell me how to handle my mate and then pull sacred duty as an out when I ask you what happened. Tell me." I was moving around the desk before realizing I was stalking him.

He circled back, his arms trading shadows to the withered, desiccated claws of his beast. "You know better than to ask me that, Sal. An oath was given. And an oath will be kept. Push all you want. You will not take that from me."

I had him pressed against the wall by his throat by the time his jaws gathered shadow and snapped around my hand. I hissed at the lightning coruscating through my bones as he shook his head, rending flesh from bone, sundering my grip. I stumbled backward, giving him the opportunity to knee me in the face. A low blow, even for him. My back hit the floor, and he was on top of me, the golden glow of his sparkly, furred arms wrapped around my throat as he squeezed. His eyes had gone pure jade from tear duct to the outer corner and wept golden tears as he wrung the life from me.

"Dammit, Sal. Get your"—he squeezed harder, my eyes bulging around the pressure as I clawed at his hands—"fucking shit together. This isn't about you. This isn't about the totoco. This is about her. You spent twenty fucking years sulking around this place waiting for her. I won't let you fuck it up."

His chipped claws dug into my flesh as my lungs burned. I could easily let my beast, who was snarling in my mind and pressing forward against the well within me, take over, but his loyalties were not mine, and he would destroy my soft cousin. When I could no longer stand the magma in my lungs, I tapped at his thigh, slapping it with what strength I had left.

He lept off of me and shoved an agitated claw through his sweat-tousled mop of curls, pacing as he calmed down. Pulling myself off the ground, I adjusted my suit, wiping the blood from my hand on the back of my pants. We glared at each other, two predators squaring off, waiting for the other to make another aggressive move. As ever, though, my cousin was the first to back down, to calm from the killer edge that pulsed within us.

"Come here, you moron. Let me heal that." He grabbed at the mangled meat formerly known as my hand. The glow of his gift lit up my flesh, and as always, the burn licked through my flesh as it knit together. When he was done and I was panting through the pain, he looked into my eyes. A lost little boy had taken up residence in the stoic face of my friend.

"You'll try?" he asked in a hushed, pained whisper.

I nodded. "I'll do dirty, depraved things to my mate, César. I promise."

He rolled his eyes and pushed me away. "You had to make it fucking weird. Didn't you?"

We both snorted a laugh, and he left while I planned the battle I would wage against my mate's nightmares.

CHAPTER TWENTY-THREE

I didn't hear the front door open, I didn't hear his stealthy footsteps down the corridor, nor did I hear him open freshly hung and oiled hinges of the bedroom door. I didn't notice him until, humming a wordless tune to myself as I finger-combed out my freshly showered ringlets, I saw him leaning against the wall, watching me with hungry eyes, a thirsty smirk on his lips and blood smeared all over his suit pants.

I squeaked in surprise, and he shifted, muscles coiling as if to strike. Something was different about him. Something dangerous and tempting rode the air between us, thick like sticky syrup. It danced in the molten heat of his black eyes, in the severe cut of his brows drawn down, as his focus zeroed in on me. It was in the sharp teeth he ran his tongue over as my startled hand flew to my shower-dampened collarbone, hidden beneath the soft cotton of one of his shirts I'd pilfered from the laundry.

I'd never tell him I had missed the solid security of his body next to me at night. I'd never tell him I missed his scent, warm and alive in the sheets beside me. I'd never tell him that I'd pulled it from the hamper as Julia carried it out this morning so I could savor his smell while I slept. Nor would I tell him that the way he was looking at me, like he was a nanosecond away from tackling me to the floor and either devouring me whole or ravaging me within an inch of my life, had my depths clenching for the welcomed inevitability of either outcome.

Instead, I turned the shock of seeing him materialize at the closed door of our bedroom into fire and brimstone. He could never know how badly I longed for him while he was gone. He could feel my wrath over it, though.

"What do you want?" I snapped. It wasn't the best I could do, but when he looked at me like that, his gaze a stroking hand over my body, it was hard to focus on all the reasons I was mad at him. When he didn't answer, I crossed my arms and cocked a hip. "Well? Are you just going to stand there and stare at me, or are you going to say something?"

The corner of his mouth twitched up, and he rolled his neck, a solid couple of pops grinding out from beneath his skin. He took a deep breath, his nose twitching with the inhale. The silence drew out between us, and I squirmed beneath his steady, unwavering stare. A twinge of fear wove into my blood. I didn't like it when he was quiet. He wasn't a quiet man. He was insufferable and sexy and made me soaking wet from the tip of my hair to the curl of my toes.

"Fine. Stand there and look like a statue. Suit yourself. You're not getting in this bed with me, though." I snorted and turned my back on him.

Never mind it was *his* bed. I slept in it; it was mine, too. He could find his own bed, preferably at the bottom of a cliff.

It was the wrong move. I should not have turned my back on him. I realized my mistake a step and a half into my journey to the bed, when my cheek met the wall as he pressed against me. My heart, the treacherous little creature it was, lurched a groaning thud, and my stomach clenched with a barely suppressed moan of delight as his nose ran up the length of the back of my neck in a soft nuzzle. His chest pressed me against the wall, ragged breaths working the bellows of his lungs.

"Oh, little flower," he murmured, hot against the crook of my neck in a tone promising reverence and debauchery.

He spun me easily, my back pressing to the chill of the wall as his nose kept nuzzling at my throat. I gulped, unable to control the twist of the fear-laced need pulsing through me, keen and sharp as the teeth he grazed teasingly across tender flesh. The fingers of one hand, tipped in the dangerous claws of his beast but not sporting the tufts of fur I was used to seeing, chased the line of the teeth. He watched me as if in awe of the way my lips parted and a soft pant escaped my lips.

I didn't like how he was looking at me. I didn't like the way it turned my legs to jelly and my insides to magma. I didn't like the way it made me feel loose and at ease. I pressed my palms to his massive chest, gave a half-hearted push, and as I expected, nothing happened. All I received was a dangerous smirk for my trouble.

"Oh, sweet little flower. How you bloom when you're mad." The hand tracing the line of his teeth wrapped around my throat and rested there with just enough tension to kick my heart rate up a few notches. "Tell me . . . can you open in my shadows?"

I pushed again, harder this time. "Oh, fuck off, Sal."

He grinned, leaned down, and nipped at my bottom lip as his knee slid up to press against the molten heat of my core. He ground up into my body, sending shockwaves of sparkling pleasure skittering from the epicenter of my body to pop and sizzle behind my eyelids.

"Tell me to stop, and I will. Tell me to keep going, and I will," he murmured against my lip, the gust of his words making me shiver with desire.

His knee kept moving, soaking the fabric of his suit pants. I didn't want him to stop. My body pleaded with its honey voice for him to keep going, no matter what lies my lips fed him.

"Fuck off," I whispered with all the bite and vigor of a malnourished and starving kitten.

The squeeze of his hand around my throat choked off a groan as his other hand dragged a razor-sharp nail down the front of his shirt I wore. Two more slices of that deadly point, and the shirt fell to the ground in a puddle beneath me.

"My gods," he whispered as if seeing me for the first time. A starved look cast down my curved and rounded body. I wanted to shy away from that gaze but also bask in it for the rest of eternity. His eyes seemed to drink in my body like it was sacred, to lap it up with the thirst of a desert in its first rain of ten years. "The teotl themselves are jealous of your beauty, my little flower. I could walk this earth for a thousand years and still not see something half as beautiful as the sight of you, dripping wet and begging for me."

I whimpered against the press of his hand, the grind of his knee against me melting away every last bit of annoyance. It shot great boulders of heavy need into me, pressing down on me until I could do nothing to stop the slow circles my hips ground against him, seeking more of the intoxicating slide and friction teasing my soaked pussy and the steady throb of my clit. My eyes slid shut as I fell into the clutches of my own greed for that slow slip.

The second his knee eased away, my eyes, glazed over with lust, whipped open, and he grinned down at me again before attacking my mouth. His tongue slid past the poorly defended fortress of my lips, and my arms snaked around his neck, drawing him into the kiss. My entire existence narrowed to the clash and dance of our tongues against each other. Small whimpers bloomed at the back of my throat as he drank from the never-ending well of carnality he had tapped within me.

Breathless, he tore his lips from mine and traced a claw around my pebbled tawny nipple. The press of that sharp point into the sensitive bud had me whimpering again.

"Tell me," he commanded in a voice sharp with the knife of his beast and with the twin lust riding his soul. When I tried to pull him closer, he pinched hard enough I was sure a bead of blood would tip my nipple. I gasped, the sound dying off into a groan as I pressed my breast into his brutality. "Wrong answer, little flower."

I didn't have time to flutter my confused lashes at him before my cheek was, once again, pressed to the chill of the wall. This time, though, his hand gathered mine at the wrist and placed them above my head, flat on the wall. "Keep those there. Do not move them."

Turning, I glared over my shoulder at him but kept my hands where he placed them. He was watching me, his dexterous hands slowly undoing his belt, letting me watch with a watering mouth as he worked it above the thick strain of his cock against the dark gray suit pants. The muscles of his arms, visible below the rolled-up cuffs of his dress shirt, flexed as he pulled it loop by loop from around him. My eyes zeroed in on the promise of the sight of his cock. When he didn't go for the button, all but gasping under the stress of his rock-hard length, I thought I'd combust.

Instead, he lifted my hair and carefully, almost tenderly, looped the black polished leather of the belt around my neck.

"Wha . . . what are you doing?" I asked, true fear lancing through me for the first time since he walked in.

He gave an almost imperceptible shudder and tightened the belt. The edges of my vision swam in inky delight as he leaned down and licked a searing line up my spine before whispering in my ear.

His body twitched, nearly pulsing with delight as he fought for breath. "Your fear tastes delicious, nayeli."

I heard the creak of the belt as his fingers flexed around it, and he finally lifted his head from the chilling trail of his tongue. "You know the words, little flower."

Words? What were those, exactly? I had a vague recollection of something about human speech being possible, but I would give anything for him to just keep touching my feverish flesh like that. To just keep doing whatever it was he wanted.

The belt loosened around my neck, and my head spun with a euphoric lightness. My hand slipped a fraction of an inch.

The crack of his hand against the wealth of my ass shook loose any last grips I had on the awareness of life beyond that moment. The sting of it raced through my body and seated itself squarely in some part of my brain I hadn't explored before. A part of my brain that was pure sensation and need. It shook loose a moan that rattled through my chest and forced itself past my kiss-ravaged lips.

"Mmm, yes. Just like that, my little flower." He groaned behind me. "Count them for me. I want to hear you count."

Another strike, this one on the other ass cheek. My fingers flexed against the intrusion of the pain as it lanced through me, but my hands did not move from the elected spot.

"One," I half panted, half moaned.

Shoving his hands between the kiss of my thighs, gathering the slick juices flowing freely. The calloused pad of his finger stroked at the insistent, aching throb of that pearl of pleasure, and I nearly crumbled into his hand. The belt tightened around my throat, bringing with it that still blackness.

"Good," he whispered into my ear. "Be a good girl for me. Take everything I have for you."

Whining, I moved my hips against his hand to chase the pleasure it promised, but it was gone before I could capture it. The belt loosened, the euphoria flooding in and washing tension from my muscles. He pulled at my hip, drawing them from the wall, the other pressing into my back to arch it out and present my ass for him. A foot wedged between mine, widening my stance. Tilting my pelvis back, I put my pussy on full display for his hungry gaze, which I felt like a tangible stroke down my shivering flesh.

"Fuck," he groaned. "Do you have any idea what you look like right now? Legs spread wide, my hand prints on your ass, your cunt dripping and begging for me. My belt around your throat."

Another slap to my ass, this one harder than the last. This one jolted my body, and I twitched with the sting. I would weather a hurricane with my hands glued to this damned wall if it would keep him going.

The press of his teeth into my side, sharp, all that of his beast, ripped a scream of pleasure and agony from my lips. My flesh parted for him, and his teeth sank into me a fraction of an inch. I stilled, a picture of a statue as the fire licking from my ribs washed into the tidal waves of pleasure. The tingle of his groaning breath against the wound had me crying out.

"Please . . ." I whispered.

I had no clue what I was asking for. No idea what I wanted. I just *wanted*. I just *needed*.

His teeth slid from me, and I was shivering, shuddering with the power of the want pressing down on me. He gripped my hips again, hard enough I knew somewhere back in my conscious self that there would be bruises in the morning. I wanted them. I wanted to wake up sore and aching from this, with his fingerprints ground into my flesh. Something about it sang in my blood as *right*. I wanted it more than breath itself and tried to squirm to make him grip harder, but he had other plans.

Another crack to my ass. The impact shook the ragged edges of my bite mark, and I moaned out, "Two."

I could hear him panting behind me. I could sense his ragged breath, just as desperate for whatever this was as I was.

Another slap.

"Three."

This time, I let the moan fall without trying to turn it into the number. I wanted him to hear how I melted into the pain. I wanted him to hear my need.

He did. Once again, his hand was on me, gathering up the dripping honey between my thighs, two fingers delving into me, his tongue sliding up my spine again. I didn't move. I fought and thrashed against the instinct to grind on his fingers. To take the pleasure I wanted so badly from him. I needed him to keep going. To fuck my aching pussy until it was crying for him and only him.

"Fuck, you are soaking wet," he groaned into my ear. His dark voice curled around my brain and stroked it as his fingers pistoned inside me, seeking that spot he was so obsessed with. I tightened on his fingers, wanting to feel every ridge and callous as it slammed into my needy depths. His forehead pressed to my shoulder as I stood still, except for the squeeze of my cunt around his fingers. "Don't come, my little flower. Not until you beg me for it."

I whimpered my protest, and he tightened the belt around my neck, choking off the sound as the black rushed in at the edges of my vision. He kept me there, hovering on the edge of bliss, suspended in the creeping blackness for what seemed like a most deliciously agonizing eternity.

The orgasm coiled to strike, wrapping around my legs, tensing and milking around his fingers. Just a little longer, just a few more thrusts of his fingers, and I would be sent into the sky, screaming my pleasure to the heavens.

I never hit the sky, though. Before I could get there, he ripped himself away from me with a vicious growl that was all Itzatecuani. The belt loosened around my throat. Then it was gone. I sagged, my forehead finding the wall, but my hands never moving an inch.

It didn't take long to discover where the belt went. Its folded length kissed both ass cheeks with a fiery lash I couldn't help but scream through. He was kind enough to pause as I caught my breath. His own breathing had long ago moved past panting; it was jagged edged growls.

"Four."

He moaned when the word dropped from my lips.

I never lost count. Not a single time between four and eight, breathing through the burning kiss of the leather striking my tender skin. By number nine, the heat on my ass joined the heat on my cheeks as tears fell. I couldn't help it. It was like something raw and bleeding broke open inside of me and poured out of my eyes. Even as I moaned out the number, the tears pooled and slid down to rain on the swell of my breasts pressed to the wall.

The tenth strike was the hardest to stand still for. It was the hardest he'd ever hit me. The explosion of sensations sent me soaring into a nebula of stars that burst from my lips on a pained, whining moan that somehow shaped itself into the number.

"Hands. Wall." He snarled behind me as his hands, once again, found my hips.

This time, I felt him lift, shifting below me with his back facing the wall. My shins found a place on his shoulders, and his volcanic breath gusted against the ocean of need at my center. His palms found a place to rest, fingers digging into my hips, above my ass at my back.

"Sit," he barked.

When I didn't move, his sharp teeth bit into one tender, puffy lip, and I cried out, my ass crashing my soaked cunt against his face. He licked, lapping at me with the raspy length of tongue belonging to his beast. He slurped and sucked at my clit. Blinding pleasure burst inside of me, and I was whimpering. I didn't mean to whimper. I didn't want to whimper, but I couldn't help it. Between the inferno on the globes of my ass, the pulsing raw thing in my chest, the crush of the stars in my head, and the twisting coils of pleasure his tongue and teeth were ripping from me, it was as close as I could get to any sound.

"Mine," he growled as my hips drifted slightly too far for his liking. He gripped them, grinding me possessively back down onto his devouring mouth.

Throwing my head back, I was unable to breathe past the crash of surrounding sensations. I used my hands as leverage when he slid three fingers into my gripping depths and pounded into me ruthlessly. I took it. Every brutal stroke of those three twisting fingers shoved me closer and closer to the edge of bliss. I wanted to flirt with it. I wanted to dance on the edge and ride it as long as humanly possible. The groan of delight that rumbled across my clit told me that Sal loved that idea or at least loved the fact that the brutality he was visiting upon my most tender of places was being met with wild abandon as I thrust myself down into him.

"Beg," he commanded into my ravaged flesh.

"Please, Itziquetzal. Please." I was weeping into the words. I wanted to come more than I wanted to breathe. I need it. "Fuck. Please let me come for you?"

The sound that dragged itself over me was half groan and half howl of delight. "Come for me, little flower. Soak my face, my beautiful fucking slut. Fucking come for me."

He pounded me harder, a small part of me wondering if I'd survive this orgasm. I didn't care. Not even a little bit. I clamped down around his hand and forced myself down as hard as I could. My heart stopped. My breathing stopped. Everything stopped as my body seized up all the discordant shards of sensation and sliced me in two with the power of the orgasm. I felt the exact moment when my heart started again, felt it pound the pleasure into every molecule of my existence in a flood that would drown the world.

It seemed to go on and on forever. Sal's fingers had stilled in me, unable to keep thrusting from the strength of my muscles flexing around him. I whimpered, chasing the tail of the comet by grinding my hips down on his fingers.

I felt when breath came back as the last drops of orgasm rippled and shivered through me. It filled my burning lungs and cooled the tears still slipping down my cheeks.

I felt dead. I felt alive. I felt every pained squeeze of my heart as it labored to catch up with me. Sal shuddered under me, as if he, too, were recovering from the most powerful orgasm of his entire life. He didn't move. I didn't move. My arms shook, the effort to hold them up against the wall a herculean one.

I felt him finally shift under me, his mouth finally coming away from the shuddering bud of flesh it had been wrapped around.

"Shhh. Shhh," he whispered against the rise of my pubis, his free hand drawing up against the back of my thigh to pet the raised welts on my ass. His fingers moved, slowly, so excruciatingly slowly. I groaned, the sensation almost too much for me to process. When he finally had pulled them from my depths, I felt the soft slide of his tongue, all his now, run along the tender, brutalized flesh reverently before he placed a kiss to my weeping cunt.

"Easy, nonayeli."

His voice was distant but so soft. I could not remember a time when he had spoken to me like that. It was like he was speaking in the presence of a god, unwilling to offend but in awe of its presence.

"Hands down."

His command was tender, and he was pulling me into his arms before I could obey. My entire body was shaking, trembling to my very roots. An adoring kiss was placed to my forehead.

"There's my good girl," he murmured against the sweat-slicked skin. I never knew how much adoration, love, desire, and worship could hide in the depths of a whisper. "I am in awe of you. You took everything I had, little flower. You are a goddess, perfection made flesh."

He carried me to the bed. A silky fur was draped around me as he tucked me into it. I whined with disappointment when he didn't immediately join me, and his dark chuckle was my answer. He joined me, his bare skin sliding under the fur blanket. Bands of iron muscles wrapped around me and crushed my back to his chest, his legs pulling mine back into his until he was curled around me. His nose was buried in the nape of my neck, his lips placing tender soft kisses to the flesh he could get to.

"Sshhh, nayeli. Ni mitz tlazohtla. Tehuan nollotzin. Amo nica in tale tehuatl."

He was murmuring in Nahuatl. The words meant nothing, but the sentiment was clear. His heart was speaking, and I shivered at the power of those simple sounds weaving a tight blanket around me.

We lay like that for a long while, his body curled around me, his hands stroking my shuddering flesh, his voice whispering secrets in Nahuatl. When I could finally form human thoughts and speech, I turned my head to him, and he smiled dotingly down to me, the oak having returned to his eyes.

"Sh—" My voice cracked. My throat worked razors through it. I cleared my throat around the vicious slash and tried again. "You didn't . . . should . . . would you like it if I . . . if I sucked you off?"

He smirked, letting it bloom into a chuckle. "No, cihuapiltzintle. I could live on the taste of you coming for me, your ass bright red, and my fingers fucking you so hard I can barely keep up." He kissed the top of my head. "No, beloved. That was for you. My reward was my name on your lips when you came for me."

When I opened my mouth to protest again, he squeezed me tight. "Sshh," he commanded in that voice that reached down into my soul and shook an errant drop of pleasure out of me.

I shivered at the sound, then snuggled into him.

The silence between us stretched out, pregnant with a sense of clean finality. As if whatever had happened between us had turned a page, this one was blank and ready for us to write something new upon it.

"That wasn't an apology, by the way," I whispered, only half teasingly.

"No . . . it wasn't." He smiled.

CHAPTER TWENTY-FOUR

S ometime in the night, Sal had slid out of bed but was back before I woke up. Curling around me like a protective shield and holding me tightly while we slept. I suspected that César betrayed my confidence when I woke, and he was still nuzzled into the back of my neck and wrapped around me. When he didn't wake as I slid from the bed, I put the thought aside. If he feared for me, I believed Sal would have held me until he was awake enough to protect me.

I went about my business getting ready while he curled around my pillow, trying desperately to ignore the aches and stiffness radiating from my delighted but battered sex and the throbbing rigidity of the bite on my side. I was sitting back on the bed when he finally roused, blearily looking up at me, fully dressed in a pair of loose shorts, a tank top, and soft-cored sandals.

He groaned and looked at the alarm clock on the other side of the bed. "You're up early, nayeli."

His voice was thick and husky with sleep.

I smiled down at him, having forgiven him for our fight from the day before. I decided in the strangeness between our rabid joining and finally falling into the arms of sleep, that his transgression wasn't as bad as it could have been. Whenever he looked up at me with those lovesick eyes, like he was in that moment, it was hard to hold a grudge against him. I finger-combed conditioner into my wet hair. "I have chores to do. And I want to get them done before it gets too hot."

"Come back to bed. Chores can wait until later," he purred, pulling at the swell of my hips where bruises bloomed like irises in the shapes of his fingers.

I chuckled and playfully tapped his hand. "If it were you, you wouldn't say that."

He smirked in defeat. He knew I was right. He never stayed in bed long after he woke up.

It struck me as odd that, the longer I stayed and the more I woke up next to Sal, the more it settled into a comfortable pattern. My deviation that morning felt like a slight against that normality and structure but also felt right.

He yawned and stretched powerful, bare muscles under the black sheets. My mouth watered to lick a hot trail down every ridge and valley.

He grinned up at me, as if sensing the path of my thoughts. "Keep looking at me that way, nayeli, and you won't be going anywhere."

I had the good sense to blush and look away. He snorted his disapproval of me not taking up his bald offer.

"I got you something." He yawned into my pillow and flopped deeper into his, snuggling it. I never thought I'd be more jealous of a pillow.

"Yeah?" I asked, lofting my brows at him, finishing the last of my finger-combing.

"It's in your nightstand."

Fishing around in the nightstand, I found a small black satchel and opened it. It was a ribbon, like the one Julia had given me for my hair. Except this one had a black edge, a white background, and featured black feathers and yellow-orange flowers in a repeating pattern. The loose-woven ribbon was perhaps two inches wide, perfect for wrapping my braids, and a little too long so I could experiment with the style.

"Is this an apology?" I asked, arching a brow at him.

He smirked bashfully and shrugged.

"Oh, good, then, if you don't know. I don't accept it as an apology."

He snorted and groaned. "Fine. Yes. It's an apology. I acted poorly."

I tilted my head, watching him. "Don't buy me things just to get me to forgive you. I'm not materialistic. But . . . you're almost forgiven."

He grinned wolfishly and grabbed me, finally dragging me down into the bed with him, and nuzzled my cheek before kissing me gently. His fingers worked into the fall of my wet hair and drew me deeper still, the kiss quickly turning passionate and heated. He was kind enough to break the kiss because I didn't have the strength to do so. He pressed his forehead to mine, both of us panting with the need coursing through us.

"I'll do better," he murmured against my swollen lips. "I promise."

"I'll hold you to that," I purred.

"I meant it when I said I would do anything to be worthy of you." His lips were a whisper against my own, a seductive temptation. I curled my legs around him, holding fast as I tried to catch my breath. "Anything at all, noyzotzon."

I pressed my lips to his, claiming that tongue that promised me everything I had ever wanted, and tore it all down as well. His tongue slid into my mouth, curling and dancing with mine. With others, it was a battle. With Sal, our tongues danced around each other, stroking and curling against each other with not a single clash of rhythm. My hips ground down against him, my body needing him to finish the dance our mouths started.

A growl rumbled past our joined tongues, and he flipped me on my back effortlessly, pressing me into the mattress with the weight of his hips. His hands gripped my wrists and held them to either side of my head.

Flashing burnet eyes fixed on me, and a curtain of obsidian locks fell around my head. "Oh, nonamic, you need to stop kissing me like you want to fuck me with the same mouth that claims to need to do chores."

He ground his thick, hard cock against my canvas-clad cleft, and I whimpered with delight. Sore as I was, every tempting swirl of his hips kicked sparks of fire into my blood, and I couldn't help it.

"Keep making sounds like that, nonayeli, and I am going to fuck you until you can't feel your legs and the only words you can think of are my name and the word please." He punctuated each thickly accented word with a grinding rotation of his hips, teasing the both of us.

It was him who finally cracked, rolling off of me with a nip to my pillowy lips. He stayed close, tracing a finger over the slight bruise that dusted my throat. There was no apology for it in his eyes. But he smiled with the memory of him tightening that leather strap just enough to smoke the edges of my vision but not enough to cut off my air completely. A delicate balance . . . much like our . . . whatever it was we were. "Finish getting dressed. And, Xochitl? When you are done with whatever it is you have on your list today, come find me. I'll finish earning that forgiveness from you."

A sweet kiss was placed on my forehead, and he leaped from the bed to disappear into the bathroom. A shaking hand touched my singed lips, and I smiled before getting up to finish braiding my hair with the new ribbon Sal had given me.

Every movement, every twitch, every jostle pulsed in my heart and flesh the memory of what we did last night, and I cherished every second of it.

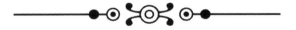

"Cihuatlatoani!" called a young girl of maybe twelve as she ran from the field gates to where I was squatting over a plaster tablet, working water out of some clay for Nopaltzin. I looked up, pushing an errant curl from my clay-slicked hands. "Tía Julia wants you to come quick!"

Concern flashed through me, and I covered the clay with a soaked cotton hank of fabric and leaped to my feet. "Show me, wewe."

I was picking up small words in both Nahuatl and, under the instruction of Nopaltzin, a few words he remembered in his native Lenca. The totoco was a melting pot of languages strung together with the common tongue of Spanish, but they were encouraged to intermingle the tongues. I learned the totoco's official term for a "young child" was the Lenca word for "child," wewe. Even the totoco's name, Lets'a Wehle, which meant Honey Moon, was Lenca.

Following the young girl, I wiped my hands on my apron, trotting to keep up. When we got to the fallow field that the totoco was preparing for the next planting, five adults circled around something. Images of the worst possible things filtered through my mind. When I stepped between them to stare down at three innocuous shoots of tenuous green stems, I was bewildered.

"Xochitl," Julia mumbled and leaned away from the plant, as if it would grow sentience and attack her at any moment.

"Julia?" I asked, tilting my head. "She said you needed me?"

"I'm so sorry, Xochi. I know you're busy, but Rafael is with Cheeno in town," she said, looking at the other cadejo gathered around for support.

"Okay?"

She pointed at the plant. "It can't be here."

"So, pull it out?"

Confusion twisted my neck and words.

"We can't."

"Why not?"

"It's rue, Cihuatlatoani," Phelix offered, as if that meant anything to me.

"Okay?" My eyes darted from face to face, trying to glean the unspoken context I was missing.

"It's poisonous to us, Cihuatlatoani," offered Emalia sheepishly, as if admitting that they had any sort of weakness was not her place to do.

"Oh! Okay. It's not poisonous to humans?" I asked, furrowing my brows, regarding the innocuous-looking innocent shoots springing from the ground.

Emalia shook her head. "No, but very poisonous to us. It can kill our cadejos and leaves us half dead."

"Okay, no problem. I'll just pull it out and toss it in the compost pile." I squatted to grip the little plant.

"No, Xochi, the entire soil around it has to be taken, too. And the roots. And it has to be burned downwind from the compound. Even the smoke can make us sick."

I frowned up at her. This simple plant could make these powerful beasts violently ill, and they were terrified of it.

"Be sure to scrub your hands and anything that touches it really well, too. Even the littlest bit could make anyone you touch sick if they aren't strong enough."

"Right, wewe, can you go get me the shovel from the tool shed and a bucket?" The young girl ran off to do as I asked, and I took off my apron and stuffed it into my back pocket to trail after me like a tail.

When she returned, I extracted the offending plant and the soil a foot around it into the bucket.

Hefting the bucket through the field and into the courtyard, I nodded at my tutor, letting him know I couldn't finish the clay. He skirted wide around me and nodded.

Once I burned the plant and buried it and its soil a hundred feet down the road to Chinameca, I washed up and went to find Sal.

I found him in the storehouse taking inventory of tools and supplies. He'd swept me into a bear hug and pressed my back against the wall, granting me a kiss that incinerated my bones.

"Let me finish up here. Tell Pastora we're ready and meet me at the gate in ten minutes." He nipped at my neck before swatting my ass, sending lightning straight to my already weeping pussy, then shooed me off.

A short while later, with a wicker basket packed into the back of his truck, I was blindfolded and grumpily crossing my arms over my ample chest. Sal assured me he'd take it off, but he wanted it to be a surprise. I kindly informed him I hated surprises.

"You never used to."

I could hear the grin in his words as we slowly rocked and crawled across uncertain terrain.

"You'd be surprised what can change in twenty years," I grumbled as a bump knocked me against the window.

The drive wasn't long, but it was like being on a boat in the middle of a hurricane, being tossed and thrashed all over. When he finally stopped the truck, I thanked god I survived with no new bruises. I reached for the door, and he swatted at my hand.

"Stay there."

Images of the crocodiles lining the river kept me from reaching for the handle again. When the door swung open, and I was pulled into his unseen arms, I gasped and flailed. His deep laughter rumbled my skin to attention as he hefted me up in a bridal carry. I felt him moving—steady, sure steps away from the truck.

The blindfold kept the light from my eyes, but the warm blanket of the sun on my skin was unmistakable. I could smell the warmth penetrating the foliage around us but could not hear or sense any water. I felt no particular tilt to the path he was taking. I mulled over the things he could possibly be leading me into as he finally came to a stop.

"You better not touch that blindfold until I tell you to, nayeli," he teased, setting me down.

My bum rested on a hard surface, and I could feel the stout stalks of plants and smell a uniquely musky floral perfume dancing along the currents of the breeze that kissed at my cheeks. I felt the crumble of the dirt beneath me, rolling it between my fingers. I was familiar enough with the dirt of the area, having learned from my tutor what to look for in the soils for the best clays. This was slightly ashy, dry, and chalky. Were we on the edge of the caldera? If we were, we must have been on a different side of the volcano than the compound. There was no other reason for the drive to have been that long.

I was lost in thought when he scooped me up again, lifting me as if my curvy body was nothing but tissue in his arms. I squeaked in surprise, and he laughed again before setting me down on a blanket. I preferred the dirt's texture. It grounded me in a natural sensation that gave me some idea of my surroundings.

"Keep your eyes closed," he whispered into my ear, his breath gusting over the shell of it, sending shivers of delight to skate down my spine.

The pressure of the blindfold fell away, but I did as I was told, letting him have this victory over my growing discomfort with not knowing where we were.

I felt his long legs bracket my own and the warmth of his body pressed against my back. His arms wrapped around me tightly, pulling my back against his chest.

"Open your eyes, Xochitl," he whispered before pressing a kiss to the pulse point right behind my ear.

One large hand came around me to toy idly with the collar-like bruise around my neck. The sensation of his rough fingertips ghosting across the sensitive skin made me shudder luxuriously.

Slowly, I did as I was asked, the white-hot golden light of the summer's day stinging my eyes at first, then blurring them before I blinked it away. When my sight came into focus, I drew in a stunned breath.

We sat atop a mountain peak, a verdant riot exploding around us, the shade of an old oak at our back. In front of us, down the mountain's slope and fading into the distance was a field of the most marigolds and poppies I had ever seen in my life. Red, orange, and yellow flower heads exploded over a blanket of green velvet. Butterflies danced in the perfumed air, and birds swooped in to pick them off. The mountain overlooked another volcano, one that was smaller than the one the Lets'a Wehle lived on.

"Sal." I exhaled as the rapturous beauty around us stole the eloquence from my stupefied tongue.

I felt the curl of his lips against the skin of my throat. "I knew you would love it."

"It's . . ." I couldn't capture the right words to describe the sheer natural splendor before me. "Sal, did you do this?"

He chuckled and curled his arms tighter around me. "I like that you think I could do something like this." Another kiss peppered my throat, and I purred in delight. "No, this is natural, as far as I know. I saw it on territory patrol years ago. This is where I would come when we were apart. When we were younger, and I couldn't see you. This is where I would come to sit and remember you."

I squirmed in his lap. This was a point of contention for us, his insistence that our playground marriage had been real and my insistence it had not. He caught on to my discomfort quickly and nuzzled the back of my neck.

"It is where I could remember you, Xochitl. I know you didn't have a place like this. It's okay." He curled me in deeper, adding his unique spice to the perfume of the marigolds floating around us.

"Why this place?" I asked softly, trying not to start an argument for once.

I wanted to enjoy this. I wanted to enjoy him opening up to me in a way that didn't make me want to claw his eyes out. My hands rose and rested over his. Our fingers naturally intertwining, I stared down at the rich walnut of his skin against my sun-kissed brass.

"There is a story. Back where I am from—"

"You're not from here?"

He chuckled and squeezed our fingers. My body relaxed into the warmth of his, the warmth of the sun, and the intoxicating scent curling around us.

I leaned my head back against his shoulder, and his chin found my shoulder.

"No, my heart. I am originally from Mexico. We immigrated here to help this totoco when I was a very young child. We stayed.

And I have never gone back. Though César sometimes goes back to see his family there."

I tilted my head to rest against his, nodding slightly. He kissed my temple, a content smile playing across his features.

"There is a story, though, that reminded me of you. About these flowers." He looked out over the fiery sunset of flowers dancing in the breeze. "Many years ago, before the Spanish Rot came to our lands and my people joined with the Nahua, there were many wars. There was a woman who shared your name and fell in love with a warrior named Huitzilin. They were madly in love, and, one day, he was called away to war. Xochitl wept for days on end to be parted from her beloved. Huitzilin, leagues away, fighting, received word that Xochitl had committed suicide. Overcome by rage and heartbreak, he threw himself into battle and was killed. When his body was taken back, his commander found Xochitl weeping with happiness at seeing the army return. He had to explain to her that Huitzilin died on the field thinking she had perished. She took his body to the top of the mountain that overlooked their village and begged the teotl, any who would hear her, to reunite them. And she took his dagger from the sheath tied at his hip and slit her throat, so they might be joined in death. The teotl were listening that day. Xochiquetzal, Huitzilopochtli, and Tonatiuh heard her prayers. They fought over which would help, and, finally, Tonatiuh settled the argument between Huitzilopochtli and Xochiquetzal. He reached out and transformed Huitzilin's body into that of a hummingbird, as Huitzilopochtli desired, and transformed Xochitl into a marigold. Now the two lovers can be seen throughout eternity together, kissing on the mountain hills where Xochitl grows and draws her beloved to her with her distinct perfume."

A soft curl tugged at my pillowy lips as he held me, telling me the story of two lovers joined in eternity. I watched the marigolds, hoping to spy a hummingbird among the blooms. "That's a beautiful story, Sal."

Turning my head, I placed a soft, tentative kiss on his cheek. Fire blazed quick and fresh in his gaze as I initiated affection for the first time since we met.

"Thank you for telling me it." I leaned my forehead against his cheek and watched the flowers dance for us. "Who is Xochiquetzal?"

He chuckled. "Ah, nonamic. I always forget how removed from our culture you are. Her name means 'Precious Feather Flower.' She is a goddess of love, beauty, and the hearth. She is also a goddess who watches over pregnant women, and those who wish to be so."

"I guess I have a lot to learn, hmm?" I grinned up at him, and he reflected my smile.

"You have all the time in the world, noyzotzon. You have but to ask, and I will tell you anything you want." His thumb stroked the back of my hand, adoration pouring from his rich chocolate gaze.

"Why me, Sal? I know we've talked—well, argued, really—about it before. But you've never told me why me."

The words poured out before I could reel them back. I didn't want to break this magical moment with another fight.

A pained smile flicked at his lips, never breaking eye contact, as he reached up to stroke my cheek. "I could say it's because my cadejo saw through to your spirit and recognized you as his mate. I could say because I love you and will always love you. But the truth, my wife, is that my blood has craved you since the beginning of time and will ache for you until the end. Is this not enough?"

My heart lurched, clenched, and shivered in my chest. I wanted to cry from the earnest, soft-spoken words that I could tell he meant with every last fiber of his existence. Sal could hide things, could keep things from me, but when he spoke with that velvety soft voice that was ours and ours alone, I knew in my bones what he said was true.

The silken press of his lips to mine came as no surprise. My body knew he would kiss me before he even moved. Slipping my arm around his back, I pulled myself into him. There was no heat to this kiss. Only the purity of emotion poured through his lips into mine. He didn't grope or grasp at my body but held my chin to his and kissed me with his entire soul.

When he broke away, with both of our eyes closed, both of us holding our breath, not wanting to break the moment, he leaned his forehead against mine. "Forgive me, Xochitl. I am not always the best man, but I am trying. I will always try for you, beloved."

He could kick cats out of trees, and I would probably forgive him as long as he kept kissing me like I mattered. Like I was all that would ever matter.

I nodded softly. "I forgive you for the other day. Not for the other things. You're going to have to find quite a few fields of flowers to make up for kidnapping me, leaving me shackled to your bed, dumping out my medication, and leaving me alone in a strange place for three damned nights."

I grinned at him, teasing him with a laundry list of his sins.

"And if I make up for those things, will you accept my mating mark?"

The hope floating in his voice was seductive.

"What does that entail?" I asked, not saying no, but needing to know what that meant before I said yes.

He smiled down, pulling his head away from mine, his thumb still stroking my cheek. "It means my beast will take you, mate you, and mark your soul as his and you, in turn, would do the same. It will mean that, even if our mate talisman were to go missing, you would still be marked eternally as mine, and I as yours."

"That . . . that sounds painful. And I don't have a cadejo to mark you with. And what mate talisman?"

He smirked. "That's not a no, cihuapiltzintle."

I poked at him. "It's not a yes, either. Does it hurt? And can I mark you without a cadejo? And what mate talisman?"

"It can be uncomfortable, from what I am told. I have never mate-marked anyone, so I don't know, obviously. And, no, you cannot mark my soul without a cadejo. It would be an incomplete marking, but it would still be there. As for a mate talisman? Have you not noticed truly?"

"That seems unfair. And noticed what?"

He chuckled again, unwound the end of my ribbon from under the braids, then pulled his own braid around his shoulder to show me the dangling feather. "The obsidian feather. It is my mate talisman. My name, Itziquetzal, means 'obsidian feather.' When we mate, before we bestow a mate mark, we give our partner a mating talisman. It is like a wedding ring. We both wear it; it symbolizes our unity as a couple. And when you give me children, they will wear a nahuali of our mate mark until they draw down their cadejos." He smiled, love pouring from his words and eyes. "The barrettes and earrings I sent to you, I made them from the pillar of obsidian in our room. The ribbon you wear in your hair, I made it for you, too."

He tucked the end of the ribbon under my braid as I swallowed the strength of the nausea clenching my stomach and shuddering of my heart. I wanted to cry, throw up, and curl into his body until I disappeared. He had given me so much, yet I still could not give him what he wanted so badly. After finding the ring, I knew that I had to escape him for the safety of his people. Annette wouldn't be far behind, and she was as unpredictable as a hungry shark.

He noticed the twist of my emotions within me—of course he did. He tilted my chin up to stare into my eyes, his own darting from one to the other as he tried to discern the shift.

"Why have you gone?"

"I'm right here," I whispered past the softball-sized lump in my throat.

"Are you?"

I hated how perceptive he was. Why couldn't he be a dense log like the other men I knew?

"I was just thinking about how it's not fair that I can't mark you, and you don't wear a talisman for me. I just wear yours. Like a dog collar."

He frowned deeply, though the expected anger never flashed in his eyes. "It's not a dog collar anymore than a wedding ring is."

"So, if I wanted you to wear a mate talisman for me?"

Excitement sparkled in his eyes, and he clenched against my chin. "Is this what you want, nayeli?"

His voice was even, but I could hear the hope and joy barely withheld from his tone.

"If I did?"

He smirked, seeing I would not let him have the satisfaction of saying yes. "Then, I would wear it with pride and be the happiest man to have ever lived."

I smirked back at him. "We'll see. And the other part?"

He kissed my nose and turned me to face the flowers again as the sun began its descent toward the horizon. "You wish to mark my soul as well?"

I said nothing, just snuggled into his body and wrapped his arms around me.

"If this is what you wish, and it is the condition of you accepting my mark, then I will speak to the teopixqui and see what can be done."

"There are other humans in the totoco. What have they done?"

"None of the humans in the totoco have asked this of their mates." He rested his head on the top of my braids. "Now, shh. You will miss the best part, wife. When the sun slips below that volcano, it lights the entire valley on fire."

CHAPTER TWENTY-FIVE

Grunting, I hefted the bucket full of soaking silty clay onto the table, where it would be worked into a pliable material that Nopaltzin and I could work with.

A sniff rang out behind me as I finally got the bucket onto the table and gingerly tilted it to dump its contents.

"Arm strength still needs work," came the gruff, gravelly voice of my tutor behind me.

"Helpful. Super helpful. Let me just get in one of the trucks and run into town to grab some. They sell that at the marketplace, right? Better muscles? I can't imagine they are out at this hour," I snapped back, shoving my hands into the squishy, wet, muddy mess on the plaster top.

He snorted and came around the other side to knead the sticky mess with me. His salt-and-pepper hair was pushed back in a dusty bandana, leaving the scar that ran from above the outside edge of his right brow down his cheek and disappeared into his sparse beard on full display.

"Is sass like that how you got your pretty new necklace?" he asked, shoving at the slop between us.

Over the long days of working with the caustic older man, I'd forged a tender truce with him. Our friendship had bloomed from a mutual love of snarking at each other. It was nice to have someone I could trade barbs with, where the highest stakes were maybe a face full of sludgy clay and a good laugh. He'd also proven so far that, whatever was talked about between the two of us did, in fact, stay between us. I had expected our initial confession by the river to make it back to Sal—had prepared for it, even—but, as far as I could tell, it never had.

"Necklace? Is there something on my neck? Oh no, is it a snake? Help me Nopaltzin! Heeeellp." I snickered as he rolled his eyes at me, flicking wet clay at me in payment for my impertinence.

"So, you two are doing better?" he asked with a cautious tilt of his brow.

This was his way, never one to hedge around the edges for long. This old dog had learned that, if he wanted to know something, he had to ask it directly, so I couldn't squirm out of the question . . . mostly.

I shrugged, unwilling to commit one way or another.

He glared at me, his hands never leaving our shared task of working the mud we'd collected and tended to for the last week. His patience was an admirable trait, a different flavor on the tongue than César's, though. Where César would wait, a calm hovering around him like a cool mist, Nopaltzin was the patience of a jaguar stalking its prey. He would watch, calculate his attack, and wait for the perfect moment to apply pressure. And, when he did, it would come in a rush, shoving his opponent back until they had to give him what he wanted. The entire time, he'd lock his gaze on you and make you squirm until you gave in.

I groaned and caved. It was no use fighting him on this. He'd just keep staring at me awkwardly until he got what he wanted anyway, and, that day, it seemed like he wanted to talk about Sal.

"We're . . . complicated," I finally huffed out, wedging a new section of the sludgy mess.

"Always complicated with you. Why is everything so damned complicated with you? Do you want his pups or not? Simple as that." He tossed a scoop of finished clay into a new bin and capped it before returning to work.

"It's not always that simple, Nopaltzin. And I don't know if I want anyone's babies." A deep sigh rattled through me, and I eased back, wiping clay from my coated fingers.

His brow shot up. "What woman doesn't want children?"

"Rude. I have more value than shitting out kids."

"Sure you do. No one said anything about your value. But, surely, he wants children, no?"

My sloppy hands found my hips as I glared across the table at him. If looks could kill, he'd have been skewered to the wall from the rage crackling in my eyes. "Is he planning on carrying them? Is he going to risk his life to push them out? Is he planning on going through hours and hours of excruciating pain, not to mention all the other horrific bodily changes? No? Didn't think so. So, his opinion as to when or if I have children doesn't count."

He snorted as if to hold the chuckle in, but it won. "All right, all right, hellcat. Claws away. I just meant that, as a tecuhtli, he must want a child to carry on his line, and since he's your mate, he can't exactly get that without your say-so."

"He doesn't get the option. He picked me, and I'm the one with the uterus. So, he'll either be happy with his choice or die bitter about it." I crossed my arms.

I had to admit: I liked when Nopaltzin was on his back leg, but the smirk of satisfaction crossing his face told me I had walked into one of his verbal traps again.

"So, you plan to keep him, then?"

Sly old fucking codger.

I groaned with resignation. Sometimes, I wished Nopaltzin had gotten less sharp with age, but from the tales I'd been regaled with of his youth, he'd only honed his skill with blade and words to an even deadlier edge.

"He can be so sweet and then, the next second, he's so damned intense. He scares me still. But . . . just for different reasons." I plopped onto a stool. Our work abandoned, he grabbed a stool and joined me. "Now . . . I'm scared of what happens when I finally let him in and then I have to leave."

He was washing his hands off in a pail of water when I said it, and his brow twitched as if he battled them to stay neutral. "Do you plan on leaving?"

I shrugged. "Eventually, I have to. I can't stay here. It's not safe."

He leaned back, his broad back resting on the wedging table as he watched me through hooded eyes. "Says who? Not safe for who? You? Him?"

Tilting my head, I watched him carefully. Trustworthy or not, he was far too slick for me to not suspect he had an angle. We stared each other down for a long time. "Both. Neither. Yes. If my mother finds me here, she will destroy everything you have here. I don't think Sal wants to recognize that. She would tear everything down to its roots."

"Strong woman, hmm?" I snorted. And he gave me a wry smirk. "You talk a lot about her, you know. I can tell she scares you, but why? From what you've said, she's a tiny slip of a woman. Liable to be blown over faster than she could throw a punch. So, what could she do? Plus, she's human. What do you think she could do to an entire village of predators?"

I exhaled, the sharp slice of my mother's voice in my mind crawling on hooks over my skin, leaving weeping mental wounds behind it. It hissed and snapped in my ears, leaving a shiver in its wake. "I don't know, Nopaltzin. I just know that she would hurt all of you if it meant getting what she wants. She would sink to any possible way of making life impossible for you to get Sal to hand me over. Anything. Even if that means tanking his business or something even more horrific. I don't think you understand how conniving she is."

He grunted and pushed away from the table. The pottery shed was not far from the kitchen-like grilling area where the fruit stores were, so when he returned with two ripe guayabas, it wasn't shocking. He reclaimed his seat across from me. The sleek snick of his pocket knife cut the silence between us, and he carved into the fruit while directing me with a subtle but meaningful twitching of his dark brows toward the water pail, indicating I should wash my hands. I obeyed, not wanting to dive into the tart fruit with cracking clay drying between my fingers. By the time I'd completed the ablutions, he'd sliced the pale white fruit in half, then into wedges, like one would an apple.

I knew what this meant. If Nopaltzin was giving me food, it meant I was about to be imparted with his "wisdom." Which, usually, was anything but wise and full of snark. I settled in, following his lead when he bit into the fruit—skin and all—letting the sweetly tart white flesh of it slide into my mouth.

"When I was young, Antu had just come to sit above us." He lofted his brows, as if waiting for the commentary on his age. It was too easy, so I declined to take it. "El Matanza was old history by then, but the scars were still scratched into the souls of every creature that crawled, slithered or walked upon the land. It was dangerous in those times for us to be us. Despite living and thriving on this volcano for generations, those dark times made it dangerous for our skins to be too dark, our feathers too bright, our spirits too restless. If we did not conform to the ideals the National Conciliation Party—our own military that was supposed to protect us—demanded of us, if we wore our tribes too close, and our feral nature too near the surface we would be whipped, beaten, starved, the women raped and the children sometimes, too. Our once beloved volcano, the gateway to our homelands, turned into a nightmare."

My eyes burned from perhaps the lack of blinking as he spoke or from the images of the strong backs and easy laughter I had been so accustomed to, bent and broken to the callousness of their own people. I couldn't tell, but I shoved another piece of the fruit into my mouth to hide and overcome the emotion as he went on.

"On the western slope, between here and Jocote Dulce, large swathes of land were cleared. Our jungle stripped bare, and the naked earth churned up to the burning gaze of the angry sun— they planted coffee on top of it." He looked at me over the skin of his forgotten fruit. The misting in his eyes was not the tart bite of the guayaba. Memory dusted the eyes that stared right through me. "Before dawn, we were led out of the shacks that dotted the landscape and forced into the fields to work the coffee plants. I remember the smell of rotting fingers, broken, bloody, withered down to the bone and yet stained by the cherries, still pulling at the branches. Still plucking the coffee from the tree, those fingers unaware that their owner was all but dead."

He inhaled a strained breath, as if he were fighting the ragged intake to go down smoother. I stayed quiet, listening to him tell me a history of this place Sal couldn't or had chosen not to share. It was a haunting, quiet tale of perseverance and pain, and I wanted to hear every slicing word of it.

"At night, when the sun disappeared and the moon was not bright enough to work by, we would be given a single bowl of rations. Whatever worm-infested, crawling thing that the overseers had decided would be our one meal after fifteen or sixteen hours of work in the burning sun." He greedily shoved the last of the fruit's white flesh into his mouth, grabbed the other, then sliced it up as he had the first. "If it was not enough, you dropped. If you dropped and did not rise in the morning, you were skewered with a bayonet. Our cadejos fed on each other, the buffet of anguish and torment so great. Those who were unlucky enough to have been paired with a white cadejo died quickly in those days. Their cadejos starved right alongside the body of its partner.

"I remember one girl, Leena—I think her name was—beautiful girl. Her family survived the longest before being brought to the camp. Hiding out in the jungle and moving often. When she came to the camp, I thought the sun itself walked among us. She had these long braids, straight down to the perkiest ass my young self had ever seen. Best ass I've seen in all my life. She was thick and curvy, like you, I guess, and she had these big eyes the color of a doe. Her spirit rippled under her skin, and even in her born flesh, she glowed golden with it. Her laughter—ah gods, I remember when I heard her laugh for the first time, it reached down my throat and grabbed me by the balls." He sighed. "Pretty sure Leena was supposed to be my mate. I couldn't take my eyes off of her, no matter how hard I tried. But Leena was a white cadejo. Her laughter died the second night, when one of the soldiers decided to put her lips to better use. My father and two brothers had to sit on me—nearly crushed me to death—to keep me from trading my shadow and tearing them apart while I listened to her screaming sobs all night long. I remember thinking they were the worst thing I'd ever heard. I was wrong. Her silence was worse. I never heard her speak or laugh again. No matter how hard I tried."

My tears had started flowing without my knowing, great silent streams sliding down my cheeks to season the forgotten fruit in my motionless hands. He stared down at his own fruit, whispering the next part to its pale flesh, as if it would hide the agony pumping through his words. As though it would somehow erase the memory from his mind to whisper it to the white flesh. "When they found her three weeks later, I really shouldn't have been surprised. She'd taken the lid to one of the cans of food we had for dinner and cut off her braids. I guess she was too scared she might survive if she used it to slit her own throat. So, instead, she braided that hair into a rope and hung herself from one of the trees."

He sniffed and leaned his head back, staring at the sun-warmed tin roof above the pottery shop. I inhaled, having starved my lungs of oxygen for far too long, not wishing to miss a single word.

"When the civil war swept through, the first thing we did was burn that entire damned fucking plantation of coffee trees. I danced in my merged skin around the flames until I thought my feet were good and cooked. And then we churned the earth, and we planted over it a marigold for each one of us that had died and a poppy for each tear we had shed."

A knife twisted in my heart. The beauty of those fields Sal and I had watched dance in the sunset hadn't just been in the fragrant blooms but in the memories each contained. I wanted to go back so I could whisper to each flower and tell them their memory lives and of how strong the totoco now was.

"I said all that to tell you that this totoco, this place, is drenched in suffering. Has been since the Spanish Infection took hold and tainted our home. But look around you, Xochi. These people, these spirits, this place is full of joy and laughter now. Nothing can kill that, nothing, and no one can take that from us again. Whatever it is your mother can do to us, she cannot destroy us. If near a hundred years of bleeding into our soil has taught us anything, it's how to thrive in adversity and how to well and truly live as who and what we are."

I fiddled with my fruit, all but a single slice left to toy with in my discomfort. How could I tell a man who had been through literal hell and watched who he was sure was his mate die that the monster that had birthed me was nothing like something he faced? How was I to look this man in his watery eyes and tell him that all the pain he had ripped up from his soul hadn't convinced me that she couldn't touch them? How did I tell him that all he did was solidify in my heart that I needed to go?

These people had come back from all of that, had toiled and bled to stay in their home, then died for it over and over again. They had fat, happy children running and playing in their fields. They had laughter and love that ricocheted off of the walls and filled every stone with joy, and all of it had come from an adversity I could only read about in the darkest of history books. They had suffered so much. They could not suffer again at the hands of my mother. Not if I could help it.

Instead of saying any of that, I nodded, letting him think what he would from that. It must have satisfied him because he slapped his knees and pushed up from his stool once again, snatching the fruit from my hands, popping it into his mouth with a wink.

"Good. Now that that's settled. Back to work. This clay isn't going to work itself, and we have work to do. And that kiln isn't going to feed itself, so you'll need to go find its dinner." Ah, there he was. I nodded again, and he glowered at me. "Knock that shit off, wewe. We don't cry over the long dead any more. You're here, be here. Anything less is dishonorable."

Sniffing, I shoved my forearm under my running nose. "Fine, but you're not allowed to tell someone things like that and get annoyed when they get a little emotional about it."

"Not allowed? Says who? Last time I checked, you weren't Cihuatlatoani here yet. Or have you decided bossing me around is cause enough for you to take your place? Gods know it's not the fucking that'll convince you. That boy's been putting in the work since day one."

Gods, does the whole totoco hear me when Sal and I fuck? I wanted to feel shame about it, but I had not a drop left in me to squeeze out. Instead, I chose fire. "Maybe. Would you even listen?"

"Doubtful. Don't listen to your mate much. What makes you think I'd listen to you?"

"I'm cuter."

He barked a loud, rolling, easy laugh. "True enough. You do have a cuter ass."

"I'm telling Sal you've been looking at my ass," I tossed back saucily as I sauntered out of the pottery shed to go find inspiration for my next attempt to leave . . . using the excuse of finding wood for the kilns to cover my actions.

"And here I thought you liked the boy and might not want both of his arms broken. Ruthless. We'll make a proper Comizahual of you yet," he said around a feral grin.

"A what?" I asked, turning back to him.

He smirked and shrugged. "Off you go. Gather me my wood and be back before the sun sets. I want to fire tonight."

Dismissed, I jogged away on my dual mission.

CHAPTER TWENTY-SIX

Every morning since that night with the belt, Sal had woken me up, dragging tender fingers over the great welts and bruises that covered the bare golden globes of my generous ass. The first morning, I had started awake with a hiss, as his lips grazed the most vicious of the stripes. A groan dripping with deep male satisfaction, lust, and something more dangerous—adoration—rumbled across the bare flesh and had me squirming. He didn't press it further that morning. He merely dug his fingers into my fleshy hips, abloom with hyacinths in the shape of his fingers, and flipped me to my belly.

Much like that morning, this morning, he worked into my welts a tingling lotion that smelled like green herbs until I was nearly panting. A single press of his lips to the small of my back was all he would give me, though, convinced I needed time to heal up. Healing was miserable, and I hated it.

Lamenting my starved body, I mulled over the items I had collected over the last few days, moving the left over cassava mixed with rice and beans sprinkled with ground iguana sausage around my plate. A plan had been forming half-heartedly in my mind over the last few days, but it felt like the wrong choice.

My fingers rose to the band of purple pressed into my skin to idly drag a finger over the flesh where, just hours ago, Sal had whispered how much he adored seeing his marks on my skin. I stood, secretly admiring my naked body, reveling in the way his bite mark complimented the dramatic nip at my full waist. The pleasure at the roadmap of his brutal love painting my figure warred with the part of me that grumbled about sticking to the plan. I watched the two combatants joust across the chaotic field of my mind.

Jumping, I shrieked like the devil had stabbed me in the kidney, when a soft kiss was pressed to the bone at the nape of my neck. A rich rum-and-spice-steeped laugh tumbled through my ears and cleared the jousters from the field as Sal slid onto the bench next to me. He took the fork from my idle hand and shoved the forgotten bite into his mouth.

He smiled, pleased with his thievery, and swallowed. "I'm going into town today to order supplies."

A tilt of my head, and furrowed brows was his answer. Sal rarely, if ever, reported his comings and goings, and I never asked.

His own gimlet gaze danced between my eyes as if searching for something.

"Oh. Okay," I said hesitantly after the silence between us got too awkward for me to tolerate.

He kept watching me. I felt like a bug under a microscope as his eyes scrutinized every twitch. I squirmed just slightly. Did he know what I was thinking about before he sat down? Did he have any idea that, behind his favorite chair, I had stashed a backpack full of odds and ends that might help me with my escape? He couldn't possibly know, right? Were cadejos psychic? I don't think I'd ever bothered to ask César.

Eventually, the tension popped unexpectedly, like a soap bubble on grass, with confetti shimmering in the sunlight. He leaned forward, his massive hand sliding across the line around my throat where he pressed another hot kiss with a soft, appreciative sound.

"Go inside and put on that dress, nayeli." His hand fell from my throat to rest over the spot where his bite mark was permanently branded into my skin as it healed.

I lofted my brows. "What for? It'll get dirty. I'm supposed to feed the kiln today."

A mischievous, wolfish grin slid over his features. "We're going into town. I have to order some supplies, and I want to show you how to get to the office should you ever need me."

"Plus, it helps that you'll be annoying Nopaltzin by taking me away today." I smirked back at him.

Those two liked annoying the hell out of each other. Over the weeks of working with him, I'd noticed the potter and Sal sparred with each other numerous times in an ever-shifting cold war.

"And it helps that I'd be annoying the old dog." He grinned and squeezed the bite mark lightly, just enough to elicit a small mewling purr of pleasure from me. His eyes grew dark and heavy with lust. "And I want to spend some time alone with my wife."

I squirmed under his gaze for a different reason and nodded my acquiescence. Anything he wanted, just as long as he kept making me fight to breathe under the weight of emotion. I was starting to like the sharp burn and slice of the press of these emotions, so different from the creature I was used to battling before.

"Good. Come find me when you're dressed, nayeli." He kissed my throat once more, stole another bite from my bowl, then pushed up to leave me to his instructions.

Less than an hour later, we were crawling down the volcano into the sleepy town that rested at its foot. His fingers were laced with mine, and we were chatting amiably. As we grew closer and closer to the town, though, conversation grew thin as a beggar, and his grip on my hand grew tighter. When I frowned down at his squeezing hand and tried to pull my fingers clear before he crushed them, he jerked my hand back to him possessively.

When he parked the truck, he reached across me and slammed my door shut as I tried to open it. "Stay," he barked, and I fluttered my lashes at him.

This was not the same man I got into the truck with. This was not the man who had whispered how much he loved me that morning. This was not the man who couldn't keep his hands off of me. This was someone else. Not even Itzatecuani had treated me like this.

I frowned up at him when he opened the door and looped his hand into the crook of my elbow to draw me out. The door closed behind me, and he backed me up against it, caging me in with the width of his massive body. "You will stay close. If I feel your hand come away from my elbow, even for just a moment, wife, you will be back on that gate again. No repeats of the last time. No running. No getting into strangers' cars. Keep your hand on my arm the entire time. Do you understand me?"

His eyes were black as night, burning a hole into my soul. His voice was dark, dangerous, and full of murderous brutality as it grated over my squirming body. I nodded, unable to do anything else. He watched me, his eyes darting between mine for a few moments, before snorting his approval and turning. His massive hand shoved mine into the crook of his arm, and he straightened up to guide us through the town.

Every store we stopped in, Sal introduced me as his wife, and I retreated farther and farther behind the mask I thought I had discarded on the hotel room floor amid the shards of glass when he and that other cadejo came bursting through my life. I smiled, shook hands, and greeted strangers behind the well-practiced face of a happy woman. All the while, on the inside, I squirmed and writhed at his shift in behavior. When my body moved and tugged at its position welded into his elbow, his bicep would flex, a steel reminder of his violent promise.

I had seen so many sides of my capricious and intense *husband*, but this was a side I had never seen before. A side of him that scared me. It wasn't the kind of fear that trickled in and wound itself around the lascivious ropes he bound me with. This was another fear, a fear that wriggled between my cells and latched on with vicious hooks. The Sal who got in that truck with me might bluster and puff up with idle threats, but the Sal who had lumbered out of that truck was a man who would deliver on them. The Sal who had driven me down that volcano would bristle at what I could only imagine was a ripe bouquet of fear rolling off of me, but the Sal glaring at a man who had stopped to introduce himself was the dangerous predator that reveled in the waves of barely contained shivering.

"Walk on, Matteo," he grunted when he'd decided the man had taken up enough of my time.

Matteo looked passively over at Sal and nodded, bidding me farewell as he did as commanded.

I turned to him, ready to make my last stand—after all, what was he going to do, slit my throat on the streets?—but the glare he gave me, the way his shoulders stiffened, and his arm flexing against my hand told me no amount of conversation would make this better. On the contrary, if I opened my mouth, whoever had crawled into Sal's skin and taken the man who licked and kissed the lines he'd lovingly carved into my skin would push the limits of what he could get away with. Something told me by the way Matteo had quickly wandered away when commanded to that Sal could get away with a lot of things in this town. So, I stayed quiet, stewed in the soup of fear drowning me as I plastered another layer onto the bulwarks of the mask I had crafted over years of dedication, and walked on with him as he went about his errands.

By the eighth store, I had wondered why he had brought me with him. If my presence here in the town, in this dress, was making him act this way, why had he even bothered to bring me?

". . . But, Mamá!"

The pitch of a young woman's voice cut through my half-hearted reverie and drew my attention away from the surly man at my side.

Looking around, I found the owner of the voice two shops down standing in front of what looked to be a seamstress's shop. I frowned as I watched the older woman, who was an inch or two taller than the young woman, bend forward to keep the conversation more private when she saw me glance up. A smile, as plastic as the jewelry around the woman's neck, came to my lips easily. I tipped my head to her, then turned my attention back to Sal's shoulder.

My gaze dipped down and cut back to the pair without turning my head. I was a master at eavesdropping by the age of seventeen. I could hear a conversation from across a room without ever giving away I wasn't listening to the person I was chatting with. Standing in the open air, while two people less than twenty feet from me had a less-than-whispered heated conversation, was a novice venture comparatively.

"Laura." She bent the name in her accent to Low-ra, like the word cow. "I did not ask you if you liked him. You will grow to like him. Matteo Santiago is a very wealthy man. He can take you from this place. Do you want to end up like your sister? Hmm? Alone, two babies on your hip, and working the coffee fields day and night?"

I winced at the familiar words. They rasped against my psyche like the kiss of a too-sharp blade, parting my flesh before I could feel the true sting.

"No, Mamá. Why do I have to marry him, though? Can't I just at least date him? See if we like each other?" Laura shifted, and I could almost feel the unease.

It had been my own discomfort not too long ago.

"Because your Papá and I said so. We are your parents. You live under our roof. Until you have a home of your own, you will abide by our rules," her mother cut back swiftly.

"I tried that. Remember?" Laura spit back.

"Oh, we remember very clearly." Her mother gripped Laura's arm with a cruel claw and shook her, her voice taking on that razor-sharp whisper yell I had heard so many times from my own. "And if you don't want to remember what happened when you finally came home, I suggest you do as you're told."

What had happened? I wanted to ask. *What had this horrid woman done to Laura?*

"I'll do it again."

Laura was much braver than I had ever been.

That thought swirled into the tumultuous currents of the thrashing waves of my mind and infected my heart with a ragged beat.

"Not likely, young lady."

Laura ripped her arm away from her mother and hissed something I didn't understand. I'd never heard those words or that phrase in Spanish before. Her mother understood her fine, though, and she straightened with a ramrod spine and glared down at the girl who shot sparks of rebellion from her entire body. The crack of her mother's palm colliding with Laura's face startled me.

Memories of the arguments my mother and I had over the years came flooding back, cackling like a horror movie's ghosts unleashed in the dark corridors of my mind. Their cracked nails clawed at the crumbling plaster of the walls. Their howls of laughter rang in my ears, gripping that shivering creature in my chest, and squeezed.

Sal led me away from the arguing pair. I felt him tugging at my arm, and my feet followed, remembering the imperative to follow and stay close, even while my mind careened down those hallways, trying to flee the memories that stalked me.

"Xochitl."

I heard the terse clip of Sal's voice above the howl of the banshee but just barely. It wasn't until he shook me that my eyes could focus on him again.

He was frowning, deep lines of anger cutting his handsome face into jagged planes of growling fury. "Pay attention, wife."

I grasped at the edges of the mask, digging my nails into it and heaving it up around the fortress of my mind. *Get it together, Xochitl, you can't fall apart here.* I needed to get far away from this place. Far away from him. Far away from whomever this man was turning into. Far away from this totoco. I was poison. My mother would come for me, and when she did, she would make that little display back there look like a pleasant walk through the roses.

"Hmm? Sorry, Sal. I was lost in thought," I said in my best impression of an absent-minded, dreamy woman.

A dark brow sliced upward, and his eyes narrowed on me, as if he could not discern if I was telling him the truth. After a moment of silence, he pressed, "And what were you thinking about, wife?"

I smiled bashfully. I knew Sal's buttons. I knew what would throw him off my trail and misdirect him to see what I wanted him to see. How could I not? Usually, it was the same burning, slithering thing crawling in my soul. I looked around conspiratorially and leaned in, letting my palms slide up the front of his linen button-down. "I was thinking of the other night."

I wanted to push on, to sell the lie better, but even mentioning what had happened against the bedroom wall felt wrong. It felt like drawing out something sacrosanct, something sacred and pure, to sell tickets to a side show. I couldn't do it. I couldn't sully that strange moment of feeling so clean and empty of conflict by dragging it out to cover this ugly, dirty feeling.

He sniffed, then narrowed his eyes on me again. He didn't push further, though. Whether he bought it would remain to be seen. He nodded finally and led me to the truck. We didn't talk all the way back to the totoco compound. It wasn't until we were safely behind the gates that his shoulders finally eased down, and I could see whatever it was that had crawled inside of him slough off into the afternoon sun.

CHAPTER TWENTY-SEVEN

It was a week later that my opportunity finally presented itself. I had minutes, maybe seconds, to slip away while the totoco unloaded the truck Sal brought in with supplies. My heart pounded so loud I was sure the totoco pooling in the courtyard and chatting in their beautiful, lilting language only missed it because of the raucous laughter from the men.

My shaking hand reached above me, and on my tiptoes, I found the tiny latch for the gate. I silently prayed to any teotl that could hear me to let this be the only hinge that stayed well oiled.

Sal must have called that goddess's eye to me when he told me of her, and she was blessing me because—Xochiquetzal be blessed—the gate swung open on silent hinges. Like a deer shooting into the meadow with hounds on my heels, I bolted into the jungle, down past the creek where I had found that cursed ring, and up the slope of the volcano's rise. Branches whipped my cheeks as I ran with every single muscle in my body. Gasping for breath, the sound of it a beacon for the world around me, I scrambled through the dense brush.

"Oh, little flower. Tsk tsk. Do you think it'll be that easy?"

His warm rum voice boomed somewhere behind me.

Fear shot through my blood. I couldn't make out where he was, though. I stopped dead in my tracks, straining to hear him moving among the stranglehold of greenery around us, but the longer I listened, the more I realized all I could hear was the sound of my panicked heartbeat.

Fuck this.

I took off again. This time, toward the caldera of the slumbering volcano. I knew there was an overlook for tourists somewhere along the lip, from the brief conversation with Julia as she showed me around. Where, exactly—and how far it was from the complex of buildings that made up the cadejo totoco's home—I had no clue. I just knew that, if I kept running toward the caldera, I would get there.

Sticks, leaves, and branches cracked under my flight, but there were no sounds behind me. No laboring breaths, nor sounds of footfalls. It could have been Sal behind me, or it could have been the whole totoco, and they could be a foot behind me or a hundred feet—I had no clue.

At least until I heard his voice again.

"Mmm, keep running, my sweet flower. When I catch you, I'm going to peel your petals down and suckle at the honey between your stems."

I shivered at the smoke and darkness in his voice, my stupid skin suit nearly purring with the sensual promise echoing through the jungle.

"I wonder if I could taste your fear as strongly as I smell it," he crooned.

There . . . off to my left. I veered harder to the right.

"I can't wait, little flower. I'm going to sink my teeth into your flesh so deep every time I smile you'll flood with the memory of how it felt when I marked you, sank my cock into you just as hard as my teeth." A pause hung in his voice, but there was no movement. *Shouldn't I be hearing movement?* "Do you remember the kiss of my fangs that night like I do? I still get hard just thinking about how your sweet flesh parted for my teeth and the way you dripped and moaned for me."

How was he closer? I swear he was just behind me and to the left, but it sounded like I was running toward him. I made a sharp left toward what seemed like an opening in the tree line, and I could barely see the bald dirt of the slope up to the volcano as I heard him chuckling deep and dark.

I grabbed a large rock and threw it the opposite way. It crashed against some branches and, seconds later, a second crash.

The growl of rage was unmistakably Sal. I had heard it too many times to mistake it for the other cadejo. It was him. He was on my trail far too closely, and this scrambling up the shifting slope would not get me further from him. My worn sneakers were sliding on the rubble far too easily.

When the swipe came, I didn't even see it. He moved too quickly, quicker than I had thought he could move. I felt the whisper of a claw across my back, but it staggered me. Barely able to keep my balance, I kept scrambling, no matter how futile it was.

The confusion almost chased away the panic when I saw the torn, tattered edges of my shirt flutter into the dirt. Sparing my bare chest with only a few seconds of consideration, I kept climbing.

I was prepared for a second swipe. What I wasn't prepared for was the sun-warmed naked body of my captor and husband tackling me to the ground. His chest bowed over me, and his hips fit snugly to my round ass.

His snarl, mixed with a chuckle, rumbled through my sweat-dusted skin as one of his massive hands slid up the nape of my neck, hesitating only a moment to brush the healing bruise that banded it, and large strong fingers tangled into the weight of my curls. I couldn't help the moan of pleasure as those fingers tightened, pressing my face into the dirt and stones beneath me.

"Admit it, my beautiful little slut. Tell me how your skin is begging for my touch," he purred into my ear, punctuating his command by tightening his grip on my hair and tugging my mouth away from the choking dirt.

All I could do was moan at the sharp pain mixing with the primal need he inspired in my greedy body.

His other hand wandered idly down my jean short-clad ass, massaging the fleshy globes that moved to press into his palm like they had a mind of their own.

I didn't answer him, though. I couldn't. What was I going to say? I couldn't trust my treacherous tongue. One minute, it was telling him to get fucked, the next, it was begging him to fuck me. Since the day I had met him, I'd suffered whiplash every second his eyes were on me and every second they were not.

My lack of comment seemed to please him. He hummed his approval as I felt the deadly tip of his claw trace from my nipped waist down my ass, then took a lazy trip up the inside of my thigh. I made a sound of protest, and he snarled again, gripping my hair harder to ensure I didn't move, pressing my face into the sharp black obsidian chips beneath me.

A strong jerk, and I felt the jeans ripped from my body. A groan fell from his lips as he looked down at my prostrate, naked body. I could imagine what he saw. My tan skin sprinkled with sweat from my run, my ass and thighs dusted with bruises from his gripping fingers. My ass cheeks were probably still sporting at least one of his handprints from last night, and no doubt the stripes he had painted there were still present. And if the stretching sparks of pain as his hands slid lovingly over my soft skin were any indication, at least a bite or two was still healing.

"Say it," he whispered, finally, after what seemed like forever. He pressed his thick cock against the cleft of my ass as he thrust his hips into mine, as if he couldn't help himself.

I said nothing.

"Say it," he barked again, jerking my head just slightly, causing him to hiss with pleasure when my ass nestled against him.

"No," I snapped back.

He growled deep in his chest, and I felt the press of his cock head testing my slicked lips. I wish my body and my mind would get on the same page. We didn't want to fuck this Cro-Magnon. We wanted to claw his eyes out and leave him for the crows. Did they even have crows in this place? I hadn't seen any.

His hips snapped forward in one powerful thrust. No matter how many times we fucked, he still filled me to the brim. I could feel every last hardened inch of his length inside me. My eager pussy welcomed its liege lord home as he seated himself to my back walls and hit that deep spot that made my eyes cross. A lusty deep moan fell from my lips and puffed up a cloud of dust around my nose. He stayed still just for a second, reveling in the fit, which we both knew was far too perfect.

Why did such a magical cock have to be attached to such an insufferable, amazing man? Why couldn't he just pick one? Why couldn't I just hold on to one or the other version of him?

My fingers dug in the dirt as he pumped into me. These were not gentle, loving strokes, no not between us. These were claiming, destructive thrusts, meant to remind me of the nights of pleasure and to quell my resistance. Each powerful, deep thrust pushed my face into the cutting shards of volcanic glass mixed with red dirt, but the sparkle of pain only made that building pleasure all the more poignant.

His massive hand gripped the still-healing bite mark and squeezed, blinding me with the venom of pain, while his plunging hardness filled me with the pleasurable antidote.

We were both panting with desire, silent as we gave in to what we both wanted on a visceral level. I could feel everything, so much brighter than with anyone else. It was always like this with Sal. It was overwhelming, the sensation of his fingers digging deeply into the meat of my ass, pulling the cheeks apart, so he could watch the filthy sight of his cock sliding in and out of my dripping wet folds. I was almost jealous of his view, wishing I could see how my hungry pussy gripped him and stretched around him. From the sound of his groan, I could only imagine how hot it would be.

One hand left my ass cheek for a millisecond as he slid a pair of fingers into his mouth, wetting them. Moments later, he pressed his calloused fingertips at the entrance to my tight, sensitive, puckered hole, and I moaned in delight. He answered my sound with one of his own, and on his next downstroke, he shoved his fingers into my ass.

It was too much. The added girth stretched me out, filled me to the very brim, and kicked me violently over the edge of orgasm. My entire body clenched around him, and my muscles rioted, slamming me back against his invading force to pump myself harder against him.

"Fuck," he whispered reverently as I came apart at the seams, screaming out my pleasure like the wild thing he made me.

The scent of blood tingled my nose, and I was sure he was just now noticing it, too. The rocks he had fucked me into had cut my face. He moved quickly, that delicious cock sliding out of me, and his hands moving me to press my back into the stones.

I was greeted with his face finally. His stern brow pulled down in concern as his thumb wiped away the blood. Both of our eyes watched with rapt attention as he brought that thumb to his lips and sucked it clean. A feral, rabid glint entered his eyes. Purpose flashed in his dark-brown gaze, and he grinned that wolf's smile.

"You wish to run, my sweet little flower? Run all you wish. I will always catch you. I will stalk you down, hunt you down, and the volcano will remind you who you belong to every time," he purred, soft and dangerous with malice as he positioned his cock at my throbbing entrance. "And you won't let César heal those, either."

He slid into me, slowly this time, straight to the root of his cock, causing a slow, groaning hiss to escape me as he leaned over me and kept whispering into my ear. "And every time you move, you'll think about my cock filling your soaking wet pussy. And we both know how you'll drip and cream with need because we both know it's always been mine. You've always been mine."

Thrusting into me, he worked my needy cunt so that every word from his devious mouth scraped my soul and burned the words into my very essence. "This pussy is mine to fuck. Mine to stretch. Mine to fill. Mine to abuse and tease and deny whenever I want. And we both know you love that."

My only answer for him was a moan as stars crested behind my eyes to form the nebula he had brought me to before. I couldn't tell him no any more. I was. I was his, as much as I hated it. As much as I loved it. I was.

A hand wrapped around my throat and pinned me to the ground as the other slid between us and tortured my clit. Every syllable punctuated by a pinch to the swollen bud. "We both know how much you love my cock buried so deep in you that you can taste my cum. We both know that you need it. We both know how much you want me to breed you and fill your womb with my get. We both know how, every night we fight, it's just your slutty pussy talking through your lips. We both know you love how hard I fucking use you. We both know that you love waking up with an aching and sore pussy to remind you of how you screamed for me. And we both know how you come undone when I leave my marks on your flesh."

The hand holding me down pushed my sweat-slick curls from my face so he could look into my eyes. He searched them for denial but would find not even a twinkle of it. He was right. I hated that he was right, but fucking Sal had become the fourth imperative in my hierarchy of needs. Sometimes, I wondered if it had replaced air, if I were honest with myself. I salivated just thinking about tasting his cum or feeling him pounding into me. Someone send a note to Maslow. Sal's cock should be around number one or two on his list.

Satisfied with my lack of disagreement, he picked up his pace and fucked me brutally into the dirt. The scent of our mutual arousal mixed with the scent of the jungle around us, the dirt at my back, at the occasional spiked scent of blood from where the obsidian cut into my soft skin. I clung to him, my hips thrashing up to meet his, strike for strike, causing the head of his thick dick to slam into my back wall. I would feel this in the morning, and that made it even better.

His hand returned to my throat, pressing, just the way he knew made me come unglued. My vision blurred, sparked with a galaxy of stars, then narrowed as the next wave of orgasm tightened like a snake, coiled and ready to strike.

"Come for me, my beautiful little cum slut," he demanded, those skilled fingers working my clit, squeezing ruthlessly, just how I liked it. "Come all over my cock. You owe it to me for making me chase you out here."

As my world blackened and became distant, I came for him. The sensation washed through every limb, drenching every molecule of my existence with sparkling gold-and-black flecks of pleasure. My body clamped down on him, and I felt his hand come away from my neck and his strong arms reposition me.

I smelled myself on the cock head that pushed past my lips and felt the chips of glass cutting up my knees.

"Drink, my beautiful flower. You've earned it," he purred above me as I took his dick into my throat and sucked with the passion and greed my dripping pussy sent up through my body.

Every long stroke of my tongue tasted his skin, my cum, and the precum leaking from his slit.

His hands were back in my hair, gripping so hard I was sure I'd be bald in a few minutes, but I wanted him to grip harder. Every flex of his fingers sent me higher and higher into the nebula curled around my head and heart. He didn't thrust, didn't shove his dick down my throat, as most guys would. Sal held on for dear life as I sucked him down like I was a dying woman, and his cum was the only cure I knew of.

When he finally filled my mouth with the sticky, salty evidence of his devotion, his roar of pleasure filled the quiet of the mid-afternoon, and the crack of his hand on my ass followed it as it rumbled across the volcanic plains.

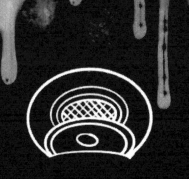

CHAPTER TWENTY-EIGHT

ITZIQUETZAL

My gaze slid lazily over her crumpled form. She was coated in dirt, blood, scraps of fabric and smelled of us. The scent of our mingled juices floated to my nostrils and filled my mind, with satisfying honey slipping into my consciousness. She had never been so beautiful as she was now, filthy, a drunk smile curling at the corners of her lips, her wild hair a chestnut halo around her head. My heart squeezed painfully in my chest as she lay back into the red dust and collapsed bonelessly below me. It chased away the spikes of rage I had felt when I saw her slip through the gate.

She gave me a glassy-eyed, sparkling smile. The feminine satisfaction and supplication in her hungry gaze made my exhausted cock twitch with the need to plant itself inside her and make her scream out her worship again. I had seen this woman in so many ways I thought beautiful, but this one, this aftermath of my brutality on her, was my favorite. I wanted to capture this moment and have it hung above my desk so that, even when I was not balls deep inside of her heaven, I could remember the look on her face when she took every last drop of my fury and twisted it into ecstasy.

I brushed a trickle of blood from a small cut running down her sweat-slicked face, needing to feel the silk of her skin under mine again. "Look at me like that more, nayeli." My voice was harsh, gravelly, and croaky from the force of my own roared pleasure.

She opened her kiss-swollen mouth to say something, but only a shredded whimper came through as she pressed her cheek into my hand. She had screamed so loudly I was sure the entire valley heard her pleasure. It made a very male place within me grunt and growl in delight at having so thoroughly fucked my wife.

When she tried to rise, her wrung-out body collapsed with no strength left in her. I knelt and sucked my teeth in disapproval. She shouldn't have to walk back to the compound, not after taking my rage and my primal need to brutally claim her. I felt the icy touch of my beast's need press my body forward and then my tongue lapped up another trickle of her blood. He howled with delight beneath my skin.

I had allowed him to ride my body too closely as we hunted her through the ravine and up the slope. The space within my soul that kept the way open for him to slip in and out of the spirit realm, one I'd usually kept a strong grip on, was wide open. His strength poured into me and chilled my blood with his presence. I allowed it. Our desires were in unison, needing to be skin-to-skin with her. To feel her breath dusting across our skin and feel the rapid beating of her heart against ours.

The image of a den filled with feathers, fur, and the swirling mists of the other land floated to my mind from Itzatecuani as our need to tend to her and show her how deeply we valued what she gave to us mingled. Yes. Comfort. Doting. Tending. We wanted to spoil our mate with our affection.

A single-minded goal formulated in our shared mind, and the ghost of his arms joined mine as I scooped her limp form into my arms and pulled her from the slope we had fucked her against.

He flashed images of her denying us the mark against the theater of our shared mind.

In time. All in time. Something is preventing her from accepting me . . . us, I murmured back to him as her head slumped against my shoulder. I felt the phantom muzzle of my beast nudge her head as

I brought us to the back gate I had tracked her through. When I looked up to catch her eye and saw her disappear behind the open gate, I knew she was running again. At least, this time, the danger to her was minimal. I will never forget the scar on my soul from the panic thrashing against it when she had run in town.

I still felt a little guilty for the way it twisted and churned in my stomach when we had gone back down the volcano the week prior. All I could think of was turning and not seeing her.

Totocan filled the courtyard, milling about, chatting as the day came to a close, and most returned from the fields and workshops they had been assigned to. The scent of dinner curled in the open space.

Deep within my mind, my beast growled viciously. I could see the flash of his fangs in the peripheral of my sight, a misty whisper of what would be truly on display if he crossed over into this realm. My greed mixed with his protective instincts of his unmarked mate into a toxic sludge that settled into my throat.

"Turn away," I barked as we stepped into the courtyard.

His influence turned the words black and powerful.

In unison, without hesitation, the totoco turned their backs to us, and I moved through, unobserved, with my precious mate curling into me and making small sounds of pleasure as I held her tightly to my bare chest. The sensation of her heated skin against me melted everything within me. She could ask me for anything, to give her the moon or rip my still-beating heart from my chest, and I would oblige her without thought. Just as long as she kept touching me, kept making those small sated sounds of pleasure she let fall from her petal-like lips. Anything she wanted, as long as she kept showering me in the golden meteor shower dusting across her half-lidded gaze.

When she licked her lips and grinned a drugged smile, I almost lost my footing and dropped her on the tile of the hallway. Teotl above, how had I lasted so many years without being near her? Even now, as I lowered her onto the bed, the absence of her skin against mine felt like a personal offense.

The sensation of a pelt of chilly fur, which had been skinned from my first hunt as a cadejo, brushed against my consciousness as he howled in my ear, as if I'd leave her there, naked and battered.

Calm down, I barked back at him as I felt his agitated pacing within me like a caged tiger. His need for her, to touch her as I touched her, was an overwhelming boulder pressing down on me.

No. Let me have this time with her, he snarled.

I felt the snap of his teeth across the gulf of the spirit realm.

I draped a fur blanket around her and tucked her into it, pushing her curls out of her face as she settled in. Her parched lips tugged mine into a frown, and I brought a glass of water to her lips. As her throat worked around the water, I couldn't help but imagine my cock filling her mouth again, and I let a rattled growl slip-free.

She smiled up at me again, twisting my heart in knots.

Mine, he howled, the weight of his expenditure of energy to form human words sharpening the pressure in my head, like the feeling of an airplane's cabin pressure changing. *Must be with mate. She needs me. Let me be with her. Selfish. Give her to me.*

He rattled around my skull, pushing at the thin veil of my control.

What do you mean she needs you? I finally asked after his insistence became too much to deal with.

She is wounded. She needs me, he whispered in a smoky voice.

Her cuts are minor. She doesn't need you to tend to them.

Not cuts. Deeper. Wounded. Let me tend to my mate.

She's hurt? Where? I cast my eyes down her form, hunting for the injury.

Let me tend to my mate. Let me care for her as you do. I will not harm her.

I frowned. Ignoring the wisdom of spirits was rarely wise. *Fine. If you hurt her in any way at all, there will be consequences.*

Leaning back, I pulled my hands from her and sunk into the space between the worlds. The sensation of the exchange between man and cadejo was like opening your arms wide at night and falling back into a pool of water. Only, this water stripped my soul from my body and let the spirit I partnered with trade my shadow for his, transforming my flesh. His ghostly form rose through the internal well of strength we both existed within and through my spirit. The misty, nebulous tendrils of his essence curled around my own and shifted through me. We were one for a split second. I fell farther into the darkness in-between, into the ancient space of the spirit realm where I would float, unaware, and he pushed through into the world.

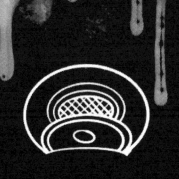

CHAPTER TWENTY-NINE
Itzatecuani

The blackness of the passage curled around me as the man pushed back and let me take over. Scent, sight, light, touch, and taste burst to life across my awareness in a cacophony as I struggled to center myself within him. Above everything, though, was her scent, floating in and out of the muddled experience that was human life.

Unlike the man, I had never been human. I had never walked the realm of earth in my own flesh. I had never experienced the world of flesh and fire until he called me up from the depths of the spirit realm and made his pact with me. Only when he had proven to me that our mutual partnership could be beneficial did I first step onto this plane of existence. It was jarring at first, nauseating and loud. The realm of spirit was one of sensation and thought, whereas the world of flesh was visceral and raucous.

She smelled of us. She smelled of marigolds and golden sunshine. She smelled of sparkling waters. She smelled of rot. The latter tainted her scent, the scent I found in the center of my being so many decades ago, and harbored within me as a shivering ember in the darkness of my realm. The scent of water was too faint, and I snapped my teeth at it, trying to chase it. It was *mine*.

I pressed a paw forward. The inky shadows hiding my form in darkness came into view, and I crouched close to the bed. I could smell her skin, her sex, everything that she was, from skin to bone to blood to the sparks swirling within her that called to mine. I needed her. I needed her with such a ferocity I wondered how any of my kind ever allowed our human partners to keep our mates from us.

I watched her grin like she was barely aware of reality and curl her fingers along the fur I had hunted for her over the years and had him craft into a blanket for her den. When she rolled over and found me instead of him, I let my long black tongue loll from my mouth to taste the air that held her scent.

She reached out, drawing her fingers from the hunted fur to curl into the shadows of mine. She stroked my muzzle, unaware of the electric sparks that danced along my skin from her touch. She could not see them. Could not see the way mates touching cast-off fire into the realm of the soul. She scratched and dug her fingers into the plush covering of my pelt, petting me like a dog.

Offended that she would see me as a pet, I huffed and nipped at the sensitive pulse point of her wrist before dragging my sandpaper tongue along the wound. My eyes slipped shut at the taste of her skin. Finally. Finally, I got to taste her, feel the essence of her body slipping down my throat to pool in my belly like fire.

It had been eons, floating in the nothing of the realm beyond, before Itziquetzal's soul called to me and courted me across the vast wasteland of the other realm. All that time without her. All that time without knowing the intensity of sensation and experience her presence could spark, let alone the lava that would course through me when I tasted her or touched her. It was all-consuming.

I turned my gaze back to her, watching the shifting heatwave mirage of her spirit floating around her body. It should have been thick, so thick I could not see beyond it. It should have been like honey flowing over her body and floating above her. But it was thin, translucent, and tattered in so many spots, rotting in others. It extended above her and around her only a handspan, emaciated and sickly.

She frowned up at me as I towered over the bed. My eyes tracked her movement. Lowering myself to eye level with her, tilting my head as I inspected her eyes, searching for the source of the rot. Her eyes had once been glowing golden lights radiating the beauty of her soul, calling to me. All that was left behind in the wake of the dawn breaking in her eyes were flecks of gold suspended in the quagmire of a brown bog.

Pressing forward, I let a paw hold down her arm to draw my tongue up her shoulder, past the throbbing hum of her throat to draw across her lips. Every inch I licked, I pressed my shadows into, letting them seep into her skin to coax out the hidden source of her soul. Licking her was like licking lightning, and I trembled with the power of it as it rolled through my smoky form. I needed more. Needed to taste her more, feel her flesh against my borrowed flesh. To feel her welcome me as she had to the man.

I felt the exact moment when my shadows penetrated deep enough into her essence. Her body stiffened beneath my paw. Rot's putrid odor crawled into my senses and twisted in my mind. I felt the ocean of anguish buried beneath her skin. I leaned forward, seeking it to see if I could find a place to excise it. There were layers to it, though. It permeated throughout her soul and left rivers of sludge coating the small sparkling parts.

Her breath hitched, the sound coated in such agony that I flicked my tongue to taste the air. Her anguish was thicker than her spirit. Coating the air around her with a delicacy I would normally salivate over. This could not be. My mate could not offer such a banquet. We failed her if such glorious pain flowed so freely.

She rolled away from me, giving me her back. Concern flashed through me. Drawing his spirit up from the well of souls between us. He clawed at the cord between us, just as desperate as I was to be near her while she radiated silent torment. I felt the tug as he struggled where I would not, his strength in spirit no where near mine. He was unaccustomed to the blackness that crept into every corner of your being on the other side. I could feel him fighting against it, trying to bring his consciousness back to the forefront, so he could at least witness what was happening.

I leaped over her prone form and settled onto the other side of the bed to stare into her eyes. The tentacles of my shadows flowed around her, stroking her spirit, trying to draw away what I could of her pain, but it was a mountain spring, unending and burbling up from fissures in her soul.

She rolled away from me again, her body shaking.

She needs me, he whispered with great difficulty across the vast gulf of time and space he existed in.

She needs us, I countered.

Let me hold her. Please. Stay close but let me hold her.

I was not above sharing the object of my obsession with him. The years of being forced to share her with others had been grueling, but with him, we were one, yet we were not. He would treat her as I would treat her. Yet, I could not find the hints of the spirit from the other realm that had drawn me to her, and without her, my comfort was a cold grip. The spirit that had woken me from my ancient slumber beneath the skin of the man had not shown herself, and without her to wrap my tendrils around, it was hollow comfort.

I sat back on my haunches, letting him rise from the free-floating well of spirit that connected me to him. He climbed up through the blackness as I fell back into it. Unlike him, though, I would remain on the surface, always close, stronger than he could ever hope to be in my element.

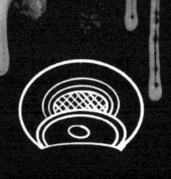

CHAPTER THIRTY

Itziquetzal

When I finally recovered connection to my born flesh, I let the feeling of icy glass that settled in my muscles from the physical transformation flee before I looked at her. My eyes were blurry, as they always were when I let him take full control. It was rare that I let that happen. The blackness remaining in my mind in place of the memory was disconcerting. Knowing I had both been in this place and time—yet not—was never a sensation I would get used to. Truth be told, it was a sensation that none of us ever got used to and why many of us chose to so rarely allow our divine realm counterparts to take control in the mortal world.

I watched her back through the blurry, watery distance until it solidified and sharpened. She was shaking. I could tell by the tiny movements that she was doing her best to hold it in, but she still quaked like a rabbit caught beneath the eye of a circling hawk.

I acted before I felt my muscles move, pulling her shuddering form against the heat of my naked body. I held her to me, worry seeping deep into me. Had I been too hard with her? I had thought that my princess bloomed under the harshest of my touches, but she was coming undone at the seams. Had the beast pushed her too hard? Had he crawled into that liminal space between her body and soul and clawed to gain purchase, like he had threatened so many times before?

"You're shaking," I whispered against the chilly shell of her ear.

Velvet wrapped each word, trying to soften them as much as I could, when all I wanted to do was rip and tear at whatever was threatening the glow I'd left her with.

She was silent for too long. The absence of her sharp tongue seeded the air with a tension that left a foreboding twist in my stomach. Something was wrong, and I had the unique sense that even the beast who prowled beneath my skin was wary of what would happen next.

When the scent of salt-kissed hot flesh wove into the tapestry of imminent dread, I stiffened with her clenched against my body. The same minatory snake that had slithered through me when I found the sidewalk she had stood on was vacant reared its mottled brown-and-black head, readying to leap like the vipers in the jungle.

When the silence drew out, and I could take the threat of the fangs no longer, I murmured her name. Coaxing her to answer me. I could feel her muscles, bare against my skin, clenching and holding on to whatever it was she was wrestling with. The tears rolled down her cheeks, splashing against my arm that banded around her.

"Xochitl." Distress guarded my voice. Desperation to know what was going on in her head seared through me, the need to hear her voice like the need to breathe. "Xochitl. What's wrong? Why are you crying?"

She said nothing, the shaking kicking up, as if she no longer had the strength to hold it in. I shifted, pulling her body to maneuver her into a sitting fetal position. I scooted so I could wrap my legs around her and draw her into my lap. The glassy, faraway look in her eye made my stomach drop out from under me.

I had seen that look once before, and it haunted me to this day. Years ago, when I was perhaps in my mid-twenties, I traveled with my father to a session of Council. They had found a cadejo who had been kidnapping women and torturing them until their spirits died. When the flesh was still alive but the soul had died, he would rip a spirit—often one that had never been human—from the spirit realm and shackle it to the dying flesh so he could feed off of the anguish of the two. It was a perversion of the highest order, and an emergency council had been called to address it.

Two of his victims physically survived his attentions, their bodies having been the host of hundreds of tortured spirits, but their own had been destroyed so thoroughly that none of us, no cadejo, priest, nor intercession with the teotl could find even a scrap of it to testify against him.

That vacant look as they sat, physically present but not attending in any other meaningful way, had imprinted on my mind in a way even my father had not expected.

That same look was in Xochitl's eye, and it terrified me.

"Wife." I swallowed past the thick knot in my throat. "Speak to me. Was I too rough? Did Itzatecuani hurt you?"

When she did not respond or move, I reached up and drew her face to stare me in the eye. A single spark flashed, weak and dull behind a film of distance.

"No," she finally gulped out. Her voice was a tissue paper lifeline in a sea of ice. "No, I'm fine. It's fine."

She was lying. I frowned, the concern clawing at my throat joined by annoyance. Did she think that was convincing?

"You do not lie well."

A wan, tired, watery smirk was my answer before she finally choked out, "No, it's fine. I'll be fine."

"Tell me why you are crying." It was a demand, one I had not intended on barking out. I wanted to blame it on the beast, but he was silent. I could feel him as a nebulous presence in the back of my mind, but he was content to watch. Her microscopic flinch was enough chastisement to make me swallow down the bubble of annoyance and forcefully soften my tone. "I should not have let him take over. He wished to be close to you. He said you needed him. Did he do something?"

The beast's huff of incredulity at being blamed for what was unfolding before us was hot in my ear.

I reached across the expanding void between us and stroked a thumb across her cheek, smoothing away one of the tears that ran down her haunted face. "Tell me, and I will do anything to dry your tears."

I was not above begging. I would throw myself from a cliff and drag my battered body across glass just to see her smile again.

"Stop," she whispered, pushing my hand away from her. Confusion danced pirouettes across the stage of my face as she went on. "I don't deserve it."

The snort that left my nose was both from the beast and me. "You do not deserve me caring for you?"

"No," she said so quickly, so clearly.

I cupped her cheek, and she flinched away from me.

I wanted to find that cliff and fling. In all my time of knowing her, in all the years I watched her, she never flinched away from a touch, least of all mine. Even when she first glimpsed the beast in his pure form, she had not reared back and away from him. Even when I came to her in my monstrous form, unable to control the battle between him and me over who would touch her first, she did not flinch away. Now, after all we had shared, she was pulling away from the tenderness I offered her.

I never understood self-immolation. It had always seemed a waste. However, at this moment, I wanted to burn away the offending parts of myself that caused this.

"Why?"

I could not control the whine from the beast creeping into the whispered word.

"Because I'm not who you think I am," she whispered back.

Hope burbled dimly on the horizon of my mind. Could it be that simple? Could it be a simple revisiting of our age-old conflict?

"We've been over this before, Xochitl. You are my wife. You are my mate. You are my heart. You might not remember, but I do. We do. We remember for you."

The beast was content with this answer, content that this same argument was one I could fix, and crept back into the mist of the spirit realm. He chuffed with his satisfaction, and I felt him retreating, images of the park and a river of black filling my mind. I didn't understand the latter, but he retreated too far away for me to keep my attention focused on Xochitl and call him back to explain.

Simple beast. The ebb and flow of human hearts had never been his expertise. They had always baffled him. If only it were that easy. The air in the room was still filled with menace, like a foul long-fanged creature lurked in the corner, drooling over the story playing out before him that he already knew the ending of.

A hiccoughing sob ripped through her throat as she finally looked up at me. The look in her eye terrified me.

"Don't you get it, Sal? I'm not who you married. You married and fell in love with a little girl who was free and wild and happy. You expected to live a life of joy and happiness with her. She wasn't a dirty, weak, pathetic thing. She was worthy of your love. I'm not. I am not worthy of anything. Not the kindness your totoco has shown me, not the love and devotion you so freely offer. I am not worthy of any of it." She was spiraling, but I could do nothing to stop it, each word sinking into my skin like barbs. "You spent years trying to get back to me, and the woman you found is not and will never be that girl again. Not because I don't want to be. I wish I could be. I wish I could be that happy girl again, but I can't. Every time I feel like I can take a step down that path again, I feel myself standing tall and then a single thing happens, and I'm right back where I started. I'll never be her again. I'll never be her again because I'm trash."

"You are not trash."

The deadly certainty in my voice was all my own. The beast had drifted away either by his own will or because I did not wish him anywhere near this conversation. This was a situation which I could not afford for him to plow through in his in-tender manner and shred her with his carelessness.

"Not even Itzatecuani agrees with you, Sal. He saw into my soul. I felt him there, rooting around. He saw what I am . . . now. Who I am. I can hear it. He's not in your voice like normal." Tears rolled down her cheeks, her eyes red and shimmering. "A mate to you would never leave her people. She would fight for them at all times, as you do. When my sister left, do you know what I did? Nothing. I did exactly nothing. It's been years since I spoke with my sister. I don't even know if she's alive or dead, and I've never tried to find out. When my father went missing, you know what I did? Nothing. I watched as he disappeared from our lives and said nothing and did nothing to find him. When I came to El Salvador, I planned on getting lost in the jungle and never going back. Abandoning my brother and mother and my grandparents. That's not a leader . . . that's trash."

I had met Elida once during my time in San Francisco. She was there the first day Xochitl and I met on the playground. She had shared the same bright and bouncy disposition of her older sister, but unlike Xochitl, she was bold and bossy. She toddled around the playground like a little general, bossing the older kids around. When they didn't listen to her, she'd bite them. She was intense and haughty. When they cried, she'd call them babies, then saunter off to find something more interesting to occupy her time.

In my years of spying on Xochitl, I never saw her again. I often wondered what happened to the cocky little girl who would fall and scrape her knees, then growl angrily at the sidewalk for having the audacity to hurt her. I had even considered bringing her here once her sister and I were settled, convinced that fiery spirit was a perfect addition to my totoco.

The news that she, as well as the father that Xochitl had told me about and had doted on, were both missing, sat in my stomach like an iron weight. The circle of love around her had tightened so completely that it had withered to just her doting grandparents, her mother, and her brother. I knew that she was estranged from her grandparents. Javier told me that, when they moved away from the neighborhood, her grandparents seemed to be ghosts of themselves without her warmth in their home. She had never gone back to see them, and we had always wondered why.

"Your sister is missing? And your father?" I asked in a stupid, pained whisper.

She snorted an ugly black laugh full of self-deprecation. "See. You don't even know that about me. Yes, Elida left when she was eighteen. She left a note saying she was moving to Japan. I haven't heard from her since. And my dad? He went missing a few months after we met. When I was a kid. I have no idea what happened to him. I never even tried to look for them." She had been rambling, pouring her soul out through her words and the steady stream of tears rolling down her stained cheeks. "Don't you see, Sal? I am nothing. It's why I keep asking you why. Why me? You deserve someone who is strong, someone who doesn't sleep with a man she hates just to please someone else, just because it's easier."

Anger burned away the heartache of her admissions, the confusion of what happened in the years I could not see her. It obliterated all thought and sound aside from the dull, hollow ringing in my ears, repeating her last sentence in my mind. The rage flashing in my eyes was the still, deadly fury all of my own, uninfluenced or assisted by the beast, that I could now feel thrashing at my clamp against his access. He heard, though. He heard it, and he was snarling and slashing at my hold on the door between us, rampaging against it in an attempt to rip through my skin and tear the throat out of the man she spoke of.

Outwardly, all I let her see was my brow ticking up and the deadly sharpness of a single word. "What."

"You didn't actually think I loved Shayne, did you?" She snorted a mirthless chuckle, and every muscle in my body stilled, ready to kill. "I hated him. Every time he touched me, I wanted to throw up, at least at first. It made my skin crawl and made me want to claw out of my skin. Eventually, I became numb to it, just letting it happen whenever and however he wanted. It was easier that way. Just staring up at the ceiling and letting him do whatever he wanted and leaving when he was done."

I felt my fingers flexing, crushing an imaginary throat beneath my fingertips.

"Xochitl . . ."

She barreled on, not noticing how her words were affecting me, nor the murder surely flashing in my eyes.

"Don't you see, Sal? I'm not who you think I am. I can never be who you think I am or want me to be. My mother has always been right about me. I am mediocre at best. I am good for only one thing, marrying someone rich enough to fulfill my mother and brother's plan, and giving them enough reason to keep me around long enough to be useful to them. I am nothing. I will never be anything. I am worthless for any other purpose than what my mother wants of me." She gasped, drawing a breath like she was trying not to choke, but still forging on as if determined to tell me everything before she passed out. "I can't even make decisions about my life on my own. Where I went to college? My mother had to pick it. Where I lived? Mother. Where I worked? Mother gave me that. I am nothing because I can't even be bothered to be independent. I am nothing but an emotional basket case who can't keep her shit together long enough to tell you I'm garbage. I am neither beautiful, nor smart, nor capable, nor thin. I am nothing but a fat, mediocre girl who has nothing special about her. No spark. Nothing. I am nothing, Sal. And you deserve *something*."

I let the silence draw out between us. All I could think of was walking out that door, getting on a plane, flying to San Francisco, and carving pieces off of her mother, brother, and that piece of shit, Shayne. All I could think about was flooding that city with the blood of anyone and everyone who had even blinked at her wrong. They had crushed her beneath their boots and convinced her she was nothing when she was *everything*.

I took deep breaths, trying to push the murderous thoughts from my mind. After what seemed like hours, I finally said in the softest voice I could muster beyond the thought of ripping flesh off of the bone with my human teeth, "Are you done?"

I was numbly aware of the bouncing of her head in a nod.

Patience. I needed patience. She did not know the depths of her abuse.

"I didn't know any of those things."

When she opened her mouth to chime in again, I glared at her in a silent command to shut the fuck up. When she made to push forward anyway, I reached out and pinched her lips closed to prevent her from going on. "Had I known those things, had I known any of it—and I suspect there is more you have not told me—I would have taken you away when you turned eighteen."

Anger boiled in my voice. I tried to hold it back, tried to kick it into the back of my mind, but it still simmered at the edges of my words. "I have kept my eye on you since I left, through Javier. I had no idea that your mother was abusing you. I had no idea that you were being raped."

She ripped her head away from my pinching fingers. "I was not being raped. I could have said no at any time."

Fire licked behind my eyes. That deadly edge bleeding into my growled words. "Did you say yes? Ever? Tell me, Xochitl, did you say yes? Even a single time. Did you ever give him your consent? Did he ever even *bother* to ask for it?"

She frowned at me, considering my words. "That's not the same thing. Rape is brutal and evil. It carves chunks off of a woman's soul. What Shayne did to me wasn't that. He never hit me. He never used force or a weapon."

I gritted my teeth, fighting the urge to lash out at something, anything at all. "Did. You. Say. Yes?"

"I showed up. He texted, and I appeared. I knew why I was going there. And I could have just not gone at any time."

I glared at her. "Could you have? What would your mother have done to you if you had not shown up when Shayne requested you perform? Hmm?"

"She wasn't abusive, Sal. She never hit me. Except for when we were younger." She squirmed.

She didn't realize how much I knew about the control her mother had on her. I was putting the pieces together, though.

The reports of her always held a strangeness to them. I didn't understand why her mother had been so integral to so many decisions in her life. I never understood why she seemed to ping-pong between one thing and another. The pieces she flung at me as evidence of her worthlessness were showing me a landscape of a mother so controlling that I was convinced there was never a time in Xochitl's life she hadn't been under her thumb.

Javier had told me throughout high school she had been a loner. I assumed that she had become an introvert. It sounded like the truth of that was that her mother hadn't allowed it. I did not like the picture coming into view. What's more, I didn't understand why. The why of a thing was often far more important than the what of the thing.

"What would she have done? Answer the question, Xochitl."

I could sense the squirming in her more than I could see it. It set my predatory instincts on edge.

"She'd have taken away my car. My apartment. Probably made me move home until I got back on track. It's not like she would have hurt me."

"That's it? She'd have treated a grown woman like a child? And if you resisted that? What then?"

"She'd send over a private security team to collect me." Her voice took on that same ephemeral whisper that set my teeth on edge. The weakness, the fragility in it made my predator want to leap on the easy kill. "And then I'd have gone away until the conservatorship could be filed . . ."

"Gone away? What does that mean?" She looked away, and I let her. I couldn't hold eye contact with her. The rage boiling in me had been lighting black flames in my eyes. I forged onward. "So, there were monumental consequences to your freedom should you choose not to spread your legs for a man you didn't want to have sex with?"

I frowned deeply.

"Yes," she murmured, seemingly deferring back to old habits, giving me the answer she thought I wanted.

I didn't believe for one second she acknowledged the abuse for what it was.

"I don't know the laws in America as well as I know them within my totoco. I don't know what this conservatorship is. However, if anyone, man or woman, had done this in my totoco, I would call it for what it is. It was abuse, and it was rape. And their lives would have been forfeited. You don't need to call it rape if you're not able to. You don't need to call it abuse if you're not able to. I will call it what it is for you. She made you sleep with a man you did not wish to. She made you think that you are nothing. She has gotten into your heart and head and poisoned you." With my strong fingers, tempered by sheer will into gentleness, I pulled her chin back to look at me, and I stared her directly in the eye, ensuring every word I spoke would get through to her. Hoping that they would help her.

"You have swallowed her poison all this time and taken it into yourself as your identity. You love deeply and with passion. Look around you, at the totoco, Xochitl. These are people hardened by life and hardened by the spirits around them, yet you have charmed every single one of them. Daily, I have reports of you. You do for others without asking for yourself. You give of yourself without asking what's in it for you. You have gone from living in the lap of luxury to living in a community that requires each member to contribute equally for them to thrive, and not a single time have you complained about what you don't have access to any longer. You were tasked with shoveling out piss and shit, and not once did you complain. You were asked to remove a poisonous thing from our fields and never once complained. You give and give and give, yet you ask for nothing in return. And when I, your mate, the man who has devoted his entire life to you and your happiness, brings you gifts, you squirm and decline them. You say you are not worthy of them, you say you do not deserve to be treated like the queen you are. Yet, you do. And you are exactly who I was meant to love."

Her eyes drifted away from me, casting themselves to the floor beyond the foot of the bed. "You barely know me, Sal. You haven't known me since I was a child."

I snorted a derisive chuckle. "You do not understand who and what lives beneath my skin, Xochitl. You have been so busy looking at all the ways I don't know you and have yet to ask or learn all the ways I do. What you know of the creatures we are could fit through the eye of a needle. You will learn . . . eventually."

She kept her eyes from me, and it made every hair on my body stand up. I was losing her to the false image she had set up in her mind of who she was. I had clawed and kicked and raged at that self image all this time, and I thought we had been making progress. It was back and, like a bad nightmare, more potent than ever. I needed her to hear me and to step away from the darkness so I could hold her.

"Xochitl." Curling my hand under her chin, I pulled her gaze back to me. "I do not have a lot of experience with abused creatures. The things you have experienced would be a death sentence among the cadejo. What I do know is that, when you sip poison in small doses for a long time, it becomes part of your anatomy. Indecipherable from your healthy system. It will make you sick at first, but, eventually, you acclimate to what could kill another person."

Searching her eyes, I watched as the small motes of gilding floating in them shimmered beneath the still unshed tears. "You have to know that, when I look at you, Xochitl, I do not just see the things you are describing to me. I see my wife, my mate, the love of my life. Someone I will spend my entire life proving myself to. You bite, and you scratch and fight me at every turn, and I love that. I love you, Xochitl. Not just the little girl who captured my heart on that playground but the woman who sits before me now. A woman who can take all the bluster and hardness of my beast and give it straight back to him. The woman who feels my claws in her skin and begs me for more. The woman who is fire and spark and bite one minute and the next is mewling and begging at the head of my cock for more, never shying away from the brutal side of me but always asking for more. I see you, Xochitl. I see who lies beneath your skin. The woman you don't even know you are yet.

I will wait for decades until you find her, but I will not allow you to keep telling me you are not worthy of me. Not because of what your mother said."

I took two deep breaths to shove down the anger at thinking that a woman tasked with loving her and raising her had done so much damage. I forged on, staring her dead in the eye as her own searched mine, as if desperate to find a reason to believe me. "My mother passed when I was a baby, but I have seen other mothers. I know what a mother should be. She should hold you when you are low and pick you up. She should not push your head underwater when you are already drowning. She should build you up, not force you to build the stones of your walls higher and higher for you to retreat behind. Your mother did this. I don't know why, I don't know what was in it for her, but she has cut you down every time you tried to stand up, and, now, your legs are broken beneath you. Let me lift you up. Let me be the rock you stand on so that you never have to hear your bones snap again."

I stroked her cheek with my thumb, meaning every last word of comfort. I wished I could do more. I wished with every fiber of my being I could reach inside of her and pull out the poison she had swallowed and wash away the nightmares she had been forced to endure. My heart bled inside the cavity of my chest for the pain that reflected back at me.

A small part of me blamed myself for allowing her so much time to be wounded and broken. I should have gone to her sooner. I should have brought her to my home sooner. I had been a fool, thinking I needed to provide for her with the same amount of luxury she had been accustomed to. Xochitl didn't care about money, she didn't care about things. She barely cared about herself. All she needed was love, and I had spent years and years, squandered in the pursuit of money that would never heal the damage the time had allowed to happen.

She nodded slowly against my palm, but I could see the thoughts zinging through her head. She was quiet, but I hoped the thoughts spinning in her pretty little head were at least being infiltrated by my words.

I pulled her into me, resting her head on my chest as I stroked through her curls. My fingers would occasionally tangle in a curl, and I carefully liberated them. I pressed a kiss to the top of her head, and she purred at the sensation. I could not help myself. I wanted to make her feel better.

I made slow, gentle, tender love to her as the sun set, drenching the bedroom in a riot of reds and oranges. I collapsed next to her body when we both had screamed our release so many times into the night that our voices were hoarse and broken.

I fell asleep next to her, my arms draped over her plush form, basking in the perfume of her skin and the record of her cries playing in my ears like a symphony of lust. I wanted to listen to that soundtrack for the rest of eternity, and I hoped that she would let me. I couldn't afford to lose her. My soul would not survive it again.

CHAPTER THIRTY-ONE

I felt hollow, empty of everything, yet the ghosts of my confession still clung to the walls of my psyche like pond scum. He knew everything, knew all my edges and darkest secrets. I told him too much. And, though we shared a passionate, tender coming together as his cum cooled and dribbled from my satisfied core, his arm draped heavily across my stomach, all I could think of was running.

It had to be tonight. I had failed too many times before. This time, I could not. This time, I had to get away. I couldn't be here when he woke up. I didn't want to see the love and adoration dim from his eyes now that he knew how weak I was. I couldn't watch his demeanor change. I couldn't stand the idea of him handling me with kid gloves. I didn't want to think of how his voice would grow soft, not with tenderness but with pity as he treated me like the broken thing I was.

Perhaps I could handle the skittishness, but if it turned to contempt—knowing I let my mother, of all people, force me into doing all those things just so that I didn't have to see her disappointment—that, I couldn't tolerate. The thought of him looking at me as I had looked at myself made tears slide down my temple as I stared up at the spinning ceiling fan. I could see he was on the razor's edge between the two when he pushed me about Shayne. I could see the revulsion seeping into the corners of those gorgeous brown eyes that stared down at me with awe as we came down from the volcano.

I didn't want to imagine a day when he realized I let Shayne fuck me for years—every other day, like clockwork—because my mother wanted it that way. I didn't want to even think of reaching for him in the dark and finding him soft and uninterested in the body I had let be used by someone I didn't even like.

So, that night was the last night I would lie next to him and feel the warm comfort of the fire we'd kindled between each other before the hearth went cold forever. At least, if I left that night, I could remember the little shreds of confetti that were the small glimpse of happiness I found for a tiny glimmer of time in this miserable existence.

I let the tears silently slip from my eyes and roll into my sex-rumpled hair as night wore into the earliest part of the morning, my heart withering and dying on the pillow where they fell.

When I heard the last of the night watch drift into soft snoring outside our open bedroom window, I brushed the last of the mourning from my eyes and began to act. Sal would wake if he didn't smell me next to him. I had counted on that and hadn't changed my pillowcase since the first night. I slid the warm pillow from behind me, not disturbing his banded arm across my waist. It would take a long time to ease out from under his arm, inch by inch, but the time it took would ensure that he wouldn't wake up prematurely.

When I finally extricated myself from his grasp and slid the pillow into my place, I padded to the door that had been replaced on quiet, brand-new hinges. Naked, his cum dripping down my legs, I paused at the door to look over his glorious nude form. I memorized the swell of his firm ass cheeks, the length of his toned legs, the slight curve to his relaxed, muscle-bound back, and the way his finger played with the fur of a throw pillow wedged where my head and hair would have been. I would hold this image in my mind until I died. Replaying it when the times got hard again.

My trek into the living room was meticulous, avoiding the tiles that rocked just slightly and squeaked just enough to wake him up. I found the bag I'd stashed behind his favorite chair and pulled from it the boilersuit he had worn to fix the truck a few days back. It was drenched in his sweat and scent and would afford me the cover I needed. He'd smell himself as he tried to track me.

I checked that the shreds of a dress were still sealed in their bag and took them out one by one. I dabbed each between my legs, soaking it in the mingled scent of our juices, then slid them back in the bag before slithering into the boilersuit, socks, and a pair of tennis shoes I had pilfered from Julia's closet. My eyes cast back to the bedroom, longing for just one more look. I even considered going back, some semi-rational part of my brain saying it was only to collect my pills. No, they would rattle too much in my bag, and I didn't know if I had the strength to walk away from him again.

My stealthy trek through the compound to the gate that led to the volcano was quick. I opened it without issue and pushed it wide. I wasn't taking this exit, though. He would expect that, since I used it the last time as well. Instead, I crouched, fished one of the scent-soaked rags from the bag, and wrapped it around a stone. The slingshot I had made from Césars "missing" rubber tourniquet and a sturdy stick I'd found was knocked with the stone, and I shot it off into the darkened depths of the jungle.

Scent trail sufficiently laid, I made my way to the gate to the fields. I'd found a path I suspected led around the base of the volcano, and, from there, I could make my way to San Miguel. I knew they wouldn't follow me as soon as I got to the road that cut between the two volcanos and led into town. Their laws wouldn't allow it, and Sal wouldn't bend them just for me, not after what I revealed. Surely not after that.

As soon as I closed the gate behind me, I ran. I didn't know how long I had before Sal woke up, but I had to keep my wits about me. The predators of the jungle were one thing, but a pissed-off Sal was another. Stopping occasionally, I shot off another scent marker toward the opposite side of the trail that would lead them away from me but keep their noses pointed where I wanted them pointed.

If they smelled me, all they would smell is the faint scent of me under the sweaty scent of their tecuhtli. At least that's what I was hoping for. I knew their noses in their fully traded form were formidable, and I hoped that the mingling of sex essence would be strong enough to cover my trail. I hoped that, by the time they found my actual path, I would be far enough beyond the borders of their territory that I could drift into obscurity, away from their world altogether.

I realized I was wrong when I had to climb. This was not a path around the volcano; it was a path up and over it. I didn't have time to backtrack, though. As I gazed between the trees, I watched a light flick on about where I thought the compound was behind me. Then another. And another. The cadejos were rousing. The warning would go out soon, and my time would count down much faster than I anticipated.

Panic tried to grip my arm with icy resolve, but I struggled past it to fire off six more scent shots into the darkness of the opposite side of the caldera from where I was crouched. Those should help a little to confuse them. I was out of time, and if the roaring in the distance was any indication, Itzatecuani had joined the hunt.

I ran as fast as my sturdy, thick legs would allow me to, ignoring the growing chafing between my sweat-kissed thighs. I'd have time to lament over the stinging later, when I was across the territory border. Not when I could just barely make out the sound of menacing roars akin to a tiger's, laced side by side with the screams of a dying man. I could see the livid yellow lights from the compound bright in the darkness. The entire compound was awake and coming for me.

I ran for at least three hours, pausing only to guzzle some water from a bottle in my backpack. I slid down rock falls and swung past low-hanging trees, with no consideration for the slithering or crawling occupants lurking in them. I ran until I thought my heart would explode from my chest and slap me in the face for the abuse I was putting it through. I ran until my lungs screamed their hatred of my entire lineage and all those that had been so disrespectful as to have borne me into this world. I ran until my thighs felt like they were on fire, not just from the chafing between them but also from the muscles deep within declaring civil war on my audacity.

I had heard the hunting parties only twice. Both times, they were at the top of the rim of the volcano, and I had hit the ground immediately. The first time, they were southwest of me, and I had to flatten myself against it. The second time, they were merely two hundred feet from me, up on the downward slope, and I'd had enough time to duck behind an unchecked growth of the lurid, red-flowered Kawinski's sage shrub. That last time was too close for comfort . . . and Sal was with them. I could feel his presence, looming dark and angry on the ridge above me as I hid from him behind the large green bush with spikes of red flowers.

They lingered there, talking in Nahuatl—I could still only catch a few words here and there—about how it was stupid for Sal to think he could sense me. I still hadn't accepted a mating mark from him, and everyone was aware that I was not a cadejo, so he could never hope to sense me if he and the others couldn't smell me. They argued and left Sal there alone as he scanned the black moonless night for me. If only he knew he was so close to finding me, and had I not heard them coming before they saw me, they would have caught me for sure. He stayed there, standing just upwind from me, for what seemed like an hour, before he finally loped off in his spirit form, hunting . . . searching in vain.

When I hit the flat road, I almost cried in relief. I had made it. I was out, and I would never see Sal again.

I should have been happy with my victory . . . I wasn't.

Regret dogged every step as I headed northeast, toward Conacastal. The weight of my remorse was heavier than the backpack with my meager possessions. It dragged at me, yanking me backward, as if to say "You're going the wrong way. That's the worst way to go."

I walked for another twenty or thirty minutes until I saw the lights of a car driving toward me. It shot past me, then turned around. Great. Out of the fire and into the frying pan.

I silently argued with the insane part of me that perked up, hoping it was Sal's truck. I had no such hopes and only prayed that it wasn't some backwoods cannibal hell-bent on sucking the marrow from my femur. My thighs took up a part in the internal monologue and grumbled something about not minding all that much as long as they could stop moving.

The car pulled up a few feet ahead of me, and the driver stayed put while an ancient woman clambered out of the passenger seat. She hunched over a cane and teetered to the back of the truck to peer into the red-drenched night.

"Are you lost, mija?" she called out in a voice that sounded like brittle, worn pages of a recipe book and the dust of millennia.

"No, señora. Just trying to get up to Conacastal for the night to catch a bus to San Miguel," I called back to her in the Spanish she had used.

She tsked, that sound a suck at her teeth as I got close enough to see the tanned, deeply furrowed face of the elder.

"Come on, then. I'll have Manuel give you a ride in. Do you have reservations at one of the hotels?"

I'm sure when I was young, I was taught never to talk to strangers and never to get into a stranger's car, but the sound of the distant howling cadejos gathered up those lessons and tossed them in the incinerator of good ideas. Fuck it. My choices were simple. If I stayed out here, on the road, they would find me. If I went with this old woman and the man at the wheel, who I assumed was Manuel, I only had a chance of being maimed. The odds were shit anyway I cut it, so I might as well take the chance and go with the less-certain one.

I climbed up into the truck, shaking my head to answer her question. I scooted across the seat to wedge myself against Manuel, who nodded to me and smiled.

Okay. So far so good. This was only a little terrifying now that I was in the truck.

"I'm Consuelo, and this is Manuel. You can just call me Mama Cee, though. Everyone else does. And just call him Manny." She patted my knee as she tucked herself up into the truck with me.

A strange sensation of butterfly wings kissing at the edges of my awareness washed over me. I brushed it off. I hadn't slept, and the adrenaline had started edging off; I could acutely feel the boulders that had taken up residence where my eyelashes had been.

The warm scent of carrot cake and freshly turned earth teased my nose in the air of the quiet cab. I smiled to myself. It was a comforting smell that wrapped around me and cradled me close.

When we pulled up to the first hotel, I hopped out, thanking her.

"We'll wait here and make sure you get sorted out, mijita," the old woman crooned.

It was a good thing they had, too. The hotel was full, and the clerk informed me they were the only hotel between here and San Miguel.

When I pushed out of the lobby, Mama Cee was leaning her old bones against the truck.

"All full?"

I nodded and sighed.

"Just as I thought. Most of these places fill up at night from tourists and the locals who just want some privacy. C'mon then. Manny and I will take you up to the totoco house, and you can stay with us for as long as you need. At least for the night."

I stopped, mid-stride. Totoco. House. More cadejos? Julia had told me one afternoon about the other totoco in their local area. She'd told me they were all bloodthirsty murderers and how their totoco had saved far too many tourists from their jaws.

I gave the old woman a once-over. Her hunched shoulders and gnarled hands spoke of years of hard work, and the dirt under her nails told me that work had been in the soil and not in the abattoir that Julia talked about. The comfort I felt in the cab of the truck couldn't have been faked, could it? My internal judge of character couldn't be so off and so wrong that I would feel at ease around this mindless murderess and her quiet but sweet friend?

That little voice growing louder and louder by the day whispered at me to run, but I could see no reason to. All I saw was a warm, comforting, elderly woman leaning against a truck, offering to keep me safe.

"You're . . ."

"Cadejo? Yes. I'm sorry, mi corazon. I thought you knew? You smell of us. I assumed you knew when you got in the truck. If I misjudged the situation, lo siento. Manny and I can go back to the totoco house and check in on you tomorrow morning if you'd like. I'd offer more, but I can't imagine another way to keep you safe without bringing you up to the totoco house."

Her words were soft, heartwarming, and tender. I could almost imagine laying my head across this woman's lap and letting her pet my head as if I were a child.

"No . . . no, it's fine. I'm not a cadejo, but I know of your kind. I just . . . haven't had the greatest of turns with them."

The woman winced, as if I had slapped her. "Itzatecuani, I'd bet, if I had a chance. I've known that boy since he was a youngster. His father was a good man, but him? He's always been a bit overbearing for my totoco's tastes. Very high-handed and puffed up, if you ask me. Could use a little taking down a peg."

Wasn't that the truth . . . Yet, even though I had run from him, hearing her speak ill of Sal twisted my guts. I could taste his smile as he pressed a kiss to my lips before starting his day. I could feel his arms wrapped around me as we lay down for the night. And, while I knew I had seen a softer side of Sal over the last few weeks, I also remembered the brutish way he pushed me around in those first few days. She would not have seen the same passionate, scorching-hot man I had, so I could understand her distaste.

She was the polar opposite of him. Where he was darkness and shadows, she was warm sunshine and rich earth. She was kindness and compassion, and he was hardness and implacability. They were as different as the sun and the moon, and I felt safe with her, at least for the night.

I nodded after carefully debating and jumped back into the truck. "I appreciate it, señora."

"Please, call me Mama Cee, dear one." She patted my knee again as we climbed back in.

Again, that strange, odd fluttering sensation kissed the back of my mind.

Soon, we were trundling up a precariously narrow, winding road that led up the San Miguel volcano.

"Do all cadejos live on volcanos, Mama Cee?" I asked, staring out the window into the darkened jungle.

"Mmm, most of them. It's in our nature. We were born of the children of the teotl, and the volcanos are the pathways between the worlds. Our kind flourished here for thousands of years. So, it is an old habit that we tend to make our homes on their slopes." She adjusted herself in the seat to the sound of popping bones. "They say that the white cadejos used to subsist entirely on the flowers that grow along their slopes. But those are old woman's tales."

In the lights of the truck, I could see the flowers as they crept past us, morning glories of some sort. It was a pretty sentiment, and I smiled softly at the idea of a ghostly white dog chowing down on the tender little buds with their faces turned up to the empty sky.

We took about half an hour to ascend the slope of the volcano. I didn't know what I was expecting their totoco house to look like, perhaps something like Sal's compound. The totoco house, as Mama Cee called it, was nothing like that. It wasn't even a single house. Instead, it was a collection of ten or fifteen small hut-like buildings, scattered haphazardly around the central anchor of a two-story Spanish colonial-style house lit from within by the warm glow of candles.

Manny slid out of the truck first, keeping the lights aimed at the house so Mama Cee and I could find our way and helped the elderly woman out before offering me his hand. Thankful, I took it.

The moment my skin touched his, I felt an instantaneous alarm bell go off that was immediately smothered with an overwhelming sensation of calm and peace. It reminded me of the way I felt on the beach when Sal held me in his arms; it was the exact same feeling.

I blushed up at Manny, whose light-mocha eyes twinkled with interest as they slid over my body appreciatively.

"Señora," he whispered as he helped me down from the truck. Guilty eyes slid to Mama Cee, who watched with a sly smirk.

"Manny, why don't you show our guest up to her room in the big house."

We both looked at Mama Cee, then at each other with a shrug, and did as she bid.

The inside of the big house was exactly how I imagined a mission-style house in colonial times would have been. All smooth white plaster walls and dark wood beams. The house even smelled old, like it had been warped into the future solely for their use. The scent of beeswax candles and drying herbs mingled with the sharp, tangy scent of adobe clay. The stairs, hand-carved and decorated with butterflies and marigolds carved into the dark wood, creaked as Manny led me upstairs to a small room with a crescent sculpture decorated with a drape of small bells hanging from it.

He paused at the door frame, letting it swing open for me. "If you'd like, señora, I can stand watch to make sure you're safe tonight."

"Oh, no. It's okay. I don't want to be any trouble," I said noncommittally, letting my backpack bounce off of the small twin mattress in the room.

"It is no trouble, señora. When one welcomes a gem into your home, you guard it against those that would steal its light," he purred softly into the gloom of the room as I found matches to light a candle on the dresser across from the bed.

I blushed and pulled on the mask I had abandoned as I settled into the life of living with a totoco of cadejos that could sniff out the smallest bit of insincerity. "You're too kind, Manny. If you'd like to, by all means. But please don't put yourself out for me."

I gave Manny a pacifying smile, and he grinned back at me. Mama Cee chose that moment to trundle up the stairs with a well-crafted but rough mug. The scent of rich spiced hot chocolate wafted over me, sank deep into my aching body, and filled the hollow spaces between the shards of my soul.

Mama Cee pushed past Manny to set the hot chocolate down on the dresser and patted my shoulder. This time, I felt the same fluttering, but it was faint, and I shot up a brow. The first time was odd, the second curious, the third not a coincidence. I wondered idly if, like César, she had some healing ability and her age was keeping her from controlling it. Despite living with them for weeks now, I was still far too ignorant of the gifts possible for the cadejo, but if César could be believed, I might be ignorant for a long time.

"Sleep well, sweet one. Manny and I will take you up to San Miguel in the morning, if you'd like." She crooned while shooing Manny out of the room. "Good night, dear." She called over her shoulder as she closed the door.

Taking a deep breath in, I collapsed onto the cold, empty bed. I stared at the steaming mug. I couldn't pull my eyes away from it. It was like everything inside of me just . . . went blank. Nothing moved. Nothing twitched. There was just . . . nothing there. I couldn't hear my heart beating. I couldn't feel that anxiety I had felt so often before I met Sal slithering under my skin. I couldn't even feel the fleshy cage that held me bound for so many years, now that he had thrown out my Adderall. I was sure that, despite my continued life, I had even stopped breathing. Everything inside of me, all my thoughts, and all my familiar body sensations were just . . . gone.

I stared at that stupid mug, taking in not a single detail for what seemed like hours, only convinced of my persistent existence by the steady image that kept me grounded in reality.

When sensation and consciousness came back to me, it was like someone had taken a long, dull hand saw and chewed up my tender skin to get to my soft bits. Pain, exquisite in its purity, lanced through every molecule of my body, every thought in my brain, and made itself a cozy little nest in the emptiness that once housed my heart. I felt like I was going to implode and vomit at the same time. A river of misery tore through my soul and geysered from my eyes to drown me in its liquid suffering. I hunched over, grabbing my knees, and soundlessly screamed a sobbing lament into my skin. The agony was so overwhelming it robbed my throat of the ability to do anything but vent the tiny cutting gasps that could squeeze past the enormity of it.

I had seen Sal for the last time. I would never feel his touch or his kiss again. I walked away from the only person who had ever seen into the shadows of my heart and begged me for more access. I abandoned the only place where I felt truly at rest. Knowing how different he would be now that he knew the truest depths of my weakness—and how different I would be to him—didn't make it hurt any less. The knowledge I had done what was best for both of us didn't ease the great pit of anguish grinding my bones clean of marrow and meat.

Sal would be able to go on. I hadn't marked him, and he hadn't marked me. He could take a true mate, one more worthy of his position and worthy of leading his people beside him. He wouldn't be burdened with a fat, half-ghost of a woman who had debased herself willingly her entire life for the meager price of the occasional pat on the head. He could have chubby, happy little babies with a woman who was strong, beautiful, and loyal like he was. A woman who was of his own kind, unlike me. She would be everything I was not and could be everything to him I could never be. She would love him and welcome him into their mating like I never could.

The idea of Sal in the arms of another woman made me gag. Sobs wracked my dry heaving form as I imagined them intertwined and moaning passionately for each other. She could make love to him in the ways I could not and give him a mating free of the burden of baggage or ignorance of his kind. She could make him happy in ways I never could.

I curled further into my little ball of torment and suffering and wept fat, hot tears into my skin for the choices I had to make, never touching the hot chocolate steaming away happily on the dresser that was unaware of the writhing creature on the bed who had given up the only scrap of true happiness she would ever have.

I sobbed until I couldn't any longer, alone with nothing but that damned hot cocoa and the boulder of lamentations on my chest, until I saw the faint glow of the dawn creeping through the small window and heard the first crowing of waking roosters. Unfocused, I stared into the nothingness I had become when the warmth of the sun crept across my numb body to urge me back into life.

"No. I won't," I told it.

CHAPTER THIRTY-TWO

Itziquetzal

Warmth suffused my limbs as I tangled my fingers around the ends of her curls in my sleep. In my dream, I was wrapped around her, clutching her naked form to my chest, my hands splayed across the bounty of her breasts. I thrust up into the tight sheath of her body as she moaned my name. She held my heart that glistened with droplets of blood and throbbed with each pump into her flesh in one of her outstretched hands. The other was stretched down her body, buried between her thighs. Her eyes radiated bright, sunlit golden beams against my skin. Marigolds with petals made of vibrant turquoise and the cerulean blue feathers of a cotinga bird bloomed around our entwined bodies as we writhed in pleasure against each other. She turned her face from me as I leaned down and placed kisses along the column of her throat that took on a honey-gold hue.

I moaned deep in my throat as I felt her clench down around me. "Noyzotzon," I murmured against the steam that rose from each kiss I placed on her skin.

She turned back to capture my supplicant's kiss, but the face I sought to ravage was not hers. The face before me shimmered in my view as a glittering obsidian mirror pulled across features that vaguely resembled my beloved. Black smoke curled around lips made of the wings of an Orizaba silk moth. They opened and let a plume of gold-tinted mist seep into my eyes.

"Wake," the voice of the mirror mask commanded in a dual voice of a man and a woman.

I sat straight up in bed, clutching my pounding heart and gasping for air.

The teotl.

They rarely visited me, and it was rarely any other than Huitzilopotchli, my patron. This was not him. I shivered in my skin and reached across the great divide within me to rouse my cadejo, who slumbered in the space between. A visitation from the teotl was rarely a good tiding.

It took seconds before I realized my bed was cold, the shock of the dream still clutching at my awareness and perception, making both duller than I was used to. When I snapped my glance to the other side of the bed, a stone fell from the cavern of my mind and crashed into the pool below my stomach.

Gone. Again.

I leaped from the bed and threw open the door to the bathroom, panic settling into my blood like great icebergs of terror creaking and snapping into smaller venomous pieces. She wasn't in the bathroom.

I flew down the hallway to check the sitting room. Maybe she couldn't sleep. She had poured a lot of emotion out, and maybe it was still troubling her.

There was nothing in the sitting room. As I looked up and down the walkway, my eyes caught on the ajar door. The world fell away and crashed into me simultaneously. My ears rang with the mocking silence of the night as it danced beyond that open doorway.

The sight of the open doorway and the chill creeping into the room finally roused my cadejo deep within me. He tilted my head back and roared, the sound of him calling the spirits of the others in his care to come to his aid. Above me and all around me, the sound of feet hitting floors before the owner was even fully roused and lights flooding in from the windows as he roared filled my ears.

I felt him push through into my skin and trade into our monstrous form. The stretch and pop of sinew and bone extending echoed in my mind, warring against the haunting silence.

My totoco, in various forms, flooded into the courtyard as I joined them. "Find her. Find my mate!"

We tilted our noses into the wind, and I caught a drifting scent of her juices mixed with mine, then ran toward it as fast as my hulking brutal form would allow.

We trailed the scent, desperation pumping into me as totoco members swarmed over the ravine and slopes of our volcano, chasing down different scents.

We searched for what seemed like hours before Kumanavai called on the wind at the peak of the caldera. I crashed through the underbrush and scrabbled up the slope to where he and another stood sentry over what they found. Blood. It was a handful of droplets spattered and smeared against the red dirt of the volcano, but it was hers. I could smell the marigold of her skin, and I was taken back to the dream. My heart felt like it had been torn from my chest and was in her palm, floating somewhere away from me, drifting farther and farther into the void between us. I clenched my hand against the stabbing torment that took up residence behind my breastbone.

The pain didn't fade, though I did my best to grind my knuckles against it to chase it from me. I couldn't afford to feel pain. I needed to find her. I needed to find her before anything happened to her. I needed to find her before she was hurt. I would not survive if she were hurt. I would not draw another breath if I found her broken and brutalized, laying at the bottom of the volcano, while I had been sleeping without a care.

My mind spiraled through flashed images of potential fates she could have met, every snapshot frame bordered by those strange feather flowers and mirrored on an obsidian surface.

"Itzatecuani."

The sound of César's voice pulled me from the images as I panted at the power of their grip. My black eyes met his soulful hazels as concern flashed across his face. He was in his human skin, and I wanted to snap and bite at him for daring not to use his powers to find her. Some small logical part of me whispered the reminder that his beast was not powerful like me but powerful in other ways. "Let your beast go, brother. Save your power for when we have a stronger lead."

His caution and even head in this matter enraged the beast in my skin, and we snapped a warning at him, gnashing the daggers of our fangs at him. He remained stalwart and implacable, calm in the face of the danger of an enraged man and beast combined in a singular pursuit of the only thing that mattered. When I did not trade my shadow, he cocked a brow and raised his hand. "Do not make me force the change on you, brother. We both know how unpleasant it is for you. Save your strength. Let the others hunt on all fours for her. You are our tecutli. Do not allow this to unmake you. Tranquílo. You walked away once, and she came back to you. We will find her and bring her back to you again."

I shivered, fighting the urge to rip his head clean from his body, soak my claws in his blood, and shove my face into the viscera of his entrails. I fought the enraged beast, who clawed and snapped, and bit at the edges of my control to stay on the surface, to stay in partial control of my flesh so he could find his mate. He was just as desperate, just as cowed by the weight of dread creeping in and eating away at the bones within us as we exchanged the shadow of our form back into the shell of my human skin.

"Here!" called Hypolita, a huntress under Ixchel's command.

I ran for her, César and Phelix following close on my tail. We ran with her over the far lip of the volcano and down into the valley between ours and the San Miguel volcano. My heart pounded closer in my chest. The pain of each drumming beat dulled slightly. A cord in my stomach pulled and twisted as we stilled over a scrabble of bushes and short trees. Night-kissed blooms and leaves were all I saw as I cast my gaze into the shadows. Something caught my eye in the darkness, but as I zeroed in on it, forcing my eyes to focus on the black of the night, nothing caught again.

It had been there. Something had pulled. Something had twisted. Something whispered on silent lips in my ear that something I should see lingered in the darkness. I stood, frozen, praying to every teotl I could name—and some I couldn't—that they would bless me and show that small thing in the dark again.

"They've found something on the other side," someone mumbled in Nahuatl, but I held up my hand to silence them.

I swore on everything I was, everything I could be, and all of the blessings that the teotls had given me that something was there. It was there. I knew it. I knew I glimpsed something in the blackness just below me, on the slope down into the heart of the valley. I glared into the night, threatening its inky depths to give up that little flash again.

I stood there, statue-still, hoping against all odds that I'd see it again or feel that twisting jerking in my stomach to guide me forward, but there was nothing but the stillness of the wind and the crawling things of the night.

She was not there. She was not hiding in the darkness. I would have smelled her if she were, but all I smelled was myself, my own fear-drenched sweat, and the exhausted sweat of my totoco.

"Mitztemoa noyollo," I whispered into the wind, hoping it would carry it to her. Hoping that her heart would hear the words and, even if she didn't understand them, that they would seep into her soul and bloom with my love for her.

Reluctantly, I turned away and loped into the darkness with the others to find another lead I prayed would pan out.

I could not afford to lose her again. Not when she had finally opened up to me. Not on the same night she had finally cracked open her chest and revealed that tender, battered heart that she had been keeping from me. I should have been more vigilant. I should have stayed up all night, holding her and whispering in her ear all of the words that dwelled in my soul for her. I should have held her tighter to my skin so that she didn't slip away. I should have done so many things, and as I raced through the dark jungle, up and down the slopes, I fought that burning stab of tears in my eyes, knowing I had, once again, failed her.

When she needed me most, I failed to hold her safe. I failed her when she needed me to be the rock for her to perch on. I should have been everything she needed at that moment. I should have held her close and made sure before she fell asleep she knew that nothing would change, nothing could chase me away. I should have been the safe harbor in the hurricane that she had brewed in her heart. I would flay open my skin and bleed across the world if it would erase that anguish and pain from her soul. I would rip my intestines out and feed them to sharks if it meant she would feel the safety she needed.

I would do anything for her. Anything at all. Any number of insane things she could ask. Just so I could see her safe and happy again. I would do it for her. I would do anything. I just needed to find her and show her that I meant it.

Dawn was drawing over the horizon by the time the totoco returned to the compound. It took three of them to pull me back into the thick vegetation when we found her trail ended at the small asphalt road that cut between my totoco lands and the territory of that vile snake, Consuelo.

César had been wise to force my cadejo across the spirit rift, into stasis, so I could not access his strength to fight back against my warriors and hunters in my desperation. He was right and wise, and I hated everything about him and hoped he fell on a viper for being right.

He had taken control as I paced the courtyard's open terrace. Hopelessness and urgent, biting fear curled in the pits of my stomach as anxiety pushed my feet to a marrow-deep restlessness. César's serene voice leaked into my ears as poisonous sludge, coating my mind and lapping at the last shreds of hope that she was safe.

"Send Phelix and Cheeno on a scouting mission. They are swift and silent. No one sees you going in or coming out. Got it?"

Cheeno and Phelix shared a glance and nodded to César as they let their ghost dogs billow into the world on a cloud of black smoke. Cheeno was a smart choice, gifted with the ability to blend into any shadow, no matter how small. Phelix may be unremarkable in his ghost form, but what he lacked in gifts he more than made up for in sheer swiftness. He was the fastest runner I'd ever seen on two legs. On four legs, none of us could keep up with him. They would make an excellent reconnaissance team.

His hand landed solidly on my shoulder, an anchor in the thrashing ocean, where despair and anger warred over the scraps of my heart. I turned to him, our eyes meeting and holding for a long while.

He softened. My oldest friend and confidant knew what this was doing to me without the preamble of me needing to explain all the gory details to him. He might not know the finer parts of what happened between us the night before, but he, of all people, knew what her disappearing into the night was doing to me.

He nodded softly, his unkempt, shaggy mop of curls dancing atop his bobbing head in the clean rays of the morning light. He leaned forward, our foreheads meeting, and my eyes slid shut as I soaked in his calm strength. I needed it. I needed to draw in that tranquility hanging around my cousin like the mantle of a teotl. Even without the howling rage of my cadejo swirling in my soul, I wanted to run across that road, up the slope of their volcano, and rip every last one of them limb from limb for even looking at her, let alone taking her.

A squeeze was given to my shoulder, and we separated. "Get some rest, brother. I'll wake you when Cheeno and Phelix get back."

I gave him a wry look. "We both know I won't sleep until she's back."

He shrugged casually. "I had to try at least, right?"

I gave him a thin smile and a conceding nod. It wouldn't be César if he didn't at least try.

"Well, instead of just pacing like a cornered jaguar, why don't you help Pastora and Ximena get breakfast ready? Hmm?"

I cast a speculative glance at the two women, who were already halfway done with the morning's meal preparation. Pastora, to her credit, seemed to ignore César and me. Ximena, on the other hand, looked as if César had suggested that I dip my balls in the beans to add a little salt.

When I blanched and begrudgingly made my way toward them, my cousin chose that moment to materialize, like an angry mother bear. "Oh, no. No, you don't. You take that sour face of yours, and you march right back to where you came from. I'm not about to tolerate you harassing us just because you got your tail caught in a door."

César gave her a scolding look over my shoulder, and she glared right back at him. Their silent stand-off over me—their leader of all things—lasted a few seconds before, to my surprise, Julia relented.

"Fine. But you will listen, and so help me, Itzi, if you step on even a single toe or drop even a single dish, I'm cutting your balls off and begging for forgiveness later."

Wild as ever. It's what I loved most about my cousin.

It was late afternoon, two days later, before our two spies came loping back into the courtyard, rising out of their four-legged forms into a plume of man-shaped smoke before stepping free of it. I had slept fitfully in small bursts, jarred awake by the slightest sound. While my balls were still intact, I couldn't say that the sleepless worry was doing my eyes any favors.

I shot up from my perch on the bucket next to the grill, where I was tasked with husking corn and cleaning vegetables for the storage shed. Cobs and husks clattered on the hard-packed dirt below me as I stalked toward them. They were both breathing hard, panting their exhaustion, their human skins already sweating.

"Report," I barked, my beast having thrown off the metaphysical shackles that César locked him behind.

I only contained him through sheer willpower.

Cheeno slid his eyes to Phelix, and they exchanged a look before the latter squirmed uncomfortably.

"Report, dammit, before I lose my mind. Did you find her? Is she okay? Tell me something."

Cheeno exhaled a ragged sound, but the usually stoic Phelix was the one who finally opened his mouth. His voice was slow—always had been—and methodical. "We found her. She's at their totoco house. And she didn't look physically wounded, from what we could see."

Cheeno cut his gaze back to Phelix, who clamped his lips shut. "That's it?" I snarled.

Again, Cheeno sighed, this time breaking his silence. "No, tecutli. That's not all. When we found her, she was flirting—"

"What."

It wasn't a question so much as a demand for him to clarify.

"She was flirting with *him*."

Him.

I knew exactly who he was talking about. Manuel. He had been a thorn in my side since I took over the totoco, and I'd wager he'd caused problems before then. He had been suspected of more crimes than I could count, brought before the Council more times than I could count, and every single time, he'd slither out from under the weight of his crimes through manipulation and convenient disappearances of witnesses.

I met him when I was still in my teens. He had been stalking the ramshackle ruins of a condemned building that teenagers liked to visit to challenge their mettle, feeding off of them. The building hadn't been in my territory, and I was the only witness to his crimes. As the rivalry between the totoco closest to our territory was ancient before my father and I had joined, I was not believed, no matter how I positioned it. The fact that, in our beast forms, we are almost indistinguishable from one another played against me, as usual.

"She wasn't flirting *with* him, Chee." Phelix cut into my thoughts with his deliberate and smooth voice, drawing my eye to him. "All we saw was him flirting with her. She didn't seem to be saying much at all."

Hope flickered up, unexpectedly, from the battlefield that had become my guts for the last ten hours. She wasn't speaking. The memory of her standing next to the toad centecpanhuia in the museum filled my mind. She had revealed that she had a keen ability to mask her emotions and intentions under duress.

That time I saw her, none of those around her noticed the way her eyes darted away, seeking any other place to lay than on the people she was surrounded by. No one else noticed the subtle way she angled her hips and shoulders away from everyone in their group. I hadn't even noticed the way her entire face seemed frozen in a single expression. I only noticed that tell when she turned on me on the staircase that first night. It was only then that I noticed the swiftness she could draw the mask down to hide from others.

If she wasn't speaking, wasn't reacting to Manny, of all people, a man I knew to be one of the best manipulators outside of those gifted by the teotl with the art of the storyteller, then, perhaps there was still hope. Perhaps she hadn't left me for him like a small voice of doubt was whispering in my ear. I'd given her fair reason, hadn't I? All the brutality I visited upon her skin and my sharp tongue. Even if she had moaned with every lash of the belt, anyone else might have seen it differently.

"She wasn't talking? Did either of you get close enough to see her face?"

Cheeno nodded as Rafael appeared at his shoulder, offering him a pair of sweatpants and another pair for Phelix, who bowed his head to the side in thanks. The two stepped into the garments as Cheeno went on. "I did. It was dodgy at first, full daylight, and they've changed things since last we were there. There are more open spaces and wider gaps between the buildings. Makes it harder to slip from shadow to shadow. And they've torn down all of the buildings that were there last time, all except the totoco house. The new ones are all aligned with north-south, barely any shadows being cast, no matter what time of day."

I frowned, considering this. The last time we had tussled, unsanctioned with their totoco, was over five years ago. My father never told me what their crime was. It most likely skirted the edge of the boundaries of the Council's laws and was intolerable to him. There had been so many squat buildings at the time, scattered along the plateau they had dug out that it had been easy for even the most unskilled shadow dancer to slip in and out of advantageous attack positions. We spent less time decimating a third of their totoco than we had to get into position. This new development meant that the rescue mission would require careful strategy.

"And? Describe her facial expressions to me, Cheeno. Leave no detail out," I said, my mind formulating strategic attack formations and tactics.

I was confident that my mate, even in her fear and heartbreak, had not betrayed me. I needed to hold on to that soft, glowing adoration she beamed up at me as I brought her back from the slope of the caldera. I had to hold on to the way she curled around me, the way she held on to me in her sleep, the way she groaned whenever I moved around on the bed, her fingers digging into my skin like she was strong enough to keep me there next to her.

We sat, heads huddled together, as Cheeno painted a picture of my beautiful wife beside that slimy beast. Cheeno painted a picture of a woman made of serenity . . . exactly as I hoped. Xochitl was a wildcat at her heart, all claws, flashing fangs, and spitting insults. She was not the soft-spoken, placid woman he described. She was holding her mask, even under the stress of Manny's significant advances. When he told me of how Manny had placed his hands on her hips to guide her through their vegetable patch, my talons slid free of my control as my beast snarled beneath my skin.

The normally chatty man went bone silent as I drilled holes into the table between us. My lip curled up in disgust, an urge to snarl I couldn't suppress. "Do you think you could draw a detailed map?"

Cheeno shrugged. "Raf could probably help me. He's the artist of the two of us. But if you need it, tecutli, I will make sure it's done."

"Good. As soon as possible." I rose, clapping my forearm to his, then to Phelix's. "You help, too. As much detail as you can manage. With the changes to the layout, we will need to come up with new siege tactics. With the added complication of extracting my errant mate, it'll need elegance."

"Itzatecuani . . ." Phelix shuffled his feet awkwardly as I lofted my brow in question. "They have kids."

I blanched, my stomach flipping. Children. They had brought children into their twisted totoco? "How many?"

He rolled his shoulders in a casual shrug that belied the discomfort dancing in his deep hazel eyes. "Six? Maybe seven. I didn't get a good count, and we didn't go too far from the main areas. I couldn't go back there again. Not after what I saw last time."

I nodded, understanding the unspoken part, the thing Phelix could never speak aloud again, the sight that had stolen his voice from us for a full year after the last time we visited that cursed place. "Any redeemable?"

He hung his head. "None that I saw."

I clenched my teeth against the prospect of what we would have to do and clapped him on the back, offering him the strength of my body when the strength of my words fell short.

CHAPTER THIRTY-THREE

*W*ake up.

The voice was so close to my ear, just inside of my personal bubble. It was a soft voice, crystalline and harmonic, but it also held a reverence a stranger shouldn't hold for me. I blinked, my eyes blurry and stinging from wringing them out to dry all night.

It had been two days since I came to Mama Cee's house. The first night and day, I stayed in my room. Manny came in occasionally, sweetly knocking on the door and whispering he was bringing me food. He'd tucked a blanket over me that first day, but when I didn't move or eat anything, he quietly brought a basin of hot water and took my shoes and socks off to wash my feet. I told him he didn't have to. He only smiled and tucked my feet under the blanket. By the second morning, he took to trying to hand-feed me. I'd churlishly rolled over and given him my back. The night before, he sat outside of my door, strummed on a guitar, and sang love ballads to me. For a man who most likely had never taken singing lessons, his voice was clear and soulful.

It was the third morning I had seen rise at Mami Cee's totoco house, so I wasn't surprised someone was in my room. I was, however, exceedingly surprised when I rose, shoving the shards of sleep from my aching eyes, seeing not a single soul in my room.

Silken fur brushed my skin, like a giant mink rubbing my arm. I jumped and squeaked in fright, my eyes darting to where the phantom feeling had been.

Calm down. You're embarrassing me, the voice chided.

Cool, cool, cool, cool. I was going insane. First, my mother, then Shayne, a pair of nightmares have a rumble in my hotel room, and I get kidnapped by the hottest man alive, who I can't avoid fighting with, and now I'm hearing voices. *Sure, this tracks.*

You're not going insane, you stupid brat. Now, get up. I am not strong enough to make you. You need to get moving. You need to go back.

"What the hell?" I squeaked to the empty room. "Go back where?"

The silence was deafening.

"H-Hello?" I cautiously asked the air.

There was no response.

What the hell was that? Or better yet, *who* was that?

I shivered in the warming air of midmorning.

When a knock came on the door, I squeaked again but relaxed as Manny's familiar, handsome face peeked around the door.

"Are you all right, sweet lady?" he asked, concern oozing into his words as he pushed open the door and slid inside with a tray of food.

"Yes, sorry, Manny. I had a weird dream is all." I huffed at my foolishness, drawing up the mask I had been using to protect myself from the discomfort of being in his presence.

The voice was probably just that, a leftover dream haunting the edges of my exhausted mind.

He smiled tenderly and sat next to my ankles on the small bed, the tray resting in his lap. "Will you eat for me today? Please? I spend all day worried about you up here. If you won't eat, will you at least tell me how Mama Cee and I can help you? It's obvious something has happened to you."

Guilt washed through me, tumbling haphazardly through my veins like marbles from a child's pocket. Relenting, I picked up a round roll from the tray and broke it apart to shove into my mouth.

What I would not do was tell these people I ran from the only man who had ever made me feel anything because I'd mistakenly let him see who I really was.

The grin that split Manny's face was broad and white-toothed. "Good. Thank you, sweet one."

He took the other roll and mirrored my actions. Settling into a companionable silence, we finished the tray of sliced meat, rolls, cut fruit, and delicious coffee. When we were done, Manny cleared the tray. "Could I perhaps convince you to take a walk with me?"

I eyed the hand he offered me dubiously. I wanted to just lay back down and disappear into the snuggly arms of the too-small bed, but he and that weird voice in my head were right. I needed to get up. I needed to keep moving. Sal would eventually find me—if he were even still looking—and I didn't want to be here when he did. These people were far too kind to deal with his wrath.

Instead of taking his hand, I dusted the crumbs off of the blanket and stood. "I think so. Maybe a shower first, though?"

That sweet smile leveled up to a brilliant, bright grin. "Of course."

Two hours later, I was finger-combing my damp hair. I pulled the long ribbon from my backpack Julia had made me and braided my hair the way she taught me. The familiar sensations of the ribbon and hair sliding through my fingers called to mind the many mornings we sat together and chatted, her teaching me Nahuatl words and me teaching her all the best English cuss words. When my fingers tangled, the lack of the ribbon with the black feathers choking their familiar movements, I sighed heavily. My eyes ghosted to where it was hidden at the bottom of the backpack, secreted away, wrapped like a thief's prize in the innocuous grasp of a cotton embroidered blouse. I longed to weave it into my hair, ached from the very depths of my being to feel the soft rasp of its rough cotton threads slide against my fingers as I wrapped it into the silk of my locks.

Tears gathered at the corners of my eyes, and I pushed them and the thoughts that brought them to my mind away. I couldn't linger on thoughts of Julia. Those would lead to thoughts of Sal. The only thing down that path was more crying and more heartbreak. I needed to forget about the forever I had planned in my head.

I was tying the bow to my braids atop my head when Manny knocked again to ask me if I was ready for that walk.

I might have walked away from the starlit forever I had planned, but I had the Right Now to walk through still.

My first daylight glimpse of Mama Cee's totoco house was like stepping into a fairy tale. The warm golden rays of the sun drenched the large courtyard. Flowers of all manners burst in a riotous dance of colors from between houses, long-abandoned vehicles, and tables set out in a picnic-like area. They pushed up between gaps of the simple planked porches of some buildings and crept up and over the walls of others. Butterflies filled the air in a hypnotizing dance of blacks, oranges, blues, greens, purples, whites, reds, and golds. I had never seen so many butterflies in a single place, not even in the butterfly gardens back home, at the California Academy of Sciences. The air was thick with them, like a caterpillar cotillion. A guitar was being lazily strummed, joined by the satiny sweet voice of a woman singing a song about a young girl who had run away with a man who did not cherish her heart. The sound filled the perfumed air with its smooth, intoxicating rhythm. Maybe it was my imagination, maybe it wasn't, but it seemed like motes of golden glitter floated in the air and danced on the unseen notes of the song.

Manny walked me through a garden teeming with more butterflies and more flowers. A vibrant border of marigolds, bronze and gold orchids, buttery calla lilies, and bright yellow daisies bordered each row of vegetables. I wandered among the beauty of the flowers, finding my feet drawn to an ambling path that curled around the flower beds and wound up the plateau.

"Ah, you have roused, golden star." Mama Cee's voice called out to me as she stepped from behind what looked to be a garden shed.

"Oh. Good morning." I let a soft, pleasant smile seep into my mask.

The elderly woman smiled back, the winkles of her timeworn face settling into a soft edge as she took my hand, as though the cane she held was not enough support. "Better not to go that way, my dear. Oh, you're safe enough on these old paths, but up that way are the old garden beds, washed out during a landslide in the rainy season not long ago. The path is dangerous and unstable. You're likely to fall off a cliff to your death."

Once again, I felt the tickle of butterfly wings dancing along my face, and it took all my effort not to let my brow hike up in question. What was this feeling? What was this strange seeping sensation I felt when she touched me?

"Of course, Mama Cee," I replied mechanically yet pleasantly as she turned me back toward the garden beds.

"There's a good girl." She chuckled, the sound like caramel warming over a toasty grill. She looked up at me as we approached Manny. "Tell me, golden star, have you considered what you will do now? I can't imagine a sweet girl like you wants to go back to that monster, do you?"

Again, the butterfly wings, this time closer. I could almost sense a cat's paw swatting at the flurry of wings as if to push them back, but, eventually, the cat's paw blew away with the wind, and all that was left was the gossamer press of wings.

"No, Mama Cee."

I didn't tell her to which question I disagreed. It wasn't important. She didn't need to know my heart was broken, and no matter what, I couldn't go back . . . nor that I hadn't decided what I wanted to do just yet.

Her soft, papery leather hand patted mine a few times, then placed my hand into Manny's waiting palm. It struck me as odd, almost like a priest placing a bride's hand into that of her groom. He stared at our hands for a moment before turning a hopeful and charming smile up at me. I let a soft smile—with no promises— cross the mask and let him guide me down the garden beds. I didn't even protest when his warm palm pressed unnecessarily into my hips to guide me through.

At the end of the garden path was a stunning lookout over the edge of the volcano into the lush jungle below. He led me to a rough-hewn bench under the explosive boughs of a flor de Fuego tree. Its deep red blossoms shaded the seat and cast it in a bloody glow. It briefly reminded me of the battle in my hotel room that brought on everything that followed. He sniffed, almost like clearing his nose, but it brought to mind the way that creature licked at the glass. Alarm cut through me for a split second before I tamped it down. There was no reason for me to stare out over this beautiful landscape and feel the icy fingers of fear lick at my neck.

Clenching my fist, I forced the feeling back into the dark recesses of my mind with the pressure of a deep breath before letting the warmth of the tropical sun roast away the last of its grip.

"This is a beautiful view, Manny."

The silence was not helping the battle with the fear waging war against my resolve.

"It's one of my favorite places to come to sit and be with myself."

The soft croon of his voice put me on edge. It wasn't like the fear losing the battle against my inner resolve. It was something else, something I couldn't quite put my finger on. It tasted of Karo syrup, meant to be sweet, but it was too saccharine and left an aftertaste in my mind of chemicals and rot.

He stood behind me, looming outside of my peripheral view. I could almost feel his hot breath on the back of my neck, and it made my skin crawl with a violence I was unaccustomed to feeling. It made me want to rake my nails—which were long razor claws in my mind's eye—across his face and throw him from the edge of the lookout. The sensation of silken fur filled the edges of my awareness, and I caught sight of opaline tufts flitting across my mental field of vision, just out of sight, but the impression clear and concise.

Manny went on, unaware of the imaginary brutality I was visiting upon him. "You'll often see the torogoz in these trees. Have you ever seen them, sweet one?"

Sweet one. It was nails on my internal chalkboard, and I bristled at it, where, just hours before, I had found it somewhat endearing. The restraint to not let the snarl of annoyance festering in my throat bubble-free had almost edged out the years of practice I had.

"No, I don't think so," I forced out through gritted teeth, struggling to hold back the sudden switch in my disposition that was both uncharacteristic of me and a bit shocking.

"If we sit quietly, we will see some." He moved out from that place behind me, that had me bristling and snapping, to sit at the far end of the bench with me. The relief from the jolting sensation of feral rage was instant, like a tight fist releasing completely, and I sagged with it.

"Then, we should shut up."

Was that my voice? It was a tinkle, a glimmering flash of silver in the moonlight and the soft brush of feathers over a sleeping face. I barely recognized it.

I spent the rest of the afternoon watching the jungle in relative solitude, Manny making an excuse to leave me after an hour or two.

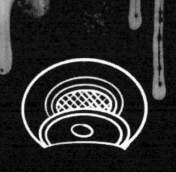

CHAPTER THIRTY-FOUR

Itziquetzal

"**R**espectfully, brother, you should have slept before we got on the damned plane." César growled under his breath from across the small plane we chartered that was heading toward Campeche, the last place I had any interest in being.

The hours ticked away so slowly. The time stretched like the fight of a cornered prey animal, scratching and yanking at the skin pulled taut around the burning embers that replaced eyes refusing to shut for longer than an hour. He was right. I should have slept. I should have done a lot of things. I should have roused the teopixqui from their slumber in the temple near the field of marigolds and demanded they prepare for the war rites. I should have stripped and made sacrifices to the teotl to bless my macuahuitl with an unending thirst. I should be balls deep in my moaning mate. I should've been exactly anywhere other than in this flying tin can, headed north to the streets of Campeche lined with its brightly colored row homes, headed to the seat of the Council.

I could see the tops of them as the small charter plane flew low. Their cheerful countenances, turned up toward the warm glow of the streetlights below us, made me want to knock them all down and shit in the debris. My black mood rolled off of me, both metaphorically and literally, my beast's foul disposition lending his smoky plume around my legs as we touched down and disembarked onto the tarmac.

César gave me a look that called me melodramatic, and I flipped him a black-taloned middle finger. He dared to snort at me as he slid into the driver's seat of the blacked-out Cadillac, me following him on the other side. He said nothing as we crept through the sleeping streets and out onto the highway that swallowed the headlights. It would be a forty-minute drive from Campeche to Edzna, where the Council, long ago, rooted its seat of power.

We were finally at the gates, being waved beyond the metal barrier that, during the day, kept the tourists from bringing vehicles into the complex before he spoke to me. In these lands, the ancestral tongue we held to was not as popular, the cadejos here preferring to cling to the Maya tongue, so he shielded his words in Nahuatl.

"Have you decided what you intend to say?" He lofted his brows without turning his head as we crawled down the narrow lane that led off into the tree line. He led the sleek black vehicle under a tree and parked it, both of us stepping out into the shadow-drenched parking lot.

I rolled my shoulders. "The truth is usually the best approach, at least with these ancient fucks. They wouldn't understand nuance or vagaries if their lives depended on it. So, the truth."

Once again, he lofted his brows at me, this time in incredulity.

"What?" He shrugged at me. I had no patience for his fucking head games. I didn't want to even be here to begin with. "Just fucking spit it out, César."

He took a deep breath and exhaled it slowly. Always so calm, my cousin. "I just know that, in this matter, you might not be the best advocate for your cause. The last time you were here didn't go that well, either."

The last time I had visited this crumbling ruin was when I petitioned the Council to allow me, a leader's heir, to take a mate without having to kill my father. I argued with them in the firelight for four consecutive nights. The Council did things the old-fashioned way, the ancient way, fashioning themselves like the teotl each of us worshipped. If you were petitioning before them, you could not eat, drink, or sleep until they'd render a verdict. Once you entered the sacbe and climbed the steps up into the Temple of the Moon, you were on the spirit's time, and you would act per their whims. As the spirits cared not for the needs of the flesh and consumed nothing, we must emulate them to prove the worth of our cause.

That last day, I had been so weak that opening my eyes felt like glass shards scraped at the sensitive meat, and my tongue felt like it was made of ancient leather. When they denied my claim, I hadn't the strength to even act on the violence that roiled in my stomach.

My mouth watered at the memory, as if preparing itself for the oncoming thirst. "It won't come to that. I don't have time for them to sit and debate."

He glared at me, crossing his long arms. I glared back at him in a silent stand-off until he finally spoke. "I think you should sit this one out. Let me speak for you. I'm not as close to it, and should they decide to say something stupid, I'm not likely to react as violently."

The laugh that bubbled up from the well between us was both mine and my beast's, an ugly, rotted thing scorching the air. "That's not going to happen."

He hitched another brow up at me, digging in his heels, arms still folded. "This isn't a dick-measuring competition, Itzatecuani. It's me stepping back from the situation, and seeing what you are too close to see. I love Xochi, and I know how much she means to you. I am not ignorant of the importance of this situation. I will fight for her with every drop of my blood. And I am willing to make sacrifices if necessary, to bring her back to her rightful place in our totoco. But, brother, this is not a request. I am telling you what will be best for this issue. We are equals."

"We are not equals when it comes to Xochitl," I snarled out at him.

"You're right. We aren't. I am not her mate. But I am the third leg in an incomplete totoco power dynamic that will never be completed in the eyes of the teotl until she is returned. I am just as invested as you are in that. And, because of that, I will speak for the totoco. I will speak for its missing Cihuatlatoani and not about the missing mate."

My cousin was one of the most annoying creature types on the face of the planet. No, not a mosquito. No, far more annoying. He was always right. The pretentious fuck sat back and watched everything. He stayed silent as things unfolded, and only when he had a good grasp of the strange little details did he bother to stand up and advocate for something. It made him insufferable.

When we were kids, I preferred to balance the scales by punching him until he bled. As adults and equals in the totoco, I was reduced in my options to rectify the great injustice of his consistent rightness, but since it concerned my mate, I couldn't hold back. The scales needed to be balanced for his audacity to be right, so I pulled back my fist and slammed it into his face as hard as I could. To his credit, he was smart enough not to act like he predicted the hit and rocked back on his heels before sniffing the blood back into his broken nose.

"I'm glad you see reason," he slurred as he healed his nose.

I responded with a grunt and a nod, not having to spell it out for him.

He spat blood on the gravel walkway as we walked down the dark path to the ruins. We passed the tiny restoration hut and into the shadows that hung over this place. The further we came toward the heart of our people's power, the more my skin crawled. When we neared the court of purification, we both paused and took a deep breath. Crossing the threshold of the temple grounds had always been unsettling for me. My will solidified, and I stepped forward into the blackness that shrouded the gathering of our kind's most powerful. The unseen line washed over me in a sensation like ice-covered cobwebs brushing my exposed body.

The barrier between the realm of our spirits and mortals was the thinnest here, having been scratched and torn at for hundreds of years, since the acropolis grounds were ceded to our people before the Conquest. Our ancestors predicted the incursion of the bastard Spanish and had gone from city to city to warn them—of course, using it as leverage. Each was offered the same deal: abandon your city to our control, and we will protect your people and house them in a safe place to keep them from the clutches of the coming invaders. Only the people of Edzna had taken that deal and been secreted into the mountains, deep in the jungle, where their tribes still live.

All those years, though, the Council had spent thinning the walls between the realms, and it produced a singular sensation that many of even our kind found disconcerting when the torches were lit, welcoming the spirits. Only during the day could humans step across the threshold and not be at risk of being immediately overtaken by hungry spirits.

César, as the speaker of the two of us, walked ahead of me and climbed the four stairs into the court of purification. Two priestesses, surrounded by flickering torches casting dancing shadows along the pale stone of the broken building, stood to either side of a silver dish filled with water.

"You come to speak before the Council?" one asked, her voice soft but made bold by the scratch of several spirits curling around her tongue.

César nodded to her, then stepped up to the bowl. She cupped a handful and washed his head, his hands, and his forearms. When she was done, the other stepped forward and handed him a sharpened jade blade and a gold basin that was the smaller sister to the large water bowl.

"Make your payment," the priestess murmured to him as the other washed me as she had César.

Her fingers caught in my braids and tugged at my scalp, annoying me further. Her finger trailed along one and traced the line of my mating talisman, and I snatched my head back. Before I could control him, my beast burst forth and snarled a snapping bite at her hands. I only missed burying my fangs into her flesh by the smallest of margins.

"Careful, Ah Kin, even on his best day, he would view that as disrespectful to his mate, and today is not the best day." César's soft voice whispered into the thick silence between us as the priestess glared at me. "Come on, Cujo, before you embarrass yourself."

He wrapped a blood-slicked hand around my bicep and dragged me back to the white faintly glowing path into the acropolis proper. As the sacbe led us past several buildings, I found the torch-lit platform of knives, and my stomach twisted. It was there I lost the bid with the lower Council members to take my mate before killing my father. I would never forget the fire dying in his eyes when the pronunciation was given, and he'd turned to clap me on the shoulder. His dark-brown eyes had held mine for what seemed an eternity, saying everything I needed to hear, yet not a single word passed his lips.

He knew how deep my love and need for my mate was. He knew I had no choice but to challenge him for the leadership of the totoco. He knew that I would not enjoy it but that I would do it nonetheless. He knew he was drawing breath at my pleasure from that moment on.

"Brother."

César's concerned voice pulled me back to the present as we climbed the staircase out of the great plaza and into the upper city. He locked eyes with me, then nodded toward the House of the Moon to the right of us. Sighing deeply, I nodded back to him as he took the lead and drew me along with him, struggling to keep afloat of the memories of my father's heart beating in my clawed hand.

We stood on the platform between the House of the Moon, where the Council held court on governmental matters and the Temple of the North, where the Ah Kin held court on matters of the spirit. On the rare occasion a matter was deemed to be an offense or a matter of both sectors of our existence, the court would be held by both at the greatest of all the buildings of the ruined acropolis: the Temple of Five Stories. I had seen only two courts be held there, and I hoped never to see them again.

We waited our turn, time seeming to shift and twist like the whims and coils of a serpent. I watched, spellbound, as César finally stepped before the assembled tribes and leaders of each. Each of these cadejo was the most powerful or ancient of their tribe. There were ten represented on the steps of the temple, arranged by seniority and influence. At the top, glaring down at the lesser tribal leaders, was the man who fashioned himself as our king, his wife, his priests, and two others whose purpose, as far as I was aware, was solely to whisper in his ear.

He tilted his feather bedecked head in question as my teopixqui stepped before him. While not unusual, after all the priests of our totocos were equal to the leaders of the totoco, it was rare that a priest spoke before the Council and not the Ah Kin. Unlike other tribes, though, I took César's position seriously, just as I would when Xochitl finally accepted my mate mark and took her position within the hierarchy of our totoco. We were equals in all things and all sectors of totoco life.

"So, the little beast sends his priest before me?"

His deep voice boomed out over the stones and echoed back to us. The flames of the torches that ringed the dais flickered and danced on the soft breeze. Shadows of beasts, spirits, and human forms twisted and writhed on the white stones in a pantomime of life.

César canted his head, watching Cadmael. Unlike how he regarded me or the rest of the totoco, this silence was pointed, sharp and slicing. It cut into the air between us, and though the elder stared down at us, César's regard cut that distance and elevation as if the two were on even footing, eliminating the old man's superiority advantage. I cut my gaze to Cadmael, crossed my big arms across my chest, and widened my stance, planting my feet on the ancient stone. César sniffed derisively, waiting for the elder to push further. His patience was both a tool of a healer and the strong weapon of a deadly warrior.

"So serious, the two of you pups," Cadmael finally relented after shifting on his feet in discomfort. He waved to push César to speak.

"We come to speak with you about the Ik'an Lepa."

His voice was a strong iron proclamation, landing solidly at the leather-sandaled feet of the assembled Council. Heads turned from the steps, whispers between the various seated cadejos in their feathered finery that mimicked that of our ancestors, like tittering birds perched atop their master's favorite gilded cage. All that power, all those gifts, and not a single one of them had used it to benefit their totocos. All sold the blessings of the spirits to pursue mortal power and influence. Short-sighted, tittering birds.

Cadmael snorted, crossing his arms over the sagging skin of his once-powerfully-muscled, dark-skinned chest. Age had not been kind to this man. My father had regaled me with stories of great battles, in which Cadmael had slaughtered creatures twice to three times as powerful as himself. But this man who towered over us could probably vanquish little more than perhaps a plantain or two. "You Lets'a Wehle have been complaining about them for decades. It's always something. They took my cow. They crossed the territory boundary to pick flowers. What is it this time? Hmm? Did they fart too close to your precious volcano?"

The tips of my fingers itched, tingled with the pressure of my beast's claws, begging to sink themselves into his wrinkled flesh and avariciously slurp at the geysers of red that would spurt from his carcass.

César, though, was a better man than me. He locked eyes with Cadmael over the distance, drawing the man to him as he spoke. His voice was soft silk wrapped around the hidden razor of an obsidian blade. "They stole the mate of our tecutli."

Gasps echoed up as twinkling, scandalized offerings from the tittering birds. Feathers of all colors and lengths fluttered and waved in the breeze. Bells tinkled as the assembled individuals leaned up and to the side to talk among themselves while my cousin waited on them. I would never understand how patience was not a recognized blessing of the spirits. While he stood, arms crossed, stoicism wafting around him like the cloak of stars above us, I shifted from foot to foot, gnashing my teeth and restraining myself from opening throats all around me.

"Enough," Cadmael commanded and stepped to the edge of the platform. His gaze tottered between César and me, a sneer pulled at his lips under his sculpted, hawk-like nose. "So, the little beast cannot even keep track of his mate? *Ha.* Proceed, Priest. Tell me what you wish to tell the Council."

His hand was on my chest before I intended to move. I felt the warmth spreading across my black shirt's thin cotton as I locked eyes with my cousin. "Calm," he murmured into my ear before turning his attention back to the Council.

He let his hand linger on my chest, his patience leaking into me and wrapping around my rage like golden shackles. I took deep breaths, centering myself and growling in my head.

"An unknown cadejo of the Ik'an Lepa began their assault on our totoco several weeks ago, when Itziquetzal's mate was attacked in her hotel room. A room in his hotel, I might add. The cadejo drew attention to us by shattering the glass wall and would have fed upon her had Itziquetzal not been there to protect her. They brawled on the beach in their beast forms, and the cadejo ran off when he was distracted by gunshots in the room. We took her back to the totoco compound to be protected. Two weeks ago, he found his mate in the back seat of one of their hunting cars, headed, at least as far as she was aware, to La Libertad. Again, had he not been there, they would have fed off of his mate. This time, though, they were hunting in Chinameca, which, as the Council knows, is part of our territory. Now his mate is being held at their totoco complex, and they have made no effort to return her nor to advise us that she is even there. Had we not sent scouts to find her, she would be another missing mate being mourned by the community."

The Council members, perched atop their stone steps, fell silent, considering what my cousin told them. Cadmael was not the

Council, and he was not my cousin. He had solidified his power through brute force, not through patience and knowledge.

"So, you come before the Council to report to us that a cadejo was hunting on unclaimed territory and attempted to feed on an unmated woman? Tell me, was she marked? Did she bear a talisman of protection? And how do we know that the driver of that vehicle was actively hunting? As you well know, the Ik'an Lepa supplements their income with taxi services between the smaller cities and the metropolis areas of your country. They have been given rights to mobility by this very Council for the last thirty years, honorably. They could have simply been dropping off a tourist and been on their way out of town when she got in the car. As for her being at their complex, perhaps she is there of her own will. I cannot imagine that a leader who willfully flouts the laws of territory by sending in scouts to another's territory is a mate who listens to his mate's needs and abides by them. And now you come before us, claiming all these ills done to your totoco by the Ik'an Lepa, yet *all* I hear is that your totoco has actively violated territory laws by infiltrating their sacred territory to spy on them." He turned away from César and leveled his piercing gaze on me. "I see now why you had him speak. Too much of a coward to spew this foolishness yourself, so you sacrifice the pride of your priest."

A snarl of warning pierced the silence that fell after Cadmael shut his annoying mouth. It took precious moments to realize that it had not been my own but that it rumbled from the otherwise implacable César. His mouth filled with the razor-sharp fangs of his beast. Cadmael was doing what few others managed to do, push my cousin too far.

"She is our Cihuatlatoani! They have no right to take her from us," he hurled back at him. "She wears a mate talisman, his mate talisman."

A woman stood, her white robe nearly translucent under the heavily tooled leather bib collar draping over her breasts. "Gentle, Teopixqui. We understand the precarious position this has placed your totoco in. It has been many years that the sacred trinity of power has not been solidified in your totoco. Even with your renowned connection to the spirit realm, I imagine this has been a hardship for you. But, please, enlighten us. What talisman did she wear? Has she been mate-marked? I am not as proficient as you, dear Priest, with the spirit vision, but I cannot see a mate mark on Itziquetzal's spirit, even with the thinning of the material world to aid the spirit sight. Does this mean that she has not accepted him as her mate?"

I heard the clack of César's fangs grinding in his jaw over the sound of my own. He drew in a deep, calming breath, and his face swirled in shadows. The sharp edges of his beast smoothed under the immense pressure of his control. When he finally turned his attention to the woman, he was the familiar, tranquil man.

"Despite his reputation as a bloodthirsty, vicious man, this woman means everything to Itziquetzal. Enough to end the life of his beloved father. His father was an honorable man, one whose spirit inspired many here and whose honor could never be said to be anything but perfect. Itziquetzal was raised to cherish his mate and honor her, just as we have been instructed to do. He wished his mate to choose on her own. He has not pushed her, nor begged her, nor tried to force her to take his mate mark. He has only offered his mate a talisman. He carved her barrettes and earrings with obsidian feathers. He had a dress embroidered and beaded for her with black feathers on it to wear to their knotting. And he hand-wove her a ribbon for her braids with his black feathers on it. She wears it daily and when she was last seen, she was wearing it in her hair. There can be no clearer mate talisman. We all would know that mark."

She smiled at him. It was an ugly and twisted, patronizing thing, as if he were a child who needed coddling. "So, she has not accepted his mate mark, and he has not accepted or been offered hers?"

Here was where the danger lay. I knew what the Council thought of humans mating with cadejos. Despite it being obvious that the line of our kind did not travel through the DNA of our human forms but through the roots of our souls, far too many clung to the idea that only two cadejos could be properly mated.

"A discussion was offered between the two, and they decided to move forward slowly, but there was an understanding between the two. They are mates. They share the same bed. She sees to the duties of a mother to the totoco, as is her place. She has never once indicated displeasure with these duties nor interest in other men. On the contrary, she gave up the luxury another man, a human man, would have provided for her in favor of being mated to Itziquetzal."

César skirted the topic. I knew he was doing his best to keep from revealing too much while still answering the questions so they would not dig too deep and find the mess he was burying.

She sucked her teeth and was satisfied, sitting with a pleased smirk. Cadmael grinned blackly down at her as she preened under his gaze.

A man on the other side of the woman rose, his bare chest glistening in the dancing torchlight. He cleared his throat, and the assembly fell silent. The long feathers on the back of the band around his head twitched as he regarded César and me. "I understand the position you are in, César. I did the same with my wife. Giving her my talisman and letting her decide when or if the mating marks would be exchanged. It is an honorable and respected tradition that has, sadly, died out in many of our totocos." He paused. The woman seated at his feet—who I assumed was his wife—shot him a doting look. He then gifted the first woman with a brutal glare. There was history there, and I had no interest in dredging up the politics of the court, so I was grateful when he finally went on. "The Council has heard what you have had to say. We have heard your evidence. None can counter your words. The Ik'an Lepa has not had a representative on this Council for at least two hundred years. We can only speculate on the potential reasons that these issues may have happened. The Lets'a Wehle do have a representative on the Council."

He paused again and looked at the ancient, withered old woman being propped up by the strength of someone I had never seen before. The woman, Amanka, was the oldest woman I had ever met. When I was a child and joined the totoco, she was already aged and fragile. She had blessed the union of my father and Antu, and that was the only time I laid eyes on her, but I remember distinctly thinking she had the bones of the earth within her to be that old and still stand on her own. Yet, here she was, nearly thirty years later, still representing our small totoco on the Council. She gave the man a toothless, weak smile, then turned her eyes to lock with mine. The sensation of crystal-clear water cooled beneath the protective cave walls of a cenote flowed over my body when her clear, youthful gaze connected. I felt her power, strong and steady with a vigor that made even my bones feel old.

When he finally went on, his voice was distant, rumbling water over river rocks muffling it as Amanka and I kept eye contact.

"What is it that you and your tecutli wish of us? And why was this issue not approached through Amanka instead of through the two of her juniors?"

César sighed. We knew this question would eventually come. We had hoped that it would have been easier, but the Council seemed especially spiteful this evening. "We did not petition our representative because, as I'm sure you can imagine, this is a time-sensitive situation. We all know the reputation of the Ik'an Lepa. Whether it is true or not, we fear for our Cihuatlatoani. We wish to retrieve her."

Self satisfaction rippled over the man's benighted face. With a sly smirk he collapsed back into his seat. Amanka's eyes never left me, but her power retracted, leaving only the sensation of being clean in its wake.

A man one step above the first woman stood. "So, have you asked for her back? It seems a simple thing. Perhaps she appeared on their doorstep, and they merely extended her hospitality."

"Ha!" snorted the woman next to Amanka. The elderly woman patted her hand and whispered something to her. The woman stood. "Amanka wishes it to be known that she is old enough to know better than to play the games of the court. She says she grants these two her blessing to retrieve the lost mate in whatever way the teotl have whispered to César is best. She will have no more to say on this matter."

Arguments erupted among the members, once again reminding me of squawking birds. It dragged on and on, César and I all but forgotten by the assembly. He looked up at me and sighed with determination.

"In payment for the grant to retrieve Itziquetzal's mate from the Ik'an Lepa totoco territory, I will dedicate a year of my services to the Temple of the North."

César bargained with the one chip he knew the Ah Kin would not allow the Council to pass up. They had courted him relentlessly in his twenties, luring him into servitude with all manner of promises they thought would entice him. They offered everything from his pick of partners among the Ah Kin to breed as many get as he wished, whenever he wished, to riches beyond imagining. None of them knew César as I knew him. The teotl had whispered the name of his mate in his ear in his dreams before he even knew if he wanted a mate or not. And riches? César had never been interested in that. He had not drawn a paycheck from the company we ran since he paid off his schooling debt. After that, he had no interest in the material goods offered to him.

He had said he would make any sacrifice necessary, and he had meant it, and I wished nothing more than to tear each down to the roots to prevent him from having to pay it.

The priestess at the top of the temple with Cadmael leaned over and whispered in his ear before he held up a hand and finally pronounced, "This is not enough. Your totoco wishes to wage war against your neighbor. You wish to take their territory, as you have always wished to do. The Council will vote on the additional payment required to give you our blessing to retrieve this woman."

Rattling filled the anger-charged silence as the members of the Council passed carved wooden markers up to him.

I had had enough. I would not allow César to sign himself into slavery nor allow them to tell me I could not retrieve my mate. This was a madness I would not countenance further. I stepped forward, joining César on the grass. His eyes met mine, silently pleading with me not to fuck up. It was too late. This was already a mistake. We should have acted instead of asking for permission. The Council was a dying power, mired in its bureaucracy.

"Cadmael," I said, casting them into silence again. I felt Amanka's eyes fall on me most of all, though the entire assembly turned to look at me. "I think you have mistaken our appearance before you as a request for permission. It is not. We came to you to do you the honor of letting you know in person that we intend to bathe in their blood, and I will personally gorge myself on the symphony of their screams should they stand between me and what is mine. I am not asking. César is not asking. We are telling. None of you will stop me from retrieving my mate—anyone who does will forfeit their right to honorable combat, and I will tear the cadejo from your soul and feed it to Tezca Tlipoca."

I turned to César, leaving the clucking chickens that were slow to react to my promise behind me. "It is time to go, brother. We are done here."

I didn't wait for him. He knew just as I did it was a dead cause. I walked away from the eruption of indignation and hollow threats that filled the courtyard. I passed through the grass-covered courtyards following the line of the sacbe, continuing to feel the soothing waters of Amanka's gaze, even though there was no way the woman could still see me.

César was quiet at my side. We did not stop at the court of purification to cleanse ourselves of the spirits, as was tradition. We kept walking, wanting nothing more than to be back in that flying tin can and headed back to the next chapter. What would happen next would require both of us to focus and unite.

War was coming, and while I welcomed it as a lover's embrace, César, the balance to my bloodlust, would never welcome the destruction that would be necessary to return Xochitl to my arms.

I should have been shocked when we got to the car and Amanka was waiting for us. Should have been, but I was not. There was a reason that Cadmael feared her above the others. She was not just powerful, she was power itself, a direct conduit to the world of the divine that gave us all of our blessings.

We stopped feet from her, giving her a respectful berth. She watched us quietly, tilting her head left, then right, leaning on the jade cane before her. She watched us in that scrutinizing way Elders would, in a way César was developing. When she finally spoke, the words formed stones in my stomach.

"The broken goddess is watching."

I had no idea what that meant, but when Amanka dissolved into black smoke and disappeared into the night, I had no opportunity to ask further. César and I exchanged looks, both shuddering our discomfort.

"Get the fuck out?" he asked.

"Absolutely. Fuck this. Fuck that. And fuck this place." I snarled back at him and escaped into the artificial safety and comfort of the Cadillac.

Neither of us said anything as we raced down the darkened freeway back to the airstrip in Campeche. Neither of us wanted to know what that single sentence—given to us by the most powerful cadejo either of us had ever met—actually meant. That was a problem for another day. Our problem for today was drumming on the horizon.

CHAPTER THIRTY-FIVE

The fourth day with Mama Cee's totoco started much like the one before. I missed my routine but was settling into a new one. I tried not to acknowledge the ever-growing pit of glass shards that every breath I took had to meander through. I tried to focus on thoughts of the next steps and my future, distantly floating in the placid seas of my mind. Once again, I woke to the strange voice in my ear telling me to wake up and to go back, but before I could wake up, it had abandoned me back into silence.

I could resist the siren call of that ribbon no longer. It had whined to me all night, whispered all the wrongness of it being left in the battered old backpack. I carefully wove the ribbon Julia gave me in with the mating talisman to hide the black feathers. No one here needed to know that the flash of white, under the vibrant reds and yellows, was me clawing to stay connected to the very thing I had walked away from and missed with every beat of my broken heart.

When I had completed my braids, I stared at my reflection in the basin on the dresser. Not a single black feather could be seen. I already felt better. Instead of my heart cascading into a dark pit, it felt cradled and held aloft, even by this tiny thread I had left to me.

I spent the morning working in the garden before lunch and then the rest of the afternoon with Alina, another cadejo in the totoco, caring for the ten children that ran wild around the slope. The children showed me how to play Arranca Cebolla. It felt good to wrap my arms around the smooth trunk of the sun-kissed, fragrant balsa tree and feel the thrum of life within it. As the children lined up behind me and pulled, I was struck by how familiar the feeling was. So similar to the pull inside me, yanking me toward the beating heart across the valley from me.

All those hours of being barked at to "up my arm strength" had apparently paid off, since it took all ten of the kids—and a little help from Alina—to pull me from my perch and tumble us all into a heap on the ground, howling with laughter.

In the afternoon, Manny came to collect me for some quiet time at our bench to watch for more birds. We spoke cordially, me avoiding commentary on my life, before coming to their volcano refuge and him promising to bring me a treasure trove of bird feathers.

When his hand drifted to touch me, his voice dipping just slightly in a pitch that was solicitous, I'd avoid it by smiling and saying something to change the subject. The scratch in the back of my mind was getting more insistent with every surreptitious touch and every stolen sniff of my hair.

When the sun set and we had watched birds for a few hours, Manny and I returned to the open area between the buildings of the totoco house. Like at Sal's compound, dinner was a communal affair. I fell in with the cadejos of the totoco easily and helped cook the meal for the twenty odd people. Mama Cee's totoco was much smaller than Sal's, but it felt more intimate. Children ran and played around the adults as we worked together, growling and posturing. Some traded shadows here and there as they chased each other.

It was relaxing, comfortable, and cozy. A feeling of familial love I had only gotten the flavor of before running washed through the courtyard as we cooked and chatted the meaningless chatter of a group of people who lived so closely with each other. They treated me as if I were one of them and not a brand-new addition. It made my heart clench with a longing I hadn't known was so sharp until

I came to this country. This family feeling was something that I'd lost so early on in my life I almost forgot the comfort it offered.

By the time Mama Cee waved me over to the open fire grill, the butterflies had gone to bed, taking the children's small raucous bodies with them.

"Help me make the cocoa, mija," she murmured.

The sensation of butterfly wings as she patted my hand tied the image of them dancing in the sunlight to my impression of Mama Cee and made me smile with a drowsy curl of my lips.

"Aye, Mama Cee," I murmured sleepily.

I didn't feel tired, though, almost relaxed to the point of sleep.

She smiled, and I saw a flash of a white muzzle scarred by a clawed hand with a malevolent grin curling around its canines.

I shook my head, trying to clear the flashed image from my mind, as Mama Cee placed a large stout, fat-bellied terra-cotta olla on the grill. I'd always loved these pots, and when Nopaltzin taught me how to make them, I was overjoyed. They reminded me of squat, fat, little old men perched atop the embers, merrily bubbling away. She set out an intricately carved, long-necked, wooden molinillo, with a rattle of its attached ring amid an army of covered jars. Then, finally, she set a metate in front of me and slid the mano into my hand.

"Have you used one before, mija?" she asked, eyeing the long porous surface and its similarly porous mate, a cylindrical tool that reminded me of a slightly misshapen rolling pin.

I shook my head, and she sucked her teeth in that unique *ts* that reminded me of the way they said my name.

She took the mano from my hand and shooed me out of the way. A small cluster of dark-brown beans, the size of the tip of my thumb, were removed from one of the clay jars. She sprinkled them on the dip in the stone tablet and eyed me to verify I was watching. She demonstrated a unique rolling, wave-like grinding pattern with the mano and ground the beans to a fine paste. The sharp, tangy bitterness of raw cocoa filled the evening air and danced with the scent of beeswax melting in with the sun-kissed flowers, redolent in the still-warm air of late summer.

"Now you." She moved out of the way and looked surprised as I mimicked her actions, though my grind was much coarser than hers. "Good. Push harder. You'll get the swing of it. Keep adding beans until the jar is gone. *Ts!* Not too many at a time, two or three until you get it right, hmm?"

She reminded me of my abuela, but the scent of carrot cake and rich earth turned the memory more tender than I remembered.

I pushed and ground as she poured coconut milk into the olla, stirring it slowly as she added a cone of turbinado sugar. As the milk warmed and softly bubbled, she added various amounts of spices and stirred. I kept grinding, watching her hypnotizing stirring, adding beans robotically as I fell into the rhythm of it.

Someone had taken up their guitar and was joined by two strangers I had not heard before. A chajcha rattle shook a beat, accompanying a throbbing drumbeat. No voices joined, though. It seemed a shame that the woman who sang that morning didn't join the enthralling sounds that flooded my senses. The gentle swish and bubble of Mama Cee's pot and the scrape and grind of the metate and mano filled in the missing chords of the song, and I felt myself swaying slightly.

"Oh, dear mija, looks like you've cut yourself," Mama Cee clucked with concern.

"Hmm?" I looked down to see beads of ruby speckling the surface of my abraded knuckles, dripping into the sumptuous, buttery cocoa paste, then hissed belatedly.

Mama Cee gathered up my hand and folded it into a clean white cloth, splashing water from a jug to wash away the blood. Once the blood was soaked into the clean fabric, she took wet hands and pushed back the stray hairs that slipped from my braided crown, the cool water dampening my eyes and forehead. "There you are, mija. All clean. Why don't you go sit down and let Mama Cee finish up, hmm?"

Alarm slithered through me, foreign and dull, like I was hearing the discordant clang of an off-key piano being struck from a hundred feet away. It barely seeped into my muddied senses. I could hear a sound like a voice in the back of my mind, like someone was talking under deep well water.

I smiled at Mama Cee and trotted off to sit at one of the picnic tables, swaying to the beat that seemed to be the only thing I could focus on. I felt like I had taken sleeping pills. Drawing in air and processing it became the only sensation I could acutely feel.

Mama Cee was humming a strange tune as she passed the mugs of hot cocoa to each member of the totoco. The tune felt like a cheese grater on my psyche, what I could feel from behind a fluffy cloud of cotton that held me back from it. She set the mug before me and patted my shoulder.

"Drink up, elentios ala nam," she purred into my ear.

"What?"

"I said to drink up, mija."

I frowned down at the steaming cup, then back up to the totoco seated around me. Only Mama Cee was still standing, leaning on her ever-present cane, which seemed longer and taller now. I frowned at it. The strange shape of it seemed incongruent with my memory of the simple wooden cane. In my dulled state, it reminded me of a twisted, snake-like staff.

Narrowing my eyes at it, I tried to focus on its blurry form.

"Drink." Mama Cee's voice floated back into my stuffed head.

I lifted my hand to grab the mug, my fingers curling around it numbly. My fingers warmed from the heat radiating from the crockery.

I lifted it toward my lips and felt a razor ripping down my arm. It cut through the floating feelings and seared a fiery path to my fingers. An image of a viper, watery and ghost-like, reared its head over the earthen mug, hissing with dripping fangs at me. My fingers cramped and then dropped the mug, unable to maintain my grip on it, and the viper disappeared like a puff of smoke. The sound of it shattering on the hard-packed dirt beneath me cut through the music, and everything went quiet.

The moment the mug dropped, my mind cleared. I felt less fogged and floaty. The fire cutting through my arm eased off to a warm pulsing, tempered by the strangely grounding sensation of silken fur brushing the edges of my awareness.

I stared down at the shattered pieces of terra-cotta swimming in the puddle of steaming liquid. The shards of the pottery soaked up the hot cocoa. I wanted to feel abashed for having broken a cup I knew had taken so long to make and for spilling the drink Mama Cee had spent so much time and expense making. I wanted to, but I couldn't. Instead, I felt a misplaced sense of victory that didn't seem centered in myself but in some unknown place that was both me and not me far too confusing for me to unpick.

"Did it burn your fingers, mija?" Mama Cee's voice was edged in annoyance peeking out from under the concern.

Her question pushed me out of my reverie. "Yeah. I'm . . . I'm so sorry, Mama Cee."

She clucked again, the sound grating on my nerves.

She opened her mouth to perhaps chastise me or say something else when the sound of a cadejo howl cut through the early evening air, the day still clinging to the edges of the horizon stubbornly. My eyes whipped back and forth between the totocan, who were all rising swiftly from the tables and bristling into their half-exchanged monstrous forms one by one.

"What? What is it?" I yelled to Mama Cee over the sudden crush of a thousand sounds where it had been so quiet before.

She hissed, "Someone comes!"

Ice gripped at my heart, but my soul, in complete argument with my heart, bloomed with delight.

Sal.

I knew it without having to see him. Sal was coming. He had found me. I knew what that meant. I knew that he would hurt these people to get to me and punish them for harboring me.

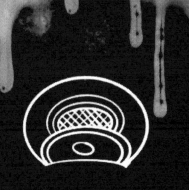

CHAPTER THIRTY-SIX
Itziquetzal

Sleep claimed me on our return flight, no matter how hard I fought it. Now that I knew what needed to be done and that there would be no assistance from the Council, there was nothing to do but set the rites and bring her back to my arms. I didn't remember moving from the plane to the truck nor from the truck to my empty bed, but when I woke in the morning to the sinking, sucking, burning knot in my stomach, I knew where I was. The other side of the bed, where she had lain, curled up next to me, was still empty. That fact twined around my bones like blackberry bushes, shredding muscles any time I moved.

By the time I made it out into the courtyard, Julia was already on her way in to wake me with a plate of food and a mug full of coffee. I smiled weakly to her, the gesture hollow and dull without the claws of Xochitl to sharpen it. Julia gave me an understanding smile and set the plate on the table as I settled myself, my long legs creaking under me as I stretched them. I mumbled my thanks as I pulled two corn tortillas to me and ate my breakfast. Eggs mixed with the last of the sausage, a fragrant rich mix of dark beans, sliced mangos and the sweet, creamy pink flesh of an anonas, the latter of which was my favorite.

Julia was doing her best to cheer me up subtly. She must have gone down to the market that morning. Of the many fruits and vegetables we grew on the volcano, anonas, with their large split cracked fruits and leathery skin, were not one of them. I smiled as I pinched a lobe of the pink flesh from the center and pulled it back. The burst of sweet nectar on my tongue edged down the vicious bite of my anger, and I slumped my shoulders as I fished out more of the delicious fruit.

I was halfway through my treat when Antonio found his way over and sat next to me. He had his own plate, absent the best part of the meal I had been served.

"Good morning, Itzatecuani," he said in a hesitant voice, testing the waters to see if I'd strangle him where he sat or hear him out. Lucky for him, Julia had made the first option far less likely. My cousin might be a bitch sometimes, but when it counted, she knew what to do.

"Antonio," I mumbled around the bite.

The sweet flavor was like eating a slice of pear dipped in raspberry and coated in cotton candy. Sweet. Tart. Earthy.

"To war today, hmm?" he asked before stuffing a bite of beans in his mouth. I nodded, devouring the last bite of the precious fruit. He pressed on after a long pause of watching me eat. "Not good."

He was stalling. I'd known the man long enough to know when he didn't want to talk about something he needed to. I groaned into a bite of tortilla and looked up at the heavens. Was it too much to ask to enjoy breakfast before I was knee-deep in bullshit and two steps from the carnage? "Spit it out, Antonio. This day is going to be long enough without you drawing it out more."

"That obvious, hmm?" He grimaced.

I glared at him.

"Fine, but you won't like it."

"I have all the confidence in the world that, whatever it is, I'll absolutely hate it."

He set his fork down and turned. "I know the teopixqui are coming down to set up for the ritual later today and that you still have to meet with your generals, but I needed to tell you the news before you heard it and got pissed at me for not reporting it."

"Stalling."

"Fine, dammit. Carmen and Izabel checked in this morning."

Carmen and Izabel were the two totocan who worked at the airport. They rarely, if ever, came back to the compound, preferring to be on their own out in the city. It suited me to have them be my eyes and ears in the comings and goings of the humans at the tiny little airport.

He had my full attention. "He was spotted at the luggage carousel with two unknown women."

I shoved a tortilla-wrapped scoop of eggs into my mouth before I reacted. I needed to save my rage and anger for the coming battle. Shayne was here, in my country. In my territory. If he was here, the only thing that could have brought him was some twisted dedication to recovering a woman who already made it crystal clear to him she was no longer interested in him. What piqued my interest most was the two women. Who were they? It seemed unreasonable her sister would be one of them without the other being her mother. Even then, Xochitl made it clear that Annette no longer spoke to Elida. What would Elida be doing with her and Shayne to begin with?

"Any idea who the women were?" I asked, doing my best to keep my beast's snap and bark from bleeding into my words.

I needed him to hold his strength and save it for when we faced a true enemy. I didn't need him bleeding it out over little things.

Antonio shook his head. "None. The description of Annette I have on file didn't match, as you've not provided me with an updated idea of what her sister looks like. I couldn't confirm there, either. One was older. Carmen says she got the best look of the two. She looked to be in her mid to late forties, with dark-blonde hair and blue eyes. The other was about the same age, with dark-brown hair, and very thin. She could be Annette? Maybe? You said she was shapely like Xochitl, neither of these women had the same figure as her."

I shrugged. "It's possible Annette could have lost weight. She seemed shapely the last time I saw her, but it has been years. Have they checked into any of the hotels? Either here or in La Libertad?"

He shook his head. "Not that I know of. Not yet. I have a request out to all of the available hotels to let us know if a group matching their description looks for rooms. They certainly didn't have any reservations under any of the known aliases or names that you provided."

Pensive, I nodded, chewing on the last bite of eggs. "Let them know that whoever is housing them will be rewarded when we are informed. I want it well known that they are not to be bothered. I need to see what they are going to do. And, if, for some reason, Xochitl wishes to return to them, I need them unharmed."

I had decided in my sleep the night before what I would do and say when my heaven was finally returned to me.

"You're . . . going to just let her go?" he balked.

"She was never a prisoner to begin with. And if our life together is going to be filled with her thinking she is, always looking for ways to run away and get hurt, then I will let her go wherever it is that she wants to be."

The words tasted like ash on my tongue.

"So, you'd leave the totoco for her?"

Antonio's shock was nearly palpable.

"If that is what she wishes, then, yes. If it is not, then, no."

Leaving my totoco for the woman of my dreams would be a hard shift in my life but not a hard decision. Xochitl was my everything, and it was time she knew it.

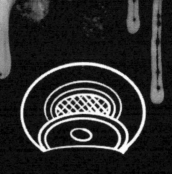

CHAPTER THIRTY-SEVEN
ITZIQUETZAL

I stepped out into the courtyard to the pulse of primal drumming. It was time. The thrumming energy was thick enough to choke on. The cadejos of my totoco pooled deep within the courtyard. Every last one of them, save for the handful of teopixqui, were naked aside from the steel in their eyes. Faces I didn't see regularly, beasts that lived in the town or deeper in the jungle that surrounded our compound, stared intently at me. Children ran in and out of the bare legs of the adults.

I acknowledged my totoco in the old way, falling to my knees in the dirt of our sacred volcano. The earth scratched my bare legs as I leaned forward, arms outstretched, and bowed my head low to touch the earth before me. As I drew my arms back, I gathered a handful of the rich, dusty red soil in my hand. Sitting up and back on my heels, I brought the dirt to my lips and kissed it reverentially. The gesture was as old as my roots went, back to before the Triple Alliance was even a glimmer in the eyes of the Azteca. The tlacualizti went back so far that none of us were sure who gave us the tradition. Hoots and ululations rang out into the courtyard, ricocheting off the walls, growing and pulsing into an unstoppable wall of power as I rose.

The teopixqui lit the sacred fires one by one as the totoco approached me on the right side. Each twined their arm into mine, gripping my strong, dirt-covered forearm with palms smeared in their blood. Each gripped it with the full extent of their strength, pressing their blood into the coating of dirt. I greeted them with "You have exhausted yourself in coming" and reached back to the waiting adept, who held out a bowl with freshly picked berries. I placed one in their mouth before they moved on. I went through the line of totocan until my forearm was dripping in blood and caked in dirt and the central fire was lit to a towering plume that stretched into the sky like the hands of Huehueteotl, the life-giving spirit of fire.

Once done with the traditional greetings, I stepped into the circle created by the totocan that would guard the compound and children in the absence of the warriors. Each stood attentively around the central fire between it and the foot-tall elevated bowls that held the ceremonial flames.

My eyes darted around the members of the totoco that had chosen to join the war party. No one had to join. No cadejo would ever be commanded to fight for the totoco. It was an honor that, in times of old, they would have fought among themselves for. Fifteen cadejos stood around me, all bathed in the warmth of the last rays of the sun and the blistering heat of the towering inferno before us.

My eyes locked with César through the angry flames, and I nodded my respect to him. César was not a fighter. He would never be a brutal war machine, having dedicated his spiritual strength to healing and connecting with the spirit realm, but he had stepped beyond the circle of his peers to fight alongside me. My heart and stomach clenched at the physical representation of his dedication to the totoco and to the safety of my mate.

The drums pounded with purpose around us, rumbling in my lungs and gripping my heart. Pipes joined the drums, singing a triumphant song, and the teopixqui began the rite in earnest by singing in the old language between gut-wrenching, wracking, emotional sobbing. Their wailing keening melted into the thrumming and trilling of the instruments until it all mixed within my blood. They sang for our coming victory. They wept for the lives we would take and the lives we would lose so that, when we returned victorious, only joy could be before us, the sorrow already having its time.

I rocked forward on my heels and felt the beat finding me. I yipped into the thick air and danced around the fire, the warriors following my lead. I stomped and skipped with one knee kicked up high before spinning clockwise with the sun. Each step was mirrored behind me as I led the warriors around the fire. Two skipping, stomping knee-up kicks. A full spin. A drop to pick up a handful of dirt to slap it on my chest while I yipped and called to the spirits crowding around us. We made three passes around the fire in this way before the small bowls of fire were brought closer to us. I was the first to taste the lick of the flame, extending my hand out into the fire, holding it there beyond the pain until I could almost feel the sizzle of my flesh. Pain now avoided pain later. If I could endure this pain, then, in battle, I could endure any pain the enemy would inflict on me.

Having cleansed my hand from the weakness of fire, I pulled away, cheers, yips, hoots, and ululations booming from the totoco as their tecutli conquered the fire first. I spun away from the first ceremonial fire to keep dancing. A quarter of the way around the fire circle, the next was set up. Again, I plunged my hand into the blazing primal heartbeat of the world and held my hand there, challenging my fear, challenging my body to endure the pain. Adrenaline poured into my body, and I could feel my heart waking to the challenge within my chest. When I could almost smell the searing flesh of my hand, I pulled away and spun onward around the circle. I stopped at every quarter of the circle, this time, to cleanse my thighs and my legs of the weakness of the flesh. My warriors followed, each one purifying their bodies of fear, weakness, and disorder, welcoming into their human flesh the pureness of spirit. Welcoming into their human flesh the immaculate state our cadejo spirits always felt, no fear, only focused strength and power.

When the warriors successfully purified themselves, we kept our dance up. We passed around the circle three more times before our armor was brought. As we passed each flame we had conquered, we were granted a piece of armor. My heart strained. If Xochitl were here, if we were not dancing this rite for her sake, she would stand behind the fires, following me as I danced. Each time I stopped at a flame, instead of the hand of a priest, she would lace the leather bands adorned with hummingbird skulls onto my biceps. If she were here, I would feel her hands slide around my waist to buckle my wide leather belt around me. If she were here, she would slide the vibrant riot of large feathers sewn into the leather of my headband onto my head. I imagined that, if she were here, a look of pride would flash in her eyes as she watched the shiver of those three-foot-long feathers wave in the breeze as I danced, my plume larger and brighter than any other, to draw the attention of the enemy. If she were here, when I knelt before the last flame, it would be her hands painting the turquoise-blue mask down my face. Her gentle fingers would paint my cheeks and forehead black and paint the taunting black bar down my chin, down my throat, and down my chest to terminate at my belly button.

I wished she were here, but soon, she would see me in all my glory as the warrior who came for her. The warrior who came to place her back on the throne, where she belonged. I ached to see her walking through the courtyard again. I ached to hear her laughter again or to even feel her claws and feel her body writhing against mine.

I rose, painted, clad in my leather armor and the fire that had kissed my skin now burning in my blood. I played memories of my beloved mate in my mind as I danced around the flames, my eyes closed to the outside world. Somewhere in the courtyard, a priest pushed slivers off of an ancient core of obsidian. Somewhere across the valley, my mate was in the hands of my enemy. Within this ring, though, I felt the usually narrow channel between my cadejo and me stretching wide like the gaping maw of an eldritch beast. I felt the waves of the beach pounding into the essence of my soul, weaving us closer and closer, called to strength by the ritual music.

I opened my mouth as I instinctually paused before one of the small bowls of fire and felt the wet kiss of ocean water pass my lips. The symbolic tears of the fallen that we may lose today, washing away my own sorrow for their impending death. I swallowed it down, letting the sensation wash through me as I kept dancing, ever-circling that towering plume of red and orange flame. Again, I stopped instinctually, the wet slither of a short braided rope of corn husks passing into my mouth. I swallowed it down, symbolically tying my fate to my cadejo. If he chose not to take up the risk of war, I would vomit it up. I had no fear of that. I could feel him. My skin was ablaze with tingles as he was all around me, within me, and outside of me, like a thick, unseen fog moving with me. He would not miss a single second of this preparation or the bloodshed to come.

My arms were outstretched to either side of me as I spun, stomped, and skipped around the flames. A wedge of sharp obsidian was pressed into my palm. My fingers curled around it as images of Xochitl flashed across my mind's eye. I saw her beneath me, beside me, holding my hand, holding my heart, bloody and throbbing raw in her hand. My beast and I were focused on her and her golden presence as I felt the first bite of the slice to my chest I cut in.

Tiny trickles of blood streamed down my chest as I kept dancing, the sounds of sobbing songs, pipes, and drums mixing in a blur with the hoots and ululations of the totoco. Next to me, each warrior did the same, focusing on their purpose and focusing on the reason they chose to join the war band. Behind me, each cadejo received their sliver of obsidian from the sacred core and, like me, sliced small cuts into their chest. Each one of us would, in their own time, slice ten small cuts into their chest, every man or woman. The last one bit into my rib a little deeper than I had intended.

My eyes were open, the world sharper, clearer. Colors were more saturated and rich. My cadejo was right there, sharing my flesh more than he would normally. We were one, where usually, we were two. I could see the energy pulsing off of each body watching us, each creature and plant around us. I could see spiritual energy waving in mirage-like ripples, even coming from the earth beneath us.

I slashed at my ear lobes, feeling the flesh part easily for the sharp implement as I did so. I felt like a tiger stretching my muscles. I felt like every molecule of my existence was finely attuned to this moment, and no other moment mattered beyond it. I felt like I could see everything and beyond as the little rivers of blood trickled down my neck and pooled delicately in the hollow of my throat before following the band of black down my chest to my navel.

I stood tall, sneering into the flames, daring it, challenging it to deny the omnipotence that I felt surging within me. I snapped the obsidian shard lengthwise and cast one blood-slicked piece into the fire. The thick liquid sizzled and popped on the black glass. I curled my lip in derision at the weakness of the flames before me as it fed on my gift of blood. I felt Huitzilopochtli riding my skin. I felt my cadejo stretching across my cells and making a home within them. I felt the power of the ancients pulsing in my blood. I felt like a god. I felt like more than a god. I felt like death itself come to collect its due.

I shoved the last shard of obsidian into the flesh between my eyebrows on the bridge of my nose and left it there, letting it rest under my flesh as I leaned back into my power and the power of my cadejo. My flesh stretched and snapped as, with a roar of powerful defiance, I opened to the shadows that engulfed me to spit up the towering ten-foot beast who was our conjoined might.

"Itech naci no Tlaltecuhtli," I snarled past my razor-sharp teeth. *I join Tlaltecuhtli in death.*

My warriors echoed my sentiment as our priests, family members, or mates pressed our weapons into our hands, and ululations of triumph echoed around me, slicing our impending victory into the book of the future.

CHAPTER THIRTY-EIGHT

The roar that ripped into the waning daylight tore me in half. I wanted to both run toward it and away from it. Instead, I stood, frozen by the inner war between my two halves, as the cadejos around me all traded shadows to their monstrous forms.

As my gaze traveled around the totoco, the enemy still unseen, I saw a lot more diversity in size, shape, and color. Three were whites. I hadn't expected there to be so many. The rest were all blacks, pooling shadows around them that dodged the faint glow of the whites. I made a mental count. About five were unaccounted for. I assumed that they went for the children as the danger neared.

And near it did. I could hear the heavy charging step of at least three cadejos in monster form and the padding soft sounds of several more in their full ghost-dog forms. They would be upon us in moments, and I took those few seconds to grab the molinillo from the grill. It wasn't a great weapon, but it was at least something.

When they came, it was like they shimmered into existence from the slim shadows that clung all around us. Mama Cee and three other black cadejos I didn't know stepped in front of me. Where the other three were tall and built like Sal, muscular and bristling with brutality, Mama Cee reminded me of César's arms.

While the warrior form of her white cadejo was as tall as the others, she was rail-thin and emaciated. Her skin was pale and ashen gray, almost green where the fur had sloughed off long ago. Her fur, unlike the thick coat the others had, was thin and haggard, as if the pelt had been thrown out in the rain and run over by rush hour traffic. Her back was crooked slightly at the shoulder like a hump, and she had a pot belly that stuck out over the small breasts barely concealed by the tufting of her ragged fur. The nails on her long, spidery fingers were cracked, and I had the distinct impression that, should she slice anyone, the infection that would follow would be instant and angry. When she turned her narrow muzzle toward me, I could see that one side of the length was marred by a deep black slash of claws that looked like it had never healed, and the other side drooped, as if she'd had a stroke.

"Go," she commanded in a snarly voice that made me nauseous, and she pushed me toward the grill.

Where her touch once felt like butterfly wings against my psyche, now I had the distinct impression of condor wings battering and beating at the walls of my mind. I wanted to vomit, but the push had me finally moving my feet, and I skittered to hide behind the tall cooking surface that still crackled with embers.

The beasts around me snarled and snapped when Sal and his totoco crested the hill and charged toward Mama Cee and hers. Sal lifted his long muzzle to the air and huffed, indulgently scenting me all over the courtyard and in the air.

"She's here," he snarled to a starved-looking cadejo who stood equal to him in height.

Sal's claws hefted a dark wooden bat, studded with shards of obsidian. Though I'd never seen him in his full, monstrous form, I assumed the other cadejo was Cèsar. Despite the jointed, jade mask that covered his face from the edge of his top lip to his tall pointed ears, he seemed familiar. The green stone flashed in the dying sunlight, the obsidian pieces embedded into the muzzle flashing with deadly purpose. His massive clawed paw clenched around a razor-tipped spear.

Sal's lip curled as he stared down at Mama Cee. "Give her to me, and I will slaughter you and your vile troupe quickly. Make me hunt her, and I will rip every limb from your disgusting form and make you watch as I tear down everything that shriveled rock you call a heart holds dear. Decide. My patience is thinner than your fur."

"Has the great Itziquetzal lost something?" she purred to him, tapping her claw against the slashes I realized matched the exact span of Sal's paw. "Could it be a girl? Not his mate, no. She was not marked. Ixpiyacoc made sure of that."

She cackled, and the sound rasped over my nerves, making me clench my teeth.

Sal returned Mama Cee's cackle with a dark chuckle that sounded like a boot crushing sun-baked skulls. "He must not have looked very hard. My mate bears my bite of lust on her waist." He snorted with laughter and let a massive taloned-hand grip to the pendulous swing of his furred balls. My stomach churned. How dare he bring up that night. Did he not feel it was as sacred as I did? "Are you still calling him that? Fire Destroyer? As if any of your grotesque band is deserving of a warrior's name. A warrior's name is a mark of honor. I see not a single beast here who still has a drop of honor to spare."

He examined the deadly edge of his flat bat weapon, boredom clear in his furry features. As Mama Cee's cadejo took slow steps backward, the gigantic black bestial forms of cadejo stepped from the thin air of shadows all around us, penning us in. "I do so hope he did touch my mate. I'd love to rip out his lungs and spank her with them for making me chase after her . . . Maybe, if she's been a good girl, I'll even let her suck my cock while I snack on his heart, so I can shit it out tonight."

Mama Cee snorted, and her eyes slid to where I was hiding, locking with mine. I saw a flash of a white glow around her eyes, then my gaze slid back to Sal.

An image of the children I had played silly games with, their golden laughter echoing over the jungle, slashed open and trampled under the foot of the totoco I had loved flowed into my mind on deceptively silent feet. But, like a flash flood, it started with a trickle and then cascaded into a torrent of blood, viscera, and screams. I watched as Tomás, a young boy of only five, ran through the stage of my mind and into a tall black monster who crouched down as if to pick the crying child up. A wicked sneer played across the cadejo's muzzle, and when the child went to rub tears from his face, it lunged. The beast's mirage snapped onto a tender chest and bit right through it.

As I panted with terror, I pressed my fists to my head, as if to smother the image. It was my imagination. It was my own mind playing tricks on me and feeding me the worst possible imaginable events. Sal's totoco would never hurt children . . . right?

"Bring her out, Mama Cee. I'm tired of waiting. Every minute you make me wait, I'll slaughter one of your pups. There's, what, ten of them now? Sounds like you have ten minutes."

The image of those sweet little kids, broken and bleeding, had me moving before I even thought of doing so. A snarl of rage ripped through my throat when I dove ahead of Mama Cee.

"Leave, Sal! I don't want you! I'll never want you. You're an absolute monster. How could you?" I screamed at him.

His obsidian eyes softened for a moment before the hardness was back, and he stared over my shoulder. He said something garbled. I couldn't understand it. Was he speaking in another language? Did the cadejos have their own tongue? Mama Cee responded to him, her words just as garbled, yet her tone was clear, mocking, and victorious. No, it wasn't another language. It was Spanish, but the words twisted and contorted into strange shapes and sounds as if battered against the rocks of an angry river. Sal looked down at me, leaning close and staring me directly in the eye. His words were slow but just as garbled.

"Fuck off, Sal! I won't let you hurt these people!"

His head snapped up, and what happened next happened in slow motion, like it was filtered through someone else's mind into mine. He lifted his massive arm, holding a deadly weapon toward Mama Cee. Fear lanced through me, fear that these people, who were so kind and gave me refuge when I had nothing and nowhere to go, would be hurt for my sake. Lightning coursed through my blood, the sensation of my ears popping violently on an airplane shuddering through my head. I expected it to burn, but all I heard was the crackling of it and felt the sparking in the roots of my hair as it rose with purpose toward Sal. My fingers curled into a fist, nails longer than I expected digging into my palm. My clenched fist slammed into the monstrosity's silken muzzle. My entire body tightened with the power of striking him.

The world caught up in a single blink as Sal rocked back on his heels, staggered a few inches, his talons coming to hold his jaw. His eyes snapped back to me. A feral snarl curled his lips.

"There she is," he hissed, triumph filling his fuzzy face. "I've missed you, noteocuitlateotl."

I looked down, an opaline glow drawing my gaze, and gasped. My arms, once golden tan, turned a pale ivory, emitting a soft, pale, golden glow and were covered in velvety white fur. I stared, turning my arms over in wonder. I examined them, fascinated by the way the fur reflected the light emanating from the skin below and scattered iridescent shards of light. My paws were tipped with long nails the color of old, well-loved gold perched atop slender fingers that flexed with power.

I took a deep breath. Where I expected to feel anxiety, only a pure, celestial calmness poured through and out of me. I felt . . . free. No, that was the wrong word. I thought I had felt freedom before. I thought I had been truly unencumbered by the things in my world, but I had never felt the sensation I felt now. It was like running out of a sauna and jumping into cool water. The burden of the years slid off of me, the tightness eased, and I drank greedily of the fresh air that pounded through my new lungs.

The sounds of battle, barking and snarling cut through my reverie. Mama Cee and César were fighting, locked behind their spears and claws entangled. Sal was pushing a cadejo with a bite mark on his head aside, as if he were nothing, stalking toward me, his dread weapon pointed down, forgotten.

"Xochi, please. Come. Let the totoco take care of them. Let's go home, noyzotzon."

His tone was soft, loving, and even adoring. Yet, the hand he extended me dripped the blood of the people who had been so kind, the people who freed me in some way I didn't fully understand.

"No," I said with absolutely no conviction. I wanted to go with him. I wanted to curl up into his arms, but nothing had changed, and here he was, slaughtering the people who saved me. "Leave, Sal. Take the totoco and go home. Leave these people alone. They've done nothing wrong. All they did was help me."

"Help you? Is that what you think they did, Xochi?" He laughed, a low, ugly sound.

I growled at him, the sound as low and dangerous as any he'd directed at me. "They did!"

The black cadejo with the bite mark on his head, lunged at Sal again, and as Sal lifted his weapon, I dove between them. I didn't know who the cadejo was, but I knew I needed to protect him from Sal's madness. His arm froze just inches from slicing my head asunder with the obsidian blades.

"Get out of the way, Xochi!"

"No! Leave! Stop hurting these innocent people!" I wrestled the weapon from him. My hands slipped on the blades and cut deep. I howled as blood pooled in my lacerated palm.

Itzatecuani snarled and yanked the marked cadejo from behind me by the throat, tossing him aside as if he were nothing more than a discarded teddy bear. A sting called my attention down to the rise of my hip, where blood bloomed from the three slashes that curled around the bone and angled down toward my lower belly . . . where the beast had almost grasped me. A sickening crack rang out as the beast slammed into the volcano's upward slope and bashed his head against a rock. Blood flowed into the red dirt in a macabre and twisted corona.

Eyes glowing a hellish crimson, Itzatecuani turned his regard back to me. Lust weaved itself into the throbbing glow as he scooped me into his beastly arms and lapped at the blood. I kicked his chest as hard as I could, trying to get free of him, but he was having none of it. A snarled growl showing his sharp canines chastised me, but I persisted.

"Why run, mate?" Itzatecuani snapped his jaws at me.

I hated seeing Sal like this. Sal, I could reason with, but his beast was another thing. He operated on even harsher binaries than Sal did. It was all simple to his beast.

"Let me go, Itzatecuani. I am not your mate. You two deserve better. And these innocent people do, too."

He snorted. "Innocent? Cadejos are never innocent, sweet mate."

"They've done nothing wrong! They are just simple people who have been kind to me!"

I thrashed, punching and clawing at his chest. I knew it was futile. Itzatecuani, unlike Sal, would never let me go.

He growled a warning to be still, I was sure of it, but I ignored him and dug my new golden claws into his flesh. He moved, shaking me like a petulant kitten.

"Innocent. Simple. Kind." His snort was derisive as he held me by the collar, dragging me behind him. He strode through the totoco house lands, taking me away from the gardens toward the path that led to the cliffs. "These people my mate associates with are vile. Evil. They are the worst of our kind."

I thrashed then, fighting his grip with every ounce of my being. That way was death, certain and unavoidable. My claws dug into his wrist, my heels into the tight-packed dirt. We entered into a dangerous game of tug of war, with his arm as the rope. I cut into his wrist, yanking him in the opposite direction, while he clapped his other hand over mine and pulled in the other.

"You're a liar," I snarled with the effort to hold my ground, even though my heels slowly skidded over the hardpan. He was toying with me. There was no way that, even in his human skin, I could hold out against him. In his nightmare skin, there was even less of a chance.

"Liar? My mate thinks I am a liar for telling her that the beasts she has laid down with are the worst of my kind? That they have violated every pact that we have made with them? That they have butchered and maimed for centuries? Sweet mate, you are blind, but I will make you see." He snorted toward the cadejo he had flung away. "See who is behind the fur and teeth, sweet mate. You recognized the bite. You knew that bite we gave him the night we saved you. So, look now at who he is."

The body was melting into the shadows around it, unable to maintain the connection to his manifestation. The exchange was slow, unlike when a cadejo did so of its own volition. The wounded scar on the top of its head was the last to retreat into Manny's tanned flesh. I stared, unsure what I was looking at, or perhaps not wanting to believe my own eyes, all strength of conviction leaving my grasp.

"Yes. You see now. That beast has wanted you for himself for a long time now, hmm? Since he smelled the buffet of pure terror throbbing through the night connected to your unshielded heart. He was the beast I dragged by the skull from your room, trying to protect my mate. The man did not wish for you to know of us so soon. No, not so soon. He wished to ease you into the world of spirits and blood. That filth wished only to feast, to add you to his pile of bones." He moved as I locked my eyes on Manny's unconscious body . . . the cadejo who had attacked me what seemed like years ago. "He hunted you, and he got what he wanted. I can smell the sick spit from his spirit coating yours from where he feasted."

I barely registered that he was dragging me down the path again. My mind was a ten thousand-piece jigsaw puzzle, tossed into the air, its pieces flung wide into the breeze, leaving only disharmonious chaos in its wake. The jealousy in his voice was confusing. Got what he wanted? What? Manny had barely gotten two unguarded words from me. Nothing made sense. The puzzle pieces were scattered, with no hope of fitting back together.

What the hell is that mammoth talking about? the voice in my head barked.

"I have absolutely no clue," I whispered to my aching, bleeding palm. "Manny didn't touch me, Itzatecuani."

A shaggy, smoke-twisted black brow cocked up as his midnight eyes regarded me, seeing into me like he had the last night I saw him. "He has fed from you, sweet mate. I can sense his spirit's tongue all over you. He might not have touched your flesh, gorged as his totoco does, but he didn't need to."

His gaze turned back to the path he was dragging me down as my mind stumbled over the idea of Manny slurping up my fear and anguish without my knowing. Is that why I had felt so drained after each of our quiet sits at the edge of the forest? Is that why, when he stood behind me, I reacted that way?

"We'll see now what you have chosen to lay down with, sweet mate," he snarled, pushing back a shrub hiding a path from view.

Panic shot through me, but it was like the stab of a plastic Halloween knife, cheap and manufactured. We were beyond the point where Mama Cee said the path should have dropped into a cliffside. Had she been mistaken?

Sounds so foreign I could barely process them drew my eyes to a slab of stonework spread out across a flattened edge overlooking the jungle's precipice.

At first the splashes of color—all manner of skin tones, bright red, muted pink, turquoise, brown and blond, and black and white—scattered across the gray stonework made no sense. It didn't seem to fit into my mind. Slowly, things came into focus as scores of eyes swiveled, tilted, and turned to stare directly at me and Itzatecuani.

The five missing cadejos and the missing children were the first things to solidify into firm shapes. Four blacks and one white, all wearing malicious, sadistic sneers. The white was kneeling next to something that my mind just couldn't put into true form.

"Look. Look how they feed," Itzatecuani's voice said in my ear, and like the inevitable crash of those pieces finding the ground, its images slammed into me.

Scattered among a blanket of the same butterflies I had danced with the first day I was here, each child was bent over the body of a woman. A fluttering swarm of rainbow wings puddled in tranquility on the shores of crimson lakes surrounding the haphazardly strewn humanity. Some women were whole, but others were in various states of dismemberment. Some had hands hacked from wrists, the flesh twitching a few inches away beside the delicate placid fan of blue wings. Some had one leg severed to the hip and the other to the knee. Scattered throughout the plateau were limbs in various states of rot, body parts cast about like shattered puppets cut from their strings. Every last limb had massive bite marks ripped through the flesh. The stench of blood, piss, shit, and gore punched me in the face like a fist.

The children were eating the dead. No . . . not the dead. Realization stole the breath from my lungs as one woman, who had half an arm left and a miniature nightmare attached to it gnawing away, turned her head to stare directly at me. I stared in horror at the reflection of a monarch crawling across the bridge of her nose to a river of cerise spilled from a toddler-sized bite above her bracken and pine bark eye. The pale ivory of her skull winked a false lash that revealed itself to be the flutter of a swallowtail.

They were eating them alive.

The scream in my throat was too mighty, too enormous to make it through that narrow channel, so it stuck there, clogged in my throat, choking me. My eyes locked with hers, and the world melted away to just her dark eyes and mine. Shapes blurred around us, her cheeks shaking with the power of some disturbance. Water splashed across my face and neck, but my eyes never left hers. Even when I was pushed and fell to the stonework in front of me, a dull sensation of heat and pressure on the back of my head, my eyes did not leave hers.

Blackness crept into the corners of my vision, and as the world faded into the peace of the inky shadows, the sounds of crunching and slurping dying out, those eyes stayed glued to mine. When the darkness finally claimed me, all that connected me to the world was the impression of her gaze.

CHAPTER THIRTY-NINE

Woodsy incense, marigolds, green things, and the rich earthy crisp scent of dark copal pulled me from the black haze. Weightlessness kissed my floating limbs as consciousness slowly filled my awareness like the sands of an hourglass. A single sharp shard mixed within those grains cutting the stream as the memory of the hacked limbs, rotting flesh, and the horrid sound of crunching filled my ears. I was back on that plateau. The children took growling chunks from the monarch-butterfly-winged women lying naked amid the dust. A pair of dark, rich brown eyes stared down from the sky above straight into my soul.

I sat up bolt-straight as a shriek ripped from my throat. A woman came to the side of the hammock I was wedged into, sneaking up on me as I panted and gasped for air.

"Shh. Shhh, Cihuatlatoani. You are safe."

Her voice was soft and strange. Though she was alone, I swore I heard three or more voices speaking every word she uttered. It was a haunting and disorientating sound. I tried to scoot away from her, but the bowed netting of the hammock swayed under my jerking muscles.

"Wh-Wh—"

"Where are you?" she completed for me, amusement curling at beautifully full lips darkened not by the slather of lipstick but by a stain, like she had been eating blackberries for years, and the juices had permanently colored her skin. "You are in the temple. The tecutli brought you here for us to care for while the warriors are still routing the enemy. Come. You have had a rough time of it. I'll clean those knuckles while you tell me a few things, hmm?"

Once I had gotten used to the strange triple speak, it became comforting. Like a soft song with backup singers or the way a hymnal was sung at the masses my mother used to take us to before she met Edwin. After Edwin, it was all discordant, joyless, soulless lark shrieks in a megachurch with the other Presbyterians. The scent of incense added to the sense of sacred space growing around me.

I slid down from the hammock, stretched my legs, and cracked my back. It was far from comfortable for someone of my shape. "Temple? So, not at the compound?"

She shrugged and rolled her shoulders under the heavily tooled leather bib collar she wore over a simple, pure white caftan. The cotton of the gown was the finest I had seen outside of the luxury stores my mother dragged me through once a month, and I longed to run my fingers across it. "In a way. In a way not. We are on totoco lands still, still on the volcano, but the temple exists on the border of the Lets'a Wehle territory and the territory of the neighboring Ulkin Sila totoco. As their totoco is very small and cannot afford to keep a full temple of their own, in exchange for certain liberties, your totoco has offered to build and maintain the temple on the border, so that both totocos may use it and house their priests here. We are in the rooms allocated to the Lets'a Wehle totoco. I thought you would be more comfortable where you could only be approached by your own totocan."

She led me to a small low table and waved me to sit. Ceramic bowls filled with all manner of fruits, both recognizable and not, overflowed the bowls. I shivered at the idea of eating anything, hearing that disgusting *crunch crunch slurp* echoing in my ears. She tilted her head and leaned back on her elbow as we both sat on the floor. "Interesting. Perhaps no food. Perhaps some atol de elote?"

Blinking at her, I tilted my head. The more I focused on her, the more I could see heatwave lines pulsing in a hypnotizing, misty, colorful display around her body like the heart of a galaxy throbbing with her at the center. She smirked quietly in return and took a stoneware bowl from atop a warming stone, waves of heat thrumming off of it. A mug was collected from the table to fill it with a warm, creamy custard-looking beverage. Memories of the feeling of my fingers forced open beyond my control kept me from reaching out to take it. Something had not wanted me to drink the last beverage I was offered. Was this the same? After all, I knew my last host far more than I knew this woman.

She smirked again, almost as if she could read the hesitation rolling off of me, just like the waves I saw drifting around her. She lifted the mug to her lips and sipped it before offering it to me. "You're cautious. A good trait to have, Cihuatlatoani. An admirable trait, even, especially for someone in your position."

I collected the mug and lifted it warily. There was no fight in my fingers, no tension in my arm as it came to my lips. The drink was warm, soothing, its heat sliding down my throat and settling comfortably in my stomach. The taste was unique, like if cream corn had seduced eggnog into a joy-filled union and birthed an adored love child. It was divine. I sipped a few more times before gifting her with a smile. "It's wonderful. Honestly."

"Thank you, Cihuatlatoani. I made it for you while she and I talked after she granted me leave to heal the fractured skull and claw marks to your abdomen. She made me leave the mark on your side, though . . . Now, let me see your knuckles, please."

She? She who? I extended my hands out to her, trust flowing between us both foreign, yet, unlike before, I didn't feel reluctant to give this stranger my faith. She sucked her teeth as she tilted my shredded knuckles on both hands in her view. One was scuffed and cut up by the stone tablet I had ground them against, the other had been mauled rudely by Itzatecuani's razor-toothed maw when I punched him.

"Care to tell me how these came to be? They will need cleaning, especially this one."

She indicated the one I ground and lofted her brows at me with a meaningful expression I didn't quite understand the depth of.

"If you tell me who 'she' is, I guess that's a fair exchange." I took a deep breath of the creamy liquid comfort's scent and forged onward. "I was grinding cocoa for hot cocoa and nicked my knuckles. Nothing too important."

She poured clean, cool water over the cuts she was most concerned about.

A tiny clay bowl—with a thumb-sized hunk of smoking resin in it that reminded me of an evergreen forest after the rain—was brought to my hand, and she whispered to it in a language I couldn't understand. It wasn't the Nahuatl that the others spoke, nor the warm rolling sounds of the Lenca. This was percussive and crisp, like Nahuatl, but had the round warmth of the Lenca words, too.

"What is that language you are speaking?"

She looked up from her bow over my knuckles. "It is K'ekchi, Cihuatlatoani. Clever of you to recognize it as different from the other tongues. It is not spoken much here, but in Edzna, it is the primary language." She blew the smoke over my skin and looked back at me. "Do you know what the awasinel was doing with the cocoa ritual?"

"The what and the what?" My blinking confusion made her titter a genial chuckle. "Sorry, I have no clue what an uh-wee-snul is. Or what a cocoa ritual is."

She smirked and wrapped a clean bandage around my knuckles. "Aa-waa-see-nul. Awasinel. It means witch. Mama Cee and her foul band of flesh devourers are well known to the Council and the surrounding totocos as a manipulative snake, and it looks like she buried her fangs deep into you. I see the evidence of her venomous gift all over your cadejo and your spirit. Recent, too." Her gaze glided to the air around me, and she sniffed in derision as if insulting whatever it was she was looking at was the best course of action to scare it off. "A cocoa ritual is usually performed before a sacrifice to the teotl. And, from the look at the strength of both your spirit and the spirit of your cadejo, I can see why she would have been tempted. I barely needed to begin the spirit sight ritual before it came into view."

She patted the unbandaged part of my hand. I balked. "My . . . My what? No, you're mistaken, uhm . . . I didn't get your name, but I'm just a human."

"Are you now?" she asked, lofting her brows and rising from the table. She tilted her head, appraising me for a long while, before she smiled again. The sensation of basking in warm sunlight suffused my limbs and brought a satisfying languor to my body. "Perhaps once. Perhaps never again."

And, with that, she left me alone, staring at the table full of flowers and fruits, stumped.

"Jesus, fuck. Can just one, just one goddamned person in this god-forsaken place speak like a normal damned person?" I asked the mango that winked its orange and red eye at me from behind a shaggy brow of coconuts.

"I wouldn't hold your breath, especially not here."

The deep timbre of Sal's voice flowed over me in the silence that followed the strange woman's exit. I expected to feel fear spike through me, to feel the biting kiss of panic, but all I felt was relief wash through me and settle deep in my bones. It felt like running through a dark forest, only to make it to the safety of a brightly lit, secure house, with a ton of locks. Safe. Secure. Protected. These words rang in my ears like a choir hymn.

I turned my head to see him leaning against a half wall of carved wooden screen that depicted jaguars dancing with hummingbirds. I expected to see him covered in blood. Instead, he was stretched out tall above me in his usual attire, a simple black cotton tee shirt stretched across those mouthwatering muscles, low-slung, black jeans that hinted at the cut of muscle at his hips that made me drool from top to bottom. His hair was loose, wet, and freshly washed. The twin black stone feathers hung from his fingers by the chain I had seen secured to his braids so often. He looked like the exact right kind of sin to condemn my soul, willingly and with glee, into the pits of hell, and I felt blasphemous.

"Can I join you?" he asked in a tone softened by exhaustion. Guilt weaseled its way through the layers of lust that folded around me like a sweet, ache-filled blanket. I nodded dumbly, unable to say anything. He was here. He was standing, now sitting, right in front of me, and he wasn't looking at me the way I thought he should. There was no pity in his eyes, only bone-tired concern as he murmured his thanks.

Awkwardly I pushed my mug full of warm atol de elote toward him, perhaps as a peace offering? Yes, it was a peace offering. As I watched the tender smile curl at his dark bronze lips and his eyes take in every movement I made, like a ravenous man who had seen nothing like it in a hundred years, I realized I wanted peace. Not just peace, though. I wanted so much more. My heart ached to hold him, to curl up into the warmth of his body the way I had taken for granted so many nights before.

The silence falling between us felt fragile, brittle, and thick with unshed words that stuck in our throats. Sal and I could be many things but awkward and quiet had never been one of them. It felt like shoving the explosive passion of us into a too-small sausage casing. We were both bursting at the seams yet too timid to be the first to break the truce. His eyes darted from my face to the drink and back again a few times before he took it and sipped at it delicately.

"I—"

"I—"

We both started at once with the same word. An uneasy chuckle passed between us as he ducked his head in embarrassment. We were like two teenage kids sitting unchaperoned for the first time, waiting to get caught and trying desperately not to do something catastrophically humiliating that we would never recover from.

"You should go first," he said to the cup before taking another distracting pull.

Yeah, like teenagers because all I could focus on was the way his lips curled around the lip of the mug and sucked at the thick, spiced corn drink. My heart angrily thrashed at the cage that dared to keep it from swimming between my thighs.

"No . . . please. You first," I breathed, my voice far huskier than I intended it to be.

He gulped and looked up at me, his eyes catching mine. His focus was singular, feral hunger throbbing within their dark depths. The bob of his Adam's apple as he swallowed hard drew my eye away from his and broke the tension that pulsed between us.

He nodded softly and set the feathers he clutched onto the table. The mating talismans. A promise ring symbolizing our relationship, and he wasn't wearing them. My mind immediately focused on them, and dread pooled in my stomach. I felt the executioner looming, saw the careening consequences of my actions barreling toward me.

He opened his mouth, and when nothing came out, he snapped it closed and then took a deep, ragged breath. Could he just hurry up already? I'd rather he just plunge the dagger into my heart all at once instead of inch by inch. He exhaled loudly but said nothing.

"It's fine. I get it," I finally spit out.

I didn't need to hear the words I already knew were coming. I had fucked up. I had acted without thinking. I hadn't even imagined a world outside of that moment when I ran. I hadn't thought through what was happening, and now he was tired of the struggle. Tired of the constant fights and the constant dramatics. I had sunk the ship on the best thing I'd ever had and only realized what it was when I lost it. I reached shaking fingers up to my crown of braids and untied the bow, unweaving the beautiful ribbon hidden under the other from my long curly hair.

I felt a bubble inside of me push and squirm and the impression of two golden eyes glaring at me as if I were the dumbest creature on the planet. My fingers fought me for a few seconds, stiffening like they had around the cup of hot cocoa, but my resolve to move forward was greater than the treachery of my own body, screaming at me to stop. If he was going to dump me—as well he should, I was an idiot—then I didn't want to drag it out. I wanted that killing blow to be swift, not saw at my soul like a hungry steak knife.

He watched me for a long time. I was almost done taking out the first braid before he spoke up. "What are you doing?" His voice was clipped, as if he was struggling to keep his tone even and at a normal volume.

I didn't look up at him. I didn't need to see his gorgeous features again, not while I was pulling his mating talisman from my hair. Not while I was struggling to just keep it together while I was falling apart quicker than the braid under my fingers. "It's fine, Sal, honestly. I understand."

"You understand what?" I hazarded a lookup into his devastatingly handsome face. "Xochitl, stop it. What are you doing?"

He would make me spell it out. He would make me say what I didn't even want him to whisper to me, let alone force my tongue to speak them. "I mean, I get what you are saying without you needing to spell it out for me. And, since I imagine you don't want me wearing your mating talisman when we aren't together anymore, I'm taking it out so I can give it back."

"Wh—" He snapped his mouth closed on his words and glared at me.

Anger flashed in his eyes, and misty glossed-black smoke shivered at the edges of the whites of his eyes.

I'd never noticed it before, nor had I noticed the way his hair moved when it was down, like molten obsidian flowing around his head. I watched the light catch on his flexing jaw as he clenched his teeth. Why was he annoyed? Did he want to cut me down himself and was annoyed I predicted this? When he spoke again, I was mesmerized by the way the words pooled in his mouth like that smoke in his eyes.

"Is that what you want?"

The black mist that floated from his mouth dissipated quickly, and I tilted my head. "Does it matter?" I asked, my fingers still unweaving the braid.

He pounded the heel of his palm on the small wooden table, shattering the now-empty mug under the force, and causing me and the coconut sat atop my mango confidant to jump. "Dammit, Xochitl, stop!"

I watched as the smoke in his mouth coalesced into the sharp blades of Itzatecuani's fangs. The moment his mouth filled with those razor-sharp teeth, the smoke disappeared. How had I never seen this before? How many times had I stared him in the mouth and watched them elongate and grow right before my eyes but never noticed the black smoke?

When my fingers didn't stop, he reached across the table and held my wrist, fury dancing in his glossy midnight eyes as he stared me in the face. "I asked you a damned question, woman. Answer me!"

My long lashes fluttered as I let my fascinated gaze dance between his smokeless mouth and his eyes. "What does it matter what I want, Sal? It's over for you, and it's my fault. I ruined us."

I'd heard the phrase "shaken" before in several situations. I'd probably used it a few times myself. I had never seen it be used appropriately. The way Sal stilled and his skin seemed to quake on his bones was something I had never experienced before. He rocked back and collapsed into his seat, thunderstruck by my simple pronunciation, ignoring the slow descent of blood from his palm to the tiled floor as he just stared at me.

I opened my mouth to go on, wanting to salt my already festering wound, but before I could say a word, he held up his hand, stilling me and killing the words in my mouth. He took several deep, grounding breaths, exhaling long plumes of the black mist before it disappeared into the brittle air. His eyes never left mine, and when I saw the flames of his rage die out and the smoke return to hovering around his mouth, he spoke again. This time, his voice was even and tinted with the exhaustion I had seen in him when he first walked in.

"I have made mistakes. I am man enough to admit this. I have acted like a beast instead of being the man you need. I thought that as long as I drew out the woman I knew you were under all the scars and layers of hurt, that it would be worth it. Only it's not. All I have accomplished is to hurt you more, hurt you deeper than you have been already. I know that the ends do not justify the means, Xochitl, I know. And, if I thought it would heal you, I would rip my own heart out and sacrifice it at the altar of your whims just to undo that pain. I cannot ask for your forgiveness. I have no right to it. Can I ask that you hear me? No more games, no more fighting, no more cat and mouse. Just . . . listen to me. Please?"

I had never heard him sound so beaten, so broken. I never imagined I *could* hear him that way. I'd never imagined the war machine that snatched me off of the battlefield and walked me into that killing field could ever beg me to just listen to him. My heart bled from the pain in his voice, my fingers going numb from the awkward position, blood draining from my face. I nodded thickly and pulled my fingers from the braids, setting them on the table. Unable to stand the agony playing on his features, I stared at the obsidian feathers.

"I have spent my entire life chasing after you, Xochitl. Twenty years running to grab your hand. I have dedicated my life to making a place for you to be happy. Everything I am is for you. Everything I have done has been for you. You and only you. There is no one else. There will be no one else for me, ever. You are the bones beneath my skin and the fire in my heart." His voice broke with the power of his emotion, pulling my eyes away from the feather and chains to connect with his as he pushed on, drawing from a never-ending pool of strength I envied.

"I need only one thing from you. I need your happiness. If that is here with me, then I will make every day from now until my last a penance, doing everything I can to give that to you. Even when it gets hard." He barked a mirthless snort of laughter that felt hollow and dry on the delicate air between us. "Especially when it gets hard. But, if it is not here with me, if standing beside me is not where you will be happy, tell me. I will take you anywhere you want to go, anywhere in the entire world. And from there, no matter where it is, I will only be a phone call away."

He scrubbed both blood-stained hands down his face, smearing the flakes into his unshed tears, and gulped down a tortured breath. "I spent a lot of time while you were missing, terrified I would never see your face again. Terrified to my very bone marrow that I would never be able to see your smile again. Terrified that I had brought you somewhere that you would meet harm. I cannot do that ever again. I cannot live with myself knowing I am selfishly binding you to my side, where you do not wish to be. You have my heart, my soul, my body, my cadejo, everything that I am and everything I ever will be. You will always have that. Nothing can or will ever change that. But if you wish it, noyzotzon, I will set you free. Just say the words, and I will make whatever it is you want a reality."

We stared at each other, the energy of our emotions a tangible thing as his shadows curled and danced around his body. I watched as tendrils of golden mist curled around me like a corona and reached desperately for him. I felt an ache within me yet not my own. A membrane between myself and something else within me thinned. The anticipation of that bubble bursting rose within me like a storm gathering in my chest, like the clean exhaustion of muscles after straining to hold a mighty weight were finally unburdened. Most of all, it felt like a steaming hot shower after a fall excursion. I wanted to lean back into it, spread my arms wide, and welcome whatever it was. I felt myself almost drunkenly swaying with the power of it. I didn't know where I gathered the strength to tether myself back to the here and now, but the grain of the wood beneath my hands and the glinting flash of the polished glass stone anchored me to the present and kept me from falling into that feeling.

Sal's face curled into a dully proud smile that confused me, but he said nothing and let the pregnant silence draw out between us before I bore the words he needed deep within his aching soul.

"I . . ."

It was a weak start. It was not what I wanted. The emotions bubbling within me were too large to sort through and too powerful to be cheapened by words, but he needed that from me. Steel flowed through that bubble inside of me and let it sink into my essence before I looked back into his eyes. I felt strong, not like I could lift a bus over my head or punch a moose but like I could stand on my own, look into the abyss and dare it to scare me.

"I spent the entire time I was gone thinking about you, Itziquetzal. Thinking about us. Thinking about all the fucked things we've done to each other and all the ways we've cut each other up. I don't want a life like that. I don't want to feel like I need to run anymore. I don't want the fear living inside of me to survive another day. I don't want to feel like my only option is to be small. I don't want to feel like I can't take up space, yell and scream, or dance in the rain or fuck with wild abandon."

I watched a dizzying array of emotions turn cartwheels over his features as he rocked with the ricochet of my words, pushing on this time, not because I was terrified that if I stopped, I'd never start again. This time, I knew I would be able to start again. This time, no matter what I told this amazing, infuriating, disgustingly handsome, devastatingly passionate man that it would be my truth, and I would mean it. I knew that I would lean into whatever came out of my mouth because it would no longer be tainted by fear, expectation, or the loss I was always terrified of happening. This time, I had the strength to be me.

"I don't want to walk away from us. I don't want to walk away from this fucked-up, crazy, intense thing that we have. I want to be that woman that you deserve. I want to be the woman I deserve to be. I want so many things, Sal. I want everything. I want to feel your claws in my skin. I want to feel your teeth on my skin. I want to feel your cock driving into me. I want to feel your mate's mark on my soul. I want to see my mate's mark on your soul. I have no clue how that will happen, but I want to figure out a way. I want to fight with you. I want to bite and kick and claw at each other. I want to love you. I want to give you everything that I am and hold nothing back. I want to give you every ugly truth and every beautiful moment of my life. I want that because you have earned it and because we deserve it."

He smiled up at me bashfully. "Yeah?"

I couldn't help but laugh. Here I was, pouring everything and then some into him, and he was sitting there with a goofy grin on his face. "Yeah. So, put those fucking feathers back on, Big Bad, and I'll put mine back on, and we can go back to kicking and clawing and biting at each other, but this time, we aren't hiding from each other. This time, I'll give you everything, and you'll give me everything."

He cocked a brow at me and looked down to his feathers. Gone was the bashful smirk, replaced by that mocking, sultry smirk I was so familiar with. "Oh, these things? Is that what that was all about?"

I glared at him, right back where we belonged. "Yup."

"Well, see, here's the thing, I had no intention of actually not wearing them. The thing is, I didn't think you were ready for the totality of the tradition." He watched me from the corner of his eye as he slid them toward me, conspiracy sparkling in his dark gaze. "See, you're supposed to put my mate talisman on me every day. Which means you're supposed to braid my hair and tie them in."

I lofted my brows and narrowed my eyes at him. "So, does that mean you'll be braiding my hair?"

He laughed. "Absolutely not. I couldn't braid to save my life."

I laughed with him, then snapped my mouth closed. "Hey, wait! Who the fuck has been braiding your hair, then?"

"Ixchel."

There was once, a million years ago, when I had access to the internet that I would surf stupid videos on YouTube. I watched a compilation of videos where people were on rollercoasters, and, on an especially scary or fast section, they would pass out. That was what it felt like when the bubble within me popped. It felt like I was rocketing through the air, hit a hairpin turn, then it all went dark.

When I came to, I was sitting on Sal's chest, his shirt ripped to shreds, tiny rubies of blood beading up on the dark skin and my lips pressed to his, devouring his with a ferocity I didn't know I had in me. I felt his fingers on the bare skin of my thighs, digging in and gripping me to him like, if he hadn't held on tight, I'd disappear into the ether.

I snapped my head up, confusion spinning in my head. "What . . . what the hell just happened?" My trembling fingers pressed the dizzy spin from my thoughts and vision.

Sal's fingers flexed against the flesh of my thigh, digging in further until it pooled around his fingers. "And when the fuck did I get naked?"

A barking, full-body laugh shook me on top of him, and he tilted his head back with it.

I poked him in the chest. Hard.

"Hey!" His laughter tapered off, but the grin stayed, pulling at his lips. "Well, you got naked when your cadejo, a possessive little thing, I might add, burst through and pounced on me. And she only let go when I explained calmly to the little ghost that I was joking and that Julia had been braiding my hair. I appreciate you coming back to me, nayeli. I'm not sure I'm ready to meet her again any time soon. She's a little monster."

His chuckle was back, vibrating his pelvic bones against the sensitive flesh of my thighs.

"My what. Wait, no. The priest said that, too. My cadejo. I don't have a cadejo, Sal. We both know that." I looked down at him again, the claw marks on his chest, my perch atop his hips, the inexplicable way my shredded clothing was laying five feet behind me and the missing chunk of time in which that had all happened . . . none of it fit together.

But the way he smirked up at me melted the confusion away. I had to trust him. I had to trust he knew what I didn't. He had been there.

"I have a cadejo?" I asked, wonder leaking into the breathy, hesitant question.

"Yes, nonayeli. It seems so." He brushed away the errant curl that had fallen into my face, tucking it behind my ear. "I always suspected, at least since we were kids. I don't know why she's just now choosing to show herself, but I'm glad she has nonetheless. It gives me hope for us."

A clawed finger traced down my exposed neck. The pinprick of pain mixed with the tightening in my chest and belly. My lips parted in a pant as he drew that line down my throat, between my breasts, and across the top of one large globe before gripping it firmly. I felt him growing firm beneath me.

"I can feel your heat, teocuitlayolca."

I tilted my head back into the sensation of his claw thrumming against my stiff nipple. I wanted more, needed more. I needed to seal the truce between us and start again with him. My hips ground down on him, the stiff fabric of his jeans creating friction that sparked fireworks behind my eyes and made me mewl like a needy kitten for more. He answered my mewls with a growl of promise.

His hand was parting my soaking wet folds when a knock sounded on the door from behind us.

"Fuck off," we both snarled at the intruder in unison.

"Yeah, I want to, Cihuatlatoani, Tlahtoani, but this is important."

I recognized Antonio's voice, even though it was muffled by the door he was smart enough to not open.

Sal pinched my clit, the fireworks turning into cannonballs as they burst behind my eyes. He wasn't stopping, so I wasn't, either. I continued grinding on him, stealing the friction from his jeans and the fingers I was forcing down on my clit. He grinned devilishly up at me.

"Not a sound, nonamic. Those belong to me and only me," he whispered up to me. I nodded down to him. "Say it."

"Not a sound. They belong to you, Tlahtoani," I whispered as softly as I possibly could.

"Good," he whispered back before he turned his head toward the door. "What is it, Antonio?"

As he spoke, he retracted his fingers from my clit, and without warning, without workup, he pistoned four fingers into my slick, wet, needy pussy. It was too much, it was just right. It hurt, it felt divine. It was everything I didn't know I needed. The burning stretch twining around the unexpected burst of intense pleasure had me snapping my mouth shut with a gust of air as I silently screamed out my pleasure.

"You remember what we were talking about before the ritual?"

"Fuck. You like that? You like being stretched wide open for me?" he hissed up to me.

He was slow. Too slow. I wanted more. I wanted to drown in the intensity of everything I felt in my heart and match it with the intensity I felt in my abused pussy. I nodded to him, unable to reliably stay quiet if I opened my mouth at all. He turned his head to the door, but his eyes were on me as he slowly fucked my clenching channel with his fingers, and I swiveled my hips down on his hand. "Yeah, what about it?"

The dichotomy between the overwhelming sensation I was feeling, paired with his calm demeanor and conversation with Antonio outside the door drove me at a wild gallop toward the cliff of an orgasm. I reached out, needing his lips, needing to feel his tongue in my mouth, claiming me. I turned his chin to me and took what I needed. He groaned deep into my mouth as our tongues danced against each other frantically. I felt his need as keenly as I felt mine, a sharp knife digging into my heart in the sweetest of ways. I wanted it deeper.

"More . . . please," I whimpered against him.

It was the right thing to say, since he grinned and pounded into me with as much force as he could manage at this odd angle. I was close. So close. It felt like my entire body would explode if I didn't come for him. He thrust deep and hard. I could feel a burning stretch around his hand, yet I wanted more, harder and deeper. I wanted everything he could give me.

I tilted back my head and came with a strangled groan as the words "He's in Chinameca" tumbled through the door. I didn't give a rotten fuck who *he* was, I just knew that I was destroyed.

"Fuck. I could watch you come for me every second of the rest of my life. Next time, though, you'll be coming down my throat. I have missed the taste of you on my tongue. I crave it like air." He growled softly.

He didn't move his hand a single inch, and as I panted against him, I was glad. When the edge of orgasm fell away, the pain sharpened.

He turned his head back to the door, his voice picking up. "Fine. Keep someone on him. I'll deal with it later."

CHAPTER FORTY

"**A**re you sure?" Antonio was leaning against the door now, his voice muffled but louder.

Sal twitched beneath me, causing me to gasp as a hot spike of pleasure coated in fiery pain radiated out from where the pressure of his stone still hand was still buried within me. His eyes cut from the door to me in a silent check to see if I was okay. I grinned down at him, tempting him by clenching my stretched thin muscles around him. A groan rumbled from his chest, then shifted into a growl as he turned to the door.

"I swear to all the teotl above and below, Antonio, if you don't fucking fuck off, I am going to shove that door up your goddamned ass." He spit. I bit my lip against the toothy smile that threatened to crack my face. He was as feral to connect as I was. I felt that bubble inside of me flexing and stretching as he turned his molten, glossy-black gaze to me. The black mist was back, floating around his mouth as he caught my eye. "As for you, my heart, I am going to fuck you until you forget how to breathe. And, if you tell me no, I'm going to make you regret it."

"Promises, promises," I purred down at him.

He flexed his fingers within me, my head dipping back, the power of the flutter within me stealing any more clever words from me. I didn't have time to enjoy it, though. He was moving again. His hand slid from my slick depths, the heat and hollow feeling making me pout and sulk with disappointment. He grinned up at me.

"Get on top of that table. Palms flat on the table. Ass up, legs spread. I want to see how you stretch around me." I blinked at him before he cracked the side of my thigh with a stern flash in his eyes. "I said move."

Oh, I liked this game. I liked this game a lot. Sal had always edged along the line of possessive and domineering, but this flavor of dominance had my toes curling and my pussy clenching in anticipation. I scrambled off of him and scurried to do as he bid, pushing the bowls of fruits and the little dish of copal out of the way as I lay over the low-slung table. I looked over my shoulder, connecting with his eyes, as I slowly spread my thighs and tipped my hips up to bare my dripping wet center for inspection.

He cocked a brow at me, tilting his head as his eyes took a slow trip from my eyes, down the hills and valleys of my lushly curved body, to the large round globes of my ass cheeks, to the small thatch of curls just barely on display above the puffy, glistening lips of my needy pussy. I imagined his fingers dragging along every inch of skin he lazily took in. I imagined the pads of his fingers tracing each line, fold, and rise of soft flesh. Goosebumps rose on my skin, my stomach clenching, my thighs tensing. He was teasing me, drawing out my thirst for him as he prowled, watching me, licking his lips like a wolf sizing up his next meal.

I knew the moment he came to what move he wanted to take next. As if he had been playing out the ways he could make good on his threat. It sparkled in his black-smoke-rimmed obsidian eyes.

"Who do you belong to?"

My mind twirled back to that same question he had first asked me as I was spread out beneath him, panting with need and begging him to just fuck me. I was so hesitant then. I don't even remember why. The words fell from my lips with no thought. "I belong to Itziquetzal and his Obsidian Beast. Who do you belong to?"

He grinned down at me, the smoke drawing in and curling around his teeth as they slowly elongated and sharpened. He dipped down, pulled a scrap of my shredded clothing from the floor, and stalked toward me. My heart pounded as our eyes locked, and he leaned over me. I felt the brush of his black hair loose on my shoulder. It teased me with its silken embrace, and the anticipation was killing me. I needed him. I needed anything and everything he was about to give me.

His breath was hot, his words full of meaning, when he whispered against my bare shoulder. "I belong to Xochitl and her golden beast. For all time. Without question. Without hesitation. Always."

My body clenched around those words and held them in an iron grip. I wanted to cry and leap on him, but instead, I cupped his cheek. Lightning clapped against my ass cheek the moment my hand raised from the table, sending fire licking up my ass and thigh. He sucked his teeth and gave me a feral wolfish grin, full of sharp teeth. "Ah-ah-ah, little flower. I said palms on the table. You move again, and you'll regret it. Now, tell me you'll be a good girl for me . . . though I do so enjoy the way your ass jiggles when I spank you. So, be a good girl, be a bad girl. I'll enjoy it either way. Though good girls get treats, and bad girls give me treats. You pick, beloved."

I moaned and wriggled my ass at him, wanting more and not wanting to push it too much. He chuckled, rubbing the stinging burn, dragging his blunt nails against it before looking back at me. He rose, still clutching that scrap in his hand, and stripped off his shirt, keeping his eyes locked on mine. My mouth watered as his skin twitched under my gaze, and muscles flexed as he pushed off his jeans. I was drooling when the thick length of his cock bobbed into view. I wanted to feel his hot flesh pressing against my tongue in the worst way. The satisfied smirk on his face told me he knew what I was craving, but the bastard had his own agenda this evening. He leaned back down, letting the silken length of his cock brush against me, as he stole my sight, wrapping the blindfold over my eyes.

"Trust," he murmured as my heart rate kicked up.

He wasn't testing me, but I certainly was testing myself. I could trust this man. I know I could.

I felt the sharp drag of his claw before the air around me shifted as he moved. My skin was alive and writhing under the sensation, as if starved for any sensory feedback, now that my eyes saw nothing but the shifting kaleidoscope of black and pops of imaginary colors. My mouth opened as I drew in a breath when the claw skirted over the aching heat of my pussy. I leaned into the sensation, needing more, craving everything that claw promised and only taunted me in giving.

The twitch of movement chased away my tormentor, though, and I pouted loudly at the loss of sensation. A dark chuckle was my answer. It was not just Sal's chuckle, though. I had become so familiar with the seamless blend of the two of my loves, hearing them weaving in and out of each other at every conversation. It had changed, though. I could make out the dark rasp of the beast and Sal's rich velvet timbre side by side. Just like the priest, like a beautiful harmony to a song.

The long sizzling length of his tongue ran from the swollen bud of my clit to my aching opening. It burned through me and seared any higher thought from my mind. When his claw-tipped fingers pried the swell of my ass cheeks apart to expose the puckered ring of my asshole to the air, I gasped and moaned. My heart pounded through my chest, desperate to get closer to the sensations exploding around me as he sucked and vibrated his tongue against my clit, his thumb pressing teasing circles into the tight rim of my ass.

"Tonight, I will have all of you," he whispered to my greedy clit, making me jerk and grip around air. He slid one hand from my ass as he spoke and dipped into my flooded pussy. "Every last bit of you. And you'll give it to me willingly, won't you?" He punctuated every dark, filthy word with a pistoning into my depths.

"Yes," I groaned huskily, dropping my head against the solid support of the table beneath me.

My hips chased his tongue, chased his finger, and tried to find more. He kept me right on the edge of tumbling into pleasure, holding me back from the ramp upward, dancing on the razor's edge at his whims.

"Mmm. That's my good girl."

He slid his soaking wet finger from my depths and pressed it to my flexing ass. His lips wrapped around my clit, and he sucked, finally pushing me off of that razor's edge and driving me down into the valley of ecstasy. As I crested the ridge, panting deep, my hips thrashing against his lips, he breached my ass and pumped his finger into the hungry depths of that dark hole. I screamed at the sensation that gripped my humanity and brutally ripped it away. I was nothing more than a panting, moaning, begging bitch in heat, pressing my ass back against the pistoning of his finger as he fucked me with it. Another joined its mate, then another, until I rocked back into three twisting fingers, plundering me for every scrap of pleasure it could wring from me.

"Come for me, sweet flower. I need to taste you come for me," he purred against my throbbing clit before latching his lips around my bud and humming into it as he pulsed his tongue around it.

His fingers in my ass pounded out a rapid pace. It was mere seconds after he commanded me to come for him before I came apart at the seams. The bubble inside me flexed and thrummed, like the tight skin of a tambourine struck on a thigh, as the world seemed to stop suddenly as every last muscle in my body tightened and clamped down. My heart stopped for an age as the ocean of pure ecstasy drowned me in the orgasm ripping through me.

I dully heard his "fuck" of pleasure. I barely even felt him move from beneath me, barely even felt the shift of heat moving away from my body over the crashing waves of mind-destroying pleasure that threatened to murder me, resurrect me, and rebirth me as pure divinity.

Slipping his sharp-clawed hands under my body, he lifted me with ease to the dresser on the other side of the room. I was perched atop it, my belly pressing into the flat surface as I dangled over it, my feet kicking to find purchase. The beast grunted behind me in displeasure, and the bowls scattered along the tiled floor. The familiar wood surface was now under my feet, keeping me propped up. His grunting turned into ones of pleasure and appreciation as I felt the beast's eyes drag over me.

"Foolish man," he grumbled, ripping the blindfold from my face. I blinked the black splotches from my vision. A black blob swam in my vision as the monster came into view. His expression passed for a harrowing grin around his muzzle full of razor-sharp obsidian teeth. "Yes, better. I want you to watch me fuck you, mate. Fuck you properly."

He tilted his head toward the black mirror standing in the corner to my right. I took in the spectacle of my riot of curls, half contained by a sloppy braid, the mate talisman ribbon dangling from it. My eye caught on the monster. Where once I shied away from him, scared of what he was and what he stood for, now I was yearning for his touch. I let my eyes travel the ten-foot length of him and lock on the massive cock bulging from the fur of his legs. I remembered it vaguely the first time I saw him, but I forgot it was that large. I took him in instead of looking at the mirror. He leaned back, pride flashing in his wicked black eyes as he crossed his arms over his powerfully muscled chest. Muscles rippled under the skin of his black-furred body, and there, between his legs, was the ebony length of him standing just as proud.

My mouth dropped open as I took in the wide expanse of his blunted crown. My eyes traveled down the impossibly thick, veined length to the flare of a swell at its base that reminded me of a firmer expanse of balls drawn up to the shaft that tapered just slightly behind it. I stared at that bulge, uncomprehending of how I had ever fit it all inside me and just sure I had never even seen that swell before.

He grinned, stroking the length of his cock, then squeezed at the flare. "I watched. I learned. My mate comes so fast when she is put to the test. I plan on having all of you as well, mate. Every last inch of me inside of you."

He stalked toward me, caressing his fist-thick bulge. "I will fuck you deep and plant my seed, and you will give the man and I get. I will fuck you every day until you swell with our child to remind you of whose cock sank deep into your soft heart and bore fruit where no other could or should have. And, when it is time, I will draw out your beast, and we will fuck under the moon, and I will mate her, too. I will write my name across her and claim her as mine. For now, you will take my cock and knot. I will stretch you wide and make you come on it until you beg me to stop. And when you do?" He pet my sensitive inner thigh with a wicked grin as he leaned forward. "And, when you beg me to stop, too tired from all the orgasms I force out of you, I will fuck you more. I will fuck you until you pass out and drip a flood on the floor from all the cum I fill you with."

He notched the wide flare of the head of his cock at my entrance. Everything narrowed to the sensation of my pussy slowly stretching around it when he eased himself into me, a gentle aching following. The pop of him breaching the tight ring of my channel made us both groan with delight deep in our throats. Secured within me, he let go of his cock, wrapped his clawed hands around my shoulders, leaned forward, holding his hips at the precipice, and whispered, "The man is sweet. I am not. You are mine. I will fuck the pussy that you have kept from me how I please. You will beg me for the pleasure of release. Say it."

"You will fuck your pussy how you please, and I will come when you say I can, Itzatecuani," I whispered, tilting my head back to bare my throat, watching the obscenely delicious sight of his black cock disappear into my golden body in the black mirror. He growled with delight and licked a hot line up my throat.

"Hold tight, little flower. You will take my knot this day."

He was true to his word. He slammed into me without the care that Sal normally would show. I gasped, that burning sumptuous twist of pain and pleasure rippling through my entire body, and I tapered off into a guttural groan of pleasure. Fuck, it felt so good. It felt so wrong. I felt full to the very brim. I felt him in my throat.

I felt him in my heart. I felt him in every cell of my body. I stilled as I got used to him, but I was feverish. I didn't know what that stretching around his cock did to me, but I was hot, needy, on the edge of going mad if he wouldn't carry out every last one of his promises.

He clenched the claws around my shoulders and sunk the talons into my skin. Little rivers of blood dripped down around the black razors. It didn't deter me. I was moving, I needed more. He withdrew to the tip, then brutally thrust back into me, driving me up against the dresser and rocking it against the wall with a clatter. The sound of wood slamming against the hard wall snapped the last tenuous thread of humanity I had clutched to, and I growled deep and low. When he pulled back again and thrust forward, I met his stroke and slammed my hips back on him. He snarled with approval, a signal he had been waiting for. His kindness was something other than Sal's, and I didn't know what I had expected from him besides that.

He fucked me in earnest, an unhinged pace of avariciousness, as if this were the last time he would ever have the pleasure of sinking deep into my molten flesh. I met him, stroke for stroke, shoving his length deep against the back of my sopping wet channel. Every time that blunted head struck the spot against the back wall, I screamed out a desperate sound as I clawed and scratched my way up that cliff face. I hovered on the edge, drunk on the mix of sharp burn and ripping tidal waves of bliss.

Beg, a little voice whispered in my ear. I barely heard it over the roaring snarls of passion falling from him.

"Please . . . fuck, please, Itzatecuani. Please let me come." I barely recognized my voice, thick with hungry rapture.

He dug those claws in deeper, and I could hear the grin in his words. "Take every inch of me," he commanded.

Every inch? Was I not already? I whimpered, begging without words.

I was decidedly not taking every last inch of him, and as he pulled me down onto that wide knot, the lava's pressure built as he rocked his hips into me, shimmying my stretched-too-far pussy around it.

"Fuck, fuck, fuck, fuck, fuck, fuck."

The word was the only word I could remember in the entire human language.

Every last drop of personhood shredded around the screaming bliss as he invaded, pushing me beyond my limits. He was snarling, growling into my skin, as we battled together to fit him all into me. We both wanted it. We both needed it. We were both starving for that pop as it finally slid home.

He was fast, swift about the command as soon as he was seated as deep as he could be inside me. "COME FOR ME NOW."

Those words wrapped around my very center and forced the orgasm from me. I did as I was told. I had no choice. The thick pulsing base within me forced the orgasm free, and I clamped hard onto him as I screamed into the void where everything else died away. All that mattered was that, even though I was suffocating under the weight of the inferno of sensation, he was still fucking me. He was still brutally pounding that head into the back wall of the turbulent ocean tempest taking up residence in the center of my existence. He was snarling words, but I couldn't recognize them. I was gone, drowning in the strength of the orgasm he conjured up from the depths.

He didn't stop. He never stopped fucking me, not even when the thick honey of his cum coated my walls. He was snarling, snapping his teeth with a loud click, as he pistoned mercilessly into me, those obsidian, razor-tipped claws never leaving my shoulders. They only dug in farther as he used them to slam me down harder and harder on his cock.

"I will make you come until your little legs are too weak to run from me again." He growled as I squeezed him blindly, rolling from one orgasm directly up the roller coaster of another.

"Please, great beast . . . please," I whimpered weakly as a third, impossibly powerful orgasm pulled at my control.

I was a bestial thing, surviving only by the millisecond at the edge of that razor between orgasms, his clawed hand pushing me over it carelessly.

"Come for me, little flower. And when you do, remember that only here, at my feet, can you come like this. Remember my cock slamming into you, coating your womb with my thick seed when you think about turning your feet to run from me again."

He kept pounding into me, kept filling my cunt with the unending stream of his pleasure. I could feel myself filling with it, trapped behind the swell of that rock-hard cock. I lost track of time. I existed only for mere seconds between orgasms he so expertly tormented me with. One after another. I whimpered weakly as I clenched down around him again. Every muscle of my body felt weak, wrung out, shredded on the altar of my penance for abandoning my mate. I slumped against the dresser. The world had gone black from my inability to keep my eyes open. I'd lost count of how many orgasms he pulled from me. I lost track of everything but the pounding thrust of him and his snarling groaned pleasure as he licked the blood dripping down my back and pooling on the dresser.

The pinching slice of his claws sliding from my shoulders pulled me back to the physical realm and out of the realm of nearly painful fullness at the center of my body. I was shivering, though I wasn't sure if it was because of the way his claws traced the streaks of blood down my spine or if it was my body reacting to having an untold number of orgasms. When the heat of his tongue tracked up my over-sensitive flesh, I knew the shiver was from the tenderness in his touch. Something had shifted in him over the last joint orgasm. Something eased, and even though this brutal creature wedged as deep as he could fit himself within me would never fully soften, it was as close as he would ever come, and I knew that on an instinctive level.

"Never again," he whispered against the center of my spine.

A toothy muzzle pressed into the skin there, in a close-enough approximation of a kiss. His hot breath, panting and as ragged as my own, gusted out against the slick of his kiss, wet from sweat and his tongue. His chest pressed against me with every breath, slowly evening out as the crazed pace of pounding eased into slow, purposeful rutting. Shadowy, silken fur nuzzled into the place he had pressed the kiss as his head rested there for a moment, drinking in the scent of my skin and the mix of our scents. He was quiet for a long while. Only the sound of our tattered breathing and the punctuation of his hips slapping against my ass bounced around the room. I almost missed his gruffly barked-out demand.

"Promise it."

It took far too much effort to turn my head and look at him. To say a feral, monstrous-looking creature, made of shadows and brutality, would ever be softened would be a mistake. Even through his fearsome appearance, I could see the fear pulling at his bestial features and the sense of being lost in the sparkle in his eyes. My heart clenched and bled for the wound that geysered from this ancient spirit made flesh that had buried himself to the hilt within me.

I tangled my fingers with his, my blood squelching noisily between the rough pad of his claws and the velvety skin of my hand. My fingers flexed, gripping him with strength I barely had left in me. "I promise you, Itzatecuani, that I will be yours forever. Until the end. If I ever run again, I will be running with you . . . not away from you."

Relief washed through the ancient creature's eyes, and he nodded, lifting our entwined fingers to his mouth to press what he could of a kiss to the bruised knuckles. Our eyes connected, and a thousand unspoken words of endearment, love, adoration, and devotion fell between us. His other hand reached out to stroke the side of my face tenderly. He had stilled in the moments between his words and mine, satisfied in his panicked rutting to be content with just feeling our twin pulses around his flesh.

"One day, my heart, I will carve my glyphs into your skin with my claws, and you will carve yours into mine." He smirked devilishly, and I shivered around him. "Until then, I will have to settle for ruining your cunt with the prowess of your mate's knot."

I couldn't help but laugh the sound a twinkling dancing bell that bubbled up from the center of my essence and turned, spinning circles around the space. I felt the twitch of his cock within me as he chuckled with me. I felt light, airy, ephemeral, and without substance yet so present in a way that felt new and clear, crisp.

He leaned forward and licked my cheek, smearing a bloodstain across it before wrapping his hands around me and pulling my boneless body from the dresser. I collapsed against him, groaning at the shift of his cock within me. He purred in my ear as he carried me, still speared on him, to a small bed on the opposite corner from the hammock I had woken in. As he lowered his massive frame on it, his back pressing against the rough blanket, I groaned again, his cock head grinding against the abused spot I loved so much.

His claw came around my hip, snaking between my legs to play at my clit. "This will hurt, my heart. But I think you will enjoy it."

I cast him a speculative look over my shoulder as he tapped, nothing more against my exhausted, overly sensitive clit, shooting grenades of pleasure through my body. I groaned, too wrung out to chase more, but still too feverish with need not to. I ground my hips down on his cock, seeking pressure and friction to match the intensity of the pleasure in my clit. He had me panting and on the edge of orgasm within seconds, on the precipice of death and rebirth.

As I opened my mouth to beg to come, he cut me off and snapped, "Give me your orgasm, beloved."

I wanted to weep, I wanted to cry into the heavens the love that poured through those simple words of command as I came for him. The moment the orgasm started, I was spinning on his cock. The pressure and pull against the knot lodged within me blinded me with a new layer of pleasure, and I screamed. My voice shredded on the power of the euphoria that the painful stretch built within me. When it finally washed over me and away, I collapsed forward onto his chest.

The silk of his fur pressed against my cheek, tickling my nose as I puffed whimpering breaths against him. Wrapping his arms around me, he pressed me into him. I smiled weakly against the strong, steady thumping of his heart. His claws tangled themselves into my disheveled curls, pulling the last bits of my braid free. I slipped into an exhausted sleep, bundled into the sleek velvet of his skin and fur, his claws gently tugging through my curls as he murmured words in an ancient language that planted seeds of love deep in my soul.

I was sure I would have woken up when he traded shadows beneath me, but when I woke, I was lying on Sal's strong, hot chest. He had propped his head up against the tiny bed's headboard. I grinned up at him and gave him what I could only imagine was a dopey smile, since it made him chuckle when he pushed the hair from my face. I tried to move, but he held me tightly, flexing against me like a vise.

"Mmm, not yet, sweet one. It has been too long since I felt your skin on mine. And, while I loved watching him abuse your flesh, I missed touching you," he whispered down to me in a satiny, cognac voice.

I loved the way his accent, which hadn't blended into the norm for me just yet, curled and smoked around the words. The dance of the black mist in his eyes and mouth played along with each syllable, and I stared up at him, suddenly fascinated with it.

After a few moments, he quirked an eyebrow at me. "What?"

"Nothing, it's just that I never noticed it before."

He tilted his head, coiling a strand of hair around one deep sorrel finger. "Noticed what, nonamic?"

"The smoke in your eyes and mouth," I said around a yawn before resting my head again on his chest and nuzzling into his warmth.

He was quiet for a few heartbeats before he purred down to me. "You see smoke in my eyes and mouth, noyzotzon?"

I nodded against his chest, listening to the comforting thrum of his heart beneath my ear.

"Interesting." He bent and pressed a kiss to my head. "You will need to be sure to tell that to the priests when you speak to them."

I squished up my face at the idea of ever leaving this tight, cramped bed. He chuckled deeply. "I know, sweet one, but your cadejo has newly emerged, and there are many questions that we need the answer to. And, as much as I would love to stay buried within you for the rest of eternity, it would be best to eventually, let him have his bedroom back."

Heat washed around my cheeks, flames licking up and coloring them. I buried my face into the solid flesh beneath me and groaned out in embarrassment. "Oh god . . . please tell me we didn't just fuck in some holy person's bedroom."

"Like absolute fucking animals, nonayeli." He snickered at me as I groaned again. "It's not the first time nor the last time the teopixqui had to wash cum and blood off their floors."

"Still!"

He laughed, curling his fist tighter into my hair to twist me up into a searing kiss, stilling my embarrassment and turning it molten in my chest. My pussy clenched down on him but found that the delicious knot that had stretched me so thoroughly had softened, nearly collapsing under the strength of my milking muscles. I groaned again, this time in disappointment, and he smirked against my lips.

"I take it you enjoyed his knot?" he asked, a sultry tease in his voice as he tilted my head back to watch my eyes.

I flushed but couldn't deny it. I loved it. I had loved every last agonizingly intense second of it. "I did."

The grin he gave me would have given the devil a shiver of delight. "I'll have to keep that in mind. As a treat for when you are a good girl for me . . . or for when I want to watch our cum flood out of you. A sight I'm still waiting to enjoy, I might add."

He raised his brow in expectation and looked down at my plush body.

"Here?!" I exclaimed.

"Oh, yes, absolutely here. Unless you'd like me to get the tape, that is."

I squeaked with fear. Never again with that damned tape. It had taken me far too long to scrub off the sticky residue. I grumbled and pushed up from his chest. I knew already that there was a tidal wave inside of me because even the slightest bit of movement already had it leaking from me. He groaned deliciously when I moved on him. I hoped he was as overly sensitive and worn thin as I was. Facing away from him, still straddling him, I pressed my hands to his knees and swiftly raised my hips.

The sensation of what felt like buckets of thick cum flowing out of me made me shiver from head to curling toes, a deeply satisfied moan slipping from my lips that echoed from his behind me.

"Fuck. I have never in all my life seen something so fucking hot. I wish you could see what I'm seeing. A thoroughly fucked, abused, swollen and gaping pussy drooling with my cum." He panted, the cock that had softened now bobbing angrily and greedily toward my cunt. "I wish I had the energy to fuck you again, cualcihuatl."

The cum drained from me; it should have just been a slow drip, but he had stuffed me so full of him that it flowed in a white river from between my thighs. A hot finger pressed against my tender flesh and played in the slick fluid, dragging it from clit to ass, and I arched my spine in aching anticipation. He hissed, and his shaking hands dug into the flesh of my hips, hanging on for dear life like me. We were ravenous for each other. Wanted more than our weak flesh could allow for.

"Thank you, teocuiteotl. I've been longing to see this sight for years. But I swear if I don't keep my hands right where they are"— he dug his fingers in to the pillows of fleshy hip again—"I will fuck you again. And if I start fucking you again, I'll never stop."

"I don't see a problem with that right now," I gasped out around the titanous weight of my need for him.

He groaned deep from the very depths of his soul. "You tempt me to ruin, my heart."

His fingers flexed against my skin, and I held my breath, willing him to move, willing him to make good on his carnal hunger to sate my own. After an eon, he exhaled and pulled me back against him, crushing me to his chest as if to hold himself back and me as well. As if he could squeeze the need out of both of us if he held on hard enough. He eventually accomplished it, but we lay like that for what seemed like hours, panting and whining against each other, knowing full well that the ravenous hunger to fuck came from the desperation within our hearts and souls, not necessarily from the tired, aching flesh we housed them in.

CHAPTER FORTY-ONE

We were curling tendrils of each other's hair around our fingers, drinking in each other's gaze, and soaking in the silence around us when the knock at the door disturbed us. It was tentative, hesitant, and soft, like the knocker had zero interest in actually knocking. My first instinct was to throw something at it and chase them away from our bubble of peace and contentment, but Sal's reluctant smile told me he knew it would eventually disturb us.

"We must eventually leave, beloved," he whispered against the pads of my fingertips as an apology before he turned his gaze to the door. "Yes?"

"It's time."

It was César's voice, soft, steady, confident in his own special, reliably serene way. However, just as with Sal and the priestess I had met earlier, I heard voices riding the harmonies of his words. Unlike them, where their second or third voice was next to their own, his was woven deep, as if the words came from the same mind, the same mouth, and the same tongue but in two very multiple pitches.

Tilting my head, I scrunched my brow as I tried to unweave how the three voices were so different. I felt Sal's gaze on my cheek, inspecting me, trying to seek the answers without asking me, content to let me tell him on my own time. Our peace was still a tender, fragile, new thing. Still pink and raw from healing over the gaping wound that had rent us apart. He would give me time, space, and support. I felt it in my bones without needing him to voice it. Whatever we had done to each other, whatever we had carved into each other had torn into us and remade whatever it was we thought we were. Its shape was still curling and obscure, but it would come into view soon.

He leaned down, pressing a heartfelt kiss to my head, and murmured something in Nahuatl I didn't quite catch before he eased me up from his chest. Strong hands pulled me into his lap. He gathered my rumpled curls into a ponytail before twisting it into a bun and tucking the end under the tight pile of it atop my head. The gentle twinkle of the chain whispered in my ear as he looped his own mate talisman around the bun to secure it. The dangle of his obsidian feather bounced against the back of my head as he peppered soft kisses up the length of my neck. His nose nestled at the top of my spine as he drank deep of my scent.

A wistful, soft groan tingled my flesh as he twitched beneath me. "Gods give me the strength to survive the temptation of my own wife. Nayeli, if you do not move, I won't have the willpower to leave this room."

Reluctantly, I slid from his lap to the grasping slide of his fingers against my thighs. My feet found the cool tile floor, and the moment weight was placed on my legs, I swayed and moaned. The aching, throbbing soreness between my legs was almost enough to have me gasping and panting for another round. The heated throb radiated from my knees to the pit of my stomach, and moaned whimpers fell from my parted lips as I tried to catch my breath. His hand was at the small of my back within seconds, offering me the strength of his body to stabilize myself.

I would feel the toll of our crazed mating for days, maybe even a week. The thought of it made me shiver with delight. Sal chuckled darkly behind me, his fingers flexing against my hip, where bruises were already forming in the shape of his claiming fingers.

"Mmm, I wish I could say I was sorry, nonayeli. But I'm not, not even a little. The sight of you weak, wobbling, and destroyed from my affections is my second favorite sight," he purred into my ear, gusting the ruined curls against my temple.

"What's the first, asshole?" I grumped up at him, not wanting to tell him I loved his teasing.

"The sight of my cum pouring from your abused pussy," he said with a wink and a quick peck to my collarbone as he passed.

"Yeah, well, now I have nothing to wear and a busted puss." I folded my arms over my chest and glared at him.

He snickered behind a large hand and fished a white gown like the one the priest had worn, the fine cotton catching my eye. When he pulled it over my head and let it settle around my otherwise naked body, I was thankful that whoever gifted the priest with this had paid attention to quality. The cotton draped over my fevered skin like the softest of silk. Anything more, and I might have been whining and squirming for a different reason. He leaned down and snatched my forgotten ribbons from the floor and tucked them into the pocket of the pants he was tugging on.

"Come, we have a date with César." He collected my hand into his and gently tugged me toward the door.

"Sharing now, hmm? That's new," I teased.

It was the wrong thing to say. He had me pressed against the door and hiked up on the invasion of his knee that ground up into my battered core within a blink of an eye. The smoke cleared from his eyes and mouth as his beast pushed forward and sharpened his features, making his words dark and dangerous. "I would sooner share the beating heart in my chest than share you with another. Do not toy with my claim on you, sweet flower. You are mine. Say it. Who do you belong to?"

"I belong to Itziquetzal and his Obsidian Beast," I purred up at him before his head came crashing down in a devastatingly animalistic, claiming kiss that stole the breath from my lungs and the calcium from my bones.

It left me panting, my head pressed against his chest as I warred with my mind to still and find shape, sound, and sight again. He chuckled and pressed a kiss to the top of my head.

He led me through the cool, shadowed hallways of the mud-plastered walls of the temple with ease. As we neared the end, I realized that all of the hallways led into the same open circular space, like the rays of a sun. Above me, the inspiration for that architecture warmed the roof's tiles as a last goodbye to the day. The sunset's warm orange, coral, and coppers whispered their imminent dazzling display through the ceiling's large open circle, feeding light into the wide-open cylindrical room.

Turning, I took in the space. The walls were white, crisp, and clean in most places. In other places, rich murals had been painted in vivid relief. One made my lips quirk up in amusement, a great, black shadowed dog with angry red eyes, surrounded by the fall of black feathers. At his feet were tiny flames scratched into the plaster. The mural had only just been started, with only outlines and a few primary colors filled in.

"Really?" I asked over my shoulder, eyeing the depiction of his beast killing Manny. I sucked my teeth at him.

Though the gesture was one of his people, it felt fitting to convey the various teasing emotions that curled at my guts. He had the good sense to at least pretend to be abashed by the display of his might. Annoying man, with his salivation-inducing hubris.

I continued my perusal of the open space. The walls without paintings held various small tables, with what looked like ceremonial goods scattered between fruits. At the center of the room was a raised brazier that held a low crackling fire kissing at its brass edges.

César's appearance should have surprised me when he joined us. The massive plume of vibrant feathers that crowned his head danced as he moved. The heavily tooled and painted leather collar that covered his throat, collarbone, and the top of his chest were stark against the image I had of this man. The glyphs on his ribs flexed with his movement. He wore an intricately woven, knotted loin cloth between his legs that terminated in heavy embroidery and beadwork. His skin shocked me the most. I had seen the skin of César's cadejo before, with its clumping fur and skin that looked rotted, but this was different. His skin reminded me of blue cheese, with deep, dark, angry black-and-green veins erupting from under his dark skin in some places, and, in others, it looked withered and dry.

Concern flooded through me as I looked at Sal. He stood beside me without a care in the world. Feeling my gaze on him, he looked down, then gave me a reassuring smile before tucking me under his arm to press me to his solid body.

Trust. The word reverberated through my mind again as César set three small stools before the flames and took a piece of copal from a bowl beneath the brazier. When he had cast it onto the flame, he finally looked up to us and ushered us forward.

We took a seat. I was tucked closest to César, with Sal on the other side of the flames. From this vantage point, I could see the dull, waxy hue of his skin and the milky film over his usually vibrant eyes. He looked dead, long since departed from this world, yet he pulled waxy lips into a comforting smile at me. All around him, a halo of night sparkled with the gems of a thousand stars, each one vivid and bursting with brilliance. I couldn't help but stare. The display around his body was a night sky we all wished we could, one day, witness. A night sky that never existed on the dull, lifeless surface of this planet. I envied whatever planet could be so blessed as to witness this display on a nightly basis.

César's voice asking Sal a question pulled my singular attention back to him as Sal said, "Mmm. Since she woke up, apparently."

"Since what when I woke up?"

César's chilling corpse face pulled into a comforting smile again, and when he opened his mouth, the stars flooded out. Though, unlike Sal's, there was an undercurrent to his voice. There, under the rich black velvet of the night sky was a flashing marbled green mist that reminded me of the jade pieces I had seen in Sal's ears and the jade piece hanging around César's neck. "I asked him how long you seemed to be acting . . . different."

"Well, it's not my fault. You guys all look different and sound different now. I'm not sure how I missed it before." I tilted my head, watching as the jade river hid between the stars. I wanted to chase it, to discover why it was being so sneaky.

"How do we look different, Xochitl?"

There! Another flash of beautiful emerald in the night sky.

I shook myself and looked away. I felt like a kitten watching a little red dot zip around the room. I was drawn so completely into the fascinating depths of the strange differences in my otherwise steadfast friend.

"Sal is mostly the same. Though, now I can see black smoke or shadows at the inner and outer corners of his eyes. It pools on his cheeks and grows and ebbs with his emotions. And, when he talks, the same black smoke comes out of his mouth. Depending on how gruff his voice is. I think, at least. I can't tell just yet what chases it away, but when his teeth trade shadows, it all goes away. So, I think it has to do with Itzatecuani. And when he speaks, I hear both of their voices now."

The two blinked. César stammered, then looked to Sal, who looked back at me. "What? Is that not . . . normal or something? I just assumed it was normal."

"No, Xochi, it's not normal at all. You said he has two voices now?" César tilted his deadhead, and I shivered.

"Yeah, when he talks, I can hear both Sal's normal voice and Itzatecuani's voice at the same time. Like they are singing a song together."

I was doing everything in my power not to look at César. The more I did, the more it reminded me of a rotting cadaver.

"Maybe it's a mates thing?" he asked, looking over to César.

"Nope," I said, popping the *p*. "I can hear it on César and the other lady. Though, they are both different in a lot of ways. They both have three voices, though."

Alarm registered on Sal's and César's face. César was the first to recover, not incredibly shocking. "What else is different about me, Xochi? And is it why you can't look at me?"

"Noticed that, hmm?" He snorted a chuckle, and I dragged my unwilling gaze back to him. "A lot. You look like a corpse. Like, genuinely, César, it's hard to look at you. You sincerely look like a dead body. Not like a zombie, but, like, genuinely, a dead body. Your eyes are the worst. It makes me want to puke. But there's also the stars. The stars are new."

He tilted his rotting head. "Stars?"

"It's the only thing I can look at. There's a halo of the most beautiful stars I have ever seen around you. And when you talk . . . Oh, did I mention the jade? That's different. The stars and night are like Sal's smoke, but not in your eyes. But there's something in your voice that isn't in Sal's. There's this hint of green that weaves in and out of the stars when you speak. I haven't seen it in Sal's voice, and I can barely see it in yours, but it's there."

César rose and walked around the circular room, pulling white curtains across each hallway except for the one we had come through. When he was done, he rejoined us. "What you are saying must only be for us, Xochi. Now, tell me, what do you see different in my arms?"

He raised both forearms, the exchange shivering through them and remaking them into the familiar shape I had seen so many times. I inspected them. Aside from the jade-tipped claws, his arms were the same. He moved them, and something sparked in the light. Without thinking, I reached out and took one of his hands, stretching it closer to the fire's light. There, shimmering beneath the black tufts of fur and sickly skin were faint glowing marks. I smoothed down the fur, pushed it aside, and leaned in closer. The glowing throbbed with the beat of César's heart in a diffused golden-green light. No, it wasn't golden-green. As I leaned forward, nearly pressing my face to his arm, I could see it better when it lit up. It was jade, marbled with golden light.

"There's something under your skin. I don't know what it is, but it's the same jade that's on your claws, but it has glowing gold veins that light up with your heartbeat." I looked up to him, meeting his milky liquid gaze. "What are they?"

He shuddered and retracted his arms from my grasp, careful not to clip me with his sharp claws. "They are the inscriptions of the teotl and my pact with my spirits. Can you see them on Sal?"

Sal uncrossed his arms and stepped around the brazier to extend his arms to me. They traded shadows slowly in a smoky plume in my hands. This was much more difficult. Unlike César, Sal's skin in his half-exchanged form was solid black and thickly tufted with fur. I pulled it as close to the fire as I dared without burning either of us and parted the fur, chasing the skin beneath. It was faint, so soft I barely saw it, but if I stared hard enough and focused on his skin, I could see the pulse of something. I traced it with my finger, finding what shapes I could. Unlike César's writing, Sal's reflected light from under his skin like a labradorite stone caught and shot back the light.

"Yes, but it's different. The same but different." Sal bent and pressed a quick kiss to my lips before he found his seat again.

"Interesting. I haven't heard of this blessing before. I will need to consult my spirits and see what I can learn of it. But it looks like you can see the spirit realm. Or at least a sliver of it. It is a very rare blessing to see it so clearly and without the need for ritual."

If César was as disturbed as he was showing, this was a big deal, and he didn't like it in the least bit.

He added herbs to the burner in the fire, where he had rested the rich incense of the copal. "I am going to draw your cadejo out now, Xochitl. It will be uncomfortable, and it will be disturbing. I have mentioned this process to you before. Usually, we do this to introduce the two spirits before they bond, so it is not as jarring for the person who will partner with the spirit. It is usually not so invasive. But you have bonded with a spirit before we could introduce you to them. Still, we must meet her, and there are some questions I have, and I'm sure you have for her."

He paused and looked at Sal. "Since you are now mated to another cadejo and this will be invasive, I have asked your mate to be here and give his consent as well."

His milky gaze came back. "Do you consent to the process? Would you like to meet your cadejo and find out her name?"

"Yes!" I blurted out, without even asking why something like this would be so invasive.

Sal chuckled next to me. "I consent if my mate consents. I trust you, brother."

César nodded and took up a blade with a jade handle, a few feathers, and an obsidian blade. "This will hurt, but you are safe. I will heal you if anything goes wrong. Nothing will, but I am telling you so that you do not panic. When you see her, do not panic. Remember that these are spirits, most of which have never held human form and are older than this earth. Do not insult her by being scared, or she will leave and never return. Do you understand?"

I nodded dumbly, expecting and waiting for the panic and the fear to grip me again. It never came. It didn't even appear when César cut down both of my arms from the inside of my elbows to my wrists. It did not come when he took up the ashes of the copal and sprinkled them in the gush of red blood. It didn't even come when he raised his cadejo arms, shimmering in a near blinding golden-white light and punched both hands into my chest. The pain from the wounds on my arms should have been nothing compared to having my sternum cracked open, but when I looked down, no blood pooled down through the white gown.

Blinking, I took in the strange sight of the man's arms buried into my chest, from fingertip to mid-forearm.

And then the world tilted, shifted left, spun, and kept spinning through brambles, tar, ice, and molten lava. It all happened so quickly I barely had time to draw in a breath to scream as the conflicting sensations slammed into me and crushed me beneath its disorienting waves. I had no clue where I was or what I was doing. I couldn't tell up from down. Was I still sitting? Was I even still on the same planet? All I could tell was that I was alive. That was something, I guess—even if I was living in an existence awash with anguish and nauseating dizziness.

As quickly as it started, it was abruptly over, and I fell to the tiled floor, panting and dry heaving into the cold tile.

"What . . . what the actual fuck, César!" I gasped out before wiping my mouth and scrambling to get to my seat again.

Before César could speak, I looked up to find his eyes, and all the air whooshed out of my lungs as I stared at the creature in front of me. It was . . . the most beautiful thing I had ever seen in my life. Waves of rainbows rippled off of it . . . her? Yes, her—definitely a her—as the light danced over her flesh and solidified it into a feminine shape. She stood so tall that the top of her head touched the ceiling, and the tall feathers cresting her brow and woven into the velvety curtain of her hair stuck up through the hole in the ceiling.

Her features were angelic but otherworldly. Her face was a mix of a placid, smooth stone mask, with the features of both bird, wolf, and human. Her lips, an ever-shifting glowing pillow of gold and opal, twitched up in a welcoming smile, and my heart lurched with familiarity and love. I had expected some biblical, crazy, twenty thousand-eyed, one hundred-winged angel, but what stood before me was a thick curvy goddess cast in white, gold, opal, and sparkling reflections of crystal.

She tilted her head, and the white curtain danced around her head like it was caught in an underwater current. When she opened her mouth, I could see rows and rows of deadly sharp teeth stretching back into an impossibly long jaw that didn't match the shape of her face. Two rows, like a shark's teeth, of long saber-like canines, capped the front of her mouth as she spoke. "I chose a form as close to my approximation of what wouldn't make you scream. I hope it is not . . . too upsetting."

I stammered. *Say something to the pretty goddess lady, dammit, Xochitl!* I thought.

"Uh . . ."

"Eloquent as always, my jewel," she cut back and chuckled.

A long, shapely leg stepped forward. As she approached, she shrunk down to my approximate height, except for the feathered crest. The crest was still a good two to three feet above her head, the feathers growing from between the strands of spun gold and opal. Jingling metal against stone brought my eye to her feet, where three bangles hung from her delicate ankles. My eye caught on the golden caps of each toenail before my gaze skittered back up her body. I had expected a goddess would be all curves, trim and svelte, but not this one. She looked like me, warm and round and strongly built, with a generous swell at her hips that promised a sumptuous bounty of backside and a set of tits that would make my mate's mouth water.

At the thought, I shot a jealous eye over at Sal. He was looking only at me, an impish grin on his face. "So possessive, little flower," he purred playfully.

The goddess before me cast her golden meteor shower eyes over at him. "Unless you plan on letting my mate out, keep your eyes to yourself, greedy man."

She bent forward a glittering breath between her face and Sal's as her intense gaze bore into him. "I kept it safe. All this time. I pulled those days like leaves from a vine and squirreled them away. Hid them deep inside the twisting brambles of her mind. Know this, stupid man. If not for me, you would have never seen her again. The heart inside of her would have fought too hard against the rotting soul of her mother, and she would have done worse to her than she did to Roberto. Remember this the next time you decide to treat my jewel with irreverence. Mate or no, I will crack you in half and slurp the marrow from your still-living bones."

I crossed my arms over my bust and scowled. "You know, I can probably threaten him all on my own. I don't need help. Plus, we have an understanding now, don't we Itziquetzal? Games, yes. Damage, no?"

The goddess did not move until Sal blanched and looked away. I snickered. Okay. I officially liked this goddess. Whomever she was, she could stay.

César looked up at the woman from where he was sitting. "What is your name, if you would be so inclined to share it, spirit?"

"I am Itzelcoszcatl. The Jeweled Rainbow," she purred down at César before sitting next to me. Sitting was a bad description. She sat in mid-air. Her impossibly long hair swirled around her, weightless, as she crossed her bangled ankles and leaned back on an invisible cushion. She lounged indulgently, like a celestial goddess perched atop her mighty throne.

"Ask your questions, teopixqui. It is uncomfortable out here. I have just awoken and still have not regained all of my strength." She examined her gold-painted nails, radiating a bright white light that made her look like the heart of a prism.

César tilted his head up at her. I mirrored the motion. "What do you mean that you have just woken? Have you not been with Xochitl for a long time?"

"Oh, yes. A very long time indeed now. How old are you now, my jewel?" she asked down at me.

"Thirty-two," I sputtered back.

"Hmm. So, about twenty-six years, then. Not very long at all," she sang back with a doting smile.

César and Sal sputtered this time. "What?" They spat in unison.

"Oh, yes. We paired together when she was barely a speck in the cosmic eye. It was just right."

"Who performed the ritual?" César gasped in an accusation I didn't like the sound of.

"No one. There was no need to draw me down to her. Her blood sang to me, and I came when I could find her. I would have come earlier, but she was hard to find." She frowned, her beautiful mask-like features contorting and casting sparks of rainbows from her eyes.

"Why was she hard to find? And what do you mean her blood sang to you? That is unheard of!" César would piss this goddess off, and some small part of me wanted to see exactly how brutal a goddess would get once annoyed.

"She was hard to find because that bitch kept planting rue all over their house. As for her blood, are you little beasts so removed from the old tales that you do not see a descendant before you when she spits in your eye?" She snorted an ungoddess-like action. Okay, maybe she was a spirit and not a goddess. I imagined goddesses didn't snort. She cast an inspecting eye over me, and I shivered under her regard. "Okay, that's fair. She doesn't look it much anymore. But, just like you, her people come from the children of Those Who Turned Their Eyes. And unheard of to you, perhaps, but not unheard of to me and mine. Don't question me, teopixqui. What you know of my kind and that which we can do and how we move among the realms could fit into the bottom of a leaky thimble."

César glared up at her, and she merely flipped her rainbow and light hair at him.

"Bitch?" I asked, finally finding my voice in this. Her eyes locked with mine. I felt like a magnet within me found its true north and was pulling me into her, seeking to be one again.

"Your mother. For whatever worth that term has. She has kept me from you all this time. With those foul pills." She spit, a puddle of molten opal splattering against the tile, then disappearing into a shimmering golden mist.

Pills. What pills? My mind worked over the information she had so carelessly tossed out at me. "Those smell like death." "It could kill us." "She kept planting rue around the house."

Rue. The vitamins. I knew my mother was a piece of work, but this? If she had been planting rue around my house when I was nothing more than a baby, she knew what it was. She knew what it would do. Had . . . had she been poisoning me my entire life? Daggers of doubt and sorrow lanced through me. One more betrayal I discovered as I learned to stand tall.

"She'd been poisoning me?" I asked in a hushed voice.

Sal's hand clamped around my waist, finding the healed bite mark easily, solidly reminding me he was right there, right next to me in all of this.

The goddess above us nodded. "Since you were about ten, I imagine? Time is different for us. I just remember, one day, I was strong in you. I could feel your very heartbeat in my eyes, even when I was deep in the other realm. We were not two but one. And then I was trapped under your skin, unable to travel through the gates to the spirit realm. I was unable to move beneath your skin. I could see through your eyes, I could hear everything going on around you, but I could not trade shadows with you. I could not speak to you. I could do nothing but ride your skin like an unseen leech."

César and Sal were both snarling and growling their great displeasure. I imagined that, if my mother had appeared at that very moment, she would be torn to ribbons as the two men fought over who got to kill her. My snarling joined theirs, much to my surprise. I imagined I should feel hollow, empty, and sad, but instead, I was angry with pure white-hot rage.

The goddess spirit grinned a deadly, feral smile that elongated her mouth to stretch across her face obscenely, showing every last one of those predator's teeth that looked sharp enough to bite through bone like butter. "I did my best to help you when I could, Xochitl. Please know I did what I could, my jewel. I pushed at every opportunity I could. I believe your thoughts called it 'generalized anxiety.' It was me trying to show you what you could not see. I remember the twist you felt when I would push, worrying that she would notice. The barbs shredded you, thinking she would use it to gain more power over you. But, until you stopped taking those damned pills, I could do nothing but push thoughts here and there, and even that left me weak for weeks sometimes."

I nodded up to her. "And my ADHD? It was all her, too?"

"No, dear jewel of mine. That is truly your core, that is and always will be with you. Your mind is a wonder. Your mind is a wonder. A thousand cosmos live and swirl in that universe within you. I have spent the years watching as the threads of life have woven themselves into new tapestries that only you could weave. Watched you conquer kingdoms and release them into freedom within a single breath. The mortal world has moved so slow for you, too slow when your mind is ticking on the timetable of the gods. If I were a beast who fed solely on the essence of creation, we would be the most powerful creature in all the realms. Your mind is a sumptuous and delicious divinity, my jewel. Even without my guidance, you see things others do not. You work through and sort the disarray of this realm with ease. I'd say maybe even let the Obsidian Beast feel your divine claws once or twice." She winked at me, and Sal made a sound that was a cross between a panting moan and a laugh.

"So, she knew the entire time? She knew what she was doing to me and to you, Itzelcoszcatl? The entire time?" I was glaring up at the spirit when she nodded.

"And to your sister, too. Same to your brother. Though, his spirit was weaker than Elida's and much weaker than I am. He withered and died before he was even out of adolescence. I remember watching him die . . . I will never forget that sight for the rest of my life."

"He was fourteen?" I asked, and she nodded.

Robert had gotten sick that year. I was sure he would die. He puked every day. He shivered and twitched. His skin lost almost all color, except for a sallow jaundice. The night he threw up black fluid, unable to breathe between the vomit, I was sure he would die. I had huddled at the bathroom's doorjamb as black leaked from his eyes and ears, a scent of rotting meat permeating the room. I quaked with him, sure I was watching my brother pass into the next world right in front of me. My mother refused to take him to the hospital. When I had run to her bedroom to pull her out of sleep, she snapped at me and told me I would wake up Edwin and to go back to bed. When I told her what was happening to Robert, she finally crawled out of bed, watched him for a few minutes, then coldly walked back to bed, saying it would pass.

I knew he was dying that night. Or at least a part of him had been dying that night. She had known, too. She knew what was happening to him. She wasn't wrong. It did pass, and she knew it would pass once his cadejo fully died within him and festered into nothingness. What sort of woman could stand there and watch her son in such agony, knowing she had brought it on, and watch such a beautiful spirit within him rot and die?

"I remember that night, too," I murmured. "I will always remember that night."

The goddess spirit shivered as if recalling the memories with me.

"If there is nothing else, teopixqui, I am still weak. And while Xochi's happiness is slowly strengthening me"—she looked to Sal and nodded in silent thanks—"she has not fed yet. You will need to feed us soon. The broken goddess is watching, and we must be strong when her eyes fully open."

My brow furrowed, and the goddess stood, took two steps in the air, then broke apart into a thousand shards of gold dripping crystal rainbows. As the crystal shards rained on me, I slowly stood, feeling whole again.

"What the fuck is the broken goddess?"

"That's something César and I are also curious about."

Sal's voice found me moments before his arms wrapped around my body to pull me tightly against him.

CHAPTER FORTY-TWO

Sal and I spent the night in our rooms, surrounded by a forest of candles. I'd never seen him cook before, but I discovered the small little apartment had a tiny kitchenette he'd slaved over for a full thirty minutes to make us a splendid meal of polenta, beans, bacon, and eggs. He'd blushed at the humble fare and made an excuse about having never had to cook before. It was sweet. Here was this big, brutal man built to rip skulls from spines, yet he had jammed himself into the kitchenette that sported a single pair of burners and a microwave to cook me a meal so we didn't need to be surrounded by the totoco as we ate. We had curled up in bed, surrounded by a nest of blankets and pillows, and talked all night. I fell asleep to the sound of his rich, rumbling baritone telling me about little things he'd learned about totoco life. Tiny little details or stories that painted a mural of his life and wove him deeper into my heart. We didn't talk about my cadejo, the rue, or my mother. We talked about everything but that, and it was the exact right medicine I needed to ease off of the cliff of dread I had climbed up to after meeting the sparkling goddess that lived within me.

The next morning, I woke to the scent of bright, vivid, clean florals drifting in and out of the scents I had associated with home: copal resin, cognac, rum, spices, marigolds, leather, and the musky scent of Sal's and my skin warmed in sun-kissed sheets. When I finally—begrudgingly—blinked bleary eyes open, I was greeted with a riotous explosion of hundreds of peony blossoms woven with the sunburst oranges of marigolds. Sal was bent at the waist, shirtless, in only a pair of low-slung black jeans that clung to his perfect ass just enough to tempt me to sin. The pucker of dimples at the base of his spine, where his muscles flexed and bent, made my mouth water. He was on his tiptoes, quietly moving among the bounty of flowers as he emptied bouquet after bouquet all around the room.

I watched him, mesmerized by his movements and the dancing sway of the black smoke that flowed over him, as he murmured the lyrics to what I assumed was a song. Either that or he was talking to himself, unaware that I was watching him. His unguarded moments were my favorite. The way the sun pooled on the blossoms and crept toward him to lick golden lines across his heavily muscled skin made my heart skip and stutter with delight. Lust mixed so expertly with deep love, a love I had only begun to plumb the depths of. A love I was confident my mate would dig trenches to deepen every day.

He turned, with one last bouquet in his arms, stalking toward the bed. His eyes hadn't risen just yet as he paid attention to where his delicate steps wove through the blooms. It wasn't until he had finally made it to the bed and spread the blossoms around me that he noticed me.

He grinned bashfully, like a teenage boy caught getting into mischief. "Good morning, princess."

His voice, wrapped in that beautiful black smoke, slithered around me, held me tight in velvet. I smiled like a drunkard and groaned softly, opening my eyes to him again. Rainbows danced over every petal of the flowers around me, sparkling like jewels in the golden sunlight. "Good morning, mate."

A sigh of satisfaction fell from his lips as he leaned forward and placed a loving kiss to my lips. "I had hoped you'd sleep a little longer."

I chuckled and scooted to curl into his warm body, taking in his handy work. "It's beautiful, Sal. I wish you could see it as I'm seeing it. It's like every petal is a crystal, breaking up the light and kicking it back in rainbows."

He smiled and pet my head as we both curled around each other and stared at the ocean of pinks, purples, creams, oranges, and green stems around us. "Maybe one day, nonamic."

We languished in each other's arms as long as possible, the sun full overhead by the time I'd finished braiding Sal's hair and attaching the obsidian feathers at the ends of each. I opted to do a single braid on my own, still weaving my ribbon in and looping it around my head a few times, before tying it off. We walked out of our rooms to the courtyard to begin our daily duties, hand in hand.

It was dinnertime before I sat again. My eyes had been constantly darting around to glimpse him as he wove in and out of the fields, the forge, the machine shop, greedy for the sight of him after my choices had denied me of it for so long. I was sitting at one of the many picnic tables when I was unceremoniously gripped beneath the armpits and lugged up into the air with ease. I screamed, and he turned me in his arms as he sat, his back pressed to the table's edge.

A swift, hot kiss was pressed to my cheek as he arranged me to his suiting on his lap, my legs spread wide, draped over either side of his. Warm, rough hands slid up my thighs to rest on my butt beneath my skirt. An amused snort left me as I glared down at him.

"You know you could have just asked," I sassed.

One hand unburied itself from kneading at my fleshy ass to flick my nose. "And then I'd miss all the spit and vinegar in your eyes while you distracted me from overseeing dinner."

I crossed my arms over my ample bosom and glared hellfire down at him, grumbling about him going the right way for a black eye. He grinned at me, his gaze wandering over my shoulder to watch as the totoco filed past the grills to collect dinner. Both hands now idly stroked the soft skin beneath my skirt.

I'd learned the night before that, though it was a tradition that the strongest eat first, Sal had changed that. On Lets'a Wehle land, the weakest ate first and of the hardiest of the foods. His rationale was solid. The totoco had more than enough resources, and if the weak always ate last, how would they ever get stronger? Instead, César, Sal, and I ate the very last.

César was not here, at least not yet. I hadn't seen him since he shoo'd us out of the temple. He had things to think about and needed to perform rituals to reveal answers.

I watched Sal's face as his fingers wandered the plains of my thighs, his gaze on the line of totocan passing us on their way to find a seat. We were given sly smile after sly smile as they went.

"None of them are mad that I made you go to battle to get me back?" I asked in a hushed whisper into Sal's ear.

He snorted and sipped his mango juice from one of the newest mugs I had brought from the kiln. "You still have a lot to learn, nocihuapiltzintle." He arched his brows and gestured to some warriors who were nursing wounds and bandages. Each of them was chatting with each other in high spirits and, from the small snippets I could pull out, regaling each other with battle stories. "The warriors haven't had that much fun in a year or two. Maybe more. Sure, they wish you hadn't put yourself in harm's way, but you gave them an opportunity to prove their bravery. Most of them were even able to take war trophies. Ixchel the most of them all. She's got an entire skin. A hard trophy to gain."

I spit my mango juice back into the mug he handed me and whipped my eyes up to him. "A human skin?!" I hissed.

He barked out a peal of deep laughter that shook his whole frame. "No, nonamic. That would be easy to acquire. No, she'll be working and cleaning a cadejo skin for her wall in the next few weeks. It's hard to capture because you only have five minutes— give or take—before the enemy spirit leaves the body for the next realm and the grip on the exchange loosens back into their human form."

Ixchel must have heard Sal speaking of her. She turned wild hazel eyes on him. Her lips were split from the bottom lip to above her left nostril from what looked like a bite, the gash held closed by the careful, strategic placement of stitches, just wide enough apart to leave a scar but not enough to let in infection. She grinned a maniac's grin at him, then settled her gaze on me. She bowed her head just slightly and to the left, thumping her chest with her fist, then turned back to her dinner mates.

"It's a warrior's salute, in thanks for the opportunity. It is a compliment," he drawled lazily as the last of the warriors passed us by. He hooked his arms into the backs of my knees, and he rose in one fluid movement, as if I weighed no more than a feather. "Stay," he barked as he set me down on the bench.

"I'm not a dog, Sal."

He turned, a playful sly grin on his devastatingly handsome face as he trotted backward. "Aren't you now?"

I frowned, grumbling about flea baths, and watched him go. I didn't like that he had changed so much. It felt like he was trying to cater to me instead of what we had promised. I'd have to find an opportunity to piss him off soon. Get the claws back out. As much as I loved waking up to flowers and him doting on me, I missed the sting of his brutality, too.

I was lost in thought, watching the delicious flow of his body under his clothes, when César dropped onto the bench on the opposite side of the table. My attention begrudgingly pulled from the tall hunk of a man I'd be riding that night, and I twisted to look at César. Best to get acclimated to his cadaver look now before the food actually came, but I was disappointed to see that, aside from the dark diseased-looking veins climbing his arms and throat and the slightly waxen cast to his skin, he was the normal César I had gotten used to seeing.

"Better?" he asked with a lopsided, clever grin.

"Much. What did you do?"

He tilted his head and exhaled a plume of night sky twinkling with stars and woven with rivulets of jade, then sucked it back in and winked at me. "There's passages in the old codexes about how to control the expanse of your spirit. No one has really bothered to try the exercises enough to master them in ages. Since before the Spanish Rot began to spread. Since the Spanish betrayed their connections to the spirit realm long before they came to our shores, we didn't need to hide it from their eyes. The skill was one of the first that young cadejo were taught, to protect themselves and their spirits. It was a lost discipline. As our people became more infected with the plague that is the Spanish religion, they lost their spirit sight, too."

Sal set a plate before me, and I thanked him with a kiss to his cheek as he sat down with us. His hip was snuggled tightly against mine as I kept chatting with César. "So, if I'm following you, the fact I can see the spirit realm isn't a blessing from my goddess?"

"Spirit," he corrected quickly. "Though, really, they aren't much different. She's not a goddess, she's a spirit, but in our lands, they are the same thing. Unlike in the lands of the Europeans. But, to answer your question, no. If you have a blessing, it's not yet revealed itself. But it is of interest that, where the rest of us have lost the ability to bond with a cadejo without a ritual, you managed to do it while you were still in Pampers. And now you also have an ability most of our people don't even have a whisper of anymore. Most of the priests have the ability, but they've trained for years to see even half of what you can see with any sort of clarity and, even then, only with extreme focus and attempting to do it. You can do it without even trying. Though, it does come with the downside of us needing to be a little more careful about how you see things."

I nodded along with him, sure that whatever he was saying would all make sense as I got deeper into training. "Wait . . . there's training, right? You're going to give me some sort of training montage, right? I have no clue what I'm doing or the rules or what I'm not allowed to do. Itzelco—"

"Do not say her name out loud, Xochi."

"Why? You say Itzatecuani's name out loud all the time."

"He's also the most powerful cadejo in the pack."

Sal snorted around a bite of ham. "It's basically a 'fuck you' to anyone who is not totoco. It says that I am so powerful that they can know the name of my spirit, and I'm not scared of them knowing it. It says that I don't give a shit what they know about me and that I'll still kick their asses into origami."

"You know you talk a lot of shit for someone who, in the face of battle, didn't even get his weapon wet," snarled the spirit within me.

It was a strange sensation to feel your mouth and tongue move without your permission and your voice to come spilling out without you telling it to. I didn't think I liked it much.

Sal's baleful black gaze slid to me, and he grinned a fanged smile. "Oh, you want me to get my weapon wet, hmm, little flower?"

César watched us bat each other around placidly with the great patience of a bedraggled nanny before he cut in with a delicate cough, drawing my attention back to him. "Anyway. What I was saying was that *she* said I needed to feed soon. And I know that feeding off of totocan is a death sentence. So, I guess I'm going to need lessons on how to feed her?"

Sal cocked a brow at the two of us, eyes darting back and forth. "Is someone going to tell me how my mate knows that? Either of you?"

César and I got awkward, looking everywhere but at him. We were about as stealthy as two neon-green signs.

"Xochitl."

Sal's bark of my name made me wince.

"It's not César's fault. See, I found Jake's ring and freaked out. And came and sat in the courtyard to be closer to other people so that, if Jake was here, he couldn't throw me in the back of a car or something." I spilled my guts. "And the totoco cleared out, and César helped me calm down, but told me that the totocan were scared of accidentally feeding on me because I was so scared."

Sal glared up at his cousin. "And you weren't going to tell me, brother? When was this?"

I winced at his accusation and steeled my spine. No more hiding. No more being scared. "It was the day of the belt."

He set down his fork and turned his full attention to me. His eyes, ringed by the floating onyx mist, darted between mine as he regarded me. There was anger in his eyes but also understanding. "That's why you ran?"

I nodded softly, doing my best not to look away from him. "One of the reasons, yeah . . . Jake never takes off that ring. If it was down in the creek, that means he was down in that creek. And the only reason he'd be back in the creek would be to spy on the totoco to find me. I had to get away before he caught me and dragged me back to them. Or worse, hurt you and the totoco."

Sal exhaled deeply, drawing in patience. "Xochitl, noyzotzon, Jake was here. That is, he had been here for a few days before. But he's dead now. Had you said anything to me, I'd have told you that." He pinched his brows. "No more hiding things."

"He's dead?" I gasped.

"He offered to buy you for a thousand dollars. He insulted my mate by stating her worth was a measly thousand dollars. He had to die." He rolled his shoulders in a far-too-casual shrug, and I stared at him.

"You can't just kill people, Sal!"

"Says who? You and Antonio keep saying this. And, yet I have. I will. I do. And who is to stop me?" He shoved a bite of food into his mouth and dismissed the idea.

"Speaking of . . ." César looked between the two of us again. "There's still the matter of Shayne, and I need to talk to the both of you about what I found today. Or, rather . . . what found me."

A fire of panic licked up my throat and was cut off by a sharp claw diving under the hem of my skirt to find my bare thigh. He rested his hand on the feverish skin, digging the claws in just enough to remind me I was here, that he was here, that I was grounded and home.

"What about Shayne?" I hazarded, my voice as thin as candle smoke.

César looked to Sal as if waiting for permission to go on. He nodded at him. "No more hiding things."

"Shayne was spotted in Chinameca yesterday. I have totocan crawling the town, but no additional sightings of him. We've beefed up the patrols along the road up the volcano, and the gate is locked at all times. If he comes, he will not catch us by surprise. What we haven't done is thought of a game plan for what happens if he does make it up the volcano."

I drew in deep breath after deep breath. "We won't go back."

My voice was steady, sure, magical. I felt my cadejo weaving into each word and soaking into the sound of my voice. I felt her inside of me, sliding through my blood and between my synapsis like a cool river washing over my skin. I felt like, if I looked down at my skin, it would sparkle with jewels as hers had.

"Then, that's what will happen. If he comes, he knows the consequences. I've already told him once, I will not tell him again. If he comes to my territory to steal my mate, he will have forfeited his right to mercy," Sal proclaimed as easily as he would decide on the menu items for the next day's breakfast.

I rolled my eyes. "And men say women are dramatic. Pack it in, Othello. Shakespeare in the Courtyard is next week."

César and Sal stopped dead and looked at me in shock. The whole totoco stopped, looking at me. "What?"

I squirmed under the dozens of pairs of eyes, then the first laugh broke the tension before the howls of laughter of the entire totoco joined in. I blushed and ducked my head in embarrassment.

"Ah, Cihuatlatoani, it's good to have you back." César sniffled and laughed with a wink.

My heart swelled with joy, and I grinned back at him.

CHAPTER FORTY-THREE

After dinner, Sal, César, and I were packed into Sal's truck and headed to the temple. I'd discovered that the temple lay down the valley away from San Miguel, on a small ridge that overlooked a blanket of trees bisected by a road that cut between El Vulcan and the Chinameca volcano. Somewhere along the ridges of the rolling foot of our volcano was the enchanted field of marigolds—that I had taken to calling the Field of Golden Memories—Sal and I had sat in.

From the outside, the temple resembled a massive reproduction of a hut, round and made of mud, with a woven, palm thatch roof. Even the double doors that led into the first atrium were hand-carved in wood and reminded me of something that a Mayan emperor would have commissioned. I ran my finger along the expertly carved and polished wood as we passed through it. A spark jumped from the wood to curl around my fingertip, like a wavering blue sprite, kissing it with a short jolt of power, then sliding back into the oblivion of the door. I frowned at it.

"What?" César asked, pausing on his journey and joining me as I examined the door.

"Nothing." I paused, drawing myself up and tapping on my inner strength. The bubble inside of me swelled with pride. "No, sorry. There's something here. It jumped up to my finger. Like a little blue ball of light. It zapped me just a little. It didn't hurt, but it was strange."

César scrubbed at his chin, examining it. "Interesting. And you've never seen it before?"

I gave him a look. "If I had, do you think I'd have mentioned it?"

He smirked and nodded, leading us back into the depths of the temple. "A mystery for another time. Though, I'm starting to suspect the more we have a true seer around, the more of those will pile up. I have to say, Xochi, I'm a little jealous. If I could, I'd crawl into your eyes and get lost in the world trying to figure out all the secrets we have lost."

"I'd like to just get through a single day without seeing something weird." I snorted at him.

"Isn't it all weird? When you haven't grown up knowing who and what you are?" He tilted his head.

The question stung. I knew he hadn't meant it to, but it dug into my skin. He was right. I had been given a gift as a young child and had it ripped away from me. I had no chance or opportunity to ease into any of my birthrights. I had been denied even the most basic of connections to my heritage, not knowing anything of who my people were or what their culture was like. Outside of this crazy new world of the paranormal, which had slowly become the norm, I knew nothing about who I was at my roots.

My mind drifted to my grandparents' smiling faces, the scents of their home and the slightly yellowed edges of my memories tugged at my heart. I didn't know where they were anymore. Did they still live in that house? Had they died? I didn't remember them being too old when I was a child, but their life was hard, even back before my mother abandoned them. I wondered if they knew. Did they know about the rue? Did they know about . . .

The bite of a claw pressing into the small of my back drew me out of my melancholy trip down memory lane. I looked up at Sal's face. Concern warred with annoyance in his deep oak eyes, framed by a swirl of midnight.

"I dislike wherever those thoughts led you," he rumbled down to me.

I offered him a thin, watery smile, and he crushed me against his body in a side hug. His lips dipped into my braid, and he murmured, "Tell me about it this evening, when I'm buried between your thighs. Until then, let's stay here, together."

Heat thumped at the ache between my thighs that I had done my best all day to ignore, but the tight sting of my core brought me back to the screaming furious fucking we had done last time within these walls. The memory of his claws digging into my shoulder as he forced me down on his knot brought a deep flush to my cheeks.

"Mmmm, that's a much better train of thought. Keep that in your mind," he growled into my ear and swatted my ass playfully.

César led us into the circular room, where I had met Itzelcoszcatl, but this time, there were more priests. The dazzling rainbow display of feathers shimmering with iridescence danced and swayed with their movement as they spoke among themselves.

"César, is this where you live?" I watched the priests eat their dinner of fruits and raw meat.

"Uh . . . yeah. That was my room you two trashed. Thanks for that, by the way. That wasn't awkward at all."

I groaned in embarrassment. We *had* trashed that room. Blood and cum coated about every surface.

"Aside from making my delightful little flower blush, why are we here, César? Why could we not talk about whatever this is in my rooms?"

Sal was getting annoyed—for what reason, I didn't know. I looked up at his eyes. The obsidian smoke was flowing like a river of tears down his cheeks and crashing like a black waterfall around his collar bones.

We took a seat with the priests as César gathered a file folder off of a table and handed it to me first. The blue folder seemed so out of place here in the temple. Its crisp, sanitary edges seemed at odds with the smell of copal and rich wood.

I cracked it open to medical reports. My name was emblazoned at the top of the first sheet of paper. Sal leaned in to examine it as I flipped through it. There were notes in English, Spanish, and what looked like maybe Portuguese? I turned page after page, not knowing what any of it meant or what I was looking at. When I landed on my blood results, or at least what I thought were my blood test results, César finally spoke.

"When I ran your test results, I got back a few strange results. Things I hadn't expected. Compounds and markers that looked odd, even for what I know now is a cadejo blood workup. So, I reached out to one of my colleagues in Boston. Jose Salazar has been a benefactor of many clinics here in El Salvador and is a brilliant geneticist. When he looked at the results, he was also a bit concerned about some of the marker results we found." He leaned casually against a table against the wall with Sal's battle depicted on it. "Neither of us expected much to come of it, so he ran it through a database to find any research associated with the genetic markers that we hadn't seen before."

Sal and I stared at César like he was speaking backward, neither of us understanding where he was going.

"Have you ever heard of Dr. James Belli, or the Pacific Center of Inter-discipline Research?" César asked.

I balked. "Of course I have. He's the doctor I went to when I was a kid. Remember I told you about the doctors my mom took me to when I got really sick?"

"When you got sick? Why didn't I know about this? When was that?" Sal snarled as his eyes darted between us.

"Not every conversation I've ever had involves you. Simmer down, Big Bad." I sarcastically soothed, patting his hand, rolling my eyes. "When I was a kid, I got really sick. I was weak and hungry all the time. I was throwing up. I couldn't keep anything down. My mom took me to a bunch of doctors, and, eventually, I went to Dr. Belli. He gave me a shot of something and prescribed vitamins. I never got sick again."

She had overdosed on the Rue. I was starving. I was dying. I don't know what he gave us, but it felt like food. It felt like joy. It made my teeth burn, Itzelcoszcatl whispered in my ear.

I scrunched my face at the feeling of her breath on my ear. "She says that she was starving and that my mom overdosed me. That's why I was sick."

César tilted his head and smirked. "She's growing stronger if she's able to speak to you more often. That's good."

Sal rubbed the back of my hand with his thumb, content to quietly listen to our discussion.

"Well," César went on, "that explains a few more things about the call I got this afternoon from Dr. Belli. He asked me if the specimen was fresh. He asked if the host was still alive. And when I told him yes and asked if the results were anything I should be concerned about, he offered to purchase the living specimen from me."

Sal was snarling a black dangerous thing. When I looked up to him, the onyx mist had disappeared, and tufts of fur had sprouted along his brow line, his sharp teeth bared in a ferocious lip curl. César seemed unconcerned and plowed onward.

"He offered me ten million dollars, plus relocation fees, to transport the specimen from El Salvador to San Bruno, where his labs are."

He tapped his jade claws on his exposed bicep as he watched the central fire. The only hint that the rage coursing through Sal beside me was shared in his reserved cousin. The priests seemed to give us privacy but also seemed like they had been informed of this, so the impact was not as devastating.

"He . . ." I couldn't wrap my mind around the idea of buying people. "He offered to buy a person . . . like it was a side of meat."

"Yes. Exactly." César sighed, and Sal shifted next to me, digging those claws into my hand as he crushed it.

I looked up at him. The anger was palpable, rolling off of him in waves. I disentangled my hand from his and brushed it against his cheek, leaning in to whisper in his ear. "Save that for later. I miss your claws, Big Bad. But, until then, calm down. I am safe. You'll never let them touch me again."

He gulped and slid his onyx gaze to me. He stared into my eyes for a long time, his features softening back into the stern man who held my heart in his hand. "Never again," he whispered back in a softly growled promise.

César let us have the time and space to process, unobtrusively watching the other priests as they cleaned up their meal. One of them was not as patient as the rest, though. He cleared his throat, and all eyes turned to him. I immediately didn't like him. He had no swirling mist around him, but his skin was stone-like and reminded me of the crocodiles sunning themselves on the banks of the river. He turned large, yellow-green eyes on me with tiny slivers of pupils to examine me as I stared at him.

"It's obvious that your mother was aware of our kind. Do you know how? You are not of our blood, yet you are here, called by a strong mate and blessed with a spirit without being part of any of the acknowledged tribes. So. Who are you, and where did your mother come from?"

I narrowed my eyes at him. Yep, I didn't like this man. "I have no clue how she knew about cadejos. She never talked to me about it. Until I met Sal again, I didn't even know about the supernatural existing. And, as far as I know, my mom is from somewhere in Mexico, or at least her parents are. They immigrated to the states in the sixties. As far as I know, my mom was born in the states? I really don't know what is true and what is made up anymore."

The crocodile man frowned and narrowed his eyes on me. "And yet you supposedly house a powerful cadejo spirit and have drawn the eye of one of the most powerful tecutli in the nations." His frown deepened as I glared daggers at him.

The bubble inside me stretched thin, and the crystalline waters of my inner goddess slipped between the plasma of my blood. I wished I knew how to trade shadows so I could rake claws across this man's face and see if that crocodile skin was as strong as the real thing. Instead, I chose words. Sal opened his mouth as I was about to unleash on him, and I had to press a hand to my mate's shoulder to still him.

"Supposedly? It sounds to me like you are aiming at something, Croc Face. So, spit it out."

He blanched a little, and César winced behind me. Right. Not supposed to tell people I can see their forms. Well, too bad. I wasn't taking it back.

"I am merely saying that it is strange that you claim that no one performed the ritual to bind you to a spirit. Yet, your mother seems to know so much about our kind. And, if the stories are to be believed, then Itzatecuani saw you as a child and claimed you as a mate even before Itziquetzal was able to make a choice on his own as a man. It seems very convenient that you have all these privileges and none of us could even confirm them."

César snarled behind me, and I held out a hand to him as well. They kept calling me Cihuatlatoani. It was time I stepped up and acted like it. I pressed my palms to the table before me and calmly rose from my seat.

Unyielding brutality. Their creatures all understand strength and power. I am here if you need it. I am not too weak to slash some sense into these pissants. I can smell them, none of them are as strong as I am, Itzelcoszcatl whispered in my ear, birthing an ugly smile to curl on my lips.

"It sounds to me like you are jealous, Croc Face. I'm not sure about what, though. Are you jealous that a spirit chose me, and she's easily ten times stronger than your pathetic excuse for a crocodile? Or are you jealous that, when I leave here, I'll have Itziquetzal's cock stuffed so far up inside of me that I'll be able to taste it? Or are you jealous that, when he falls asleep at night, he'll be thanking the teotl that I didn't suck his spirit out through his cock? Which one is it?" I stalked toward him, hunting him through the room as he slowly backed away from me, cornering himself against a table. I pressed him into it, grinding my cotton skirt-covered hips into his. I took deep inhales of his fear-laced scent. It didn't squelch the twist of hunger in my stomach, but it still made both myself and the spirit within me purr with triumph. "Or is it that you're jealous of Itziquetzal getting to get down on his knees and bury his face in my pussy whenever he chooses? 'Cuz I gotta say, Croc Face, as ugly as that face is, not even a glazing of my cum would make it pretty enough for me to let you at me. So. How about you spit it the fuck out. What's the issue."

"Holy fuck," César groaned behind me in a whisper.

"I'm a lucky fucking man," Sal replied with a thump I assumed was him punching César.

I only had eyes for my prey, though. I could almost hear his heart slamming against his ribs as I snorted his scent, and he stammered. "I'm just saying that it's awfully convenient and asking if may— maybe your mother . . . maybe . . . maybe she did something to—"

I slammed my fist into the table next to him, making him jump.

"Don't ever question my mating again." I sweetened my voice as I eased away from him, gently rearranging and sorting out his leather bib. "It's just not good manners, my dear Croc Face."

"His name is Cypriano," someone pitched in from my right.

"I rather like Croc Face. It suits him."

My voice was saccharine and soft as I pushed away from him.

"He does bring up a good point, Cihuatlatoani. While your mating is obviously a true love match blessed by the teotl, it does not eliminate the possibility of your mother having something to do with it," a woman offered as I padded back to Sal.

He looked like a man starved of pussy, and I liked that look on him. Where this titanium spine had come from, I didn't know, but I knew I liked the feeling of it.

I looked back to Nebula Woman, the priest who had been so kind when I woke up. I softened immediately. She was not saying these things to harm me. At least that was the instinct I had about her, unlike Croc Face, who left a slimy feeling on my skin whenever he looked at me.

"It's possible. I wouldn't put anything past that woman. If she can kill a cadejo in the chest of her only son, poison her daughter for years, and force her into a relationship she didn't want for years to her benefit, then she could be capable of anything."

"We've gotten off topic," César said, drawing my attention up to his waxen face. "Regardless of what Annette did or didn't do, this doctor trying to buy cadejos is concerning. Especially knowing that he had treated Xochitl when she was a child. I'd like to question you and your cadejo about what you remember about these interactions. If you would be so inclined, that is."

I paused, looking inward for her answer. She squirmed inside of me, not liking the idea of revisiting the memories of being trapped, but she relented. "Fine, but I swear to fuck you aren't punching your slimy claws into my chest again. We'll talk like civilized people. No chest punching."

I turned to Sal, César chuckling to my side, and kissed his cheek. "Don't go anywhere, Big Bad. I'll be back in a while."

César and I retreated to his room and began the arduous task of reliving memories I would rather have let die in the past.

CHAPTER FORTY-FOUR

A week passed since César's bomb of information about my childhood doctor. A week Sal and I did everything short of digging the information from my brain to avoid letting me think about the many twists and turns and potentials that Annette could have been up to. It had become hauntingly clear that my mother knew a lot more about the world I was now a full part of than she let on, and it was not put to good use. The lingering questions we still had were about me. It felt better to center my thoughts on how things applied to me versus how many ways my mother could have fucked me over.

The nightmares had started two days ago, or so I thought. I woke up with a sweaty start, being violently pulled into Sal's arms and crushed against his naked, panting chest. At first, he said nothing, just let both of our racing hearts calm down. And then the questions came. At first, it was hard. That lingering dread associated with the idea of losing him to the darkness of my past consumed my will to talk and to keep our promise to each other.

He'd spanked it out of me, chasing every last thought aside from bending to his will from my mind, and when I finally relented and told him I had dreamed that I woke up in Shayne's bed, under him, shackled to the bed and unable to feel Itzelcoszcatl anymore, he held me until the sun rose. When I woke up this morning the same way, the determination on Sal's face scared me. He needed blood and fear to quench his thirst for vengeance, and I needed his arms.

We had been at an impasse for far longer than I had liked, but at least, when it passed, we were on the same side again.

I had not expected him to take a deep, grounding breath after I tried to apologize for the nightmare disturbing him.

"It's not the first time," he whispered into the crown of my curls. "I just hoped that, with everything settling down, they'd stopped."

Ice washed over me as my entire body paused. "What?" I asked in a half whisper.

"You've had them since you first came here. I assumed that maybe it was just the change of scenery. I thought maybe you were too scared of everything around you to not be haunted in your dreams." He nuzzled his nose into the knotted pile of spirals. "It's been a few days now. You haven't had one since we came back from the temple that first night. I thought maybe they'd gone away."

"You never told me."

The fragility in my voice made him squeeze me against his naked skin.

"No . . . I didn't. I didn't want to face that they might be of me. And, when we started fresh, I didn't want to bring them back by talking about them. And I'd hoped that they were gone for good." His thick fingers pet the length of my hair as he spoke, calming me and pulling down the ruffled spikes within me. "Do you remember them? When you're awake?"

"No . . . not usually. If you didn't tell me I had them, I'd say this was the first one I'd had in a long time." I puffed out on an exhausted exhale.

He nodded against my curls and pulled me bodily on top of him, where he wrapped the iron bands of his arms around me and squeezed me until we fell asleep again.

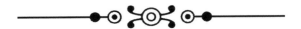

We were back up on the caldera, just us two practicing. He had told me I needed to learn quickly before my cadejo became too weak to feed without aid. So, here we were, away from others, staring at each other. His instructions made little to no sense.

"Reach out and touch her" was about as useful as telling me to paint the stars, and I was getting frustrated.

Sal shoved a hand through his ruined braid. Okay, maybe the trip up to the volcano wasn't a complete waste of time. I hadn't minded pushing him into the obsidian he'd so callously ground my knees into not too long ago, when I rode him until he was clawing at my thick thighs and filling me with his pleasure again. His hair might have gotten ruined when I'd ground atop him, or it might have been when we'd both gotten annoyed at my lack of progress, and he decided the best way to inspire me was to bury his face between my soaked thighs and make me sing like a motmot. The way the red dust and flecks of obsidian clung to his sweat-soaked, bare chest and dusted in the midnight curtain of his hair made me lick my lips with hunger.

He quirked a brow at me and smirked. "Settle down, temptress. Keep looking at me like that, and we're going to be late. I need you to be able to feed yourself before we leave this ridge. Even if that means I have to decline the way your lips are begging me to choke you on my cock."

"Mmmm," I purred up at him, tracing my finger up his abs.

The security of being one with my cadejo unlocked a thirst for my mate I had no idea was even possible before. Or maybe I had just finally found a place where I felt safe, protected, and secure. Maybe it was that my bones were getting stronger and planted more firmly in the earth every day. Whatever it was had me ravenous for him at all times, and I could barely go a day without tasting his skin.

"Promises, promises."

He growled at me and kissed me with a ferocity that melted my body against him. Too early, he ripped away from me and panted against my lips. "Please, nonamic. Mercy. Do this for me."

I sulked and nipped at his lip. "Fine. But only because I can tell César I finally won our bet."

"What bet?"

"Oh, I bet him two hundred dollars that I could make you beg before the end of the month. I won." I winked.

"Fucking César."

I laughed. The twinkling sound of two crystals lovingly rubbing together danced on the warm afternoon air. "I'm joking. Now, think happy thoughts, or I'll never get to figure this out."

I closed my eyes and took a deep breath. My mind opened, and I traced a mental finger against the bubble I learned was the barrier between Itzelcoszcatl and me. She moved against the barrier, like a hand pressed against the shower curtain to touch the skin of the person inside of it. She pressed against the barrier, and for a moment, she slid her fingers into mine. Sparks like bursting gemstones popped in my consciousness, and I reached out, imagining the opal-skinned arms of the goddess mirroring my unseen arms. I pictured Sal in front of me, delicious muscles flexing in the sunlight, and traced my imaginary finger over his chest.

A pulsing aurora borealis shimmered in my mind, and I opened my eyes. He was staring at me, a smile on his hammered bronze lips. All around him waltzed that aurora in a rainbow of colors, each wave tipped in a golden mist.

"Good. Now, draw it to you." He stepped closer. As he moved, the waves of color pulsed with his heartbeat. "Slowly. Draw slowly."

I imagined those mirrored hands dipping a finger into the pulsing kaleidoscope ocean and drawing back. I imagined the maw of jagged teeth opening and a long tongue flicking out to lick the dripping paint of pure happiness from my fingers. The moment it touched my mental tongue, I felt it wash through me, like taking the first sip of hot chocolate after a blisteringly cold winter's day. I shuddered, a sensation like a stomach rumbling shivered through me.

So hungry, she murmured in my ear.

"Again. More this time," he barked at me.

Again, I extended my vision of my arms side by side with her opal-skinned arm, and, this time, instead of a single finger, I dipped my entire fist.

"Easy. Slow. Take your time. Your prey is not running or fighting. Take this time to be sure about the amount you take. Remember, what you draw off, you are taking from your prey. Until you can learn to use your gifts to seed the flowers of your meal and harvest it like a farmer, you will need to be conscious of how much you take. Too much and your prey will be damaged beyond repair."

The moment he said that, I shook the hand dipping into the honey jar of his emotions and withdrew it like it had been bitten.

"Sal! What if I take too much? What if I hurt you?"

Concern replaced the consuming hunger that made my teeth itch to sink into something.

Without hesitation, he was pressed against me, a hand cupping my jaw and lifting my eyes to his. His voice was soft, a small whisper of silken night brushing my lips, as he hovered over them. "Take as much as you need, hungry little ghost. I have more than any man could ever hope for. Every day, I see your smile fills me with more joy than any creature on this planet has any right to keep to himself. Keep smiling, keep laughing, keep fighting, keep biting, and I will be your banquet for the rest of our lives if I need to be."

My heart clenched in my stomach, and I felt the burning prickle of tears forming in my eyes as I stared up at him. A future as long as time stretched out in his glittering deep burnet eyes, and I wanted it. I genuinely wanted to be right here with him for every last minute of it. Smiling, I nodded to him as he pressed a soft kiss to each of my glistening eyes.

"Now. Try again," he purred down at me before stealing a quick peck and stepping back again.

Bolstered by his faith in me, I reached out with my imaginary arms, both hands caressing his form. I didn't have to wonder if he felt them. The shiver that rippled over his skin and thickened in his jeans told me he could. When I found that aurora again, I thrust my fist into it and clenched it around the dripping artist's palette, wavering around him. I drew it back to me, and I saw the moment it left him. He swayed on his heels, the aurora shimmering and quivering under the weight of my mental tug, dimming just slightly. I watched in wonder as I drew the happiness away from him and let it slide down the mouth within my soul. Warmth suffused my limbs, chasing away any ache, innervating my nerves, and making me bounce on my toes with bubbly giddiness.

A twinge of concern at how it affected me had me casting my eyes back to Sal to check on him. The light display that burst from him twisted my guts with hunger and the aching weight of untainted elation. I had thought the undulating, shifting colors were bright before, but they exploded in a riot of a blinding, vibrant, throbbing rainbow. I wanted to laugh. I wanted to scream. I wanted to do everything all at once. Instead, I settled for running into him and throwing my arms around him.

"I did it!"

"That you did, hungry little ghost." He flicked the tip of my nose, gazing down at me with pure adoration. "Now, before we are even later, let's get home. I need you showered, dressed, and thoroughly fucked before seven. Not necessarily in that order."

I grinned and threaded my fingers into his, swinging his arm as we traveled down the path toward the compound. "Where are we going?"

He snorted. "Nope. It's a surprise."

"I hate surprises," I said, screwing up my face in annoyance. I had started to like Sal's surprises, but I was absolutely not going to tell him that.

"I thought we talked about lies," he said with that old wolfish grin I loved so much.

"Fiiiiine." I sighed. "Maybe a little hint?"

"Keep asking, and you're getting a hood for the drive," he grumped down at me, though I could see the way his lips were fighting a smile.

"So, it's a drive? So, the fields? No. Can't be the fields. No point going out there at night. Hmm. Not the temple. There'd be no point in keeping that a surprise. Into town? Why would we go down there? And why would that be a surprise?" He was trying so hard to keep a scowl on his face, and the more I pushed, the more he was almost winning. So, I pushed harder. Much harder. "Oh, I know! You're finally going to follow through on that date night with César you promised me? I'll be sure to shave all my bits."

He growled, and I danced away from his grabbing hands. "Catch me if you can, Big Bad," I teased with a wink as I took off running. "And no trading shadows! It's not fair!"

"Oh, little flower, haven't you learned by now? I never play fair. Run, run, run, little flower. When I catch you, I'm putting you over my knee until you beg me to stop."

He made good on that promise, though I was just sure he had timed that. I had no delusions that, even in his human skin, he could fully chase me down, but he let me have the illusion of winning until I was tossing open the front door of our rooms. I was about to celebrate my victory when the iron of his massive arm wrapped around my stomach and pulled me back into the marble slab of his body.

His teeth—thankfully human—buried themselves into the flesh of my throat with a growled, "Mine." He lifted me off the ground as I struggled, dragging me toward the bedroom. Every time I kicked, he bit down harder.

He fucked me into dizziness on the tile floor of the hallway, neither of us able to resist long enough to make it to the bedroom. He was a cruel taskmaster and waited until after I was a boneless, spent, and well-satisfied mess to darken my ass cheeks with his hand prints.

Two hours later, I met him in the living room in a new dress I had found on the bed, this one embroidered with dazzling obsidian-beaded feathers. Joining them, unlike on my other dress, were iridescent beads. Some bordered the feathers, some wove in and out of them, and some made up entire feathers. It was a beautiful pairing of our two essences, and I loved it. I had pushed my curls into some semblance of manageable, and the two obsidian feather barettes he had given me held back half of the front of my hair assaulting my face. I so rarely got to wear them, but they paired so beautifully with the dress he had chosen.

He was dressed up as well. A black button-up was tucked into dark charcoal slacks, rolled up at the sleeves and a matching charcoal vest buttoned up over it. I wanted to tear it all off of him and bruise my knees on the tiles, worshipping that gorgeous length he had hidden away behind those mouthwatering slacks. When my eyes traveled down his body, they caught on the black fabric in his hand, and I frowned.

"What the hell is that?"

"Oh, did you think I'd forget, nayeli?" He sucked his teeth with a grin that promised he'd walk me himself through the gates of hell and drop me off into the flames.

"You aren't serious?" I laughed, mistakenly stepping backward.

His prey drive flashed behind his glittering obsidian gaze, the pools of black smoke making the flash even more menacing. It made my heart race with unspoken, lascivious promise.

"Oh, I'm very serious. Don't run, nayeli. I'll chase you. And, when I catch you, my plans will be ruined, and you'll have to make it up to me. Be a good girl, and you'll get a treat."

I forced my legs to stop moving. I wanted to be his good girl. I liked being his bad girl, but I loved being his good girl. I loved the way he moaned those two words when his hands were buried in my hair and pulling sharply as praise rained down from his lips.

"Good girl, Xochitl," he purred, slipping the black bag over my head.

The world went black, and all I could latch onto was the scent of his skin, the warmth of his breath, and the sound of my heartbeat. When he pressed a kiss through the fabric to my lips, I swayed with the powerful need to follow, to curl up at his feet and do whatever it was he wanted.

Two hours later, I was on the edge of my seat. Every time I had opened my mouth to ask if we were there yet, he'd pushed my panties aside and pinched my clit. He never let me get too close to the edge, though, even when I asked silly questions like why the sky was blue, just to earn another pinch that I'd grind down on. By the time he was opening my door, I was ready to knock him down and tear off his clothes, but the sounds and smells around me drew my attention away from him and to what I could sense around me.

Itzelcoszcatl writhed with delight beneath my skin, like a fish swimming in a plastic bag fresh from the fair. I couldn't see the aurora bursting around me, but I could feel its twists and turns flavoring the air like cherry Jolly Ranchers, making my mouth water.

Sal's hand taking mine and drawing me slowly toward an unknown destination had my senses trying to split themselves between the buffet that I could feel peppering my skin with little sparking kisses. I stepped up when he whispered for me to do so, stepped where he told me to, trusting this man who I had somehow been blessed to have barge into my life like a bull in a china shop, shattering all my expectations, preconceived notions and fears, only to glue me back together with a solid sense of self and a slowly growing deep abiding love for me.

When he gathered me into his arms and pressed me against him, I almost tripped. Nervous laughter bubbled on my lips, and soft yellow light filled my eyes as the bag was pulled away. I blinked, trying to draw shapes into solid form again.

It was the square we danced in, filled to the gills with people, all joining the dancefloor as the band finished their preparations for the evening. The string lights seemed so much brighter than I remembered. The stars hung close in their seats in the velvet sky as if whispering conspiratorially about the scene they knew was about to unfold. Happiness flowed all around me, floating on unseen breezes, twisting and twirling on currents of heartbeats. I smiled up at Sal, who had eyes only for me, like he did that night.

"Eat up," he murmured. "Slowly. And not too much from one person. If you feel stuck or need help, just tap my hand. I am here. I will keep you from hurting anyone. Little sips. There's enough here for you to sample everyone without hurting anyone."

The strange rumbling stomach that lived somewhere in my throat and heart growled with appreciation for the bounty before it. I needed to trust, and I needed to have faith I would harm no one. The consequences of drawing too much off of a single person could be catastrophic. César had told me a little about it over dinner, how a white cadejo could leave a human unable to ever feel joy again. The thought of walking around this beautiful world, unable to feel happiness, a blank, gray slate until you finally died, sounded like true hell. I never wanted to do that. Even the thought of feeding off of someone's happiness made me squirm with unease.

Sal's arms wrapped around me and held me tight to him as the music started. I focused on the hands that itched in my psyche, flexing them to test my dexterity. I could do this. I could feed my goddess and prove to myself I wasn't a monster who would steal a person's only reason for living. He swayed us, moving my body with his to the music, as I reached out a tentative psychic hand into the first light field. It tasted different from Sal, somehow less bright and sumptuous. But, as I licked it off of that imaginary finger, it still washed through me like the kiss of a warm hearth.

I watched, taking in every microscopic twitch of the man I had drawn from. I waited, breath catching in my throat, to see if he swayed on his feet, to see if my nibble was too much. My eyes grew hot and itchy from my intent, unblinking stare. When his rich, burbling laughter drummed through the thin space between us as his date swished her hips and bumped his on purpose, I finally exhaled. He was unharmed. From the looks of it, he hadn't even noticed the predator in his midsts.

Confident I could draw off of a human without hurting them, I cast those two hands in different directions, dipping into the hearts of two people at once. A tingle ran up my spine, and Sal's fingers dug into my hips, pressing me against his body in case I needed his support. I didn't, but I would never turn away the press of him against me again. I rested my head on his chest.

The bubble between me and my cadejo thinned, and I felt her surge within me and around me. I expected to feel my skin ripping and the exchange happening, but she kept herself close to the surface without pushing me into a trade. She took over from there. I watched as that goddess of rainbows and opals danced unseen between the writhing bodies and laughter-filled faces. I watched as her tongue slid out, a hunter among the sheep that had no clue how close they were to a walking death consuming them for eternity. She was polite, at least, dragging a golden-tipped claw up the bared thigh of a woman, unseen and easily dismissed as a gust of wind. When the woman blushed with delight at her dance partner, Itzacoszcatl moaned—or was it me? Sal's fingers gripping my thigh said perhaps it was both—as she ran her tongue from her clavicle to her ear. I felt the heated zing of the energy rumbling through our connection.

She was an unseen primal spirit unleashed on the unsuspecting populace, hunting through the crowd, sampling their essence indiscriminately. I almost wished Sal could see what was in my mind. Orgies would look tame compared to the stalking, white-and-gold creature with deeply rounded, plush curves and honey tipped breasts bared to the night sky, purring with lavish delight as she fed freely for the first time since the two of us bonded. At least, as far as I knew.

When she was done and satisfied, the grueling empty hole within me sealed shut, capping her thirst for more. I imagined a delicate golden chain between us and pulled it back.

Clever girl. You learn faster than even our mate gives you credit for. Fine, I won't gorge myself on these creatures. For now. Perhaps next time, you will let me run free and slake my thirst. I heard her purr as she slid back into the depths of my soul, once again, unseen but felt.

"She is fed?" Sal asked when I gripped his vest and drew myself up for a kiss.

I nodded into his lips, not wanting to leave them ever again.

"Good," he murmured into my mouth and dipped me backward. "I remember this night so well. Do you?"

It seemed like decades ago. Another lifetime, another me entirely. I imagined a fragile woman on the verge of shattering into a thousand pieces under the weight of all the pressure that belonged to everyone else. I imagined the dark stranger who made that fragile, brittle woman shiver with delight and the guilt that pulsed through her in just accepting his kindness, let alone his adoration.

"I do," I whispered, the magic of that night resurging to grip us and drown out the rest of the world.

"I remember thinking there couldn't be a more beautiful woman in the world walking toward me when you got out of that cab. I felt like lightning had struck me." He swayed slowly to the song, one hand on my ass possessively and the other thumbing the line of my jaw. "And then you danced with me. I remember the feeling of you in my arms felt like home."

I blushed, remembering what had been running through my mind. "And then I ruined it by telling you I was engaged."

He playfully sucked his teeth, tipping my head up to look him in the eye. That eternity stretched out between us the moment our eyes locked. "I already knew. I heard how hard your heart had been pounding when you told me. And I thought to myself, 'This woman is here with a stranger, telling him she is engaged to another man. Anything could happen to her. And she wants to be here so badly. And, yet she's willing to throw that all away to do the right thing.' I remember thinking that you had the heart of a lion in your chest, and I was smitten. I wanted so badly to tell you who I was to you. But I wanted to earn your love. I wanted so badly just to beg you not to run from me."

"I'm pretty sure you like it when I run from you." I grinned up at him, the bubble of emotions building within me unable to shut the hell up.

"Oh, no, little flower, I *love it* when you run from me. I would run my legs to nubs chasing you all over the earth if I needed to. I would chase you into the gates of the deadlands. Wherever you go,

I will be there. Always." He sealed that promise with a tender kiss that poured his love into me.

I swam in the sea of his overwhelming adoration, letting it fill me from toe to brow. He didn't deepen the kiss like I expected him to. I expected him to ravage my mouth, but he kept the kiss heartfelt, and it made my own swell within my chest.

When he pulled away, I was dizzy and short of breath, my hand drifting from his shoulder to my head to keep it from spinning off my shoulders and floating into the atmosphere.

"Xochitl, my beloved flower."

He called my attention back to him, love sparkling in his eyes as he searched mine. He was nervous. I could feel it shivering in his muscles as he tried not to crush me against him. He fished something from his pocket, then took my hand and folded my fingers around the cool stone. I broke eye contact to stare at the baby fist-sized clear quartz breaking the light into a thousand shards of rainbows.

I stared at it for a long time as the memories of a sun-drenched park and three knobbly kneed kids, flooded back in perfect clarity. Tears burned at my eyes as the memories of our time together as children washed into me.

I remembered. I remembered the serious young man, kneeling in the grass, asking me to marry him. I remembered the ridiculous ceremony performed under a tree and how a strange, overwhelming feeling had overcome me, and I had to run off, run away from him before . . . I didn't even know what would have happened, at least then, I didn't.

Itzelcoszcatl purred within my mind. Her velvety fur curled around the memory, reminding me of a dragon wrapped around its horde protectively. Her molten gold heart pounded and throbbed around the memory. *This was mine. All I had. All I could live off of. It belonged to me until you released me again.* Her voice was full of soft reverence, love, tenderness that seemed so sharp on a creature so primordial. *Now it is ours. Cherish it as I have.*

Tears slipped down my cheeks as I looked up at Sal's face. He brushed one away with the rough pad of his thumb as he hiked his slacks up and got down on one knee. A small box magically appeared in his hand while I was staring at the stone in my hand. My breath caught in my throat. My heart was freaking out, running around, screaming and thrashing against my ribs, trying to burst free and scream its joy to the entire world.

"Xochitl Angelica Esparza, we've done this before, but, this time, for real. Will you marry me? Will you be my mate, my wife, my partner, and equal in all things? Will you let me catch you for the rest of our lives?"

His voice hitched, caught on the titanic weight of the emotion rolling off of him. I saw it, saw Itzatecuani curling in a great black plume of smoke behind him, and the aurora of pure joy was almost too bright to even see through.

I couldn't reply. Emotion constricted my throat. So, I did the only thing I could think of . . . I ran. Or at least, I jogged. He growled a laugh behind me and ran after me. When he got close, I sped up. When he got too far behind, I dropped back. We played cat and mouse all the way to his truck, where I let him finally catch me. His teeth were buried in my throat with a possessive growl, and his hands were hiking up my skirt to dive under my panties and find my center. He didn't push it further, just claiming and holding tight to his prize. I moaned against him, my body wedged tightly between his truck and his equally unyielding body when he fluttered soft kisses up and down the column of my throat.

"I'll have my answer, little flower," he groaned into my ear as I pushed my ass back against the stiff length of him.

"Do I need to spell it out for you, Big Bad?" I twisted, facing him and jumping to wrap my legs around his body. Any other man, and I wouldn't have had the confidence that he'd catch me. Sal did, though. Sal would always catch me. "I will marry you on one condition, Itziquetzal Almendárez."

"Name it. Anything. I will give anything to be yours." He panted into my lips.

"Will you take my mate mark into your spirit?" My hips ground down on him, daring him to deny me.

"I'm pretty sure that's my line, little flower. But, yes. Of course. I am yours in all ways, forever."

He kissed me then, cutting off any additional discussion, and I drowned in that sea and pushed into him my own. I held him close, my heart bursting with everything I felt for him. I wanted to die in his arms, but most importantly, I wanted to *live* in his arms. I wanted to be his everything because he was my everything. All the cuts and scrapes that brought us here, back to this little street, into this puddle of orange-yellow light, didn't matter, but they would always be part of the unique story that was us.

We made love until dawn, not even bothering to make it home. We crashed into his suite at his hotel and devoured each other with the passion and hunger of two people finally allowing themselves to want everything that they always dreamed of but thought they could never have. Sometime between streetlights and the break of dawn, we made a few plans, and a beautiful, simple gold band was slipped onto my finger. I didn't need more than that. I didn't even want more than that. I had him in every way that counted. He had me in every way that counted, and soon, we would be emblazoned upon each other's souls for all of eternity. I fell asleep tangled in his limbs and dreamed peacefully of our future together.

We woke to a jarring ringing of the phone next to the bed, tangled together like necklaces tossed into a jewelry box. Sal groaned into my breast, where his head still rested, while I slapped at the offensive ringing. Somehow, I hit speaker phone.

"Sal? Xochi?" César's voice called out.

"What?" I asked with a voice still hoarse from screaming my ecstasy all night.

"Xochi, is Sal with you?"

"Where exactly do you think I'd be with my mate sounding like that, brother?" he growled without lifting his head. "Make it quick. I'm not done ravaging her just yet."

A long, suffering, exhaled sigh came through the phone.

I could almost hear him thinking about how much he hated us. Good. Let him hate us. I was just fine with that as long as I got to keep testing exactly how much torment I could take from the naked god stretched out over me.

"Did Jamal happen to crawl into your truck?"

Jamal was Ximenia's brother's son, a young ten-year-old cadejo. A rascal who loved playing hide-and-seek . . . especially when no one knew he was hiding. It was his favorite thing to do, scare his auntie and mom into hysterics, who would try to hunt him down, only for him to jump out from behind some shadow they hadn't searched. More than once, he'd mistaken me for his mother and pounced from the shadows to knock me down.

"No, not that we saw, and we've been here all day," Sal said around a massive yawn as he stretched. He pressed lazy wet kisses around the hill of my stomach, fingers walking across the silken expanse that pebbled and tingled for him.

"Can you go check? Just to be sure."

"César, if you ask my mate to move even an inch, when we get back to the compound, I'm kicking your ass," I moaned. "He's not with us. He's probably just hiding. He'll turn up."

"Good bye, César," Sal hissed and reached over me to rip the phone from the wall before he dipped below the covers to make me sing again.

CHAPTER FORTY-FIVE

"So, if we invite the Council, too, how many people would that be?" I asked, scratching my head and staring down at the scribbling on the notebook between César, Julia, Sal, and me.

Julia groaned. "Too many. Do we have to invite them?"

We sat in the courtyard, after dinner, soaking in the beautiful weather of the early evening, planning out the wedding that was far more complex than I wanted. Sal insisted the wedding be a massive affair, according to tradition, and even though I groused about not needing a big fuss over it, he only dug his heels in even more.

Julia had not helped. As soon as she spotted the gold band on my finger at lunch that afternoon, she proclaimed with a vicious growl she would "take the eyes of any bitch who thought she was in line for the procession."

I still had not a single clue what that meant, but I was getting the idea it was something akin to a bridal party. She also backed Sal's camp of having a massive event. César and I groaned when the chalkboards, notebooks, and chess pieces came out. Where exactly Julia had been stashing this mini Pinterest board, I had no idea, but, apparently, she had been planning my wedding longer than I even contemplated it as a possibility.

When I'd asked if it was appropriate to sit around the compound and plan a wedding, while the rest of the totoco scoured the landscape for Jamal, Sal had assured me he would be located. I still wasn't comfortable with the idea, especially after Sal had come back from his own excursion into the jungle to search for the young boy. We'd had a tense discussion settled by Sal commanding that we could not stop time for one misbehaving child. He'd tried to smooth it over when I told him to get fucked if he thought I'd be so easily quelled in my concern for our people. His eyes softened as he stroked my cheek, crooning that cadejo children often spent a few nights in the jungle when they were young and newly merged with their spirits and that it was common for them to need space to commune.

I was still not convinced. Guilt twisted through me in the slow creeping choke of kudzu, and I gnawed on my lip with indecision when left too long with my own quiet thoughts. Sal knew cadejo children better than I did or ever would, but some small part of me still wasn't sure he was right. Even Itzelcoszcatl twisted within me in conflict with her primal instincts to protect and hunt.

"We could opt out of inviting them to the ceremony, but they would want to be invited to the feast afterward, and I know that at least a handful of the older members would insist on attending the mate marking ritual." Sal scrubbed his hand down his face.

We had been at this already for three hours, and I had an itch to run and not be caught this time.

"Wait. What?" I whipped daggers at him, scowling. "Attend the what now? Come again?"

"Yeah . . ."

I glared between César and Sal. "Were either of you going to tell me that I have to fuck my mate in front of an audience? At any time before the actual event?"

"To be honest, Xochi, I fully intended on keeping my fat mouth shut until the very second you couldn't back out," César said in his easy, unruffled manner.

The stars made his proclamation even more irritating somehow.

Sal squirmed under my inspection, unwilling to admit anything. He suddenly stood. "It's getting chilly. Why don't I get you a blanket, nonayeli?"

He was trotting away before I could even smack him. "None of that 'my princess' shit, Itziquetzal—what's his middle name?"

"Rojelio."

"Seriously?"

"Si." Julia hissed the s, grinning.

"None of that 'princess' shit, Itziquetzal Rojelio Almendárez! I expect answers when you get back!" I shouted after him from across the courtyard.

He paused at the door and smiled, "Anything you wish, nonayeli," he shouted back before disappearing into the apartment.

The three of us laughed as the courtyard filled with the puddling headlights of a car coming up the road. Several members of the totoco had gone into different towns that dotted the base of the volcano and should have returned at any moment. All three of us looked to the car as it parked at the gates. I frowned. That was odd. Usually, the totoco vehicles would pull off into the worn grass. The only time vehicles stopped at the gates or beyond it was when there was trouble, if someone were hurt, or if they were unloading something.

"I bet Rafael got into another bar fight," César quipped as he rose from the table. "Send a group of caged-up cadejos out on a mission, and they will find trouble . . . or manufacture it."

"Or Ixchel finally castrated Antonio." I sighed and rose with him before joining him in a stroll toward the gates, expecting to have to bandage up one of our hapless totocan.

The closer we got, the more tension knotted in my stomach. I reached out to Itzelcoszcatl to run a finger over the thin membrane between us.

What is it? I asked her in a soft voice.

She squirmed against the membrane, pulsing a thrumming sense of danger. *Run.*

And then she was gone. I felt the pressure on the membrane as she pushed off of it to float back with speed to the spirit realm to hide. It was the first time since we had been properly introduced that she had ventured back into her native realm, and it made me more uneasy. I reached out and caught César's arm to caution him. His hazy hazel eyes fell to my hand, and he snapped his mouth closed on any question, as if he felt my trepidation through that single touch.

Three doors opened on the black town car that bled into the growing night, but the headlights were so bright I could see nothing.

"Angie."

My name on that voice curdled the air and sliced pounds of flesh from my arms. I knew that voice. My bones knew that voice. I couldn't breathe. My lungs refused to expand, calcified in my chest.

Shayne. Shayne was here, and he wasn't alone. Two massive men, easily six-foot-four and ten tons of stupid, flanked him as he came around the front of the car.

César growled next to me, and I barely registered the sound, my eyes locking on the specter of my nightmarish past, one I had hoped had found its grave.

Outlined by the car, Shayne looked like everything the movies thought an angel would look like. Tall, well muscled—but not from having ever worked a single hardship in his life but rather solely crafted for vanity. His blonde hair wasn't in his usual spiked style. Instead, it was natural and floating around his head in a carelessly coifed faux pompadour. Nothing about this man was effortless. He'd spend more time in the bathroom than I ever had. A sharp, tailored, soft gray linen shirt clung to his chest, drawing the attention up to his sparkling summer sky eyes creased at the corners, with a sleazy two-hundred-dollar-an-hour rented smile.

"Who is this?" César snarled next to me.

Shayne tilted his head at him, ever the actor. "You must be the man that took my wife. I had tried to be a good man, even sent our agent to negotiate with you. I assume you killed him since he never came back. Shame, really."

"Shayne," César growled. "You're not welcome here."

The sound of soft footsteps behind me rang in my ears, but no one reacted to them, and they retreated.

I was stuck. The images from my nightmares crashed into me, threatened to melt the hard-won steel spine, and petrified my muscles. All I could see was him shirtless, thrusting above me while I floated above my body, screaming at myself to slit his throat but unable to move. I wanted to move. I needed to move. I screamed inside my head to just *move*.

"That's fine, pal. I'll just take my wife, and I'll be off. You can go back to licking rocks or whatever it is you people do." His cornflower-blue eyes turned back to me, and I felt every molecule of my skin scream in protest. "C'mon, Angie, let's go."

I didn't move. I couldn't move.

"Angie, don't make this more difficult than it already has been." When I didn't move, he nodded to the two, who leveled their guns on César. "I know bullets won't kill these guys. Trust me, we've already tried. But rue darts will work just fine. Now, I've come for my property. Get in the fucking car, Angie, or I'll kill your little lover."

Rue. Darts.

Shayne knew.

"You knew?" I gasped out in a voice as thin and small as a single dandelion seed dancing in a hurricane's rage.

He laughed. "Of course I did. What the fuck do you think I was paying your mother for? It certainly wasn't to fuck you. You're the lamest lay I've ever had. Now, get in the fucking car. I won't say it again."

He knew. He knew. He knew. He knew.

Those two words echoed and clanged about in my head like church bells.

"I'm not your wife."

Whose voice was that? Whose voice was so tight, so starved for a grip to cling to? It couldn't have been mine. I hadn't heard that dried leaves in an autumn gale voice in so long that I didn't even recognize it.

The laughter was mirthless, cruel, and twisted as it crawled from between Shayne's perfectly moisturized lips. "Of course you are. Your mother signed the papers and the marriage license two weeks ago. Cost a pretty penny, but it was worth it."

Did he mean her purchase or the price of whomever was corrupt enough to accept a power of attorney signing a prenup and marriage license for an absent party? It didn't matter.

"I'm not your wife," I repeated, trying to convince myself this last salvo, this last brutalization of my agency, wasn't real.

"Oh, Angie. Still dumb as ever. Of course you are. Now, get in the fucking car, Mrs. Ellington."

Footsteps again behind me.

My eyes slid to César. I had known this moment might eventually come. I had feared it and eventually ignored it, hoping that, for just once in my miserable life, I could truly be happy. And now, here I was. Itzelcoszcatl had fled, and I had a choice: César's life or my own. It was a simple choice. The one thing I could count on was that, even if I left with Shayne, Sal and César would come for me again. I had faith in that.

Solid in my faith on how this would need to happen, I finally took a deep ragged breath and took my first step toward Shayne. The moment my foot fell, I knew it was the right thing to do. I might be grinding shards of glass into the pads of my feet as I took another step, but it was the only way. I didn't want to think about the alternatives. I didn't want to fall down the warren of things that could happen. I saw only one timeline, and I needed to have faith in that.

"Stop where you are, Xochitl."

Sal's voice rang out from behind me, deep and dark, but without the added gravel of Itzatecuani sharpening the edges.

We all turned to him as he stalked shirtless toward us. His eyes were locked on Shayne, the midnight smoke barreling down in livid black torrents that billowed behind him, almost obscuring the sight of the blooming hellebore that puddled around Julia's aura. She must have snuck away from the confrontation to fetch him. I wanted to kiss her. I decided, if I managed to get there, Julia would never get a single word of complaint from me, no matter what manner of wedding-related shenaniganry she wanted to get up to.

Shayne sneered. "Two? Really, Angie? I knew you were a whore, but who knew there'd be two that would want to have a dead fish in their bed."

One of the guards turned his gun on Sal, but Sal kept coming. Small plumes of dust whispered in the light of the headlights, drawing my eye down his body to his hand, where he clutched a freshly shorn blade of obsidian that cut into his flexing fist. Anger vibrated off of him, dark and dangerous. If Shayne had an inkling as to what Sal was capable of, he'd be smart to piss himself . . . Shayne was not smart.

"Ah-ah-ah. Stop right there, pal. There's no reason to die over a piece of ass. That one behind you seems cute enough. A little rough around the edges but better than a fat girl, right?" Shayne chuckled at his lame joke. "I know she's not much to look at, but she's well trained, and I don't want to have to go through all that again. So, just let me take her off your hands. Not like she could be doing much good here. She's completely talentless. Can't even suck a cock without teeth."

Sal was stalking Shayne. I could see it in the way he moved, slowly but with purpose. It reminded me of the way he had stalked Manny on the ridge that day. It reminded me that, behind his teasing grins and molten kisses, the man was deadly from his head to his bare toes that curled in the dust as he advanced with the patience of a jaguar.

"Sal . . . don't. He has rue," I whispered to him as he drew near.

Shayne laughed, the sound a cheese grater to my frayed senses. I wanted to cry, but I couldn't. I would never show Shayne my weak side. I would go with him if it saved Sal and César from being hurt, but if he thought he could hold a comet on a leash again, he would find himself renamed Chicxulub quickly.

"Shoot him. I'm tired of the bugs in this backwater bullshit," Shayne said, as if dismissing the lives it would affect.

Sal was all action, having drawn close. He moved in a stunning flash of black flames rippling off of him. I'd never seen this side of his aura, but there it was, burning hungrily at the air as he snapped his wrist and slid the obsidian shard across the throat of the guard closest to us, the one who had his gun trained on him. The guard dropped his rifle and grasped at the geyser of ruby that shot into the night, as if trying to shove the spray of life back into his already-dead flesh. The other guard was fast but not as fast as Sal. He was the smartest of the three. Instead of aiming the gun at Sal, he aimed it at me.

My world narrowed to the barrel of that gun. Even though she had retreated to the spirit realm, I wondered if the amount of rue in the darts would kill Itzelcoszcatl.

Sal slid to step in front of me as the gun fired. That eternity I had seen unfold in his eyes snapped with the sound of my high-pitched scream. César wasn't moving. Why wasn't he fucking helping? The dart landed with a thunk into Sal's side. His eyes followed it, the silhouette of the dart casting a deathly shadow that stretched and wavered in the strange light. The grin that pulled at Sal's features turned my blood to ice, and I felt terror squeeze my throat.

A simple lunge forward, and, once again, a ruby spray spattered against my mate's gorgeous, smoky skin. He didn't even spare a single second of attention on the man as he turned to Shayne.

"I was very clear."

The economy and grace with which he prowled toward Shayne had me moving. I dashed forward, falling on the body of the guard where I had seen a K bar jutting from his boot. I pulled it, my heart—finally figuring out that I needed it—pounding viciously. I was without my cadejo for the first time in a long time, but I needed to end this for me, Xochitl, before I could figure out what the hell was with the abandonment. Mirroring the stances Sal had taken, I stalked Shayne before Sal finished his statement. "On what would happen if you came here."

I launched myself at Shayne, knife bared and aimed at his heart. Sal intercepted me with shocking speed. His steel-and-flint eyes locked onto mine. "No."

He gently extricated the knife from my hand before he turned back on Shayne.

César was at my back, pulling me away from the two men. "He needs to do this. He is not looking to just save you from everything, Xochi. That man raped his mate for years. He needs this." His milky hazel eyes met with mine.

I needed this, too. I needed the catharsis of taking Shayne from the world and letting him know it was me who did it. But had Sal let that information fester in his soul all that time? Had it writhed and bit at his soul like it had mine? I turned and watched Sal toss the handle of the knife to Shayne. I tried to squirm free of César's grasp. Sal would get hurt. He'd already been shot with rue. There was no way he could access the strength and power of his beast to end this quickly before Shayne hurt him.

Images of Sal covered in his own blood, dying, as Shayne dragged me into the car, filled my mind, and I struggled harder. César held me tight, giving not a single inch. For a man who looked like a corpse, he was alarmingly strong, capable of restraining me with little of an effort, and I hated him for that. He could at least do me the dignity of pretending to struggle.

Shayne jabbed at the circling Sal, who dodged away with no issues. The two men circled each other, Shayne doing his best to find purchase in the flesh of the stalking predator. I could do nothing but stand there and watch, tears burning in my eyes. A sob choked from my lips when Shayne caught a lucky shot to Sal's bicep, and a dribble of red blood leaked down the slopes of his muscle. Sal's eyes found mine, absolute terror sliding through me.

He smiled a warm, doting smile so out of place in the feral face of a brutal man on a mission. It was almost like he couldn't help it, the very sight of me forcing his lips to smile.

Shayne took the opportunity to charge him, the steel of the blade flashing in the headlights. Sal didn't move, not even an inch, until the last moment, when his arm snapped up and wrapped around Shayne's throat. His gaze slid begrudgingly from me to lock onto his prey, following the line of Shayne's arm where the knife was buried in the meaty muscle of Sal's upper thigh. A maniac's grin shredded my mate's wild face.

The sickening sound of fabric shredding and flesh parting for the wicked bite of obsidian rent the air, followed by Shayne's scream as Sal dragged the blade he'd shoved into Shayne's dick. He took his time with it, Shayne choking on his screams, by the time Sal made it to his stomach. The blade caught and snapped on Shayne's ribs. I stood there, too horrified and scared to even fight César's grip on me, as Sal dropped him. Slick, wet, sloshing splattered against the spotlit soil where Shayne fell.

César's grip eased, and I jerked free, running to my beloved. My arms were around him before I collided with him, his lips on mine before I could get a good hold of him. He kissed me with all the brutality and desperation of a man dying. I kissed him with all the frayed nerves and terror that had built up in me and the horror of potentially living a life without him so close to having forever. He moaned into my lips, crushing me against his heaving chest.

The sensation of the shard of obsidian slicing down the back of my dress should have been a shock—or should've concerned me. Not even the smooth kiss of the night air against my bare skin as Sal peeled the petals of my clothing away from me was a distraction from the stability and security of his lips devouring mine. The sleek hiss of my dress joining the gasping, sputtering body of my ex-fiancé didn't pull me away from Sal's lips.

Only when he growled into my lips and turned me roughly, pushing me to my knees over Shayne, did I let his lips go. My honeyed gaze met with the wavering light in Shayne's eyes, and

I saw his spirit hovering around him. It was a sickly, disgusting, putrid black, mottled with rotting green-and-white sores, oozing psychic pus along the mirage. Nothing there sparked beauty or mercy in me. And the fear I held for him loosened and sloughed off into the night like the shed skin of a snake.

When Sal's thick, hard cock invaded my depths, I kept eye contact with Shayne. I buried my hands in the bloodied mud that pooled next to him and rocked back into the thrusting. The sweet slap of my ass against Sal's hips was an ancient song, and I fell into it with every beat of my heart.

"I'm only a terrible lay when I'm forced to fuck half a man," I hissed into Shayne's gaping face as Sal pounded into me with all the force of a man possessed.

It was not a romantic coupling. It was not a sweet coming together of two bodies or even the measured merging of brutality that was us fucking in the temple. This was different. We both knew what this was. He was pounding into me to show the man who had taken so much and continued to take so much from us what it looked like when my true mate fucked me over his defeated body. And I was fucking him back to show myself that, no matter what Shayne had said of me, no matter what he did to me, I was not there and not that woman anymore.

Shayne's chest rattled with blood-filled gasps, and I leaned forward, the tips of my breasts dragging in the crimson catastrophe that was his chest, as Sal fucked me up that rabid cliff to orgasm. I wanted to taste the last breath of this horrible man who had taken so many things from me and was stealing the chance of sleeping in the arms of my beloved, too. I wanted to feel the last spark of his life leave his body.

I sealed my greedy lips around my former fiancé's blood-smeared lips, moaning into a mouth I had never kissed with passion. Sal growled behind me, digging his iron fingers into the swell of my hips hard enough to leave bruises I would wear with delight in the morning.

Shayne shivered, whimpered into my lips, and I could feel it, right there on the edge of his consciousness. He knew he was dying. He knew there was nothing to be done about it. He was clawing through, struggling to hold on to the last seconds of his life.

He could have them. But they would not be peaceful.

"Fuck me hard, Big Bad. Come deep inside of me. I want to tell our children they were conceived on the corpse of the man who thought to control their mother," I purred the silken lover's words against Shayne's blood-smeared lips.

Sal groaned and jackhammered with stunning precision that exact spot deep within me he knew drove me mad. I curled the fingers of one hand into Shayne's hair as he tried to turn his head away from me and ripped it back to look me straight in the eye. The slow slither of my other hand dove into the viscera of his organs and slid around, searching for the pulsing center of him. With dexterous fingers, I pushed past the torn edge of his diaphragm and felt the strong constriction of his heart. I wanted to hold it as it beat its last thump, with my fingers wrapped around it, holding it with a delicate touch. Once again, I pressed my lips to his, grinding down on the tender flesh and drawing air through Shayne's mouth, robbing him of it. His arms flailed and flopped, trying to swat me away, and I caught one in the hand that had gripped his hair, bending it at an odd angle to give me better purchase to force my hips back against Sal.

I felt the shuddering of the broken man below me right as I crested that hill and clamped down on Sal with a strangled cry. My fingers echoed every spasm of my pussy, crushing that lump of muscle between cruel digits. My sucking, panted, ecstatic cries drew the last breath from him, his heart sputtering out around my clenching fingers, and he stilled under me as I felt Sal wash my channel with his pleasure.

We both panted, ragged, unwilling to move. What we had done was beyond civility, beyond the natural boundaries of polite society. I wanted to feel bad for it. I wanted to feel shame crawling in my heart, but I didn't. I didn't even feel bad that I came as I sucked in the last breath of a man I had once promised to marry. That breath squirmed its way through my body and settled in my psyche in a heap of molten iron that drew itself into my bloodstream to fortify me.

Without pretense, I rose, dusting the red dirt from my knees, and stared down at the bloodied body before me. Someone was talking behind me. Someone was shuffling around, but my eyes were locked solely on the broken doll spilled out on the ground, replaying the small bits I had learned from him.

He had known the entire time. Flashes of our lives together burst in my memories. The first time we had gone out together, he'd taken me to a business dinner with him. He sat me right next to the man he'd told me was trying to outbid him on a merger with another tech firm. He'd told me to be friendly with him. He'd slipped me champagne after champagne until I was laughing with the man. The more I laughed, the more he had withdrawn into himself. I'd gotten drunk and assumed my lame commentary put him off. I remembered feeling like I could conquer the world that night, and I'd only felt higher when Shayne had spent an hour praising me for being exactly what he expected. Those words now felt dirty and tainted.

I knew what he had been doing. He'd sat me next to that man as a warning, having me drain off his happiness and joy, any scrap of positive feelings he had, to make him weak. He hadn't been praising me; he'd been praising his latest acquisition for accomplishing the goal that he'd paid so dearly for.

Every single interaction I'd had with others, he had been twisting and using my cadejo. He'd force-fed her right under my nose, without me even realizing who and what she was or who and what I was. I had been a weapon to him. That was all. Just a SIG Sauer with a pussy for him to fuck when the night was over, and he'd squeezed every last bit of use out of me in other ways. No wonder Itzelcoszcatl had run. She didn't want to be used anymore.

Tears burned at my eyes again, liquefying the grisly sight before me and threatening to breach the walls of my eyelids.

Fingers like iron wrapped around my throat and pulled me to my mate. The press of his hot tongue chased the crystalline tear up my feverish cheek.

"Only I'm allowed to make you cry," he purred in a voice drenched in midnight.

I smiled weakly and collapsed into the pressing squeezed security of his hand, needing to feel the rightness of it.

"So, uh . . . that happened."

César's voice broke the brittle reverie of the moment, and I looked to him over my shoulder. He looked awkward and uncomfortable, with the totoco standing in a semi-circle behind him. I probably should have felt some semblance of propriety, what with standing here naked, covered in bile and blood, cum leaking down my legs, and being held by the throat. I didn't, though. I couldn't even muster a single scrap of shame to spare them.

"Our Cihuatlatoani has tasted the breath of her dying enemy!" whooped Ixchel from behind César.

My mentor stood quietly, tracing his eyes from my face to the body at my feet. His voice was soft but rock-hard, like always. "And created an heir on the roots of her fallen enemy."

"That's a bit presumptuous. And Sal killed him. I didn't," I said awkwardly, my eyes darting between the stoic tower of Sal and the bouncing, bloodthirsty maniac.

He flexed those steel bars of fingers against my pulse points and smiled a rabid smile down at me. "You allowed me to wound him, but you are the one who plunged your hand into his chest and stilled his heart." He flicked his tongue out and tasted Shayne's blood on my lips. "Seeing you sucking the life from him like a tzitzimitl was the third hottest thing I'd ever seen in my life. Tell me, nonamic, will you ever stop finding new ways to twist my balls and force me to come for you?"

I pressed into his titanium-banded grip, letting my vision swim black at the edges, before leaning up to whisper against his lips, "Gods, I hope not."

I kissed him then, smearing the blood of the man who had used me as an unwitting slave into his lips, as I drank his love from him.

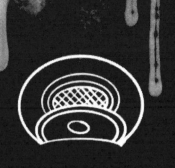

CHAPTER FORTY-SIX

ITZIQUETZAL

She had astounded even me in her ruthlessness. I'd never thought a woman could reach into the bones of the earth and draw up the wild bloodlust of our ancestors in such a way. Ixchel had been the only woman I had ever met who could match my mate in thirst at that moment. Watching her wrap her lips around that centecpanhuia's mouth at first had twisted my guts in jealousy. Poisoned words floated in my mind, questioning whether she still had feelings for him. But when he pulled his head away from her, and she snarled and ripped a chunk of his hair from the root to force him back to her, I almost lost it. I'd buried myself so deep inside her I thought I would be lost to the tight, wet depths and die happily to the embodiment of vengeance I had speared on the length of my cock.

When she rose, deadly purpose flashing in her honey-kissed eyes, I could not see the shimmering of her cadejo and realized that brutality was all her own. A mild twinge of concern twisted my gut, but the pride I felt, knowing the woman who would stand beside me as my equal and guide my totoco was as parched for justice as I was, made me fall head over heels for her even more. I didn't think it was possible to fall for her every single moment that her eyes met mine, but I kept finding new reasons that my heart's song would always praise the goddess made flesh, who had given me the honor of standing next to her for the rest of eternity.

She would protect our people with the last pump of blood in her veins, she would carve chunks from her own flesh for our get and for me. She would give me everything and demand I gave everything to her in return. And give, I would. Every last breath would be in service to her if she let me.

The totoco had witnessed her trophy, too. If any had any doubt this woman I pulled to us from the outside world, with outside ideas and no knowledge of our roots, could lead them, they'd buried that deep and would be too scared to speak it into the wind. She stood before them, hair blowing in the late-night breeze, lavish rolling hills and valleys of her full figure on display, blood smeared obscenely from cheek to throat, a glove of brilliant crimson blood covering one arm, bruises from my fingers adorning her hips, my cum leaking down her thighs, and a ferocity in her eyes that made even me wish to bow to her. She had taken in the last breath of an enemy, one that none knew the true depths of his depravity, but they all knew this man had not treated their Cihuatlatoani well. They all knew that she had suffered in some way under his hand.

Not surprisingly, the first of the totoco to move after the declaration of her trophies were the women. The women of the Lets'a Wehle tribe had always been the boldest of us when it came to tradition. Ixchel was the first in line, asking to share her kill. It was an old tradition, one I didn't even know the roots of. One that was more animal than human. I moved to help her, trying to ensure that she knew how to navigate these waters, but my beloved little flower bloomed without the care of a gardener.

She leaned down, her cadejo finally having returned, it seemed, her jaws trading into those multiple rows of teeth that only she seemed to have, and tore off a mouthful of Shayne's thigh. She spat it into her hand, and Ixchel kneeled before her, opening her mouth wide and letting my flower feed her part of her trophy. When each woman had blood dripping down their chins, the men finally followed, kneeling before her and murmuring their words of loyalty and fealty while receiving their portion of the kill. The women did not need to utter words of promise to their Cihuatlatoani. Unlike men, their bond to each other was unbreakable, rooted in the ancient matriarchal roots that wound through them.

I was the last, following César in supplication to the woman who captured my heart before it had the opportunity to even think of another. My beast squirmed in my chest, too large with the pride he, too, held for his mate. He had chosen Itzelcoszcatl long before she found a body to partner with, or at least, so he bragged. I suspected that, given the nature of my flower's beast, the opposite was true, and some things about male pride were universal. She did not spit the chunk into her palm and feed me like the others. No, not my flower. She had sunken into her connection with our world seamlessly, from timid shaking leaf to proud oak, by her own merit. Slipping her finger under my chin, she guided me to my feet as I towered over her, then wrapped her bare arms around my neck and drew me down into a ferocious kiss, where she finally shared her trophy with me.

My heart, once a solid stone in my chest, now brought to life by the bite and claw of this amazing creature, slammed painfully into the cage of my ribs. I kissed her until I was forced to swallow and thus break the dance of our lips. I rested my head against hers for a long while, relishing the feel of her warm body against mine, the scent of her skin mingling with mine, and the feel of her breath against me. She shivered, and I imagined the adrenaline of the moment was wearing off. She wasn't a seasoned warrior. She knew instinct and not how to manage the drop from war.

I gathered her in my arms, lifting her with ease. I loved the solid weight of her in my arms. If only she'd let me carry her more.

I decided as I walked her toward the apartment that, when she finally fell heavy with our child, I'd carry her everywhere. She'd not be allowed to step a single foot from the bed the entire time our child grew in her, or I'd turn her over my knee and spank the fight from her. The thought of her hissing and spitting mad to get back on her feet made me grin. I stuffed it back down quickly. I didn't need her to know just yet.

Her head was already lulling against my blood-spattered chest when I lay her down on the bed and tucked her into the blankets. She fussed a little, wanting me to join her. I had to deny her, though. There were things I needed to settle before I could finally slide in next to her. I kissed her fussing lips.

"Sleep, nonamic. If I come back, and you are awake, you won't like the consequences," I growled, tucking the blankets around her.

She screwed up her face in an adorable twist of pure stubbornness. True to my word, I ripped the blankets off of her, forced her on her belly, and delivered three sound, strong swats to her ass. When I was done, I tucked her back in, kissed her forehead, and barked, "Sleep."

She huffed, then hunkered down into the blankets, finally. My little spitfire flower. Always fighting me. I'd have it no other way. I was halfway to the door when her small voice called me back.

"Sal?"

I turned, leaning against the door, glaring at her, prepared to be forced to spank more sense into her. I quietly ticked off exactly how many swats she'd get before I buried my face between her thighs. But, when my eyes met hers, she was not the steel goddess who had fed my people from her own mouth. She was a small, scared, shivering creature who looked far too fragile, dwarfed by the enormous bed. My heart broke and my will with it. I padded back to her, sliding in under the blankets to wrap my arms around her.

"I can't stay long, nayeli. I need to see to a few things before we sleep, but I can stay for a little while," I whispered, tucking her head under my chin and holding her tightly. I pressed her to me like I had the first night we danced together, finding all those emotional burs and stroking them back into place. She burrowed into me, burying her nose into my chest and sobbing quietly. I clucked quiet *shhh, shhh, shhh*s to her but let her weep.

She had learned so much about herself she should have never known. Things no human should ever know about themselves. She had learned so many horrible things done to her without her even realizing it. I feared that, if and when she ever stared down the evil that was her mother, she would learn far more. I hoped that, when she did, I would be strong enough to push the shattered pieces back together.

She cried into my skin for a good while before my little soldier abruptly sat up and snatched something off of her side of the nightstand. Dizzy from the wild switching of emotional outpouring, I blinked and stared up at her. Fire licked at her golden eyes, and I saw the shimmering sun of her cadejo swimming in her irises. Her face was set in ironclad determination.

"Here." She shoved something into my hand, and I stared dumbly at a blister pack of something. When I looked back up at her, lost, she grumbled. "Men! Look. I'm ready. When you're ready. I'm giving you my pills. You tell me when."

I stared into her eyes, trying to keep the emotions battering my mind from bleeding into my face. She couldn't be serious? Was she serious? Was she giving me control over when we had a child? The trust was hypnotizing and delicious but terrifying. She could know none of that, though. She couldn't know that the thought of her waddling around, back aching and massive with my child, made my balls clench with need. I wanted to watch her grow with my get so much I could almost taste it.

I slowly ripped my gaze away from her and back to the pills. A wicked grin pulled up at my lips as I hefted the pills in my palm, then crunched them into my fingers. "I am a greedy man, nonayeli. I have waited twenty years to have you to myself. I think I'll take a few more years or so of having you all to myself. Maybe."

I winked at her. "You'll never know if I'm giving you the sugar pills or not. From now on, at breakfast, you will come to find me. You'll get down on your knees and beg me to breed you."

She was shivering in my arms for a different reason, squirming as my voice dripped with the dangerous promise of Itzatecuani.

"Maybe that day, I will. Maybe that day, I won't. You'll beg nonetheless. And I will give you your pill and maybe you will find out if, that day, I will fill you with my get or not."

She groaned and writhed against me. I needed to get out of this damned bed before I buried my cock in her again, ignoring the unwelcomed pressing matters erupting into our lives. I needed to know how he found the compound. I needed to know how he got up the road unannounced. I needed to know a great many things, and César would have been collecting the information I needed to make the next move. Her mother would not catch us unaware. No one would catch us unaware ever again if I had anything to say about it.

Most importantly, I needed César to see to the seeping creep of the poison meandering down the lane of my blood toward my heart. Its slow progression was stealing the strength from my limbs. Had Itzatecuani not abided my command and retreated to the spirit realm when I saw the dart guns, we would both be writhing on the ground now, fighting the passage into the next world.

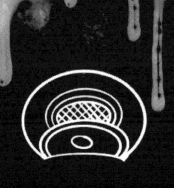

CHAPTER FORTY-SEVEN
Itziquetzal

I lost an hour holding her to me until she was finally snoring against my bicep. I wished I could stay there for the rest of the night but had to pull myself out from under her.

I found César right where I thought I'd find him. A smart man would not have let me abandon her to trace him down at the temple. No, he was hunkered down with Ixchel, Julia, Nopaltzin, and Rafael, sharing a late-night snack of honey-covered fruits while they huddled.

They didn't bother to drop their conversation when I slid in next to Julia, who slid me a mango, which I bit into appreciatively.

"Might want to be careful, Itzatecuani. She's far prettier than you. A few of us might easily be convinced to stab you in the throat to let her take the prime seat," Ixchel said, tossing a nut into her mouth with a playful wink.

"If she'd let you get to me, I say have at it. You're right. She's far prettier than I am."

Anyone else making such a threat would have probably found themselves shredded to ribbons, but the hellfire that was Ixchel would always get away with too much.

I lofted a brow at César, and he nodded to Ixchel and Julia. The two peeled away from the four of us and went to stand guard. Ixchel at the window of Xochitl and I's ground-floor rooms, closest to the gates and Julia with her butchering knife at the front door of the apartment. Just in case. The women of the tribe would be Xochitl's retinue.

She'd be insufferable when she figured out what had changed, but it was exactly as it should have been. She had proven her merit and taken her place as the final leg of the tribe's structure required to make us solvent in the eyes of the spirits again. Whether she took my mate mark was inconsequential. She had proved her service, her strength, and her dedication. I could not be more proud of the woman she had become, and I was eager to see her bloom further.

César pushed up from the table, taking up his medical bag to come around to my side. He kneeled in the dust of the hard-packed courtyard and took out various instruments I had no idea the use of. A hiss of reproach was his answer as he prodded the swollen, angry red knot under my skin, where the dart had penetrated.

"Do we know how he managed to get up the volcano?" I asked around a mouthful of mango, trying not to grind my teeth as he slid a needle into the hole left by the tranq dart.

César nodded to Rafael, who blushed. "That . . . was my fault, tecutli. Cheeno was on guard this evening, and I . . ." The man blushed and hung his head for a second before gathering his courage and forging on. "I pulled him into the tree line and had his cock down my throat when the car went through. We didn't notice until it was too late. I'm sorry, tecutli."

I watched the man, staring directly into his eye, trying to find any indication he was covering for his mate. Rafael had come a good way from the terrified man who had appeared with Cheeno in our territory. He had refused to even hold his mate's hand, where eyes could see them when they first came. Now, he was willing to admit that not only had he been the reason for an enemy finding their way to our gates but also admitting to the same amount of loving passion that the rest of the mated and paired couples did. I was proud of him for finding his courage and being honorable enough to admit to it.

I nodded gruffly. "You both should have known better. I will wait until the morning for your Cihuatlatoani to wake, and the three of us will find a suitable punishment. It does not look good for you to have to force her to make her first act as your Cihuapilli to be to dole out punishment. The shame of it will be great."

I lofted my brows at him. Rafael was a human who might not understand all of our ways, but he understood the shame would be something both he and Cheeno would need to overcome on their own. I warned him only so that the two could collaborate on ways to gain the favor of their new Cihuapilli. Not that, with her soft heart, Xochitl would hold a grudge too long.

He was wise enough to hang his head and nod.

"Good. Now, go tell Cheeno I said to find another guard for the rest of the evening and rest up with your mate. I imagine the two of you will not get much rest. Your Cihuatlatoani has sharp claws and a long memory."

His dark eyes widened, and he nodded before trotting off to find his mate.

Nopaltzin was wise enough to keep his eyes trained on Rafael's back before opening his mouth. "Still scaring the man? We both know that Xochitl is as soft as the flower she's named after."

I snorted a laugh. "Yeah, but it'll give Cheeno something to comfort his mate over, and we both know how Cheeno dotes on him."

Nopaltzin grunted a laugh and leaned back in his seat, eyeing me carefully, César still working on my wound. "You remind me of your father more and more every day. Smart and focused like him but with the cunning and prowess of Antu. They did well with you, boy."

"You'll need to take charcoal and come to the clinic for a flush. A couple hours in the dialysis chair should fix you up. You were lucky. They are using some sort of synthetic-compounded rue and not the real deal." He pushed up to stand, pushing his hair out of his face and tucking the latex gloves into a bag. "I gave you a shot of steroids. Should keep you on your feet until tomorrow, but don't put it off too much longer, Sal. I'm serious. You're going to

484 | N. Cáceres

start deteriorating quickly if we don't get you in and your blood flushed."

I nodded to him. I'd go the next afternoon, after I got the search parties' reports and settled my mate's mind some.

"Does she know?"

The gruff, solid voice of the Elder drew my attention back to him.

"She knows many things. Be more specific, Old Dog."

He crossed his arms and watched me, silence stretching into the expanse between us. I hated when he did this. Ever since I was a child, training for battle at his knee, I hated when he waited for you to catch up instead of explaining himself. I sighed heavily. "About what she did? I don't think so. How could she? She doesn't know the ways of our people enough to know the depth of the bond of shared kills."

He glared at me, waiting. I ground my teeth. If César wouldn't punch me. I'd punch the Old Dog in the face a few times for his impudence. "No, I don't think she knows that crushing his heart and devouring his last breath ended him on this plane as well as the next."

Long ago, our people believed that the house of the soul was in the heart, and the last breath of a dying person was the soul escaping the prison of the dead flesh to begin its journey to the deadlands. By crushing his heart in her hand as she came, Xochitl had forced his soul from his body. By inhaling and devouring that last breath, she had ensured Shayne's spirit would never walk this plane or any other plane of existence ever again. She had ended his cycles, as if he had never existed. It was the most powerful trophy of battle a warrior could take. One that required a depth of mercilessness many didn't have in them.

"Glad you could join the conversation, boy. Thought I had praised you too quickly," he snarked.

I smirked at the older man, a sad smile weighed down by the anchors of ancient memories. He tutted and looked to César before going on. "The teopixqui is unwilling to spit it out, so I will. When

I was out this evening, unlike the rest of the mutts, I kept my eyes open and unclouded. I saw a few of the stragglers from Ik'an Lepa. I got one alone, promised him I'd let him suck my cock if he was a good boy. Young one. Maybe mid-twenties. Thought he could easily get one over on an old codger like me."

That was a mistake, a mistake I would never make. The old man of the totoco was long in the tooth for our kind. I wasn't sure his exact age, but he looked to be nearing the edge of fifty. Whatever his blessing had been, it had given him strength and nimbleness even Amanka could not claim. I hadn't tasked Xochitl with learning pottery just because I thought she needed a hobby. Nopaltzin had been a general under my father and Antu, his best, but had retired from the totoco's war ranks when I had taken over. He still trained many of the younger warriors when it was time. I knew he would protect my mate while I was busy running the mining companies or managing the totoco's affairs. It helped that he was also the wisest of the ranking members.

"I pulled him into an alleyway and had a very long conversation with him about being a useful citizen." His knuckles, still shredded from said "conversation" cracked as he flexed them. His intense gaze fell on me. "He let me know that we didn't get them all. Not even a fraction of them. We might have gotten the younger get, but there's still at least thirty totocan that stay off compound, hunting."

I snarled, anger kicking into my chest. I hated that we had to return so many spirits to the other realm that day, especially spirits bound to children, but the rot of feeding on flesh could only be flushed out by plunging the spirit back into the well of the spirit realm. To hear that we hadn't even crippled them, and they were still out there to spread that infection, made it worse. Thirty more would scatter across Central America to seed the addiction of feeding from the pure source of the spiritual energy we craved. I could only hope that the Council would be more judicious in their culling of the practice soon.

"And did he know where they are holed up?"

Nopaltzin shook his head. "Tried to get him to loosen up, but aside from teeth, nothing shook loose. We've got him in the old hut near the mouth of the caldera creek, though. We'll see if the acidic waters on his feet inspire his memory after a few days."

I grinned at the man. He might accuse me of being cunning, but this cadejo was much worse than I was. This man knew patience and how to stretch out a single session to get what he wanted. I wished he would reconsider taking his rightful place as a general, but I had asked him so many times over the years that, if I asked again, I might be on the receiving end of that cunning and patience.

I nodded to him. "Keep me up to date."

I expected him to leave, but when he didn't, I tilted my head in question. He exhaled long and stared me dead in the eye. "You'll keep her? She's a challenge to your seat. She hasn't spent much time with the totoco, but they see who and what she is."

Perhaps I had selected too good of a mentor for my mate. Jealousy twisted my guts. He was everything I wasn't and just enough of a threat as an unmated male with whom I could see the easy air she forged turning into more. But his concern wasn't one of interest; it was a concern of hierarchy. The totoco had the chance to see the way her unleashed cadejo felt on their senses. Even I could feel the power rolling off of her. It had been ages since a white cadejo found a home with our totoco, and with a spirit so strong and the opposite of my strength, he wasn't wrong. She was a threat to my position. She could easily challenge me for tecutli and, if trained properly, might even win. Spirits followed power, cunning, creativity, and strength, not just animal instinct.

"She'd have to kill me to be a true threat." I leaned back, watching Nopaltzin with a new, more wary regard.

"She would." He looked me up and down as if weighing my chances against my mate. "And if you keep pushing her, she might just have a reason. Walk careful with that one, boy. That beast in your soul has picked a worthy mate. She is as strong as he is and can command the loyalty of your people just as he can. She doesn't even need to try. And if he pushes her too far from his hand, when he pulls it back, he's likely to find a stump."

I grinned. He wasn't telling me anything I didn't already know. "It's what I like most about her."

He snorted. "Just as insane as your father. Never thought Antu would find a worthy mate. Gods know her first wasn't truly worthy. But when your papa went against her in that fight and didn't hold back, she didn't on him? Never thought we'd get the blood and jizz out of the courtyard stones. Glad to see the apple doesn't fall far from the tree."

He nodded to me, cutting the conversation off as he rose and left César and me to watch him strut away.

"If I didn't like that old fart as much as I do, I'd use his head as a footstool," César grumbled, and I couldn't help but laugh.

"Yeah, well, he's loyal, and he's useful and if you took nothing away from that, you should have taken away that he'd bleed for cihuapiltzintle without a single thought. Which, if Shayne showing up is any indication, might be of use to us." I slid my eyes back to my cousin and sighed. "How does a gringo like that know so much about us?"

César tapped his nail against the wood of the table, a gesture that never meant good tidings. He was quiet as he processed my question. I wished I had Xochitl's gift to see the eddies and tides of a person's spirit. I wished I could see the inner workings of my soft-spoken cousin. Even after years of growing up together, he was still a mystery.

"He said he had been paying her mother. The doctor who contacted me to buy a living specimen was a doctor that her mother had taken her to when she was younger. It's obvious that her mother knew of us and what we are from the start. Why else would she keep rue around the house? The question is, which came first? Xochitl's cadejo *or* her mother's knowledge of who and what we are? And if her mother knew of who and what we are before she gave birth to Xochitl, how did she know? Is she one of the lost that fled? Are her parents cadejos? What is her connection? And if it was her mother who told this doctor of who and what we are . . ."

"How many others has he told, and what has he done with the knowledge?" I finished for him, and he caught my eye with his.

"Exactly." He sighed heavily and leaned back, his gaze tangling in the stars above us. "I don't like the implications, Sal."

"Me either," I said low and dark to the skin of the fruit I had devoured.

His gaze fell back on me. "Not just because Xochitl was being used by an outsider for her feeding power. Not just because she was hurt in the way she was hurt. But because of what the implication is. Are there others? Are there more of our kind in servitude? But, even more, I don't like the timing."

I cocked a brow at him. "When exactly is it a good time for our people to be used as slaves to the greed of the white man?"

He rolled his eyes at me. "Not like that, Sal. Jesus, you really have gotten melodramatic in your old age. I meant because of the bells."

"The what?"

"With all the other news, I hadn't gotten to it just yet. While you were in there, comforting her, Honoria came by." Honoria was a priest up at the temple, a refugee from the Usulutan totoco, who had been devastated by the violence against the tribes in Honduras. "She said she was cleaning the temple and found tufts of hummingbird feathers leading out onto the steps. When she followed them, she found a pile of hummingbird heads. No bodies. Just heads. And then there were the bells. The rest of the priests swore that they had been disturbed by the sound of rattling bells throughout the temple. No one could find the source of them, but they all agreed they heard the same thing. A full minute of rhythmic bells. They said that it sounded like someone was dancing in the solar room, covered in bells. And, when they went to investigate, no one was there. But there was this . . ."

He reached into his pocket and fished out a teardrop-shaped metal bell crusted over with the patina of age. It tinkled lightly as he set it on the table. "They found this in one of the hummingbird's heads."

I pushed it around with the blunt tip of my finger. "And what does it mean?"

He rolled his shoulder in a casual shrug. "I don't know yet. But it would be wise of us to use the opportunity of having the Council attending the wedding to ask some of the older Ah Kin and maybe even Amanka."

I fought the shiver that ran down my spine at the mention of the ancient representative of the totoco. She might have been loyal as the roots of a tree, but she was too old and knew too many things for me to be comfortable around her.

"And how do you propose we corral Xochitl into letting us investigate during her wedding? Better yet, do you have any idea how we are going to convince the Council members, especially Cadmael, not to want to witness the marking? We both know she's not going to accept that." I crossed my arms and glared at my cousin, who was full of so many great ideas that night.

"Maybe. She let you fuck her in front of the totoco and didn't seem too phased by it. Maybe we—oh, I don't know—just tell her what's supposed to happen and let her decide? I'll be honest, brother, I would not put money on Cadmael winning in a war of wills against her. She's cut her teeth against you and won. He might be the self-styled king, but she's something much more. Maybe we just let her deal with him."

"Do you want blood at my wedding, brother?" I laughed, the sound rolling through my entire body at the vision of my beautiful bride knee-deep in Cadmael's gore.

He smirked a mischievous grin and shrugged again. "There was going to be blood at the wedding regardless of what happened. It's just a matter of how much at this point."

"Fair point." I chuckled. "I'm making Julia tell her, though. I want to be able to have children with her eventually, and she'll castrate me for sure if I have to tell her that she's going to have to trade her shadow fully with her cadejo for the first time and be mated by Itzatecuani like that in front of others after we use our claws to carve our mate marks into each other's skin."

"Oh, yeah. She's going to fucking murder you. Does she even have a mate mark yet?" he asked, tracing my body in search of any hint of it.

"Not as far as I know. I'm going to suggest just simple gold bands and her initials. At least until she can ease into this a little more. A month is not enough time for her to settle in and learn her nagual. And it's okay. I'll let her even bite me if that's what she wants to do. Doesn't matter much to me how I wear her mark."

César shuddered. "Seriously? Are you insane? Have you seen her cadejo's teeth?"

I flashed him a maniacal grin. "Fucking hot, right?"

CHAPTER FORTY-EIGHT

It had been two-and-a-half weeks since the night Sal proposed. It had also been two-and-a-half weeks since Jamal was last seen. The cavalier nonchalance with which the totoco had initially approached his absence had been whittled down to a sharp, biting, ever-present panic that undercut every interaction. Every car that came up the ridge caused butterflies to dance in our collective bellies. Perhaps someone had found him. Every hunting party went out into the jungle, sure they would be the team to finally find him. Every twig that snapped could have been him. Every animal cry in the night could have been him.

His mother had to be sedated by César multiple times. Her panic and anguish had kept her in a constant state of half shadow, burning her spiritual energy at both ends. If he had not sedated her, she would have worked herself into a coma, both her mortal energy and her spirit's energy sapped by the constant, futile running and hunting.

Having had spent more time in the jungle, I learned quickly how to ride as a passenger as Itzelcoszcatl loped into her full ghost skin, hunting for any hint of the boy. Even a whisper in the wind of his laughter would have drawn her to him. My born flesh carried a rugged map of scratches, cuts, abrasions, and all manner of other small injuries sacrificed up to the whims of the dense, tropical forest, hoping it would yield its hostage or some vestige of his path.

It never did.

I returned from one such fruitless hunt. The strength of Itzelcoszcatl's spirit form was dizzying at first. Where I had expected the perspective to change, I had been shocked to find that, at eye level, her shimmering white head could easily rest atop my born flesh's head. Sometimes, I wished I could see myself in her skin through someone else's eyes. She was massive, as big as Cheeno's Jetta that I brushed past, leaving my scent mark. But none of the vehicles here were shiny enough to see a good reflection, just the impression of a white blob.

Exhausted, I stopped as a familiar scent tickled Itzelcoszcatl and I's nose.

What is that? I whispered to her.

A growl rumbled through her as she pushed back, and I sprang forward, flowing into the world on the wings of dancing raindrops, washing the fur and spirit back into the spirit realm.

My body felt wrung out, hollow, and dragged down with bone-deep weariness as I reached up to take a sheet stored on the gates for the hunting parties to slip into. I wrapped it around my body as I walked.

My toe collided with a box, and I stumbled a few steps to the orchestra of rattling. Tucking the last edge of the sheet around me, I squatted to examine the cardboard box. There was no note, no addressee on the outside of the folded closed box, so I shoved my hands between the flaps and opened it.

My heart stopped when the afternoon sunlight danced into the dark crevice and revealed the simple orange pill bottle and a folded note. I didn't need to open either to know what was in the bottle. Rue pills. The same ones I had taken every day for over a decade. I would know their exact shape in a sea of pills.

Shaking, I snatched the note from the box, as if the pills would grow sentience and bite me if I moved too slow.

I expected some wild supervillain's prose to meet me, a demand for something in return for the boy's life. In my soul, I knew Annette was here, and she had Jamal. He could not have gone missing this long without her involvement. I didn't expect the reasonable, curling, beautifully penned note.

Angelica,

My beautiful daughter. I have missed you so much. I've tried to call your cell phone, but I haven't gotten through. Your sister and I are staying in Tamanique. We would love if you joined our guest and us for dinner soon. We are so eager to see you again.

I've left some of your vitamins, I know how you get when you haven't been watching after yourself.

Hope to see you very, very soon.

Love,

Mom

Another time, another place, another me would have crumbled at the implied threats scratched between the letters. I was no longer Angelica. I was no longer the beaten and broken dog lapping at her heels for a crumb of a treat. I was Xochitl, Cihuatlatoani of the Lets'a Wehle, but, most importantly, I was my own person, and my bones were as strong as the earth beneath them.

I crumpled the note in my hand and stalked toward the apartment. I would change and go after Jamal and put an end to this. A soft press to the mental membrane within me told me she would be with me. Tired as she was, she would fight beside me if I needed her.

I was tossing clothes onto the bed when I felt his presence. I flicked my eyes up to take Sal in. His hand was wrapped around his stomach, still nursing the rue burn inside of him. He'd spent every day at the clinic on a modified dialysis machine, trying to clean his blood of the traces of the toxin.

"Going somewhere, nayeli?"

His voice was casual, relaxed, and without worry. Too much so.

"Tamanique."

His brows rose, and he tilted his head to examine me. "And why is my flower racing off in such a rush to the sea?"

"I'm going after Jamal."

I didn't want to give him the details. He would try to stop me. It was his job as my mate to stop me from doing stupid things, but I was going whether he liked it or not.

A concern laced growl rumbled from his lips. "You've found him?"

I didn't answer, just tossed the note to him as I clipped a bra around my stomach and turned it. "I know her, Sal. This is no coincidence. She all but says that she has him."

His eyes darted across the page, gobbling up the words, as I shoved my arms through the arm straps and hoisted my breasts up into the cups. "She says Elida is here, too."

Hope dawned on his face as he looked up to me. "Do you think she is? We can rescue her, too, bring her to the compound, and help her detox like you did."

I didn't let myself process that part of the note. I'd let it bounce right off of the wrath-born armor I curled around myself. Could I really bring Elida here? Was she even truly with Annette?

I let the golden drops of hope from the dawn in Sal's usually turbulent face trickle into my blood for but a second before I shook my head violently. "No. I don't think so. Annette knows how much I love Elida. It's just a ploy. Some twisted manipulation to get me there faster."

"You're not going."

It wasn't a suggestion. It wasn't a question. It was a divine commandment, as if him merely speaking the words into the air made it so. Had he forgotten who he was talking to?

I snorted and pulled on one of his shirts. "Good luck stopping me. I'm getting pretty good at fast exchanges. Care to race, Big Bad?"

"Dammit, Xochitl. I'll tie you to the fucking bed if I have to. You're not going."

"I am. And hot. Hold that until I get back."

I was hopping into stretchy bike shorts and pulling on a skirt over them. If I would have to run with Jamal, I didn't want to be slowed down by thigh chafing.

"Xochitl. I mean it. You're not going. You don't know what you are walking into, and you're already exhausted. You've been out searching for him every day from sun up to sun down. You barely eat, you barely sleep. You're in no shape to fight her off if she tranqs you." The muscle in his sculpted jaw ticked as he held back for a few moments. "I can't lose you again."

"You won't lose me, Sal. I'm taking Nopaltzin's gun. She might be a monster, but even monsters aren't bulletproof." I pushed up off the bed, having strapped on my running shoes.

So aptly named. The last time I had them on was at the Ik'an Lepa totoco house. Blood was still flaked in the soles.

He caught me by the arm, his grip weaker than it should have been. Chips of obsidian rimmed by plumes of black smoke bore into me. "If you're determined to go, I'm going with you."

"You're still not healed up yet, Big Bad." I rested my palm on his chest, leaning up to place a soft kiss to his lips. "But compromise? I'll take Ixchel with me."

He considered my offer, his fingers digging and flexing into the flesh of my arm. "Ixchel and Cheeno. And me."

I frowned up at him. He would not let this go. "Five minutes. If you three aren't ready and loaded into the truck in five minutes, I'm leaving without you."

He nodded, the compromise a fair enough one for him. I'd intended on taking Cheeno with me anyway. His ability to slip in and out of shadows would help steal Jamal away without risking the young boy being hurt.

Gods. Had Annette pumped that young boy up with rue, I would rip her limb from limb and savor every last scream.

True to my word, in exactly five minutes, I was firing up Sal's truck. Only Ixchel had gotten in by the time I put it in drive and was trundling down the dusty road.

"Dammit, Xochitl!" Sal yelled as he ran full speed to catch me, with Cheeno close at his heels.

I didn't stop. I'd warned them. Five minutes, or I'd go without them. They tossed gear into the open back of the truck, and Cheeno hoisted himself up. Sal, ever Mr. I Have To Make Things Harder On Myself, aimed for the front seat. Ixchel was polite enough to slide over and push open the door for him but, with great amusement at her sprinting tecutli, didn't even encourage me to stop. She may have even casually leaned on the gas pedal thigh a hair.

Sal was spitting mad and cussing up a storm by the time his massive frame swung into the cab and slammed the door behind him. "Seriously? Fucking seriously, Xochitl?"

"She said five minutes," Ixchel chimed in happily.

"I did, indeed. Not my fault you're bad at time." I shrugged.

"And running," Ixchel put in helpfully.

"And running," I confirmed.

"Twenty."

"What?"

"Twenty." He exhaled through puffing, ragged breaths. "It's how many stripes I'm going to paint on your ass with my belt when we get home."

"Awwuh, he says the sweetest things to you, Cihuatlatoani," tittered the maniac in dutch braids next to me.

"Doesn't he just? He's a real dream boat." I rolled my eyes at Sal's embittered scowl. "Buckle up. I learned to drive in San Francisco, so . . ."

"What exactly does that—"

Sal slammed her back against the seat, forced her into a seatbelt and himself into one, too. Gods be with Cheeno. San Franciscans believed in offensive driving as a prime directive.

CHAPTER FORTY-NINE

I was not surprised at the home we pulled into. It was a
lavish, sprawling Spanish-style mansion on the edge of a
beachside cliff. Ixchel whistled her impressed enthusiasm.

I glared at it. It wasn't even a little bit shocking Annette would
pick a home so far out of the price range of the locals, which some
foreign millionaire visited once or twice every five years.

"Remember the plan."

We'd spent the entire drive, zippy as it was, formulating a plan
and having Sal growl about it. No matter how he cut it, I would
have to go in alone, even if just for a while. He hated that, but there
was no way around it.

Ixchel and Cheeno crawled out of the truck, and Sal went with
them as I made my way to the front door and knocked.

My beast thrummed close to the surface, a hair's breadth from
pushing forward to rend the world on the edge of her fury. I drew in
a breath, brushing my mental hand against the bubble in my mind
between us. It throbbed back, filling me with a sense of steadfast
preparation. Images of mist rolling off of a granite mountain face,
a graveyard of broken arrows at its base, wandered through my
mind, and I nodded to myself. I was ready for this. Most likely,
that was a lie, but there was no way forward without going through.

Nerves gripped me and raked razor-sharp claws down the soft
metal of my internal armor. I fidgeted with my skirt, fingering the

embroidered black feathers that adorned the body of the otherwise simple cotton.

Minutes drew out in perfect silence as I waited. My mother was many things, but a manipulative mind game master was her chief achievement. A full five minutes ticked by, my mind crawling like a colony of ants with nerves, before a massive man with an assault rifle casually hanging from his chest opened the door.

His eyes darted around and behind me. "Alone?" he asked in thickly accented English.

After weeks of being so submerged in switching between the rolling undulations of Spanish, the crisp sway of Nahuatl, and the warm burbling creek of Lenca, the jagged chop of the English language was jarring. It sounded like a knife and fork on an empty plate, sawing away at imaginary vegetables.

"Yes," I ground out, the word feeling like a stone on my tongue.

The man nodded and stepped aside. "You are to go through the family room, into the kitchen, and out onto the patio."

I wandered through the house in the direction he pointed, toward the massive wall of glass facing out to a stunning view of the ocean crashing against unseen rocks below. I felt every watery fist pumping into my soul.

"Angelica! Oh, sweet girl. I've finally found you!"

The sugar in her voice dripped and fell to the ground like honey-flavored acid. A matching plastered-on doting smile spread across her bird-like features as she walked toward me, arms spread wide as if she truly expected me to hug her.

I stepped back, avoiding the leech of her arms, and glared. "Annette."

"Oh, come now, you must give your mother a hug!"

She tried again, getting within a foot of me before Ixchel, my self-appointed Eagle, melted out of the shadows and extended her arm to keep Annette away from me. The command was clear without Ixchel needing to say a single thing. Annette's gaze slid from me to Ixchel, and the mask wavered, rage and indignation at Ixchel's audacity to stop her rippling across her features. To Ixchel's credit, the withering glare that would have melted my bones only a short while ago only made her smile that maniac's grin, as if daring my mother to do her worst. Annette slid the familiar mask back across her features like a well-loved glove and smiled softly to the insane woman, who, I knew for a fact, was looking forward to making a belt for her cadejo skin armbands from my mother's hair.

"Well, hello, dear, I didn't see you come in with Angelica. I'm Annette Yarbrow. I'm so glad to see Angelica has found a little friend. I've been so worried about her since she disappeared." A sad, forlorn look crossed her avian face. "She's not well, you know. It's not her fault."

"I know who you are," Ixchel said in a ferocious accented voice.

I'd never heard her speak English. It was grating to my ears. Ixchel had always reminded me of a movie clip of a black panther. Smooth, rolling, velvety, with a hint of dangerous promise, and the way she talked reminded me of the rolling jut of the shoulders of a prowling cat. Hearing her speak the chopped, clipped, and ugly words of English—even in her liquid accent—made my ears hurt.

Annette was done with Ixchel, clearly realizing she wasn't getting anywhere with her. Her eyes met mine, and I saw the derisive disgust flash in them as she took me in. What would she see? I wondered. Would she see the breathtaking way my skin had been burnished in the sun? Would she see the beautiful wrapping weave of the mate talisman ribbon that bound the crown of braids wrapped around my head? Would she appreciate the craftsmanship of the hand-embroidered cotton skirt bearing those black feathers? Would she recognize the hours of time that went into dying and weaving my cotton blouse? Somehow, I doubted it, and she didn't wait long to comment on it.

"Angelica . . . you look . . . right at home."

She almost lost the act, almost. Her gaze slid back and forth between Ixchel and me, as if trying to find her next soft fleshy spot to strike.

I didn't give her the opportunity.

"Where is Jamal, Annette?"

The steel in my voice was borrowed. I imagined Sal gripping her throat and snarl down at her. His presence somewhere in the shadows that stretched across the wooden deck, hovering over the edge of a sea cliff, a dense canopy overhead, gave me the courage I needed to bolster my armor. I knew he was watching. I knew Cheeno crouched with him. I felt weak in her presence. I could feel the old me whimpering in a corner, begging me to back down, to avoid the argument and the strife this would cause.

Her gaze settled back on me, leveling me, taking me in completely.

I had changed since she last saw me. Not just the clothes and accessories. I had to bank on the idea that all the pounding at my psyche had forged me into a stronger creature, recognizable even to those who were used to the meek woman they had known last.

"Now, Angelica, there's no need to be rude."

"Xochitl."

"Excuse me?"

"Xochitl. My name is Xochitl. You'd think the woman who named me would know what my name is." I crossed my arms over my ample breasts and widened my stance.

I doubted Annette would bring a fight, not like Shayne. And while she had one hired goon running around with an assault rifle, I had three very pissed-off cadejos. My money was on the two silent, slinking shadows stalking somewhere within the house, searching for Jamal and Elida.

She snorted a black, fetid sound. "I didn't name you. I cried every day when I was pregnant with you. I didn't want kids. By the time you came into the world, kicking and screaming, I hadn't even thought of a name. Your father named you after his mother and sister. There was more to it, though. Xochitlte-something. I had to cut it down. Though, that's neither here nor there."

I tilted my head. This was the first time I had ever heard of my father's family. "And what happened to him?"

That saccharine sweet smile crossed her lips again, all pretenses of the controlling mother I had known and the doting mother she attempted to present stripped away. I had no idea the depths she could crawl down to. I wondered if I really wanted to know.

A wine glass, filled with deep burgundy wine, was taken up casually in her hand as she smirked at me. "You know what happened to him, Angelica. He was deported and chose never to come back. He'd rather live in a shithole country like this one than have to deal with the little monsters he spawned."

Ixchel snarled softly to my left. She knew what this woman had done. How she had kept me under control. As my Eagle, a position I was learning meant that she was always armed to the teeth and no more than twenty paces away from me. She also knew the finer points that would be peppered in as a cautionary tale that would travel through the tribes attending the wedding. Her and Cheeno, who we had agreed would act as Sal's Jaguar when he had regained his honor, would make sure of that.

"So, you knew exactly what you were doing to me? You knew what you did to Roberto?"

Why was I asking? Why did I want to know? Why was I even bothering to listen to her? Maybe some small part of me wanted, hoped, and needed her to redeem herself. Maybe, just maybe, if she said something, any little thing that justified what she had done to us, maybe it would seal the massive gash in my heart she had left. Maybe I could move forward without the constant fear that those around me would see how worthless I was.

"Robert was lucky. I was able to purge him completely. You and Elida were a little more stubborn." She looked behind me to the gathering shadows around Ixchel, who was practically foaming at the mouth to sink her teeth into her, hearing the callous and dismissive way she talked about murdering a spirit.

I heard the thug she had hired moving deep in the house somewhere. I hoped that sound was him being put down by Cheeno and Sal to rescue Jamal.

Her caramel-and-acorn gaze slid back to me, and she crooked that scimitar brow at me that, a few months ago, would have brought me to heel with no other words needed. Straightening my back, I used her own tools against her. Gone were the days I served as a simpering dog at her feet. I would not be tugged around by an unseen leash, just to avoid the lash of her wrath. I pulled to myself the images of Itzelcoszcatl, regal and ferocious in the temple, letting that sense of imperial superiority reflect across the mask I drew up.

Staring her down, I imagined balancing a massive crown of feathers and gems glinting in the waning sunlight. "Where are Jamal and Elida?"

"Come sit down, have a glass of wine. I'm sure Elida will be around soon." She moved to the glass-topped deck table before I had time to register what was happening.

The crack of the gun going off ricocheted around my head and rattled loose that old fear. Memories of a wire hanger slicing into the flesh of my thighs made me wince more than the yelp behind me and to my left. My eyes slid to Ixchel, who clutched her stomach with a bloodthirsty, maniac's grin painted across her face. Blood wept between the wedge of her fingers. Her teeth were chattering, snapping, and clicking in excitement and anticipation of the fight to come, as if chewing on the agony of the gunshot to fuel her furor. Her eyes laser-focused on my mother.

Peace flooded through me, wrapping me in icy cold arms. "If you shoot again, Annette, I will not wait for you to tell me where they are. If you shoot my people again, I will bathe in your gore before the sun sets."

"Your people?" A dubious yet amused expression twisted her elegant features. "Your people?" Laughter, dirty and ugly, skittered out of her thin lips. "Oh, that's very rich, Angelica. I'm getting bored, though, and we have a flight to catch. I've been in this god-forsaken country long enough. Come drink the wine."

"Do you really think that's going to work? I mean, honestly, Annette. Do the math here. You seem to know a decent bit about what kind of creatures we are. There's no chance you really think that I am going to just curl up at your feet again." A thump rattled the wood of the deck, drawing my eyes to where my feet were.

"Because, Angelica, it's what you do. It's what I've trained you to do. You are nothing but property. A trained poodle that will dance to my tune when and where I tell you to. I own you. I rented you out to the highest bidder, and I pride myself in customer satisfaction." She fluffed her ego like an inflated car salesman at the end there, and it made me want to wretch.

I turned to the bleeding Ixchel, sliding my gaze silently down below me. She gave a tilt of her head and stepped back into the shadow of an oak where she disappeared. "Shayne is dead, by the way."

I sneered down my nose at her, conjuring the image of my cadejo, a goddess who waited on a razor's edge, pacing in my mind, waiting to leap through my skin, and shred the woman who had tormented us both.

"Good. He was a bit of an annoyance, anyway. Always whining about how you gave him sad eyes. He was too soft to keep one of you on a leash. I'll be able to make a better sale now."

"Are you truly not listening? I'm not going back. Not today, not tomorrow. Never. And if you think you are going to drag me off, I assure you, you aren't going to make it out alive. Neither of us will if it comes to it."

"Is that so?" She tsked, a sound so similar to the sucking of the teeth of my people that I wanted to rip the sound from her lips for blaspheming the beautiful sound. "Well, Angelica, if that's your decision. I can't make you come with me. You've made it more than clear where you stand. And, as you said, I am at a disadvantage."

She clucked a few times and slid a pair of sunglasses back on to her face.

Was that it? Was it really going to be that easy? An uneasy relief slid into my bones, and I watched her with speculation. She elegantly collapsed into a deck chair like a smug, self-satisfied queen mounting her throne, swirling the wine in her glass. I felt her eyes on me the entire time.

"Shame, though. I thought you loved her more than that." She sipped slowly.

I noticed with an internal frown that, all this time, she hadn't mentioned Jamal. Was she holding him out as a pawn?

Out of the corner of my eye, I saw Sal's massive body take up the frame of the wide-open, telescopic sliding glass door. His eyes, frothing with rabidity, connected with mine, and he shook his head in two quick, nearly unnoticeable shakes.

"What."

It wasn't a question. I threw back at her when my attention came back.

"Elida. I thought you loved your sister more than this." She pushed her glasses up on her face. The saber plunged successfully on its target.

"What do you mean?" I scratched out beyond the boulder that settled in my throat.

"You didn't really believe that note I left, did you?" She snorted a laugh. "Had I known you were this dumb, I wouldn't have even bothered. She's not in Japan, you idiot. I rented her out for experimentation when she was of age. She was much less interesting a subject than you were, but she fetches a pretty penny nonetheless. But, with you playing rebel in the jungle, I had to drag her down here to ensure you'd come quietly."

She paused, tapping on her chin. "Actually, I think I'm totally done with you mangy dogs. I should thank you, really. It's been a lot of work to train you to fetch. I'll just have her throat slit and move on. Robert is already broken of his little issue."

The taste of fresh blood and flesh washed through my mouth, making me salivate, as the three rows of shark-like teeth erupted through my gums, and I felt my legs fight the stretch of my cadejo pushing to the surface at the mention of the dead cadejo so callously thrown at us. Before I could register the command from brain to limbs, I snatched the delicate, narrow wrist of the woman I had once called mother.

Let me out! Let me out! Itzelcoszcatl bellowed, thrashing against my tenuous hold on her.

Not yet. Sal didn't find Elida or Jamal. We have to wait for Ixchel and Cheeno, I hissed back.

"Where are they?" I growled, the sound conjuring the image of desert-parched bones ground beneath the crush of stones.

Annette slapped at me, pulling a canister of mace from her purse that lay slung haphazardly on the table and spraying it in my face. I huffed, sniffed, and sneezed the noxious gas. It tingled, like the bubble of hydrogen peroxide on an abraded knee. I recognized the sharp green, almost citrusy herbaceous scent of rue floating in the air. Before I could laugh in her face, an iron grip took my shoulder and shoved me back from her.

I scowled up at the mercenary who must have pushed past Sal when I caught my balance, narrowing my eyes on him. "I'm sorry for your mistake."

Cheeno was on him before I could even finish my statement, his blood-red eyes glowing like a neon sign, even in the lurid light of the day as he stepped from the shadows. The scent of spoiled meat mixed with the herby scent of the rue, and no one moved. No one except Ixchel, who stepped into the fray from the same shadow. She would not let the Jaguar get in licks where she could not. She had traded shadows and stalked down the guard in a hunting formation with Cheeno. The plan was to eliminate any threats after searching the house. My mother was my concern. The scent of fear, pure and primordial, permeated the deck as the two massive, shifting, swirling, dog-shaped shadows herded the now three mercenaries away from us.

If the Jaguar and the Eagle had returned, that meant their hunt through the house and below it was unfruitful, and we could move on to the next phase of my plan.

Sal had not moved, but I could feel his rage as a palpable entity, aching to bathe in blood and rejoice in the carnage he would reap. Images of a battlefield deep in the jungle, frantic with the cacophonous clamor of weapons meeting wood and leather shields, screaming, yelling, and my mate's drunken roaring laughter as he tore through the bodies of his enemies filled my mind. My cadejo was preening over the viciousness of her mate, longing for a time when she could lean back on a rock, sunbathe in the light of the summer, while the red mist of battle peppered her skin. As much as I would have shrunken from the idea a few months ago, I had to admit the idea of it made my knees a little gelatinous.

My gaze turned back to my mother. She was holding the rue mace like a holy talisman that would keep her safe from me. "If only you hadn't poisoned me my entire life and made me nearly immune to rue because my tolerance is so high. If only," I murmured past the rows of teeth in a faux wistful tone, mocking her.

"Drink the damned wine, Angelica, or I'll give the order to kill Elida." When I didn't even wince, she forged on. "If you do as you're told, I'll make sure she gets out even. I'll send her down here to them. Let them have her."

"Bargaining already? That was quick. I was almost looking forward to shock and denial. And I thought you said she was here, mommy dearest." I crossed my arms over my chest and watched her, feeling the press and swim of Itzelcoszcatl behind my eyes, like a prowling shark trying to get into the diver's cage. "You don't have her. You're just trying to get what you want. Now. This is the last time I will ask. Where is Jamal?"

She laughed. "Oh, Angelica. Do you really think I want you? No one actually wants you. You're a grotesque monster who sucks away the one thing that no one wants sucked. I only want the money. You're a means to an end." Her greasy falcon's gaze turned to Sal, a man so far out of her league—when compared to the paunchy Edwin—that it was almost insulting to let her look at him. "Tell her. We both know you don't actually want her. What's your angle, hmm? Want to breed a few more of her? I know her kind isn't exactly common anymore."

He tilted his head. Sal was the most dangerous when he was quiet. She had made another mistake by calling his attention to her. "She is everything I have ever wanted. I would tear the heavens apart just to hear my name on her lips. If she gives me get, I would be a lucky man. If she does not, it does not matter. I have bled the life from my own father just to have a chance at standing beside her. So, yes, harpy, I will fuck her and fill her with my cum whenever she wants, and I will count myself as blessed every second she lets me breathe in her general presence. And the only reason you still stand here long enough to flap your cock holster is because she's deemed it so. Don't test my patience."

She laughed—actually had the audacity to laugh at him. Rage boiled in my blood. My eye caught on something, drawing my attention down her body to the slight twitch and shake of her hand around the canister. She was terrified. Absolutely terrified. She was fighting it, clutching the useless mace in a death grip to hide it, but living with creatures that fed off of fear and terror made you notice those things. My eyes narrowed on it, and I felt my cadejo lick her lips and the edges of each tooth at the weakness she found in her prey. She may feed on happiness, but she was just as harrowing a monster as the rest, perhaps more so.

I tilted my head, letting my scrutiny catch up on Annette's eyes. "Show me. I assume that, if you are, in fact, renting her out for a fee, you have some evidence she is still alive. So. Show me."

"Drink the wine, and I will," she snapped back.

I summoned the imaginary, shimmering, rainbow hands in my mind and stroked her cheek with them. Seeded the hope that I would actually behave. I had been practicing, but my skill was still not as finely honed as I would have liked. Some of the others could, in their shadow-traded form, manipulate the emotions of humans to the exact specifications they wanted. I could only twist and push and tug in my human skin, not yet skilled enough to do more.

"Show me the pictures and tell me where Jamal is, and I will call everyone off and go willingly. Quietly, even. As long as you keep your bargain, I will keep my mouth shut and do as I am told until I die." I let that imaginary hand stroke and pull, her eyes glimmering with greed.

"It's a beautiful pool, Angelica, you haven't even noticed. It's really very rude of you, you know," she hedged, the words bolstering a dangerous slice to them.

Sal was twitching behind me, itching to stop me. I really must have been stupid before Itzelcoszcatl came into her power, if they all thought I was this stupid. She didn't have Elida, I was sure of it. She wouldn't be avoiding the torment of showing me some horrible picture if she really did have her.

"Drink the wine, you stupid mutt, or Lacey and I will fill that pool over and over again," she hissed in a whispered threat.

My eyes slid to the eternity pool that sat on the edge of the deck for the first time since I stepped out onto the patio. Annette was losing her touch. Back in San Francisco, had the pool boys allowed that many leaves to float on the top of her precious pool, she'd have had them fired. It took milliseconds for me to notice the dark shape wobbling under the breeze-swept surface.

I didn't think. I didn't even let it process. I was running before my cadejo registered what I was seeing. The surface of the water breached easily as I dove in after the boy's sunken body. Strong strokes brought me to the bottom as my arm wrapped around Jamal and kicked off the flat bottom. The weights around his waist dragged and scratched at my skin, making it feel too tight.

I gasped at the surface, rue-filled water rushing toward me, carrying the true weight of the precious cargo I carried with me. I had always known, had always worried Annette would do something horrible to the totoco. I'd spent so many nights agonizing over the potential angles she would take. I never suspected her cavalier disregard for life would see a precious child drown in a pool filled with rue. She hadn't been satisfied killing Jamal. She wanted to drown his spirit with him. My chest collapsed in on itself with the enormity of the sacrifice.

I was dragging him up and over the lip of the pool when Sal reached us. "Get back." I gasped as the water dribbled into my mouth, setting it on fire. "Rue."

The sound of Jamal's corpse rolling onto the wooden deck twisted my stomach and gagged me. His poor little body was pockmarked, as if he had been dipped in acid and infected with some flesh-eating disease. I knelt next to him, my entire being shaking, Itzelcoszcatl a silent witness huddled in the corner in awe of the sheer horror before her. I let my hands run along his body, twisting into the ropes that bound his legs and hands together. He had fought hard. They were dug so deep into his flesh I struggled to free his limbs and settle them peacefully next to him. Next were the weights, massive plates thudding heavily on the wood beneath him as I unwound the ropes. All the while, behind me, my mother's muffled voice rattled on. I heard nothing she said. None of it mattered.

My shaking hands fixed his hair, settling it on his black-veined forehead. I rose, turning my head away, unable to look at him any longer. I couldn't memorize the horrifying death mask of a child I knew to be so full of life. I snagged a towel from a nearby chair and looped it under his arms.

"Take him to the truck."

My voice was a solitary leaf, brittle and light, on the raging power building within my heart.

"No, Xochitl . . ." Sal said.

My eyes locked on to Annette.

No more. There would be no more crying children. No more shaking, cowering kids in corners of apartments. There would be no more dead children.

Let me out. Itzelcoszcatl crooned in my ear. *It tingles but does not burn.*

Step-by-step, I stalked her. With each footfall, I could feel myself stretching, my eyes sharpening, blood seasoning my tongue as shark teeth formed in my jaw. I felt my curled locks ripple into a crown of long plumage atop my head. My sight narrowed to one eye as Itzelcoszcatl took the other. We were two spirits existing on the same plane, and I had never felt more like the righteous hand of the teotl.

"Drink the fucking wine, Angelica! Or I'll shoot him!" she screamed as I got within clawing distance, my gold-tipped, knife-like claws clicking in the sunset.

"I was going to walk away, let you wither and die in your joyless dried-up husk of a body. But this? This, I cannot abide. You can strike at me, degrade me all you wish, but you will never harm my people and live," I purred in my own voice.

An opalescent-furred arm, rippling with strong muscle, shot out and grabbed her by the wrist that held the gun.

"Nor mine," my cadejo crooned in her bell-like, songbird voice.

Annette wriggled, trying to yank her arm free of my iron grasp, like a fish on a hook, knowing it's for the pot.

Searing heat announced the shot before the sound of the gun going off hit my ears. Magma flowed from my left shoulder, and the grin splitting our merged face was malignant, pure, and without fault.

"You will not need this because you used them to offend the flesh of my jewel," Itzelcoszcatl whispered down in a lover's croon to the struggling woman before pulling her arms wide into a mockery of a crucifixion.

She kept pulling, our muscles straining as our claws dug into the tender flesh of her inner elbows. Her screams came quickly, almost drowning out the twisting, gut-wrenching sound of the bones slipping free of the shoulder sockets. The flesh strained and shuddered before finally giving in and ripping free of Annette's torso. An ocean spray of blood showered us as she dropped to the deck. The two arms were chucked carelessly over the side and into the waiting bosom of the ocean below.

We were not done with her yet, not by far. Our knees caged her in and pressed firmly to the bleeding stumps as we bent over her. "And you will not need these because you refused to see the suffering you birthed."

I felt myself push forward. Itzelcoszcatl's dagger-tipped paws exchanged into my own stubbed fingers. I wanted to feel this. I wanted to savor the sensation as my thumbs dug into the sockets, pressing the solid ball as I spoke with my own voice. "Your life is not ours to take in this life, but we will find you in the next. You will never know true rest. You will spend eternity as our favorite prey. We will hunt you throughout the ages and find such glorious ways for you to die every single time. Hear this in that rotten thing you call a soul. Carry it with you into the next life. We will always find you. We will mark your suffering across the echoes of time. We swear this."

When the orbs of her eyeballs popped beneath my thumbs, I sighed with satisfaction and pushed up to stand, turning to Sal, who was staring at me as if I were a goddess who just stepped forward from the heavens. Behind me, an aria of primal terror shrieked and writhed. It was the most beautiful sound I had heard. It reached out and stroked the primordial creature within me, piling wood on the pyre of our righteous, burning anger.

"Bind her wounds. I'll carry Jamal's body to the truck," I snarled through my shark's teeth at him.

"She's not dead yet," Ixchel commented, stepping through the doorway to the house, a shirt tied tightly around her torso, picking at her teeth. Cheeno was on her heels.

"Oh, I'm aware, but this kill is not mine. This belongs to Jamal's mother and father. She has taken their son. The least I can do is bring him back to them and deliver her for their justice."

I took one last look at the woman who had birthed me into this world, one last look at the creature she had become. Ruby beads dappled her creamy white silk charmeuse dress. Shimmering rivers of thick slime spotted with blood ran down her pale cheeks into her screaming mouth from empty, angry mangled sockets. It was a fitting appearance, the outside finally depicting the horror I had always seen peeking around the corners of her public mask.

"She came with Shayne's assistant Lacey. Find her. She helped Annette snatch Jamal. Punish her as you see fit."

I felt the bloodthirsty grin that crossed Ixchel's face, and the grim, determined mate to it on Cheeno's as they accepted my order.

I turned my back on her, closing the book of Angelica. There were no more pages I wished to read, see, or carve out anew. I was Xochitl, as I was always meant to be. And I would embrace my new life, love, and family with both arms and my eyes turned toward the dawn.

I stalked down my mate, slowly letting go of my hold on the shared flesh form. The burn in my shoulder would need attention as soon as we got back to the compound.

When I reached him, I let a bloodied finger trace down his jaw line. "I need to shower before I get in the truck . . . Care to join me?"

He groaned and nodded. "I found a bathroom while searching."

"Elida?"

He sighed and shook his head. "If she was ever here, there's no trace of her now."

CHAPTER FIFTY

Two-and-a-half weeks later...

I paced the living room floor. Why was I so nervous? Nothing would change. Nothing would be categorically altered by the end of this day, yet I felt like I was standing on the edge of a mist-blinded cliff, being told to take just another step forward. My stomach was tying itself into a menagerie of balloon animals. I felt dizzy and nauseous and sluggish, like every paced-out slap of my feet took twice the effort. My eyes kept darting to the window, waiting for the sun to drop closer to the horizon. It hung, frozen in place above the horizon line, mocking me with its teasing descent.

"You're going to crack the tile," Ixchel drolled from the earthen lip of a jug, the chilled drink a gift from one of the Ah Kin from Edzna. I narrowed my eyes on her as she sheepishly put the jug back in the water to keep it cool. When I narrowed my eyes at the out-of-character expression, she quickly tossed it aside with a simple roll of her shoulders. "It's true, though. No amount of walking around will make the sun set faster, Cihuatlatoani. So, sit. Drink. Breathe your last bit of single air for a while."

The apartment was bustling with the totoco's women and a few of the visiting dignitaries, including the ambassador to the Council for the totoco, Amanka. I'd learned that Amanka, unlike the rest of the totoco, did not live within our territory but in Campeche, near the seat of power for the tribes.

Tribes.

That was still settling into my brain, that it wasn't just a cluster of them here in El Salvador. They stretched from the Alaskan coast to the tip of Chile, with small pockets of totocos controlling even smaller territories around volcanic vents. Amanka was the grandmother of the former totoco leader, Antu Silan Ulap. My brain had done cartwheeled pretzels, trying to figure out how the grandmother of the woman who raised Sal was still around.

The ancient woman flicked a mysterious smile at me as she sat in a place of honor in a chair someone had brought in for her, as if she knew I was still trying to work it out. She patted the seat on the couch near her, and I trotted over to her to sit on the floor, a custom I had learned was appropriate when an elder matriarch was in attendance. Her wizened, withered hand found the top of my lavishly braided head tied up in an equally elaborate style. The top half of my braids were pulled back and folded over itself to a handspan, then wrapped with a vivid red cloth with bells at the end. The tails of the cloth dripped down on either side of my head, jingling as I moved. The edges of the braids had been fed through a small golden bell-shaped piece and hung in front of my eyes. Those same ends had then been dipped in gold dust and were brushing the tip of my nose.

"Have your stars been read yet, sija?"

Her eyes were bolted to me. I could move anywhere, and they would follow. My eyes drifted up to the massive tree growing around the woman's spirit. Blooms and fruits of shapes, colors, and styles I had never seen before sparkled in the low light of the living room. The others were smart enough not to stop their conversation as I sat at the elder's foot. I shook my head, the bells tinkling in the air.

Her gray-and-white-head bobbed with a slow nod. "That boy was never one to let the stars dictate his life. When he came back to us and told us he had found you—so early, no less—we all told him the stars said he would not marry until he was much, much older."

"Technically the stars were right." I grinned up at her.

Our eyes met, and she leaned in, searching my gaze for something, before she grinned and sucked her teeth. "Never thought she would come out. She was so content to lounge about."

"Who?" I asked, fluttering my gold dusted lashes.

Her age-thinned lips tipped up, and she tapped me on the nose. "You're not the only one, sija."

Julia and Pastora both warned me not to talk too long with Amanka. They said she had lost too much of her human spirit and walked too closely in the spirit realm. If I spoke too long with her, I'd go insane.

"It's time!" screeched Julia from behind me, dragging me away from the antediluvian woman.

I shot to my feet and adjusted the buttercup-yellow cotton robe and the red-tasseled sash tied around me. My eyes darted out the window, where I saw Ixchel dashing out to light torches. One by one, the crowd of women filed out of the apartment to take hold of the offered torches.

And, so it started. The women led me, some playing instruments, some singing, some dancing, to the small round hut that had been built over the last three weeks, beyond the tree line, deep into the jungle, away from the compound. Dirt and leaf litter shifted under my bare feet as we approached the fire-lit clearing.

A massive copper tub had been set up outside of the hut and was steaming in the early evening air with hot water. A hundred people, some strangers, some totoco, surrounded the small clearing, but my eyes fell immediately on Sal.

He stood tall, his long straight black hair hanging in a polished midnight curtain around his bare shoulders. Stacks of dark bronze sheathed muscles flexing in the warm glow of the torches, and a different sort of fire burned in his dark eyes. The world fell away and blurred into nothingness as we stared at each other, at our forever. Time stretched out between us, and I saw the life we would build together coalesce into a shimmering white light of promise. My heart lurched, squeezed down hard on itself to keep from exploding with the enormity of the love I had for him. I wanted to cry. I wanted to shout.

The Ah Kin and teopixqui were speaking, giving a blessing, but it sounded like bees hovering around the open blossoms of a marigold field. My entire existence had, once again, narrowed down to the way his beautiful full lips tipped up at one corner in an inviting tease.

Hands gently guided my robe off of me to let the fire-kissed night dance across my naked skin. I felt Amanka's silky paper skin take my hand and guide me to the tub where Sal was also headed. We eased our naked bodies into the bath, the sound of the audience turning their back on us to give us some modicum of privacy filling the clearing as the priests circled, singing the blessings and prayers for a happy marriage and fertility.

Sal mumbled something to a priest as she passed, who asked him a question. I tilted my head in curiosity.

"She was asking if I wanted to add a blessing to open your heart to, uh . . . another wife down the line." He had the good sense to look apologetic on the priest's behalf.

I snorted. "I'd cut your balls off before you ever even thought of bedding another woman."

His deep, baritone laughter filled the warm night and tapered off into a wicked grin. "There'll be no need for that. My heart and balls have belonged to you since we were children. It will always belong to you. You are my everything."

I scooted closer to him, letting my hand slip as close as I could to trail a teasing path up his calf. We weren't supposed to be touching just yet. This was supposed to be cleansing, but all I could think of was crawling into his lap and getting very dirty. "Oh, Big Bad," I breathed softly. "I love you, too."

His eyes went glassy, sparkling with affection and the seeds of unshed tears. "I've waited twenty years to hear you say that, noyzoyzton."

The urge to slide into his lap was almost too much to resist, but Amanka was at my shoulder again, that timeworn hand slipping under my armpit to urge me to rise. An older man I'd not met just yet did the same to Sal. We were pulled apart, our eyes lingering on each other as I was taken into the hut we would be locked into after the ceremony, to get dressed.

I was led to a small woven mat to stand close to a slumbering hearth. Ixchel, the fire runner of the totoco, appeared with a small bowl aglow with a tiny flame.

"Light the hearth from the fire of the temple," Amanka crooned, passing me the bowl. I took a brush of straw from the small table next to me and lit the ends. "Let the fire warm this home and kindle new life in heart and womb."

I winced. *Yeah, not likely on the latter there.* Despite me adhering to Sal's new pill rule, as far as I could tell, he was still giving me birth control and not the sugar pills. Though, every morning, I'd kneel at his feet and beg him to give me a child, his finger pressing the pill into my outstretched tongue felt like a supplication. And every morning, he'd drag me back into bed, and we'd worship at the altar of each other's pleasure.

As soon as the flame caught, the women were an orchestra of movement. Dressing me and adorning me in the finery I was to wear up to the ceremony on the lip of the caldera. Before I knew it, I was dressed in a simple, long tunic-style top, split from the mid-thigh to my waist and an embroidered skirt that had bells fringing the hem. The ends of my hair, both the ones at my forehead and the ends of the rest of my curls, were dipped in gold and shaken just slightly to free the excess. My feet were painted red on the soles and gold on the tops to above my ankle.

A conch shell was blown outside of the hut, and I bounced on the balls of my feet as we all filed out of the hut, me leaving bright red footprints on the packed earth floor. Ixchel and Cheeno would stay at the hut. Their shadow forms were already seated on their haunches, like two temple dogs guarding the entrance to the cosmos. They would protect the now-sacred space from interlopers, both of the realm of flesh and the realm of spirit, so that, should an heir be conceived that night, it would be blessed and untainted. I couldn't help but pat the two ghost dogs on the head like loyal dobermans as I passed them.

Nopaltzin stood next to a small stool, a sling tucked over one shoulder. So far, this was the only part of the ritual that had gotten a side-eye from me. I hesitantly mounted the stool and leaned up onto his back as gingerly as I could. I had been assured that the elder cadejo was far stronger than he looked, but he was approaching fifty, and I was not a dainty flower.

"You can do better than that, girl. Get up there," he growled, hefting me up onto his back for a piggyback ride.

The sling came down around my bum, and I was secured to his back. I felt ridiculous, but this was a tradition Sal's people had observed back before the Triple Alliance. The bride was to be carried to her groom on the back of her father or a priest. Nopaltzin had claimed it as his great honor, and I didn't want to argue with him. He had become a fatherly figure, anyway.

The climb up the caldera rim from the wedding hut was an agonizing trek. I was sure, at any moment, Nopaltzin's back would give out, and we'd tumble down the slope into the benighted bushes. It never did, though, and to my surprise, every step toward the rim of the caldera, his back straightened more and more until I was gripping on to keep from sliding.

When we arrived, safe and sound, he let me down, placing a comforting hand on the top of my head. "I've been proud to know you, Xochitl. You have brought light back to this totoco. You will have my loyalty unquestioning until I pass from this realm into the next. Now, get up there and make that man remember why he is lucky to have found you before I did."

His sentiment twisted my heart into the first petal of a flower, and I sniffed back the threatening tears to take the last five steps up to the rim of the volcano my totoco called home. This long-dormant beast was the conduit for us between the spirit realm and the flesh. It was only fitting that, as I brought the last piece necessary to solidify the compact between that realm and this for the totoco, we would seal that union on its lip, staring into the throat of the sleeping giant granting us a safe home.

Sal and I were seated on a mat, surrounded by the flickering flames of torches and the watchful eyes of our guests. The Ah Kin of Edzna lit the copal behind us and intoned the last of the blessings and prayers as Sal and I watched the attendees.

Amanka was at my side again as I rose. A copili of fiery feathers from an aracari, vivid magma iridescence of scarlet macaw tail feathers, mixed with the beautiful shimmering black feathers of roosters and a trogon bird, was handed to me. The leather band had taken me the entire two weeks to carve and paint, laboring over it for this exact moment, when I would place it on Sal's head. I held the headdress aloft for the guests to see and stepped up to him. Love and adoration shimmered up at me from his burnet gaze. I lowered it and placed it on his head, adjusting the centerpiece of glimmering jade to rest above his brows. Crowning him Tlahtoani of the Lets'a Wehle tribe.

I felt the pleased tremble of the sleeping giant underfoot as the image of a pleased smile amid a conflagration of cheerful flames wavered in my mind. My beast turned within me, eager for her part but also eager to taste the air that sparkled with spirit energy as they drew close to this sacred moment.

He smiled softly, his hand snaking around my ankle in a silent comfort and thanks for the symbolic acknowledgment of his leadership of the totoco. I indulged in the sensation of the rough pads of his fingers dancing from my heel to my ankle before I moved to sit again. That soft touch turned steely as he held me still.

"My gift to you, nonamic," he purred up to me as Cadmael handed him a box.

Two jade bangles were removed, and as he delicately latched them to my ankles, my breath hitched. A matching pair of gold anklets joined them before the box was placed aside. I tested their weight, savoring the way the gold sounded clinking against the jade.

"They are beautiful, monamic," I whispered.

He pulsed his fingers at my ankle before finally releasing me to sit next to him again. Our eyes never left each other, hungry to just look at each other as we traveled the journey to the end of that night together.

"I'm afraid my gift is far less beautiful," I said as Amanka brought the large wooden box with my surprise for him. My mouth was already twitching, fighting off the smile as I placed it in front of him.

A cocking of a brow was given to me, and he flipped the lid open. The raucous laughter pouring out of him filled the entire valley in a blitz of joviality. There, in the box, was an expertly stuffed seagull, its head turned to stare accusingly at him. He lifted it from the box and held it aloft as if it were the Heismann trophy. Peals of laughter joined his as totocan, who had heard the story of us meeting on the beach, got the joke right away. Some guests shuffled awkwardly, but this was for us. Seagulls could live . . . for now.

"I shall treasure it always, nonamic," he gasped out when he finally caught his breath.

The gifts kept coming, Julia bringing a blouse and skirt to lay in front of me. Nopaltzin brought Sal a new cape and hard leather armbands I had commissioned for him. The guests brought gifts of all sorts, from pottery to gems to gold to a dizzying kaleidoscope of brilliantly colored feathers. When it was finally Amanka's turn, she laid before us a set of gorgeous gold earrings that had shells dangling from them.

Sal stiffened, and I looked from him to Amanka.

"They were Antu's. They were returned to me when she passed into the next realm. And now, I gift them to the woman who takes her place with honor."

Sal rose, taking the old woman's hand in his. "You do my wife and me a great honor, elder. Thank you."

She patted his cheek and then kneeled between us as he sat. Ancient weathered fingers, like the roots of the tree that grew in her spirit, grasped the cape that now hung around Sal's brawny shoulders and the end of my tunic. She whispered something I couldn't understand, though it sounded like the lines to a beautiful poem that made my heart clench with emotion, as she tied the ends of our garments together. She knotted it once and then again, symbolizing the union of first the man and woman and then the two spirits residing within us.

Hoots and cheers rose from the cadejos around us, pronouncing us officially married. The tears threatening my eyes all night finally fell as the big body of my husband scooted closer so our knees touched.

"What did I tell you about crying?" he whispered above the ululations of the crowd as jugs of pulque were passed around and jovial merriment rang through the bowl of the volcano.

The echoes ringing back at us sounded like spirits from beyond, crying out with the same jubilation as those here with us. I gave him a watery smile, and his thumb caressed my cheek to rub the tear away.

Long poles were slid through the ends of the small platform under our mat. Under the cover of our marital knot, Sal gripped my thigh as we were lifted into the air, and the descent back to the marriage hut began. I swayed with the journey, my eyes finding their place glued to his. Fires banked in his eyes, and I could only imagine he saw the same reflected at him in my golden gaze. Covering his hand with mine, I squeezed, our fingers tangling naturally with each other.

The short climb down gave us little time to fan the glowing, ever-present embers of our ardor, but by the time we were lowered off the shoulders of the totoco, I was clenching and nearly panting with the need to wrap myself around him and feel him brutally thrusting within me. The way he growled low in the back of his throat, an ever-present thrumming need, answered my own.

A massive bonfire was lit behind us. Guests made their way to where they wished to observe, casting a menagerie of shadows across Sal and I.

His palm found my cheek, and I leaned heavily into it. "Are you sure?"

His soft rum-and-spice voice rumbled through me, and I nodded. This tradition went back thousands of years. I did not want to be the one to break it. Not then, not ever.

His hand found mine, our soft human fingers holding on to each other, his gripping tightly as if to say "You got this."

I knew the next step. We had walked through the ceremony a hundred times. I didn't have to run a mental finger across the membrane between us. She had been present the whole night, just under the surface, itching to burst forward. I felt the liquid sensation of warm water coursing down my arm and the sharp bite of my nails being pulled out into the gold-tipped, white-furred claw I had been practicing to manifest. He matched me, arm trading his shadow into the onyx-furred nightmare that had so often stroked me into a bloody, panting, keening mess César had to sheepishly heal.

He nodded softly and turned me to face him, our knees kissing beneath the tied double knot as the priests circled us. Oils and herbs were pressed to our skin and head, incense brought close as words fell on us like a shower of rose petals. Sal's arm moved first, drawing sharp claws down the sides of my skirt to shred it and let it puddle around my bare hips. I wanted to shiver, my bare skin pebbled by the sensation of a thousand eyes pressing in close.

I followed his lead, letting my fingers grow long and sharp, dragging them down the edges of his pants, then pushing them away before crawling into his lap, my knees finding the side of his hips. When his furred arms came around me to scoot me closer so our hearts could beat close to each other, I almost purred, his heat chasing away any visible fears and reluctance. Let them look. Let them see how much we love each other.

An obsidian claw tipped my chin up so he could watch my eyes as the other cleanly bisected the back of my tunic, my own claw mirroring his motion as the knotted material puddled in our laps. Hunger flashed in his eyes, and I was sure my own reflected back at him as his lips crashed into mine. Our tongues tangled with each other, chaos and need guiding their warring dance as they slid and entwined with each other.

We were breathing raggedly by the time we pulled ourselves away from the kiss, hearts slamming in unison against the bars of our chests, foreheads pressed to each other, trying desperately to ground each other. Naked need thrummed through us like a sizzling pulse of raw electrical currents trapped on the precipice of falling into the pandemonium of something so much bigger.

Sal groaned, pulling me into his lap and stealing another kiss. He wasted no time, and I needed no time to ease into this rabid connection. He dug into my thighs and slammed my dripping heat down onto the thickness of his cock. We both froze, panting and groaning at the sensation of coming together. We had not been allowed to fuck for two whole days, and it felt like an eternity since we had sunk into the simple joy of each other's bodies.

I was the first to break the reverie, rolling my hips against the stiff intrusion of him, grinding it deeper into my tight depths. His breath caught in his throat, his fingers pressing my flesh.

"If you keep moving like that, nayeli, I'm going to lose my fucking mind. My divine golden goddess, I can barely keep my head on straight around you as it is but being away from your pussy has me on the edge of absolute madness." He buried his head at the base of my neck and bit down hard, his blunt teeth clamping down on the flesh and making me want to both squirm and still for him. He pulled away far too soon, licking and kissing the throbbing flesh. "And I intend on at least keeping my wits long enough to mark you, finally."

I panted against his lips. Drawing in deep drags of air to cool my inferno of need. When I could finally feel myself beyond the vast pit of desire, I nodded.

My clawed arm reached out, brushing velvety, silken fur across his bare, sweat-glistening chest. I traced my golden claws across his skin as he did with me. We teased each other, building up the bank of volcanic pressure and need between us. When I could take it no longer, needing to move—or I'd be the one going insane—I stilled my claw and began the marking. I let the tip sink into his skin right above his heart but did not move it, just let the ruby drop of blood bead up around the gold. As the blood pooled around my claw, I watched, dumbstruck with awe as smoke pooled in the depths of the blood.

"I wish to give you my mate mark. Do you accept it?" I asked in a hushed, reverent tone.

That moment was the moment we had been dancing around for what seemed like years. Even our audience seemed to go stark-still, no conversation or movement to disturb this sacred moment. I couldn't meet his gaze, my eyes catching on the bead of blood with the swirls of ink. This was not just Sal's turn to speak; his cadejo spirit could easily reject me at this moment. Fear and uncertainty twisted in my guts.

"I am yours. I accept your mark into my soul, sweet flower," he whispered. The smoke in his eyes cleared, and his teeth smoked to the long daggers that had nipped and teased me so often. "And I accept the Jeweled Rainbow's claim on me. From now until the end," the husky voice of his beast scratched out.

I wanted to sob, I wanted to cry with joy. Instead, I focused all of my efforts on not shaking as I carved the sigil the priests had helped me craft as my mate mark into his flesh. The shimmering rainbow of my beast rippled across my hand and danced with the black smoke that fell from the cut. It needed to be deep, deep enough to cause a vivid scar, one that could not be healed and one that would last for the entirety of his life in this body.

When I was done, I looked up into his burning dark gaze. He was so still, so quiet at this moment, but pure hunger radiated off of him. Need so untainted that it made my breath catch, and he groaned when my pussy clenched around him.

His black-furred, clawed hand came to the flesh between my breasts and rested there for a long time, his other hand squeezing mine so hard it felt like he'd break the bones.

"This will be the only scar I ever allow you to suffer," he murmured as a promise to my skin before he met my eyes.

Nodding softly, I accepted his oath, even though there was no way he could keep it.

"I wish to give you my mate mark. Do you accept it?" he asked, his voice thick with unvoiced emotion, whispering the words that would bind our souls and the spirits within us.

"I am yours. I accept your mark into my soul, Big Bad." Fire seared my gums as my beast didn't even bother to wait for me to ask her for her decision. She was just as eager as I was. "And I accept the Obsidian Beast's claim on me. From now until the end," she snapped, as if biting the air with each word.

He shivered, Itzatecuani pressing too deep at first, unused to being gentle in his handling of my flesh. He had become bolder and bolder as our time together grew longer. The stinging burn of his claws dragging through my skin had become an erotic sensation, my hips jerking in response, fighting for the delicious match to the pain that coursed through me as he carved his mark into my skin.

Just as his had, when I looked down at the tight, burning slashes in my chest, I saw my cadejo seeping into my blood. Iridescence and gold flakes swam in the streaks of red as they coursed down my skin. The feel of my blood slipping and sliding down the fevered flesh drew a shivered gasp from my kiss-brutalized lips.

When he was done, he panted out a huff of exertion, and I couldn't help but circle my hips, grinding the head of his cock deep into that spot I loved so much. He tipped his head back, groaning, as both of his hands gripped my hips and forced me down harder on him.

I watched him, our eyes intent on each other as my hips drew slow circles onto him. Shimmering mist grew around me, pulsing with veins of gold and shot through with rainbows. Darkness coalesced and pooled in smoky tendrils around him, flames pitch-black, eating the light cast by the mist around me and gathering behind him. I felt the exact moment when Itzelcoszcatl stepped free of my skin. It felt like a great hole opened up in my stomach and poured free the contents of everything that made me. Sal stilled under me, both of us riveted by the display before us.

No forms were taken. Though I expected to see the great goddess I had witnessed in the temple, here, she only gave her misty form a hint of solidness. The impact of her presence in the world was the sensation of hysteria edging the overwhelming burden of a happy moment, juxtaposed on the flash of shark jaws, the glittering of knife-like claws. The smoke behind Sal shuddered and advanced on the glimmering white mist retreating a step as the darkness stalked it.

Sal gripped my hips and pounded up into me, claiming my attention as the shimmering mist played cat and mouse with the darkness. Calloused fingers wrapped around my throat and tightened as the brutal blackness reached the mist and collided into it, Sal's cock spearing up into me in one deep, claiming thrust. A deep, guttural moan trembled on my lips as the two polar opposites writhed in the air beside us.

I needed more, wanted more, and I would take it. My hand found the throbbing red mess on his chest and pushed, flattening him against the mat, my glittering twin following.

"You are mine, great beast. And you will worship me as I deserve." Itzelcoszcatl's bell-like voice filled the pregnant silence as she surged forward, and I did as well.

My eyes connected with Sal's. For a moment, the tiniest of fear that, without his beast pushing his hunger for me, passion would not bank the flames in his eyes. The visceral need that shimmered back at me gripped me and stirred my hips to slam down on him, grinding his dick deep into my tender, feverish folds. My blood-soaked hand found his throat and squeezed like he so often did to me, smearing his blood in a lurid scarf.

"Run all you wish, creature of mist and fury. You are never getting away from me. In this life or the next," Itzatecuani's voice rumbled back.

Sal surged beneath me, mimicked by the surging of his dark beast, and pinned my shoulders to the mat, my legs wrapping around his brutally pistolling hips. I was so full of him, barely able to breathe around the intensity flooding the too-small clearing ricocheting back and forth. Our unleashed spirits soaked into our skin, then volleyed back to them in an unending circuit of primal lust.

"We will bathe in the blood of our enemies, rend the foundations of this world, and crush it beneath our feet, my mate," she answered as I turned swiftly between deep pounding thrusts to get on all fours.

Sal didn't miss a single desperate stroke, seating himself so deep I swore that I felt him in my lungs.

He gripped my hair, pulling my head back, speaking his own words, not the words of our beasts. "You were mine before the children of Raax Pek'u were even conceived, and you will be mine until the sun dies in the heavens."

"And you will be mine until every spirit in this world and the next disappears," I scraped out between panting moans.

He pulled more, lifting me from the mat to my knees. The hand in my hair slid around my throat, and iron fingers gripped and squeezed. His voice was hot in my ear as the blackness stalking the edges of my vision matched the one that stalked the fire-licked edges of the clearing after the slash of opaline claws. "Every breath is mine. Every heart beat is mine. You live and die in my arms alone. You bleed and moan in my hands alone."

The toothy maw of my beast manifested as it bit down within the nebula that hunted it. A howled moan of pleasure rippled through the blackness and my husband as I reached between my legs and squeezed his pendulous balls, carefully pulling him to plunge into my gripping depths. "And your pleasure belongs to me. You will thrive and wither under my stewardship. You will kneel and worship at the altar of my pussy and fill me with your sacrifice."

Shuddering behind me, he nearly crushed my wind pipe in his hand as the other slithered down my body, smearing the gold-and-crimson blood down my feverish flesh to dance his fingers across my clit. "I will worship you always, my beautiful golden goddess."

A grin of triumph, unseen but shuddering through the charged energy of my beast as the inky ball of smoke struggled at the stress of a pressing claw, signaled her victory over the Obsidian Beast. Sal shivered from head to toe. He lifted me and turned me to face him before seating himself deep inside again as he went to his knees with me in his lap. His thumb stroked my jaw as we feverishly rode each other. His eyes locked with mine, and he whispered his supplication again. "I will forever worship you, sweet golden goddess."

As we climbed that hill together, his hand found mine and gripped my fingers, as if we would spin into the cosmos should we not hold on for dear life. Pain coursed through me and mingled with the sweet ecstasy of his throbbing cock thrusting inside of me. We came together, roaring our pleasure into the night, pressing down on the raw, jagged nerves sliced open by our devotion.

As the stars popped and sizzled in my vision, he drew my lips to his, his other hand cupping my cheek tenderly.

"Mine," he whispered his promise.

"Yours," I answered.

CHAPTER FIFTY-ONE
César

I smiled softly, a tender curl of my lips as Cadmael fitted the last brick into the entryway of the ceremonial hut my cousin had been sealed into with his mate. After the performance the two gave, they deserved the privacy. Guests were already murmuring at the ferocity of their mating and the strength on display from both of their spirits. Good. Let them see how his choice was perfect and that the tribulations they had both endured to finally be here on that night were worth it.

He had fought so hard for her. My heart ached with the memory of long nights sitting quietly with him as he stared into the depths of the cosmos on the roof of the totoco compound building. Over the years, it had been a steady sight. If Itziquetzal was ever missing, you could find him staring at the stars, mourning the absence of the woman who was now wrapped in his arms.

My heart had broken over and over against the tides of his longing. I knew that, to have the woman he loved with every grain of his existence, he would have to kill the amazing man who was his father. So, I was happy to turn my back on the symbolic cave we had built for them to finally seal their mating.

A barb of jealousy shredded a secret corner of my heart.

The spirits within me thrashed in a whirlpool of sensations and images, an image of the stars rotating and spinning in the night sky, flashing across the theater of my mind. Time slid effortlessly through the images, like a boat slipping silently through the moon-kissed river of the sky. I felt their urgency, their insistence, and eagerness.

I slid my hazel eyes shut as I conjured the image of the woman I had only glimpsed that first night the teotl stirred around me. A gift, a treasure granted. The well-worn edges of the memory slid into my mind's eye without trouble. The rich, sun-kissed, unblemished skin, still supple with an untouched youth. The sparkle of her deep brown eyes was the color of the most luxurious of woods. In the memory of her, her hair was blown back in an unseen wind, the thick black sheet flirting with the gust coquettishly. She sparkled with joy and happiness I longed to share with her.

"Lost in thought as ever, young priest."

The gruff voice of the self-styled king ripped me unceremoniously from the face of my promised mate.

A dark frown carved itself into my features, and I had to wrestle with myself to force placidity back into them. Since Sal was mated, it was my turn, and the interruption had soured my mood.

"Not so young at all, Cadmael," I volleyed back at him before taking a torch offered by an initiate to help lead the procession back to the compound courtyard to start the feast. "It is good that you came. You do our totoco a great honor. Thank you, Elder Cadmael."

Cadmael matched my pace, staying at my elbow as the guests were led away from the quickly escalating volume of Sal and Xochi's marital bliss. His soft, sandaled foot was careful not to disturb the sticks and leaves beneath us. Cadmael was ever the hunter, trained so long in the old ways, when we were more predators than men. He might have traded his spears and arrows for a crown of feathers and gold, but he would always default to the stalking of his prey, even if the prey was a political rival instead of a startled turkey.

"Of course, tlamacazto."

One of my beasts snarled and snapped at the disrespect of the lesser title. He knew damned well that I had not been an initiate in almost fifteen years. He had attended my initiation. He had gawked and bleated his spleen over the inequity, that one so young should be blessed with more than one spirit, whereas he was the elder and most powerful of us and had only one. Greed would always be Cadmael's greatest vice. "You will repay my kindness by speaking with the Council members and me. Now that your totoco is whole, your place in the Ah Kin is solidified as well."

I clenched my jaw. It was not a request; it was a demand, and it slithered up my skin like a river of acid. I had no interest in spending the evening of my cousin's wedding with this pompous ass. There was no wriggling out of it, though, no matter the words I could craft. With Itziquetzal and Xochitl walled up in their hut, I was the only one left of the totoco's leadership to stand for the Lets'a Wehle, so I politely nodded and followed him to the table of honor set out for the visiting dignitaries.

Seven representatives, not including Amanka and Cadmael, had trekked to our volcano, and they all sat in their finest sacred regalia of their station. A menagerie of luxurious and vibrant feathers danced in the soft late summer breeze. Jade, obsidian, red obsidian, bloodstone—and more exotic stones whose names I couldn't remember—glimmered in the torches' warm light. We had opted not to light the strings of light bulbs that normally illuminated the courtyard, in favor of the more traditional open fire to celebrate the Tlahtoani and Cihuatlatoani, observing the old ways of marriage.

The greetings between us were formal, with no simple hellos and salutations for these pillars of ancient tradition. When they were finally over, I sat and cast my eyes over the feast the women had prepared. The cadejos lazily enjoyed it, with no true appreciation for the labor that went into the rich soups and lavish meat dishes that spread out across the table.

"I have been told by Honoria that you observed an incident a few weeks back at the temple. Is this true?" Chimalmat, a representative of one of the many Honduran totocos, asked, placing a bite of turkey on her pillowy lips.

I watched her for a long moment. If there was one thing I had learned about the Council, it was that nothing was ever simple and that the opening salvo to the conversation was far too blunt to be a simple question.

"We did. Hummingbird skulls and a bell were found."

Julia appeared at my elbow and handed me a glass of strawberry-mango juice. While the others might have indulged in the pulque flowing like water through the raucous festivities that almost dulled the sound of the Council members right before me, I would not. I had to stay sharp. With only the Eagle, the Jaguar, and myself to watch for the totoco while Sal and Xochi were confined, I could not afford the distraction.

"A bell? Intriguing," another woman chimed in. I had only met her once, but her name rattled in my head like loose marbles from the spirits that spun within me. Itotia. The dancer. "Are you aware of others receiving these gifts?"

I narrowed my eyes mentally but showed no signs of interest or discomfort. I had picked up a few tricks from Xochi, her skill at obfuscating her emotions behind an imperious mask ever impressive. "I am not. We have been a little consumed with preparing for the festivities."

"Of course, teopixqui. We appreciate your hospitality," Amanka, our totoco's representative and grandmother to our former Cihuatlatoani, said to soothe the air of accusation that Itotia had left hanging. "It has been reported to many of us that there have been strange occurrences in many of the totoco villages all over the peninsula."

I tilted my head at the ancient woman and bowed it in supplication to her superior station. Sal, Xochi, and I might run this totoco, but when Amanka was present, she outranked all three of us put together, as the eldest and wisest woman in the totoco. "Please, Elder, if you would be so kind. I am curious to know more."

The rest of the Council was mollified by my traditional stance. That's all these predators lusted after, a return to the old ways and respect they had earned solely by being the eldest or by being the most ambitious. Unlike Amanka, none had earned their seat on the Council through adherence to the spiritual paths of our people, nor the strength of their beasts.

"Many, including Itotia and Chimalmat's totocos, have reported finding bells raining down on their villages, as well as hearing loud bells. Many of them said it sounded like someone had strapped ayoyotes of bells to their ankles and was dancing right outside their door. Yet, when they opened the door, there was no one there, and the bells had moved to sound farther away."

As if summoned on command, someone danced by with those same rattling anklets on, holding up a pair of doughy effigies of babies and spinning with them. I frowned, letting the emotion bleed through my otherwise passive features to indicate that their presence was inappropriate to the austerity of this meeting. The dancer took their dough babies and wandered back into the writhing crowd.

"This sounds like a simple spirit manifestation," I cajoled, though my spirits churned and throbbed a vitriolic disagreement in my stomach and heart.

"We thought this as well, teopixqui."

This time, it was Sanse, a cadejo from Belize. His dark eyes and skin had the images of my promised mate bubbling up in the back of my mind. Soon. She would be mine, soon.

My thoughts drifted to wondering what the press of her lips against my skin would feel like, and when I came back to the present, he was mid-sentence.

". . . completely black."

"I'm sorry, Elder Sanse, I could not hear you over the music. Can you humor me and say again? I am sorry for my inattentiveness."

Being so deferential in my own home, on my territory, had my predators bristling under the strain of it.

He curled a honey-sweet smile, as if he knew what had drawn my attention away. "I said that the night of the bells, the skies over Edzna went completely black. Not a single star to be seen."

That now-familiar frown scratched deeper into my face. One of the key features of Edzna that drew our ancestors was the clear night sky views of the stars. As a young initiate, I had laid on the grass in the great plaza between the acropolis and the Nohochna for hours, gazing up at the brilliant blanket of the diamond-dusted black sky. I had been nowhere else in this world with a night sky to rival the grandeur of Edzna's.

"Was there—"

"Before you ask it, no, there was no fog. No weather to obstruct the view. No low-flying aircraft. The stars were there, clear as ever, and for a full half-hour, the sky went as black as our beasts. And then the stars were back," Cadmael said.

He had the manners of a self-inflated drunken bull. How he had ever been appointed to his position was still a mystery. I could not imagine the man suave enough to charm anyone to vote him into the place of power, let alone unofficially crown him for life.

"And the Ah Kin? What say them on this matter?" I asked, hedging my tone to not sound accusatory. The Ah Kin should have taken this issue upon themselves. It was surely a message from the teotl.

"They say that the only thing the spirits will say is that the broken goddess is watching." Cadmael leaned forward, gauging my reaction.

Amanka's words the night we had gone to Edzna came flooding back. She had known before the rest of us.

An image of a bronze-skinned leg, adorned with red paint that traveled up to the ragged shredded flesh, where the white of a femur winked in the night sky, flashed before my eyes, but before I could scrutinize it and examine it, it was gone again. The spirits within me shivered, neither of them responsible for the image and conveying such with the sense of dread and unease that filtered through our bond.

They pulsed and throbbed with concern, but there was a third presence, one I had never noticed before. The sensation of wings brushing my cheek, light and airy, heralded its return to my consciousness, and with it, the image of a twin temple set atop a mountain of red stairs framed by monarch wings.

Templo Mayor.

"I will commune with the teotl and see if they are willing to spare me a vision to assist in our hunt for answers, Elders," I assured them as I rose from their table. "Enjoy the feast."

I had to go to Mexico City.

ABOUT THE AUTHOR

N. Cáceres is a proud Latina and Indigenous woman who was born and raised in San Francisco, California. She grew up longing to paint magic over the world with a love for stories that have teeth, grit, and complex characters. Somewhere along the way the chase for the mighty dollar took over that whimsical desire but when it finally returned, it was in the form of a burning compulsion to tell stories that bite back. (We recommended a cream for that but she's too stubborn to listen so instead of the cream she chose attacking an innocent keyboard.)

She wanders the wilds of California with a book in one hand and some form of caffeine in the other. Usually, can be found near some sort of body of water or another. Do not approach. Or do, who are we to tell you what to do? No one. That's who.

You can connect with this creature by visiting her website: www.authorNCaceres.com or find her on any social media by the handle: AuthorNCaceres.

ACKNOWLEDGMENTS

To Chris: Shut up. Of course you got a mention. Thank you for being my friend for so many damned years. Thanks for listening to me work through all of the little pieces of this story and tolerating me when I told you you didn't know anything about romance.

To the amazing Elle: Thank you for bursting into my life, throwing coffee all over it and dragging me out of my self doubt. You've been a constant on the road to making this book a reality. Whenever I stumbled or doubted, you were there to cuss me out for being dumb and it's what I needed.

To Rowan: Your spirit, your soul has kept me warm when it got cold. Thank you so much for being the very first fan of Sal, even when others were telling me he was a problem, you got him. You understood the fucked-up layers that made him wonderful. Thank you for being part of this process and for letting me be part of yours.

To Azalea: My dear, your gentle ferocity has made me giggle and holler so many times I cannot even begin to count them. You are my favorite teddy bear with teeth. And don't you ever forget it.

To The Council: You are always there when I need a little warmth to come in from the cold to. Thank you. I cannot express how lucky I am to call you my friends. Each and every single one of you can be counted on no matter what is going on. I can't wait for our Golden Girls moment.

To my editor, Samantha, who is reading this right now and frowning at my grammar: Shh. You leave my pretty words alone, dammit! Thank you for believing in me, this book, and this project. And thank you for having patience with me when I barked at you for touching my pretty, pretty sentences . . . even though I paid you to do that.

To my community: I hope the gift I delivered to you soothes that brutal, jagged piece of your soul like it soothed mine to write it.

COMING SOON

Fire on the Horizon Series
Obsidian Feathers
Jade Soul
Steel Claws
Dusk of the Fifth Sun
Spiral Heart